Handsome as sin.

With those words running through her head, Irene couldn't help but notice the athletic grace with which he moved, the perfect way his elegant clothes fit his long legs, lean hips, and the width of those shoulders Clara had so admired. As he halted before her desk, she noticed the pale, clear gray of his eyes and the black lashes that surrounded them, lashes far more opulent than any man ought to have. He might very well be, she realized in dismay, the handsomest man she'd ever encountered. How could she not have noticed that fact the day before yesterday? Maybe she'd been working too hard.

He gave a slight cough, reminding Irene that she was staring. Not that all her scrutiny had done her much good, for as he lifted a slim portfolio of black leather and placed it on her desk, she realized she hadn't even noticed until that moment he'd been carrying such an item.

Irene gave herself a little mental shake to bring herself out of this sudden and most aggravating appreciation of the duke's masculine assets.

By Laura Lee Guhrke

ATTENTION: ORGANIZATIONS AND CORPORATIONS
HarperCollins books may be purchased for educational, business, or sales promotional use. For information, please e-mail the Special Markets Department at SPsales@harpercollins.com.

LAURA LEE GUHRKE

The Truth About Love and Dukes

AVONBOOKS

An Imprint of HarperCollinsPublishers

This is a work of fiction. Names, characters, places, and incidents are products of the author's imagination or are used fictitiously and are not to be construed as real. Any resemblance to actual events, locales, organizations, or persons, living or dead, is entirely coincidental.

THE TRUTH ABOUT LOVE AND DUKES. Copyright © 2017 by Laura Lee Borio. All rights reserved. Printed in the United States of America. No part of this book may be used or reproduced in any manner whatsoever without written permission except in the case of brief quotations embodied in critical articles and reviews. For information, address HarperCollins Publishers, 195 Broadway, New York, NY 10007.

First Avon Books mass market printing: April 2017

ISBN 978-0-06-246985-4

Avon, Avon & logo, and Avon Books & logo are registered trademarks of HarperCollins Publishers in the United States of America and other countries.

HarperCollins is a registered trademark of HarperCollins Publishers in the United States of America and other countries.

17 18 19 20 21 QGM   10 9 8 7 6 5 4 3 2 1

If you purchased this book without a cover, you should be aware that this book is stolen property. It was reported as "unsold and destroyed" to the publisher, and neither the author nor the publisher has received any payment for this "stripped book."

For my father, whose courage, resilience, and optimism inspire me every single day. I love you, Dad.

The Truth About Love and Dukes

Chapter 1

*H*enry Cavanaugh longed for a well-ordered life. As the Duke of Torquil, he had many responsibilities, and they would have been easier to manage with a private life that was well-ordered and predictable. Unfortunately for Henry, he had two unmarried sisters, an impecunious younger brother, and a hopelessly indolent brother-in-law. He also had a pair of nephews who adored driving nannies away and a mother with artistic inclinations. A well-ordered life never seemed quite within his grasp. Henry mourned this fact on a daily basis.

Today was no exception.

"Jamie, really," he said, frowning at his late sister Patricia's husband as the other man's twin sons entered the room, whooping like savages. "Is a bit of peace and quiet at the breakfast table too much to ask?"

"It is on this particular morning, apparently," his sister Sarah put in, pressing her hands to her ears.

Jamie gave a shrug as he reached for the marmalade, seeming disinclined to check his sons as they ran behind his chair around the end of the dining table. "Nanny Smith's gone. Crept away with her things before dawn this morning, leaving only a note behind. What's a widowed father to do in such circumstances?"

"Nanny or no," Henry replied, raising his voice to ensure he was heard above the din, "your children are your responsibility, and not, I should think, a particularly difficult one to manage."

"Says the man with no children," Jamie countered as he spread marmalade on his toast. "Wait until you have sons of your own in the nursery," he added, waving his knife in Henry's direction. "You'll sing a different tune then."

"I doubt it."

Across the table, his brother, David, gave a laugh. "And your duchess, when you find her?" he asked. "What if she proves difficult to manage?"

"That won't be a concern. When I marry, you may be sure I will choose a wife whose views are in accord with mine. Especially when it comes to the raising of our children."

"Oh, that's what you'll think. But once the honeymoon is over, you'll find your notions of accord were an illusion. After six years of marriage, I barely get an agreeable word out of Carlotta."

Henry could have pointed out that very few people got an agreeable word out of Carlotta, but just then, Colin gave a shout, snatched two slices of toast from the sideboard, and tossed one to his brother, Owen, and Henry decided that if Jamie wouldn't manage the boys, he would have to do it for him.

"That will be enough, gentlemen," he said as he stood up, his voice carrying all his ducal authority and cutting through the boyish ebullience of the twins. "Colin, Owen, cease this gamboling about the dining room at once."

The boys went still and a blissful silence came over the room.

"You will go down to the kitchens," he went on, "and ask Mrs. Deal—politely, mind you—to make you a proper breakfast. Afterward," he added with a pointed glance at Jamie, "your father will take you for an outing in Hyde Park, and I will commence a search for your new nanny."

The groans the twins gave at the notion of yet another new nanny were stifled by Henry's arm stretching toward the door. "Out," he ordered and the two boys obeyed immediately. They even managed to maintain a respectful silence all the way to the baize door at the end of the corridor, but a muffled whoop just before the door banged shut told Henry that this enjoyable silence would not be shared by those below stairs, poor devils.

"Well done, Henry," his sister Angela approved, looking up as she turned the page of her morning newspaper. "Something needs to be done with those boys of yours, Jamie."

"Hear, hear," Sarah and David echoed together, and faced with the staunch disapproval of his relations, Jaime had the grace to look abashed.

"They've become absolute hellions, I know," he said, gave a sigh and leaned back, raking a hand through his brown hair. "Patricia was much better about keeping them in line than I. On my own, I'm not sure what to do with them."

"Do what most widowers do," David said carelessly. "Send them to school."

"Should I?" Jamie looked doubtful.

"Why not?" David gestured to the footman for more kidneys and bacon. "School would sort them out soon enough. It kept all of us on the straight and narrow path. Well, two of us, anyway," he added with a glance at Henry. "Torquil was born on the straight and narrow, and I doubt he's ever veered off of it."

Henry paused, thinking of his one and only deviation from the straight and narrow, a deviation his siblings and the world knew nothing about. "And I never shall," he said after a moment. *Not ever again.*

"Anyway, I'm not sure school's a good idea," Jamie murmured, reverting to the subject at hand. "The boys are only eight."

Henry did not miss the questioning glance Jamie sent in his direction.

"If you think it time for the twins to go to school," he responded, "I will stand the fees, of course. But in my opinion, you are right to deem them too young yet. They should wait another two or three years. In the meantime—"

"Good Lord!" Angela's sudden ejaculation inter-

rupted Henry before he could underscore the importance of discipline and routine to a peaceful home. And
when he turned toward his sister, her dismayed expression reminded him that perpetual drama, not peace,
was the routine, at least in his household.

Angela leaned forward in her seat, a frown drawing
her dark brows together. "It can't be," she murmured,
still staring at the folded-back page in her hand. "It just
can't be. Mama would never . . ."

Her voice trailed off, but just the mention of their
mother was enough to send a ripple of disquiet through
Henry. As far back as he could remember, Mama had
always been his idea of the perfect duchess—a gra-
cious hostess who worked tirelessly for charity, con-
versed intelligently on any subject, and performed her
many duties in exemplary fashion. She was, in fact, the
only member of his family who had never given him
cause for concern. Of late, however—

"Don't keep us in suspense, Angela," Sarah's voice
cut into Henry's uneasy thoughts. "What sensation
about our family has *Society Snippets* printed this
week?"

David made a sound of contempt. "That scandal rag?
Why are you reading that, in heaven's name?"

"I—" Angela paused, turning to Henry, and in her
eyes, the same pale gray eyes as his, he could see the
reflection of his own growing apprehension. "This is
Mama's paper. I saw her reading it last night. On my
way into breakfast, I found it with the morning papers,
so I took it. I fancied it might be amusing to read a
scandal sheet at breakfast. Amusing?" she repeated,
her voice choking on the word. "What was I thinking?"

"Whatever you've read that is causing you such distress, you'd best tell me," Henry advised. "Then, and only then, can I do something about it."

"I'm imagining things, I'm sure," she said, but her voice was unconvincing.

"Perhaps." He braced himself. "But tell me anyway."

She nodded, lifted the paper higher, and began to read. "'Dear Lady Truelove—'"

A groan from David interrupted. "Do stop, Angela. Every time I visit my club, it seems the lads are reading that woman's column—aloud to each other, if you please. Deuced distracting—"

"David, stop rattling away," Jamie admonished. "I fear something serious is in the wind. Keep reading, Angela."

Angela cleared her throat and began again.

"'Dear Lady Truelove, I am a lady of good society, highly placed within the *ton*. It is because of my rank that I find myself in an unbearable conundrum, and I am writing to you in the hope that you can help me resolve it. When I was young, a girl of only seventeen, I married a man twenty years my senior. I was not in love with this man—'"

Angela broke off, her cheeks pink, clearly embarrassed to be reading such an intimate account aloud. In the pause that followed, she looked at Henry again, and the uneasiness in his guts deepened and spread.

"Go on," he said, his voice hard even to his own ears. "Read the rest."

Angela's gaze dropped again to the newspaper in her hand. "'Nor,'" she continued, "'was I even particularly fond of him. I agreed to his proposal only at the behest of my family, for he was considered an excellent match for me. After many years in this loveless union, and having borne five children, I found myself a widow, and until recently, I was content with my situation. But now, in the autumn of my life, I have fallen in love, truly and completely in love, for the first time. The man whom I hold in such passionate regard, however, is not of my station. He is a painter, a brilliant artist—'"

"What?" Sarah gasped. "So the gossip about Mama and Foscarelli is actually *true*?"

Henry glanced around and appreciated that his youngest sister's shock seemed to be shared by everyone at the table. But for his own part, he was not all that surprised. Loath as he was to admit it, the signs his mother was embroiled in an inappropriate liaison with the Italian painter had been there for months, yet he had chosen to believe his mother's recent lessons in the painting of oils were borne of a desire for artistic expression, rather than desire of a more primitive kind. Suspicions to the contrary had been rattling around in the back of his mind, but he hadn't wanted to acknowledge them. He thought of his own past indiscretions, and he appreciated just how his father must have felt on his behalf a decade ago.

Slowly, he set down his knife and fork. "Go on," he said again, and Angela complied.

"'For many months, I have tried to deny my feelings for this man, but I have come to accept that they are too strong for denial. He has proposed honorable marriage, and everything within me cries out to consent.'"

Honorable marriage? Henry rolled his eyes. There wasn't anything honorable about Foscarelli. He was a lothario of the worst description.

"But what does she mean to do?" Sarah cried. "She can't really be thinking to marry him. He's *Italian*." The last word was uttered as a devastated wail.

"'Needless to say,'" Angela continued, "'my family would not approve—'"

"She's right about that," David muttered.

Angela paused again, giving an exasperated sigh. "If all of you keep interrupting, I shall never come to the end of this narrative. Do be quiet and listen." She leaned forward in her chair and went on, "'So, my dear Lady Truelove, the dilemma I face is this: should I suppress what I feel and refuse this man, as honor dictates? Or should I surrender to love, accept his proposal, and allow myself to be happy?' Signed, 'A Lady of Society.'"

She lowered the paper, and in the silence that followed, all of them glanced at Henry, waiting for him to speak, reminding him of his duty as head of the family.

"We don't know that this lady is Mama or that the artist in question is Foscarelli," he pointed out, trying to sound reasonable and logical, but the mere voicing of that man's name in connection with his mother sparked his outrage and threatened to send reason and logic to the wall. And the idea that such a scoundrel would dare regard himself as worthy to marry their mama brought all Henry's protective instincts to the fore.

Still, as tempting as it was to find the notorious painter and thrash him within an inch of his life, Henry knew his first priority was to reassure his siblings, then determine the true facts. "That man has been linked with many women of society other than Mama," he went on. "Sometimes accurately, and sometimes not, I imagine. As for the letter to this Lady Truelove, I daresay it is an invention, the product of a journalist with a vivid imagination and a salacious mind."

"But the similarities are so striking," Sarah said, her voice faint. "If this is Mama, and if she were ever to marry that man . . ." She stopped, clearly too overcome by the horror of such a possibility to continue.

"Any similarities have no doubt been taken straight from the gossip columns, Sarah," he pointed out. "Mama's lessons in art have been fodder for the gutter press all season, and that has obviously provided this Lady Truelove with the inspiration for her latest fictitious offering."

They all nodded in agreement, but Henry didn't know if any of them were reassured. He certainly wasn't.

"I suppose we ought to hear the rest," David said with a sigh, gesturing to the paper in their sister's hand. "Carry on, Angela."

Their sister gave him a blank stare. "Carry on with what?"

"It's an advice column, isn't it? What advice did this Lady Truelove have to offer?"

"It doesn't matter." Henry pulled the newspaper from Angela's fingers, and set it to one side of his plate to be taken away by the footman, who would toss it into the dustbin where it belonged. "Let's not validate this socalled journalist with another moment of our attention."

Despite his own words, Henry couldn't resist a glance

at the paper beside his plate as he picked up his knife and fork, and the reply of London's most sensational columnist made him feel even grimmer than before.

My dear lady, in matters such as this, what else can one do but capitulate to passion and follow one's heart? Life is a short and often painful experience, and we must take our joy where we can find it . . .

He looked away, suppressing a sound of disdain. Following one's heart and capitulating to passion sounded so exciting, so appealing, but as he well knew, the reality of such a course was painfully different from the romantic picture painted by lurid writers such as this.

The silence at the table pulled him out of his contemplations, and he looked up to find that no one had resumed eating. They were, instead, staring at him.

"Mama is a sensible woman," he said, impelled to offer further reassurances. "And discreet. She would never allow her private life to be put on display by writing such a letter. And however similar this fiction might be to her own situation, she'd never follow this silly woman's advice anyway."

Those words were barely out of his mouth before a pointed cough intervened, and all five of them looked up to find the housekeeper, Mrs. Jaspar, standing in the doorway.

She turned to Henry with an apologetic look. "Forgive me for interrupting your breakfast, Your Grace," she said, "but Her Grace, the Dowager Duchess, is gone."

"Gone?" Henry frowned at this imprecise choice of words. "What do you mean? Gone where?"

"We don't know, Your Grace. But she is not in the house."

"She's probably gone out. It's a bit early, but—"

He stopped as the housekeeper shook her head, her face taking on an apologetic cast, and he knew there was more to this than a shopping excursion or visit to a friend.

"Mrs. Norton—that's Her Grace's maid—never goes up until Her Grace rings the bell," the housekeeper explained. "But when the clock struck half past ten, Mrs. Norton decided it would be best to go up and take a peek, as Her Grace might have been taken ill, you see. When Mrs. Norton went in, she found Her Grace was not there. The bedsheets had been turned down just as they always are, but the bed's not been slept in."

"She's done it, then," Angela cried. "Oh, God, I knew it the moment I read—"

Henry arrested this flow of words from his sister with one hand. A lack of discretion, even in front of long-trusted servants, was never a good idea. "And are you absolutely certain, Mrs. Jaspar, that our mother is not in the house?"

"Oh, yes, Your Grace. We would never presume to worry you with a matter such as this before having a full search of the house. Mrs. Norton says a valise, a hatbox, and some of the Duchess's clothes are missing. And there's this, found on Her Grace's mantelpiece."

Henry rose as the housekeeper approached his side and pulled a folded sheet of paper from her pocket. She placed it on the table, and he took it up, breaking the seal as he resumed his seat.

As he read the lines penned in his mother's hand,

his anger widened to include not only Foscarelli, but also the scandal-mongering woman who dispensed reckless, radical advice for the sole purpose of creating sensation and selling newspapers.

He knew, however, that he had to contain his outrage for the sake of his siblings, and he folded the note with slow, deliberate care. After tucking it inside the breast pocket of his morning coat, he looked up, his gaze skimming past Angela's white face to rest on the housekeeper who had moved to stand again by the door. "Thank you, Mrs. Jaspar," he said. "That will be all."

After Mrs. Jaspar had left the room, Henry turned to the remaining two servants hovering nearby. "Boothby," he said to the butler, "have my carriage brought around. Samuel," he added to the footman, "have my valet fetch my hat and stick. I'm going out immediately after breakfast. And close the doors behind you, please."

"I'm right, aren't I?" Angela murmured after the butler and the footman had departed to carry out his instructions. "She's gone off with that man, hasn't she?"

Henry pressed his tongue to his teeth, working to find a palatable reply, but in this case, there was none. "I'm afraid so, yes. They seem to have eloped."

A sob from Sarah flared up his barely contained anger and put Foscarelli's health decidedly in jeopardy. "I will take care of this," he said. "I will find Mama and bring her back before she can complete the foolish course she has embarked upon."

"If you can," Angela said before Sarah could reply.

"But if you fail, Mama will become the laughingstock of society."

"Not only Mama," David added. "By doing this, she subjects the entire family to shame and ridicule."

With that, Sarah began to cry in earnest. "This is my first season," she wailed, "and before it's even over, my mother has gone off with a man nearly half her age, a man who isn't even a gentleman. I shall never be invited to any ball or party of significance again. How shall I even hold up my head in society? And what of marriage? She talks of her happiness, but what of ours? If she marries that man, she risks my social position and my matrimonial future, and Angela's, too. How could she do this to us?"

"Do not make yourself so uneasy, Sarah," Henry advised. "Even if Mama has been as reckless as you fear, none of you will suffer for it. I promise you that."

"Even you won't be able to prevent her from being laughed at, and all of us along with her," David pointed out. "Not unless you can stop this elopement altogether, and it's seems too late for that. You can't chase her and her Italian all the way to Gretna Green."

Henry cast his brother a glance of impatience. "Mama is fifty years of age. She has no need to sneak off to Scotland in order to marry. Foscarelli is somewhere here in London, so they probably intend to marry here, perhaps at the Registry Office, since I daresay he's a Catholic. Let's hope that is the case."

"Hope?" Sarah echoed in tearful disbelief. "You talk as if there could be a worse alternative."

There were several, but Sarah was an innocent, and

he refrained from voicing the more unsavory ones. "They could be thinking to go abroad and marry there," he said instead. "The Continent is much more lenient than England. Here, the law requires fifteen days of established residency before a license can be obtained, and I'm not certain Foscarelli has his own establishment. The man has no family here, and he seems to live off of friends, floating from one residence to the next every other week or so—at least, if the gossip can be believed."

"The gossip might be out of date," Jamie pointed out. "He may have established residency and obtained the license already."

"He may have done," Henry acknowledged, "but I doubt it. A man like that would never pay the fees for a license and sign the lease for a residence unless he was certain of Mama's consent."

"And before agreeing to marry him," Angela added, gesturing to the paper by Henry's plate, "she was clearly waiting to see what this Lady Truelove would advise."

"Then the woman did tell Mama to marry him?" Jamie asked.

He reached across the table for the paper so that he might read the columnist's reply for himself, but Henry flattened his hand over it before the other man could pick it up. "She did, but let's not dignify this column by giving it our attention."

Jamie acquiesced, once more sitting back in his chair. "Still, whatever the woman's advice, we seem to be taking it for granted that marriage is Foscarelli's intent, but I'm not sure the man's even that honorable.

He could simply have Mama holed up with him some-where—"

"That's enough, Jamie," Henry cut in with a glance at his sisters. "There are ladies present. And there's no point in speculating at this stage. Now," he added, rising to his feet as the doors opened and Boothby came in, "I believe my carriage is waiting."

He started to move away from the table, but then paused, studying the newspaper that was causing everyone such anxiety. He'd thought to have the footman throw it away, but upon reflection, he deemed it best to take it himself, keeping it—at least for the moment—from his distressed siblings. And he might need to refer to its contents later. He took it up, and started for the door.

"But Torquil," David called after him, "what are you going to do?"

"Find Mama, of course," he replied as he walked out. "That is," he added under his breath, "if I'm not too late."

No matter what the situation was at present, he knew there were various steps he could take to resolve it or mitigate the damage, and he contemplated them as he went downstairs.

If, despite his conclusions to the contrary, Foscarelli had already obtained the license, the damage might well be done, but if so, the marriage could perhaps be annulled. Making a mental note to consult with his solicitors about that, he paused to accept his hat and stick from the footman waiting by the front door. If annulment was not possible, then paying off the groom to move abroad and stay there was the only other option.

On the other hand, Jamie could very well be right about Foscarelli's true motives. It wasn't hard to imagine that scoundrel putting Mama up in some seedy flat in an obscure part of London, with no intention of marrying her at all. If so, a demand for funds to keep the whole thing hushed up would no doubt be forthcoming.

Either way, the family would be supporting a worthless cur of a man for the rest of his life unless Henry could prevent it.

To that end, his first step was to find his mother, which would necessitate the employment of private detectives. If it was determined that she'd gone abroad, there was nothing more that could be done until she returned. If she was still in England, however, private detectives would find her, though it might take days, or even weeks. Unless—

Henry paused by his carriage, struck by an idea, and he looked again at the newspaper in his hand. He glanced past his mother's question and the columnist's ridiculous reply, his gaze coming to a halt at the bottom of the page.

Are you suffering the pain of unrequited love? Are you baffled by the unaccountable behavior of the opposite sex? Are you tormented by an affair of the heart and feel there is no one to whom you can turn for understanding and advice? Fear not. Lady True-love can help. You may write to her through her publisher, Deverill Publishing, 12 Belford Row, Holborn. All letters will be answered, and will only be published by mutual consent.

As Henry read those words, he wondered if a method of finding his mother more expedient than even London's finest detectives might just be staring him in the face.

Chapter 2

Publishing a scandal sheet was not for the faint of heart. It required a shrewd head, an unsentimental heart, and a thick skin. Fortunately for the Deverill family and for all the avid readers of *Society Snippets*, Irene Deverill possessed all three of those qualities. She was also blessed with a sense of humor, and there were days when Irene found that trait to be the most necessary one of all. Today was one of those days.

"Mr. Shaw," she began for the third time, hoping she could at last succeed in getting a word in amidst the angry stream of criticism from the irascible, elderly man seated on the other side of her desk, "I do see your concerns, but—"

"The *Weekly Gazette*," he said, referring to the paper by its former name, "was a newspaper, young woman, and its purpose was to convey to the public serious and important events of the day in East and Central London. But now? Now, thanks to you, it is nothing more than a . . . a purveyor of scandal and titillation."

Irene tried not to smile as she studied the prim mouth of the man opposite. A bit of titillation, she felt, would do Ebenezer Shaw far more good than the liver pills sold by his company, but it wouldn't do to say so. "I realize the changes I have made may be a bit unsettling—"

"Unsettling?" Mr. Shaw tossed his copy of yesterday's edition on top of her desk. "Gossip columns, fashion news, advice to the lovelorn . . . what's next? Reports of England's haunted houses and a weekly astrology report?"

At once, Irene's imagination began to envision a series of articles on England's most haunted places—Jamaica Inn, perhaps, and Berry Pomeroy Castle, the Tower of London . . .

She glanced past Mr. Shaw to her sister, Clara, who was seated by the door, clipboard in hand. Clara, who acted as her secretary, perceived the meaning in that glance and scribbled a note. With that, Irene was forced to abandon the delight of contemplating future issues of *Society Snippets*, and return her attention to one of the less appealing aspects of her profession: pacifying irate advertisers.

"The paper may not be the same sort of publication you began placing advertisements in twenty years ago," she said in her most placating tone of voice, "and the content may no longer be to your taste. Or mine," she added hastily as he opened his mouth to give his opinion on that score yet again. "But neither of us can deny the results. Circulation has risen 300 percent since the changes to our editorial content were implemented ten months ago."

Clara gave a little cough. "Three hundred and twenty-seven percent, to be exact."

Irene lifted her hands in a self-evident gesture. "There you are. Shaw's Liver Pills must surely see the benefit of such a massive increase in our readership. More people are seeing your advertisements than ever before—"

"We cater to a certain class of clientele." He drew himself up with injured dignity. "The people who now read your publication are not the sort we desire as our customers."

Irene could not understand what difference it made to Shaw's what class of clientele purchased their liver pills as long as those pills were paid for in ready money, but she knew it wouldn't do to say so. Before she could decide how best to proceed, Mr. Shaw spoke again.

"Our annual advertising contract is coming up for renegotiation, and I feel that before we can do that, the problems I see must be addressed."

"Of course," Irene agreed. "What is it you wish me to do?"

"Do? Do?" Mr. Shaw's eyes bulged as if he couldn't believe she'd asked such a preposterous question. "Isn't it obvious?"

"Not to me," Irene answered truthfully. "How can I alleviate your concerns?"

"Return the newspaper to the way it used to be, of course."

Irene cast her mind back five years, to her grandfather's death and her father's attempts to run Deverill

Publishing on his own. Those attempts had been dismally unsuccessful, for her father had a serious fondness for brandy and no talent for business. As a result, the prosperous enterprise built by the two previous generations of Deverill men had collapsed with breathtaking speed. Within four years, their entire income had been obliterated, the publishing offices on Fleet Street forced to close, and most of the presses and equipment sold at auction for a fraction of their value. Their home on Belford Row, their only remaining property, had been mortgaged to pay debts.

It was at that point that Irene, well aware from managing the household just how precarious their financial situation had become, decided something must be done. Insisting that her father take care of his health and leave the worries of the business behind, she had taken over the *Weekly Gazette*, the only remaining vestige of her grandfather's once-vast newspaper empire. With much grumbling from her parent, she had moved Deverill Publishing into the family library, added a door to the street, and turned her father's study into her office. She had then changed the name of the paper from the *Weekly Gazette* to *Society Snippets* and transformed it into a scandal sheet. In less than a year, thanks to Lady Truelove and a few other inventions of Irene's imagination, the paper had become a raging success, the family business had been saved, and the days of irate tradesmen, demanding creditors, and perpetual skimping on coal and butter were over.

Mr. Shaw might—for reasons she couldn't fathom—wish to return to a time when her little weekly had discussed "serious and important events of East and

Central London," but she vastly preferred a profitable publication, a household that could pay its bills, and a tidy nest egg in the bank. Irene thought of the 327 percent rise in the paper's circulation and reminded herself there were other advertisers besides Shaw's Liver Pills.

"I'm afraid," she said, giving Mr. Shaw her prettiest smile, "what you are asking for is not possible."

The bulging eyes narrowed. "Perhaps it would be best if I spoke with Mr. Deverill about this."

Her smile faltered a little. "That's not possible either. My father is ill, you see."

"Ill?"

"Quite ill," she added, reminding herself that wasn't really a lie. To her way of thinking, if a man spent most of his time in an inebriated condition, he was suffering from an illness.

"Your brother, then. Surely Jonathan Deverill must now be in charge, if your father is ill."

"My brother is out of the country. Since finishing at university, he has been . . . ahem . . . seeing the world."

That was, she supposed, the best way of putting it. No need to mention that Jonathan and Papa were not on speaking terms, and hadn't been for three years now.

Mr. Shaw's gooseberry-green eyes narrowed. "Then, we are back where we started. I shall need to speak with your father. I really must insist."

Irene stiffened.

"Uh-oh," Clara murmured, perceiving the telltale movement. "That's done it."

With an effort, Irene kept her smile in place. "Shaw's has been advertising with our newspapers for many years with great success. Like my father and grandfather before me, I have always regarded your company as our most valued and important client." She paused, waiting until she saw the gleam of satisfaction in the eyes of the man across from her before she spoke again.

"But," she went on as she rose to her feet, "I believe it might be time for both of us to reevaluate the strength of that relationship."

"I beg your pardon?" His astonishment would have been amusing if it wasn't about to cost her the newspaper's greatest source of revenue. "You would sacrifice our business without any attempt to address our concerns?"

"I believe I have made that attempt, but you do not seem to agree, so I fail to see what else I can do. The loss of your business shall be a terrible blow, of course, but I cannot allow advertisers to dictate the editorial content of the newspaper. It would set a most dangerous precedent." Her smile was still pleasant as she came around her desk and crossed to the door of her office. "I'm sure you understand," she added and opened the door, glancing at her sister.

Clara took the hint at once. Setting aside her clipboard, she rose. "I will show Mr. Shaw out."

Irene mouthed a heartfelt *thank you* to her sister as Clara took the spluttering Mr. Shaw firmly by the arm, much as a good nursery governess might have done, and escorted him out of the office.

Irene watched from the doorway as Clara led Mr. Shaw past the printing press and the long table of type-writing machines. Those machines were silent now, for the three journalists on her staff were off pursuing the investigations that would comprise next week's edition, and there was no one in the office save Clara and her-self. She continued to watch until her sister had ushered Mr. Shaw out to the street, then with a sigh of relief, she stepped back and closed her office door. Only after she had resumed her seat did the ramifications of her decision hit her, and her relief was displaced by a sudden throb of panic.

She slumped forward with a groan, plunking her elbows on her desk, thinking of all the revenue she'd just tossed out the window. "Oh, dear God," she mumbled, rubbing her hands over her face, "what have I just done?"

If Shaw's could not be replaced, and soon, the loss to the paper would be enormous. They might be making a profit now, but Irene knew how easily they could descend back into destitution if she did not take care. And while genteel poverty made for romantic stories in the paper's fiction section, it was too much a part of Irene's recent past for her to find anything romantic about it. In fact, the possibility that her decision might return her family to that state made her feel slightly sick.

Still, what was done was done. The question was what to do now. With that reminder, Irene lifted her head and reached for notepaper and a pencil.

Within three minutes she had scribbled down the names of twenty companies that might be suitable replacements for Shaw's Liver Pills, and her innate optimism began to return. There were a dozen or more possible prospects in her mind, but before she could write them down, there was a tap on her door, and she paused, looking up as Clara once again entered the room.

Her sister's big brown eyes were wide and her lower lip was caught between her teeth. Irene felt compelled at once to offer reassurance. "It'll be all right. I already have a plan to make up the lost revenue. We shan't miss that old curmudgeon and his liver pills in the least."

"I know." Despite those words, her sister did not look reassured.

"I shan't let us descend into poverty again, I promise—"

"I know, I know."

Irene frowned in bewilderment. "Then what has you looking as if we're headed back to queer-street?"

The younger woman leaned back in the doorway, casting a glance into the room behind her, then looked at Irene again. "There's a gentleman out front," she said in a low voice as she approached Irene's desk, a card in her hand. "He wants to see Lady Truelove."

"And I'd love to own a unicorn," she whispered back, smiling, her good humor restored. "We shall both be disappointed, I fear."

"This is serious, Irene." Clara held out the card. "This man isn't some nobody from nowhere."

Irene stood up, shoved her pencil behind one ear, and took the card from her sister's outstretched fingertips. Plain and white, it was unadorned but for a thin silver border and a coronet watermarked across its surface. She didn't know one coronet from another, but she knew the feel of expensive, high quality paper.

"Duke of Torquil." She read aloud the black copperplate words printed over the watermark, and as she spoke, yesterday's Lady Truelove column flashed through her mind. She looked up to meet her sister's apprehensive gaze with a dismayed one of her own. "Good Lord."

Clara nodded, confirming that they were both thinking along the same lines. Even if one didn't own a scandal sheet, it wouldn't have been hard to guess the identity of the "lady of society" who had fallen in love with an artist, and upon receiving her letter, Irene had known at once who she was. Gossip about the widowed Duchess of Torquil and famous Italian painter Antonio Foscarelli had already been bandied about in several scandal sheets, including her own.

"Even so . . ." Irene paused and swallowed hard, looking again at the card. "Why should the Duke of Torquil want to see me?"

"Why indeed?" a hard voice intruded, and Irene looked past her sister to find a man standing in the entrance to her office, a man whose tall form and wide shoulders seemed to fill the doorway. His face was one of finely chiseled features and gray-blue eyes, but it was also a face of uncompromising lines and implacable resolve. In those brilliant, pale eyes, there was the unmistakable glint of anger.

She could make a fair guess as to the cause, and she felt a sudden shiver of apprehension. As a woman in a man's occupation, however, she knew she couldn't allow herself to be intimidated by anyone, so she tossed the card aside, lifted her chin, and met his hard gaze with an unwavering one of her own.

He glanced over her in the toplofty way so characteristic of the nobility, and one dark brow arched upward as if the woman before him was not quite what he'd been expecting.

"Your question is an excellent one, madam, and a telling one, too." He removed his hat and bowed, that icy gaze once again meeting hers, and as he straightened, a grim smile touched his lips. "Lady Truelove, I presume?"

HENRY HAD ONCE been afforded the dubious honor of meeting a lady novelist, and in the vague recesses of his mind, he had assumed Lady Truelove to be cut of a similar cloth—a plump figure swathed in rubbed velvet and lashings of jet, middle-aged, with frizzy, henna-dyed hair, and a simpering mouth.

Now, however, seeing London's infamous columnist in the flesh, he appreciated how inaccurate the picture in his mind had been.

For one thing, Lady Truelove was not middle-aged. She was perhaps twenty-five or -six, no more. She was clothed not in velvet and jet, but in a serviceable white shirtwaist, plain gray skirt, and dark blue necktie. Her hair, piled high atop her head in a careless sort of chignon, was not henna red, but a deep, rich blond that gleamed in the dim light of her musty office. Her figure, tall and shapely, was nothing like that of the rotund creature he'd envisioned. Instead, this woman was like a Gibson drawing come to life.

Though not yet invited to enter the room, Henry did it anyway, for he had little time for ordinary civilities. As he came in, the brown-haired wren of a girl who'd greeted him upon his arrival dipped a bow, begged his pardon, and murmured something about bringing tea. Ducking past him, she departed, closing the door behind her.

Henry returned his attention to the woman behind the desk, and as he crossed the room toward her, he noted another sharp contrast between her and the novelist of his acquaintance.

This woman was beautiful.

Wide eyes in a heart-shaped face stared back at him, hazel eyes surrounded by thick lashes much darker than her hair. In the tawny depths of those eyes, he could see a riot of rich colors that made him think at once of the woods at home in Hampshire, of dappled sunlight falling on moss, bark, and lichen.

He lowered his gaze, taking in as much of her figure as he could see above the desk, and as he noted her full bosom, tiny waist, and generous hips, he felt another glimmer of surprise. Such a sensuous figure usually owed more to artifice than to nature, and yet, her clothing was not the sort worn by women who favored tight corseting, bust improvers, and other such falderals.

Given the beauty of her face and the exquisitely feminine lines of her body, her surroundings and her attire seemed even more incongruous. This wasn't the sort of woman who ought to be wearing the uniform of shop girls and typists, slaving away in an office. Such a splendid body belonged in a boudoir, its curves tantalizingly visible beneath a layer of sheer silk chiffon. Those gold tresses ought to be loose and falling around her shoulders, not piled up in a haphazard mass of curls. She should certainly not be at a desk with ink-smudged cuffs and a pencil stuck behind her ear.

"You are laboring under a misapprehension, sir."

Her voice, cool and prim, brought Henry out of

this somewhat erotic reverie and reminded him of the business at hand. "What misapprehension is that?" he asked.

"You seem to believe I am Lady Truelove."

"It seems a reasonable assumption, given what I overheard just now. Do you deny it?"

"I see no reason to confirm or deny anything . . . to an eavesdropper."

"If you don't wish your conversations to be overheard, perhaps you should close your door. However," he added before she could make any further efforts to divert the conversation to his behavior, "I can understand why you wouldn't wish to admit your identity. If I dispensed the same abysmal advice to the British public that you do, I should be loath to admit it, too."

Despite his attempt to provoke her into defending herself and her work, thereby ending any tiresome arguments about her identity before they could begin, she did not rise to the bait.

"I have the authority to speak for Lady Truelove," she said instead, "which is why my secretary brought you to me."

If she wanted to deny being the notorious columnist, so be it. "And you are . . . ?"

"I am the publisher of *Society Snippets*."

This woman was the publisher? He'd been led to expect a man in that role, and he had to smother a laugh, appreciating that at this point in his day, he ought to be taking the unexpected in stride.

She frowned at the stifled sound. "Something about my position amuses you?"

"I wasn't amused, madam," he hastened to assure her. "But there are times when a man is reminded of how absurd life can be."

"You find the idea of a female publisher absurd, do you?" she asked, her tart voice indicating she'd taken offense, and he realized that he was conversing not only with a female publisher, but also a suffragist.

"I confess, I do." He cast another glance over her and thought again of sheer silk chiffon. "In this case, at least."

She bristled at that, but he scarcely noticed, for his body was beginning to respond to the direction of his thoughts, and he was too occupied with bringing it back under his own regulation to pay much heed to her sensibilities.

If he was having lusty thoughts about suffragists in neckties, he reflected in some chagrin, it had clearly been too long since he'd had a woman. If this sort of wayward thinking continued, he might be forced to take a mistress or stop procrastinating about finding a suitable wife.

"I'd have thought a duke would have the good manners not to stare at people."

Her acerbic comment about his manners brought him out of his reflections with a start. "Forgive me," he said, striving to remember civilities and offer an excuse for his preoccupation to the irate beauty of the poisonous pen. "You may attribute my thoughtless words of a moment ago to my . . . ahem . . . confusion."

"Confusion?"

"Yes." He set his hat on one corner of her desk, then drew the previous evening's edition of *Society Snippets* from the breast pocket of his jacket and refolded it so that the front page was visible. "The masthead of your publication states that one Edwin Deverill is the owner and publisher," he said, pointing to the bottom left corner of the page. "Are you Edwin Deverill?"

That took some of the wind out of her suffragist sails, he noted. "I daresay I am old-fashioned," he went on before she could reply, "but to me, Edwin seems an odd name for a woman, Mrs. Deverill."

"Miss Deverill," she corrected him at once, her pointed chin jutting up a notch. "I am Edwin Deverill's eldest daughter."

A spinster as well as a suffragist? And she offered advice to the lovelorn? This situation was sliding from absurdity into farce.

"My father," she went on, "has passed all duties of this publication to my care. Any matter that concerns Lady Truelove, you may share with me, and if I feel her attention is warranted, I will bring the matter to her."

Despite this pretense, he knew what he'd heard. She was the infamous columnist, and he saw little point in beating about the bush with her. "Then I shall come straight to the point of my call, Miss Deverill. My mother is missing. She departed from her home in the middle of the night, alone, declaring in a note to me of her intention to elope with a man."

"A travesty, indeed."

She said nothing more, and Henry felt his resentment returning. "Her family is worried about her."

"Of course. In what way can Lady Truelove and Deverill Publishing assist you?"

"My mother gave no indication of her intended destination. Perhaps you can tell me where she has gone?"

Miss Deverill shifted her weight and looked away, straightening the blotter on her desk, an obvious attempt to stall for time. "How should I know your mother's whereabouts?"

He opened the paper to the appropriate page and began to read. "'Lady Truelove can help. You may write to her through her publisher, Deverill Publishing, 12 Belford Row, Holborn.'" He looked up. "I am hoping in her correspondence with you she may have given some indication of her intentions or whereabouts."

"She did not, not to Deverill Publishing anyway." She paused again, this time to tidy the papers on her desk, then she looked up. "Lady Truelove is employed by this paper, but her correspondence is her own business."

"Miss Deverill, your words to your secretary a few moments ago could only have one meaning, and I do not have the luxury of pretending otherwise for the sake of your sensibilities or to preserve your pseudonym. In your role as Lady Truelove, you have clearly been in correspondence with my mother, and I need to know any information she may have given you. I am particularly anxious to locate her and be reassured that she is all right."

"Locating a person who is missing would seem to be the purview of the police."

"My mother is the Duchess of Torquil. A matter such as this cannot be taken to the police."

"Private detectives, then."

"I have every intention of engaging the services of private detectives, but such inquiries take time. By the time detectives discovers her whereabouts, it could be too late."

"Too late?" She frowned as if she actually found those words bewildering. "Too late for what?"

"To stop the elopement, of course. Thanks to you, my mother intends to make what can only be viewed as a grievous mistake, and I intend to persuade her to reconsider, if I can. In your correspondence, did your advice to her include a recommended location for the nuptials? Did she give you a forwarding address? A date she intends to wed? Any information at all?"

She tilted her head, studying him thoughtfully. "Why do you consider that your mother's marriage would be a mistake?"

He stirred, growing impatient, for he was not here to answer questions, but obtain answers. "It is not surprising, I suppose, that someone of low social position would fail to understand why this elopement would be disastrous, but that makes it no less so."

She stiffened, seeming affronted by what was an obvious fact. "Of all the snobbish, arrogant, condescending remarks I have ever heard . . ."

Her voice trailed off in a splutter, her mind clearly having run out of disparaging adjectives, and he took advantage of the momentary silence. "Tell me what you know."

She did not reply. Instead, she pressed her lips together, glaring at him.

He dropped the newspaper onto her desk and leaned forward, flattening his palms on the desktop, his eyes staring down the resentment in hers. "I was not making a request, Miss Deverill."

"That's a pity," she countered at once. "For I don't respond well to commands."

"And I don't respond well to unnecessary intransigence."

"It is not a matter of intransigence. Even if Deverill Publishing was aware of your mother's whereabouts or was privy to her plans, I would not be at liberty to reveal any of that to you. *Society Snippets* promises its readers that the information conveyed to Lady Truelove by those who seek her advice shall be held in confidence. While I can understand that you are concerned for your mother's well-being and have apprehensions—however misplaced—about her decision to wed—"

"Misplaced?" he interrupted, giving an incredulous laugh at her choice of words. "Do you have any idea what my mother's marriage to Antonio Foscarelli would do to her life? To her social position? To the position of her family? While we are on the subject," he added before she could answer, "do you ever consider the disastrous consequences that may result from the advice you dispense so carelessly?"

"There is nothing careless about Lady Truelove's advice, and on her behalf, I resent your accusation, sir."

"Resent it all you like, but it's clear you have no consideration for the lives you may ruin."

"Or perhaps I simply don't define ruin the way you do."

Henry's mind tumbled back into the past, and the image of a shopkeeper's dark-eyed daughter flashed through his mind. "Being trapped in a union all of society would view as a disgrace, a union where the two people have nothing in common but their mutual passion—that is not ruinous in your view?"

A hint of color came into her cheeks at the mention of passion, but she did not address that aspect of his point. "Unlike some, I don't view the opinions of you and your precious *ton* as something to worry about."

Henry shoved thoughts of Elena and his own stupid mistake back into the past where they belonged. "You say that only because you are unaware of the power we wield. You have no idea what it would be like to be in her shoes, how it would feel to be shut out of—"

"Oh, but I do know," she assured him. "I fully comprehend what it means and how it feels to be cold-shouldered by your set, believe me. And I don't care a jot."

Despite the defiant declaration, there was an unmistakable hint of bitterness in her voice. Another time, he might have been curious enough to explore the reasons for it, but just now, he had more important things to consider. "Even if that's true, Miss Deverill, my mother is not you. Her life is not like yours, and you have no idea what your advice will do to her. Nor, I suspect, do you care."

"That is not true! I—"

"It's a sensible outlook, I suppose," he interrupted, ignoring her protest, "if one is a newspaper hawker."

"Better to be a newspaper hawker than a lily of the field like you," she shot back, those tawny eyes flashing gold sparks, showing that Miss Deverill possessed not only a stubborn streak, but also a temper.

"A lily of the field?" Henry thought of the duties that filled his days and worried his nights, and he almost wanted to laugh. "Is that what I am?"

"You toil not, neither do you spin, yet you believe you are entitled to wield power over the lives of those around you."

"I believe that I am entitled to wield that power because it is borne of my position. I am a duke. With a high rank comes high responsibility. That is how the world works."

"Not my world."

"I'm sure, but might we leave a discussion of that fact and your world for another day?"

"Certainly," she agreed at once, gesturing to the door behind him. "I'm sure you have important, ducal things to do, like attend balls and go to race meetings. While I, on the other hand, must attend to the insignificant little task of earning my living. So, by all means, take your leave, sir."

"Balls? Race meetings? Does that encompass the entirety of your knowledge about a duke's duties?"

"Well, those things do seem to be the greatest preoccupations of your set. And the appropriateness of who marries whom, of course."

Despite the pert sweetness of that last comment, her resentment was palpable, and he wondered if in addition to being a newspaper hawker, a suffragist, and a spinster, she was also a Marxist. "You have no grasp of what being a duke means."

"And you have no grasp of what it's like to earn one's living."

"Nor do I wish to."

"A declaration that does not in the least surprise me. From the look of those clothes, work wouldn't suit you."

He opened his mouth to fire off a reply, but as badly as he wanted to set her straight about the duties required of men of his rank, a glance at the clock on her wall reminded him of his priorities. Unfortunately, he still didn't know anything more about his mother's plans than he had when he'd arrived here. "It is clear you are unaware of the many responsibilities of the nobility, Miss Deverill, but much to my regret, I do not have the time or inclination to instruct you on the subject. Finding my mother is the only thing I care about just now."

"And in that regard, as I have already said, I cannot help you."

He studied her face and knew he was wasting his time. Whether because she genuinely did not know his mother's whereabouts, or because she was refusing to part with the information because of her misguided prejudice against his class or because of some absurd notion of journalistic integrity, he could not be sure. But whatever her knowledge or her motives, she was clearly not going to be of any assistance to him.

"Then, I shall bid you good day." He gave her a bow, took up his hat from the desk and turned to go. By the door, however, he paused, one hand on the knob, and he turned to look at her over his shoulder. "But before I go, there is one thing I should like you to consider, if you would."

She looked at him as if she'd rather swallow poison than consider anything he might have to say, but he forced himself to wait, and after a moment, her curiosity seemed to overcome her resentment. "And what is that?"

"I should like you to consider what impact your decisions may have on the lives of other people. If my mother suffers ridicule and condemnation because of you and your publication, what responsibility do you bear? If her life is ruined, what consequences should there be for yours? Given the part you will have played in her downfall, what punishment will you deserve?"

She inhaled sharply. "Is that a threat?" she asked, her chin tilting up in defiance. "There is nothing you can do to me, sir."

"You think not?" He gave her a pitying smile. "Oh, my dear Miss Deverill."

His words, soft and dangerous, caused a flicker of concern in those tawny eyes, a reaction he found quite satisfying under the circumstances. "If my mother corresponds with you in future," he went on as he donned his hat, "I doubt you will inform me of the fact, but I hope you will have the courtesy to tell her that her family is worried about her and would like news of her. And by the way," he added as he opened the door, "I am not a 'sir.' That title is reserved for knights. I am a duke, and properly addressed by a commoner such as yourself as 'Your Grace.'" With that, he walked out and closed the door behind him, leaving her no chance to reply, which he could only deem a very good thing. In dealing with a woman like Miss Deverill, any man would be wise to ensure to always get in the last word. Otherwise, she'd devour the poor sod for breakfast.

Chapter 3

In all her twenty-six years, Irene had never known she possessed a hot temper. She'd always considered herself a levelheaded sort of person: calm, steady, and reasonably good-natured, but as she watched the door swing shut behind the Duke of Torquil, she felt anything but calm and steady, and she realized she had been quite mistaken in her own character.

She wanted to go chasing after him and tell him just what he could do with his pointless forms of address and his condescending manner, but she could not seem to move. Her feet felt embedded in the floor, her body burned as if on fire, and her blood seethed through her veins like lava. All in all, she felt like a mountain in the full throes of a volcanic eruption. If smoke had started billowing from her ears, she would not have been surprised.

"Oh," she said, a huff of air that seemed dismally

inadequate to the situation, but there was no other satisfactory outlet for her feelings. The knowledge that her outrage was of the impotent variety only served to increase it. "Oh!" she said again, her hands balling into fists. "What an awful man!"

The door opened, and Clara came in, a tea tray balanced on her forearm. She stopped by the door, glancing around in surprise as she shifted the tray back to both hands. "He's gone already?"

"Unless he's lingering in the outer office like some harbinger of doom," Irene muttered, scowling, "then, yes, he's gone. Thank goodness."

Her gratitude at the man's departure did not seem shared by Clara, who looked inexplicably let down. "And I fetched tea from the kitchen and everything," she said, lifting the tray in her hands a bit higher as she came into the room.

"He wasn't worth the trouble."

"Irene, how can you say that? He's a duke."

"A duke. Well, my word and la-di-da." She pressed the back of her hand to her forehead. "I shall need my smelling salts in a minute. I'm that overcome."

Before her sister could reply, there was a tap on her open door, and she looked up to find Annie, their parlor maid, standing in the doorway.

"If you please, ma'am," she said, dipping her knees in a quick curtsy, "Mrs. Brandt's compliments, and I'm to tell you tea will soon be ready for you and your guest in the drawing room."

Irene and Clara exchanged bewildered glances at this message from their housekeeper, but it was Clara who spoke first. "Annie, I already had Mrs. Gibson make tea for us. As you see," she added, nodding to the tray in her hands, "I've brought it here."

"Begging your pardon, Miss Clara, but Mrs. Brandt what says I'm to take that away and have you bring His Grace to the drawing room. She's ordered Mrs. Gibson to make him a proper tea."

"A proper tea?" Irene echoed, her anger fading into a sort of amused irritation. "Heavens, does that mean we've been having improper tea all these years? Who'd have thought?"

Clara laughed, but Annie didn't. Jokes were wasted on their parlor maid, who took everything said to her at face value. "Mrs. Brandt says a duke what comes to call ought to be given a proper tea. She promises she'll bring it in once you've brought His Grace upstairs to the drawing room."

"The duke is gone, Annie," Irene explained patiently, gesturing with her hands to indicate the lack of that august presence in her office.

"Oh, ma'am, Mrs. Brandt will be ever so disappointed. She told Mrs. Gibson to put sugar icing on the cakes and told me not to worry about serving. She'd wait on the duke personally, she said."

"Wanted to see him for herself, no doubt," Clara murmured.

Annie nodded, looking sorrowful. "It was a right disappointment to me, Miss Clara, I don't mind saying."

"There is no need for disappointment, Annie," Irene assured her as she came around the desk. "You are more fortunate than you could imagine. Please go back down to the kitchens and tell Mrs. Gibson she doesn't need to put icing on the cakes—"

"Now, Irene, let's not be hasty," Clara cut in, shoving the tray into Annie's hands and hooking her arm through her sister's. "It seems Mrs. Brandt and Mrs. Gibson have gone to a great deal of trouble. I should hate their efforts to be wasted."

Irene sniffed, but she allowed her sister to propel her out of her office, out of their former library, and along the corridor to the stairs. "In any case, I doubt even Mrs. Gibson's sugar icing would have impressed Lord Insufferable."

Clara laughed. "Oh, dear, he seems to have gotten under your skin all right. But, Irene, you can't call him Lord Insufferable. He's not a lord. He's a duke."

She waved a hand, not needing another lecture about proper forms of address. "A minor quibble, Clara. Lord Insufferable is a title that suits that man admirably."

"Still, it's a shame for poor Annie," Clara said in a whisper.

Both of them glanced back, but the parlor maid had already vanished behind the baize door that led down to the kitchens. "I wouldn't want to be the one who has to tell our temperamental cook and grenadier housekeeper that their efforts to impress a duke have been in vain," Clara went on as she and Irene continued up the stairs and entered the drawing room. "Now, Irene, you must tell me everything."

She gave her sister a rueful glance as she sat down on one end of the horsehair settee. "Must I?"

"Was he so very horrid?" Clara asked, sinking down beside her.

"Worse."

"Did he come about his mother?"

"Yes. She's eloped with the Italian, apparently."

"So she did follow your advice? You weren't sure she would, if I recall. Oh, won't this make a sensation for the paper?"

"Yes," Irene agreed, but the word was barely out of her mouth before the Duke of Torquil's question rang in her ears.

If she suffers ridicule, disgrace, and pain because of you and your publication, what consequences should you face?

The question was nonsense, of course. A mature woman like the duchess would surely appreciate all possible consequences of the choice she was making. Irene could not be held accountable for those consequences.

"But why did Torquil want to see you?"

She had no chance to answer, for Mrs. Brandt arrived at that moment with a laden tea tray, and Irene shoved the duke's accusatory words out of her mind.

"Tea, miss," the housekeeper announced as she entered the room. "Mrs. Gibson's made some lovely iced cakes today. A pity His Grace won't be able to enjoy them," she added, making no effort to hide her disappointment as she set the tray on the tea table beside Irene's chair.

"A great pity," Irene agreed with cheer as she reached for the teapot and the strainer. "But please thank Mrs. Gibson, and assure her we shall enjoy the cakes enormously."

The housekeeper didn't seem at all gratified to hear it. Still looking quite let down, she left the room.

"Well?" Clara asked the moment the housekeeper was out the door. "Why did the duke want to see you?"

"Why does it matter?" Irene countered as she strained tea into two cups and added sugar.

"I can't believe you'd even ask me that," Clara said as she took the cup and saucer Irene held out to her. "Of course it matters! He's a duke."

"So?"

"Irene! You know I read about the doings of the aristocracy in *Society Snippets* every day. So do you."

"I read our paper because, as the editor, doing so is one of my responsibilities. It's different for you. Your job as my secretary doesn't require you to read what we publish."

"But I like to read it. I like gossip." She lifted her round chin a notch as she sat back with her teacup. "Especially about handsome dukes and their scandalous mothers."

Irene wrinkled up her nose in distaste at her sister's description of the duke. "Handsome is as handsome does."

"Oh, stop! You sound like Papa's Cousin Martha."

She did, a fact she found terribly disheartening, but she turned away, pretending vast interest in the cakes Mrs. Gibson had taken such pains to decorate. "Either way, I didn't think him particularly handsome."

"Tell it to the marines! You know as well as I do he was handsome as sin."

Irene made a face. "I doubt that man would know a sin if it bit him. He's so stiff-necked, he ought to be a vicar, not a duke."

"If he was a vicar, no woman in his parish would

ever miss services." Clara sighed, fanning herself with her free hand. "So splendidly tall, and with such wide shoulders."

Irene groaned. "Oh, Clara, don't be mawkish."

Clara was undeterred. "Beautiful eyes, too. You must have noticed that much, at least."

Beautiful or not, the thing she'd noticed most about his eyes was how disapprovingly they'd studied her. Everything about her appearance had been dissected, judged, and no doubt found wanting. Just the memory of his disdainful gaze made her feel hot and angry and thoroughly stirred up all over again.

"As for the rest," Clara said, her voice intruding on her elder sister's thoughts, "you enjoy hearing gossip about him and his set as much as anybody, Irene. I know it, whatever you say. Why, changing the newspaper to a scandal sheet was your idea."

"I'm glad so many people enjoy reading about the doings of dukes, believe me," she answered, relieved her sister had abandoned talk of the Duke of Torquil's eyes and shoulders. "But for my own part, I couldn't care two straws. And why should I?" she added, feeling prickly all of a sudden. "It's not as if they care about us. Lilies of the field, all of them, and so I said."

"Irene, you didn't call him that to his face?"

She wriggled a little at her sister's appalled expression. "I might have done," she muttered, tugging at one ear.

Clara stared at her, shaking her head. "The Duke of Torquil is wasted on you. If a rich, handsome duke ever came to call upon me, I'd die of happiness."

"No, you wouldn't, for you'd be forced to listen to the horrid things he says," Irene countered and took a cake from the tray. "You should have heard him today, talking about how his mother's marriage to Foscarelli would be beneath her, and such a horrible blow to her family."

"Well, that sort of thing is bound to cause a scandal and have an impact on all her relations."

If my mother's life is ruined as a result of your advice, what responsibility do you bear?

Heavens, she had to stop that man's words from rattling around in her head. Irene suppressed an oath and took a bite of her tea cake. "Still," she said after taking a moment to savor Mrs. Gibson's lemony sugar icing—if not the reason for it, "the duchess is capable of deciding for herself who to marry, isn't she?"

"The duke is no doubt displeased over the match. And he's obviously concerned that his mother is being taken advantage of by Foscarelli."

"Perhaps, but when I wrote back to her, I did point these things out, and I advised her to consult her solicitors, draw up a marital settlement, and tie up the money. I don't know if she did so in the end, but I was very clear about it in my correspondence. And from her words to me, it was obvious she is fully aware of the impact her choice will have upon her family. As for her son, I don't see how his disapproval is of any concern to us."

"It isn't, I suppose, but still—"

"She's a grown woman, and seems to have sound judgement and plenty of good sense. Yet her own son seemed to think her incapable of choosing for herself what man to marry. Would you truly want a man as overbearing as that paying you his attentions?"

"Well," Clara began, but Irene gave her no opportunity to answer.

"It's understandable he would want to know where his mother had gone, but even after I explained that our paper must keep such matters confidential, he still expected me to tell him. No, wait," she corrected herself at once. "He *commanded* me to tell him."

"Then it's obvious he doesn't know you," a long-suffering male voice uttered from the doorway, and both Irene and her sister looked up as their father was wheeled into the drawing room by his valet. "For my part," he added as Sayers maneuvered the wheeled chair into a place by the settee, "I gave up ordering you about long ago. I recognized it as a futile effort about the time you learned to walk."

"Very wise of you, Papa," Irene assured him. "Wouldn't you agree, Sayers?"

The servant, whose countenance Irene had always likened to Lewis Carroll's Mock Turtle, bent to secure the brake of the chair before he answered. "I would not presume to say, Miss Deverill," he told her as he pushed a stool forward and eased his master's foot onto the padded velvet surface, an action that solicited a growl of pain from the older man. "Sorry, sir."

Mr. Deverill waved aside apologies. "Just bring me the brandy, then you may go."

Irene frowned a little, watching him as his servant moved toward the liquor cabinet. "Papa, you should be having tea at teatime, not brandy. And anyway, Doctor Munro has forbidden you the brandy. It makes the gout worse, he said."

"Nonsense. Munro is a sour old goat, and a teetotaler besides. Of course he'd try to keep me from the brandy. Now then," he added before she could argue, "would it be the Duke of Torquil who's ordering our Irene about?"

"The same," Clara said. "How did you know?"

"How do I hear anything in this house?" Mr. Deverill gestured to the valet approaching with the brandy. "My daughters never tell me anything, that's certain. Servants, thankfully, feel that the master of the house, even if he's in his dotage, should be informed when a duke comes to call. Put it there, Sayers," he added, taking up his filled glass and gesturing for the valet to put the bottle on the table.

"Papa, really," Irene began, intending to remind her father again of the doctor's orders, but he cut her off.

"No lectures, my girl. I'm sixty-two years old, and I'll have my brandy if I want it. Like your duchess, I don't need my children making my decisions for me."

"And Papa wonders where I get my stubborn streak?" she said to Clara, earning herself a glare of disapproval from her parent.

"So where is His Grace, then?" Papa asked, glancing around. "Surely you invited him up for tea?"

"Surely I didn't," she countered breezily as she settled back in her seat with her teacup and cake.

"Really, Irene, where are your manners?"

"My manners are perfectly acceptable," she countered, feeling a bit prickly still. "The duke didn't come to pay a call or have tea."

"Given our social position, and the fact that I've never met the man, I already concluded that much," her father answered, downed the contents of his glass, and reached for the bottle to refill it. "So why was he here?"

Irene explained, but her father didn't seem any more enlightened. "So his mother's gone off with an artist? But why would he come looking for her here? What makes him think you'd know her whereabouts?"

"Because she's one of Lady Truelove's correspondents and her letter was in last evening's edition," Clara explained. "But Irene sent him off with a flea in his ear, apparently."

"Lovely." Papa set aside the bottle and took another hefty swallow of brandy. "Now we're insulting dukes and turning them out of the house. That will certainly not bode well for my efforts."

"What efforts are you talking about?" Irene demanded, sitting upright on her seat. "Papa, what are you scheming?"

Her father shrugged, trying to seem nonchalant. "I have been in correspondence with the viscountess, that's all, hoping to interest her in you and your sister."

Irene groaned. "Really, Papa! What do you hope to achieve?"

"She might be able to persuade her husband to bury the hatchet. They're both nearing eighty, you know, and your mother was their only daughter. We might be able to broker a peace."

"Peace? With Viscount Ellesmere? Not likely. My maternal grandfather, I daresay, would like nothing better than to see our lot at the bottom of the sea."

"The viscountess seems open to the possibility of a truce, and she thought she might be able to exert some influence with her husband. If so, it could mean a world of difference to both of you. You could perhaps have a season, go to balls, find husbands."

At twenty-six, Irene knew she was most decidedly on the shelf. Clara, four years younger, might have a bit of time left, but it didn't much matter. Without dowries, neither of them was likely to find a respectable husband, regardless of how many balls and parties they went to, but her father spoke before she could point that out.

"A duke," Papa said, giving her a frown as he swirled his brandy and took another generous swallow, "could be very helpful to my cause, if we could get into his good graces."

Irene shot him a wry look. "Not to crush your hopes for our future, Papa, but having me in the Duke of Torquil's good graces is about as likely as flying pigs."

"What did you say to him? Gave him your cheek, I suppose?"

"Not at all," Irene said with dignity, but Clara ruined her attempt to prevaricate.

"Well, you did call him a lily of the field," her sister said, causing their father to groan and pour himself another glass of brandy.

"All my good work undone, likely as not," he muttered, shaking his head. "It won't matter a jot if you're a viscount's granddaughter if you insist upon snubbing dukes. Really, Irene, must you air your opinions at every opportunity?"

"Oh, I couldn't help it, Papa! The man was so damnably arrogant. And besides, my description of him was apt. I doubt he does any work at all."

"Nor should he," her father said severely. "It would

be unthinkable for a gentleman, especially a duke, to work. It's beneath him."

"Yes, so this particular duke reminded me while looking down his nose and oozing disapproval of me and my profession."

"You can't blame him for that, since a woman isn't supposed to have a profession," her father retorted, leaning back with his glass. "You should be going to parties and juggling the attentions of young men. Not slaving away in that musty office you've made out of what used to be our library."

Irene did not reply, for what was there to say? Her father had never been good with either money or the lack of it, a fact her brother Jonathan had attempted numerous times to remedy without success. A violent quarrel on that topic three years ago had resulted in the banishment of Jonathan from their house and the tearing up of every letter sent by him to their father in the aftermath. Her brother had taken off for America, his present whereabouts unknown, and their father, as if to prove his son wrong about his abilities, had begun speculating wildly with what money they had left. If Irene hadn't intervened, they'd be destitute.

She noted how his hand shook as he refilled his glass again, and she appreciated—not for the first time—that if food was to be put on their table, and if tradesmen and servants were to be paid, she would have to be the one who provided the means. She also knew from past experience that attempting to make her parent accept the hard realities of their life now was as much a waste of breath as telling him not to drink.

"Be that as it may," she said instead, "the duchess's

life is her own business, and if the duke doesn't like the man she chooses to marry, the duke shall be forced to lump it."

"Good heavens, Irene." Her father stared at her, appalled. "You didn't tell him that?"

"Essentially, yes."

Papa groaned. "What will Ellesmere think if he hears about this?"

"Nothing he wasn't thinking already, Papa."

"Yes, but Irene," Clara put in before their father could answer, "the duke does seem to care very much about his mother. You may find his manner arrogant, and even discourteous, but surely worry accounts for that. And it doesn't mean you ought to behave in kind."

Irene felt a stab of guilt. "Really, Clara," she said with a sigh, "it is so aggravating when you decide to be my conscience."

"Someone has to be," her father put in. "Otherwise, God only knows what you'd take it into your head to do. Start a revolution or resume working for the vote, or some other ghastly thing." He shuddered and took another drink.

"I fully intend to march in the streets and champion the vote for women whenever I have the chance," Irene answered. "But at the moment, managing the newspaper takes all my time."

"That is one point in its favor, I suppose," Papa grumbled. "It keeps you away from politics."

Irene made a face at him as she stood up and walked to the secretaire. "As for the rest, neither of you need accuse me of being uncaring, for I have every intention of telling the duchess of her son's visit to me."

Clara shot her a startled glance. "So you do know where she is?"

"I do. A letter from her arrived this morning from a London hotel. I haven't had the chance to read it yet, but I shall do that now, then offer a reply, informing her of her son's visit to me and his concerns about her. I shall also recommend she communicate with her family post-haste."

"Really, Irene," her father said, "I don't understand you. If you have had a letter from the woman and you know where she is, why didn't you convey that information to the duke?"

"Because Lady Truelove promises confidentiality to all her correspondents, Papa. You know that."

It was Papa's turn to make a face, one that made him look as if he'd just eaten a persimmon. "Don't go quoting that abomination you've created in my presence."

"It puts food on the table, Papa," she said as gently as she could.

"There are other ways to do that."

Irene would have appreciated his suggestions on that score a year ago when creditors were threatening to take their home and all their furnishings, but when she watched him down the remainder of his third glass of brandy and pour a fourth, she reminded herself it did no good to fire off tart rejoinders and be cross. "Either way," she said instead, "I have given my word to my readers to respect their confidence, and I won't break it."

"But, Irene, he's a duke."

She was becoming quite tired of that particular refrain. "I don't care if he's the Prince of Bohemia."

Her father gave her an unhappy look. "It would grieve

your mother to see you display such irreverence for the aristocracy."

"Would it?" Irene countered with asperity. "I think Mama displayed an admirable irreverence for her aristocratic family when she had the courage to follow her heart and marry a man of the middle class. And since the viscount and all Mama's family turned their backs on her from the day of her wedding and I've never met any of them in my life, I don't see why they ever deserved her reverence. They certainly don't deserve mine. Or yours."

Pain shimmered across her father's face at this reminder that Mama's family had deemed him so unworthy of her, making Irene regret her words at once. "I didn't mean—"

"I know what you meant, my dear," he said, cutting her off mid-sentence. "And I am grateful for your loyalty to my side of your family tree. But my dear child, it doesn't do to have such blatant disregard for the aristocracy. They are very powerful, and their influence is mighty."

"Yes, so His Grace took pains to remind me."

"Did he, indeed? And what was your response?"

She grinned. "What do you think?"

Her father sighed, shaking his head. "One of these days, Irene, your cheek will be your undoing."

"I'm sure you're right," she said, trying to look suitably chastened. "But really, Papa, duke or no, what can that man possibly do to me?"

artist, but had ensconced herself in a suite of rooms at Thomas's Hotel in Berkeley Square.

Immediately upon the departure of the detective, Henry called for his carriage. While waiting for it to be brought around, he wrote a letter to his solicitors, giving them Foscarelli's address and instructing them to open negotiations with the Italian. Buying off Mama's lover would be, he had no doubt, an expensive proposition, but to avert the looming disaster, he'd write the check happily.

Once in his carriage, Henry ordered his driver to take him to Berkeley Square, and during the short ride, he read the dossier the detective agency had compiled for him about Miss Irene Deverill, her family, and her newspaper. That particular request had been an impulse on his part, for his heated conversation with the woman had sparked not only his ire, but also his curiosity. She had also evoked in him certain other emotions, those of a darker, more erotic nature, but he knew he'd do well not to explore those particular feelings too deeply.

It was just ten o'clock when his carriage pulled into Berkeley Square. Thomas's was a small but comfortable hotel located on the north side of the square. It was considered to be somewhat old-fashioned, but to Henry's mind, that was a point in its favor. Upon his arrival, he inquired after his mother, handing his card to the concierge. "Please have the duchess informed of my presence and inquire if she will receive me."

A footman was dispatched upon this errand, and though Henry wasn't at all sure his mother would see him, a few minutes later the footman returned, affirmed the duchess was receiving, and gestured toward the electric lift tucked discreetly behind a trio of potted palms. "If you will follow me, Your Grace?"

He was led up to a suite of rooms on the second floor, and though he knew his mother had taken no servants with her, not even a maid, it nonetheless seemed incongruous when she opened the door to him herself.

"So you've found me."

That cool greeting did not bode well, nor did her equally cool demeanor. No one had ever thought he and his mother bore much of a familial resemblance, for the duchess was diminutive, sweet-faced, and amiable, and Henry, as everyone knew, was none of those things. Right now, however, there was a determined line to his mother's jaw and a guarded cast to her countenance that reminded Henry far too much of his own character for his peace of mind. Still, given the current circumstances, he could hardly have expected her to welcome him with open arms. "Did you think I wouldn't find you?"

She gave a sigh and opened the door wide. "No," she admitted as he came in. "Although I did think it might take you a bit longer than it has."

"I daresay, since the nuptials haven't yet taken place."

"A fact that fills you with delight, no doubt."

"I find nothing delightful in this, Mama," he assured her as she led him into the suite's small sitting room. "We have all been concerned for you."

"There is no need to be." She gestured to a pair of moss-green settees, and when she sat down upon one, he seated himself directly opposite. She gave him no chance, however, to begin the eloquent speech he had been preparing since her departure Tuesday morning.

"Henry, I know your intent is to change my mind about

my marriage, so allow me to save you the trouble and spare us both what would surely be a quarrel. I shall not change my mind, regardless of your efforts."

"I am not here only for that reason, Mama. I am also hoping to persuade you to return home. A hotel cannot be as comfortable as your own home, especially with no servants to attend you."

"Now that you know where I am, I shall send for my maid. She is all the help I need for the present, since this situation will not be for long. Antonio secured the lease on his own flat here in London yesterday. A fortnight from now, he will be able to obtain the marriage license and we can be wed."

Though this news confirmed his earlier prediction of Foscarelli's actions and further cemented his low opinion of the other man's character, it was nonetheless a relief, for it meant he now had two full weeks to change his mother's mind. Despite that, he knew he had to tread carefully, and he decided pretending a lack of knowledge about the other man was his best course. "I take it Foscarelli had not previously had a fixed abode in town?"

His mother's nose wrinkled at the implication. "You make it sound as if he's been indigent."

Not indigent, Henry wanted to say. *Just low enough to sponge off his friends as long as possible.*

Wisely, he didn't voice that opinion. "Not at all," he said instead, but he must not have sounded convincing enough.

"It is the season, Henry. You know how difficult it is to find rooms in town. It's only because it's nearly August that he's found rooms of his own at all."

Henry didn't debate the point. "Of course," he said politely. "But if we may, could we discuss your living arrangements rather than those of your . . . ahem . . ." He paused, grasping for a description of Foscarelli he could manage to utter without choking. "Rather than those of your acquaintance? There is no need for you to stay in a hotel, Mama," he added. "You have a home."

"Where I would leave myself open to the continual arguments of my children over the course I have chosen? I think I would prefer to remain here. Thomas's is a perfectly respectable establishment."

"If one is a tourist, yes. But not if one already has a comfortable home a mere five blocks away."

His mother drew herself up, the morning light through the windows glinting on her steel-gray hair. "When a woman has chosen to elope, there is no going back."

At that somewhat melodramatic declaration, Henry had to suppress a sigh. "You aren't married yet."

"Which is why I am here, and not already living with Antonio in our new home."

"New home?" Henry stared at her, dumbfounded. "You intend to live with him in a Camden Town flat?"

"Why not? It is a full-service flat." There was a hint of amusement in her blue eyes that told him she was teasing him a little, but she spoke again before he could reply. "You may rest easy, Henry. Antonio only leased the flat to apply for the license. We shall sublet it. But I could hardly expect you to welcome him into the ducal residences after the wedding, so I have made an offer to purchase a very comfortable little villa for us. It is in Chiswick, on the river. Once the wedding has taken place, that is where we shall begin our life together. We shall travel to Italy in the autumn, for he does so want me to see Florence, and I have never been—"

"Mama, please," he cut in, unable to bear it. "You talk as if you and Foscarelli shall be a pair of young newlyweds on honeymoon. You are fifty years old, not nineteen."

"So I am too old to see the world?"

"You know what I mean."

"I do. What you mean is that at my age, I should not be prone to the reckless actions we all take in our youth."

He stiffened, all his defenses rising to the fore. "Just so. God knows, when I was nineteen, I was unbelievably foolish. My passion blinded me to the consequences of making a rash marriage to someone far beneath my station. But I was paid out for my folly."

"You married the girl in honorable fashion."

"Honorable?" he echoed, his voice scathing even to his own ears. "Making a marriage so wrong that I had to conceal it from the world, hide it even from my own family? Putting my own wife away in a cottage in the country, sneaking away from Cambridge to visit her . . . yes," he said with bitterness, "I was so honorable."

"You loved her."

"Did I?" He shook his head. "No, infatuation is not love. Passion is not love. Lust"—he forced the word out—"is not love. Do not paint a romantic picture of my actions, Mama, or attribute to me honor that I did not possess. I married Elena because I wanted her, and I could not have her any other way." Guilt and regret felt like a weight against his chest, making it even more incumbent upon him to steer his mother from the mistake she was about to make. He leaned forward in his seat, considering his next words with care. They had never spoken openly of his clandestine marriage a decade ago, but though he hated doing so now, it was necessary.

"It only took eight weeks for our mad infatuation to die. Eight weeks, and then there we were: two desperately unhappy souls with nothing in common but the ashes of a dead passion, caught for life in the consequences of our—my—mistake. For it was mine," he rushed on as she tried again to speak. "The power in the situation was all mine; she had none. Papa said she was my ruin, but—"

"Your father was an unyielding man who could see no way but his own. And in this, he was wrong."

"I know that. Elena was not my ruin." He paused, swallowed hard, and met his mother's gaze. "I was hers. Is it any wonder we were unhappy?"

"Stop, Henry," she cried, her voice sharp. "Please, stop this. I cannot bear to hear you berate yourself this way."

He could have continued in this vein. He could have asked her what she and a man so different from herself would share, work toward, and talk about once their passion had cooled and they discovered there was no foundation beneath it. But he refrained, for the point had been made, and hammering it to death would serve no purpose.

"Until this wedding takes place," he said instead, "would you at least consider returning home? We have friends and acquaintances who live in Berkeley Square.

You are bound to be seen coming and going from here, if you haven't already. What do you imagine our friends will think to see you slipping in and out of a hotel two blocks from your own residence? Or worse, what if they see that man coming here to visit you?"

"Heavens, Henry, you make me sound notorious."

"You soon will be, I can assure you, if you follow through with this elopement."

His mother sniffed. "That would say more about the quality of our acquaintances than it would about me. My true friends will stand by me. The rest don't matter."

That sounded very much like the lofty sentiments Miss Irene Deverill had trotted out two days before. Fine enough in theory, he supposed, but wholly untenable in reality.

Still, as he studied his mother's resolute expression, he decided another shift in tactics was in order.

"Have you thought of how this will affect the marital prospects of your daughters?" he asked.

"Of course I have."

"Then you know your marriage will considerably diminish their chances of making a good match themselves."

"That depends on one's definition of a good match, doesn't it? I would say that because of my marriage, my daughters will soon be able to determine which gentlemen of their acquaintance genuinely care for them, and which only care for their position in society."

"As if position is not important."

"Henry, do you really think worrying about my matrimonial future or even that of your sisters is your most vital concern?"

That took him back a step. "Of course it is of vital concern. You are my family."

She leaned forward, close enough to put her hand over his. "My dear, perhaps instead of worrying about my matrimonial future or that of your sisters, you should be considering your own. Elena passed away eight years ago, freeing you to marry again. David is your only heir," she rushed on as he opened his mouth to reply, "and he is married six years now, with no children. You must marry again. You know that."

"I am well aware of my duty, Mama. There is no need to remind me of it."

"Falling in love is not a duty, Henry."

"Are we back to talking of love?" he countered. "Forgive me, but I thought we were now talking of marriage."

His mother gazed at him with sadness. "Oh, my dear," she said, "I begin to fear the romance you once had in your soul may be irretrievably gone."

"If so, I cannot help but find that a good thing." He met his mother's unhappy gaze with an implacable one of his own. "We both know the task of choosing one's marriage partner is a serious business for people like us, Mama. It's not a frivol. Marry in haste, repent at leisure may be the course you seem bent upon, but for myself, I will not choose it twice in one lifetime."

"We love who we love, Henry. Love can't bend to one's will."

"Stop," he said fiercely. "Stop speaking of my marriage to Elena as if I had no choice. I forgot who I was, and where my duty lay, and I allowed passion to dictate my course. The result was tragic for all concerned.

Do not spare me or excuse me, for I certainly shall not spare or excuse myself."

She studied him for a moment, opened her mouth as if to argue further on the topic, then closed it again, much to his relief. "Very well," she said quietly. "Just which young ladies of our acquaintance might enable you to do your duty most commendably?"

He ignored the acidic note of her voice. "I am considering several, but my matrimonial future shall have to wait until yours is settled, so stop trying to deflect the conversation."

"It is settled, my dear boy, whether you like it or not. Fifteen days from now, Antonio and I will be married, and try though you will, you cannot stop it."

That remained to be seen. "I assume Foscarelli has the blunt to support you?"

"Why? Are you threatening to cut off my portion if I marry him? Now who's behaving as if I'm nineteen?"

Henry was shocked. "I have no intention of cutting off your allowance from the estate, Mama. I know you do not need it, but it is yours by right. I cannot imagine any circumstances in which I would ever deny it to you. On the other hand, I confess I am not thrilled it shall end up in the hands of a man who cannot seem to support himself, much less a wife."

"Really? That will be news to David and Jamie."

"It is not the same thing, Mama, as you are well aware. Jamie and David are family, and their allowances from the estate are a given, as is yours. Antonio Foscarelli is not family."

"He soon will be. Still, you have no need to worry

that my allowance from the estate shall be needed to support him."

"Yes, no doubt because he is counting on a substantial marriage settlement from me."

"Not at all. There will be no need for you to give him any money."

"No need? Mama, if you're saying he isn't to receive a penny, I heartily endorse that decision, but I have the uneasy feeling that is not what you mean."

"It isn't. I am settling a sum on Antonio out of my private funds as a dowry."

Henry wasn't surprised by this news, but nonetheless, his guts twisted into a sick knot of dismay. "I see. So you have already visited our solicitors and drafted the marital agreement?"

She gave a little shrug. "I mentioned to Antonio that you would expect one to be drawn up."

That wasn't the same thing, but Henry refrained from pointing out the fact. "And what," he said instead, "was Foscarelli's reply to that?"

"He's not fond of the idea."

"How shocking."

She seemed to miss the sarcasm. "His people don't believe in that sort of thing, and frankly, neither do I. Most people don't. It's a very modern view, Henry. Formal documents and discussions of money . . . I cannot help thinking it sordid. Besides, the law protects my property well enough. The Married Women's Property Acts—"

"Mama," he cut her off, "the law as it stands now is all very well, but in practical terms, it's a sticky wicket, particularly if people separate later. A prenuptial agreement would do no harm."

"I refuse to enter my marriage anticipating its demise."

Henry took a deep breath, reminding himself it was best to fight one battle at a time. A marriage settlement only became relevant if he couldn't stop the marriage from happening. "You say you intend to settle a sum on him. How much?"

"Fifty thousand pounds."

The enormity of the sum sent any notions he had of being calm and reasonable to the wall. *That swine*, he thought, rage rising within him as he appreciated how Foscarelli must have worked on her to persuade her to such an exorbitant amount. That worthless, fortune-hunting swine. "God, Mama," he managed after a moment, "that's nearly half your fortune."

"I'm well aware of that. But offering a dowry is perfectly acceptable, as you know. A man can't be having to beggar pin money from his wife each month."

"Yes, yes, God forbid fortune-hunters be kept in check with a pesky allowance."

"Really, Henry, must you be crass?"

"Yes, Mama, it seems I must, if only to prevent you from being a fool. You know you will have to sell out half your personal capital to raise that amount of money?"

"Of course."

"I do not understand you, Mama," he muttered, raking a hand through his hair, trying to think. "Why not just put him on a quarterly allowance? Why does he need a dowry at all, especially such a vast one? Fifty thousand pounds is an enormous sum. Why would you—"

He stopped, realizing in a sudden, horrific flash of insight what his mother was doing. "My God, you're spiking my guns."

She looked away, staring down at her fingertips as they idly traced the intricate embroidery of a sofa pillow. "I don't know what you mean."

"Yes, you do. I came here assuming you weren't aware of the true nature of his suit, but now I see that I was mistaken. You know full well what sort of man you are marrying, and you don't care." He gave a laugh of utter disbelief. "Your motives for being such a fool prove you an even greater fool. You realize that?"

He regretted his words at once, even before she spoke.

"If you insult me again," she said, her eyes narrowing, "this discussion is over."

Henry rubbed his hands over his face, cursing himself for being so blind that he hadn't put a stop to the Italian's machinations months ago, cursing his usually sensible mother for being so damned foolhardy, and cursing Lady Truelove for aiding and abetting it all. It was several moments before he could trust himself to speak.

"Let us leave off discussions of money for the moment," he said, working to think. Talking his mother out of this could not be accomplished in one conversation, that was clear. He needed time, and as much information as he could glean. Only then could he figure out how to prevent her from taking the foolhardy course she was bent upon. "Where are these nuptials to take place, if I may ask? Neither the ducal chapel nor our parish church shall be appropriate under the circumstances, since he is a Catholic."

"You say that as if it's akin to having the plague."

"If he had the plague, I would celebrate," Henry muttered. "Are you prepared to convert? You'll have to, you know. Or he will."

"There is no need for conversion. We shall not marry in any church, but at the Registry Office. You are welcome to come, though I'm sure you won't wish to."

"Oh, I will be there, you may be sure. If only to object when the magistrate puts the question."

"Henry, I have made my decision. These attempts to bully me into submission are futile."

"Bully you?" Henry was affronted by the accusation. "God, Mama, are the suffragist views of Lady Truelove contagious? What is all this talk of bullying and submission?"

"I had plenty of that sort of thing from your father," she went on as if he hadn't spoken, her voice growing markedly colder as she mentioned her late husband. "Over twenty years of it, in fact. I don't need to tolerate it from my son."

"That is not fair, Mama."

"As you already pointed out, I am fifty years old, so I fail to see how my choice of whom to marry is any of your concern, Torquil."

The use of his title and the withering tone of her voice were too much to bear. "Because I love you, damn it! That makes it my concern."

Her gaze softened at once. "Oh, my dear."

He looked away, feeling suddenly awkward and vulnerable, the two emotions he despised above all others, and he was compelled to move onto safer ground. "It is my duty as head of the family," he said in his best ducal voice, "to do all I can to ensure the well-being and security of all my relations. That includes you, Mama." He looked at her again. "Could you really expect any less of me?"

"Dearest Henry," she murmured. "Of all my children, you are the one who has always worried me the most."

"I?" He stared at her, astonished by this revelation. "Why, in heaven's name?"

"Because you fight so hard against your own nature."

He stiffened. So much for safer ground. "I have no idea what you mean," he lied.

"Yes, you do. Ever since you were a boy, you have striven to be the son your father wanted you to be. But he was an uncompromising sort of man, with a rigid sense of duty, a cold heart, and a puritanical moral compass. He did his best to make you the same, and any influence I may have had over your early life was blunted by him at every turn. When he and I discovered your secret, that you had broken free and married a tobacconist's daughter, it was the shock of his life. I, however, was not all that surprised. There is an element of me inside of you, you see." She smiled a little. "I've always known that."

"And you think that particular part of us a good thing? Mama, my passion for Elena was a disastrous mistake."

"I know you think so. But I cannot agree. You loved her, I know it. Despite what you say or however you may define the emotion, you loved her, and to my mind, love is never a mistake, even if it brings pain, even if it does not last."

He exhaled a sharp sigh. "Perhaps that it so, Mama, but marriage is not like love. Marriage is permanent. If it proves a mistake, there's no getting out of it, not for our sort."

"Yes, but it is possible to have both marriage and love, my dear."

He gave an unamused laugh. "Yes, well, that is the trick, isn't it?"

She reached out, her hand closing over his. "Elena has been gone eight years, your father nearly as long. I know you are wary of trusting your own judgment in this, but can you not now open your heart again to the more tender emotions of life? For I fear if you do not do it soon, you may not be able to do it at all."

This conversation, Henry decided, was accomplishing nothing. "We seem to be talking in circles." He pulled his hand away and rose. "Therefore, I shall take my leave."

"Oh, Henry, don't go all prickly and stiff and act as if you have ice water in your veins. I know you too well to be deceived. All I am trying to say is that while I know you will never be the sort to wear your heart on your sleeve, don't bury it so deep that you suffocate it to death."

"My heart, since we are talking of it, is suffering at this moment. On your behalf, Mama. No, wait," he went on as she tried to speak. He had one card left to play, and he needed to play it while he could. "Allow me to finish. As I said, if you stay here during the next two weeks, people we know will observe you coming and going from this hotel. They will come to call; they will question you."

"I shall tell them nothing."

"Then they will draw their own conclusions and spread those conclusions as fact. And you can be sure whatever the talk, it will not reflect favorably upon you, your daughters, or any of your other relations. Wouldn't it be better to just come home? Stay in your own residence until . . ." He paused, working to force the words out. "Until the wedding?"

"And listen to you disparage Antonio to me at every opportunity in an attempt to change my mind about him?"

"I won't do that. I give you my word I will not speak ill of him in your hearing. And I will make certain the other members of the family exercise the same restraint."

His mother might be acting foolishly at the moment, but she was not, as her next words proved, a fool. "You may not disparage Antonio in my hearing, but I have no doubt you will nonetheless make every attempt to change my mind and circumvent my course."

There was no point in denial. "I will do that, Mama, whether you come home or you remain here."

"True." She paused, considering, and after a moment, she nodded, much to his relief. "Very well, then, I will return home."

"And will you promise me that you will be discreet in regard to your marriage plans until the wedding has taken place?"

"There's hardly any point to that now, since everyone is bound to guess from Lady Truelove's column that I am the woman who wrote to her about him."

"People may guess, but until the wedding, they will

not *know*. And in the interim, I should like Sarah and Angela to enjoy what remains of the season."

"Very well. You may be assured of my discretion. I will arrive home this evening, in time for sherry before dinner."

Relieved, he bowed. "Then I shall see you this evening." He turned to go, but he had barely reached the doorway before her voice called to him.

"Henry?"

He paused to look at her over his shoulder. "Yes?"

"I don't suppose it shall make any difference to your point of view about this situation, or your low opinion of him, but Antonio makes me very happy."

"If that is so, I hope I can find some consolation in the fact."

With that, he departed, and though he had achieved one of his objectives in coming here, the other still loomed over their future like an impending storm, and he had no intention of giving up.

On the other hand, he doubted that hammering home the Italian's many flaws, offering up the reports of private investigators, and presenting his mother with the gossip column accounts of Foscarelli's past activities would accomplish anything. She knew what a scoundrel he was, that was clear, and the harder he pushed, the more likely she was to dig in her heels. But to sway her against this marriage, what other options did he have?

"Your Grace?"

"Hmm?" Startled out of these contemplations, he looked up to find his driver beside him. He'd been so lost in thought, he didn't even remember taking the lift down to the foyer or exiting the hotel, but he must have done both, for he was now standing on the sidewalk, his brougham in front of him and his driver holding the door open.

"Sorry, Treves," he said and stepped into the vehicle, his mind still racing to decide his next step. Fortunately, he'd barely settled back on the seat before inspiration struck.

He wasn't likely to have much success in persuading his mother against the course she'd chosen, but he was not the only person she might listen to. "Take me to my solicitors, Treves," he said. "Asgarth and Hopwood, 17 Norfolk Street."

Chapter 5

"No, no, this won't do at all." Using a fat lead pencil, Irene crossed out yet another paragraph of the typewritten column that had been handed to her a short time ago by the young woman sitting across from her. "No one cares a jot about Lady Godfrey's pet parakeet. You're Delilah Dawlish, London's most sensational gossip columnist. You're supposed to titillate your readers, not bore them to death."

The young woman on the other side of the desk, whose real name was not Delilah Dawlish, but the much more prosaic one of Josie Blount, grimaced at this criticism. "It's rubbish, I know," she said, "but there's not a speck of interesting news to be had just now. The season's nearly over. Until the Glorious Twelfth when the house parties start . . ." Her voice trailed off and she spread her hands in a gesture of futility. "There's just nothing new to talk about."

"There must be something more interesting than the death of a parakeet." Irene tapped her pencil against the pages on her desk, thinking hard. "What about house parties, since we're talking of those? Anything newsworthy there?"

Before Josie could answer, a tap on her door interrupted, and Irene looked up to find Clara in the doorway. "The Duke of Torquil is here to see you."

Irene groaned. "For heaven's sake, what does that man want now?"

"Now?" Josie sat upright in her chair, her keen eyes narrowing with speculation as she studied her employer, her excellent investigative instincts aroused. "The Duke of Torquil is here? And he has been here before?"

Irene shrugged, hoping to downplay the matter. "He came the day before yesterday, around teatime."

"The Duke of Torquil coming to see the editor of this very newspaper," Josie said, her voice holding an undercurrent of excitement that Irene perceived at once.

"Oh, no," she said, shaking her head. "The Duke coming here is not going in your column."

"Look at it this way. He's more exciting than Lady Godfrey's dead parakeet."

"Not one word, Josie. Not one."

The journalist sighed. "Oh, very well, but why the secrecy?" She paused, glancing over her shoulder to the open doorway behind Clara, then back at Irene, her gaze turning speculative. "It's about his mother, isn't it? It must be. What else could he want?"

"My head," she answered at once. "On a plate." Before the other woman could ask any more questions, she stood up, holding out the sheets of paper. "We're fortunate you have two days until press time. Give me something worth talking about, Josie."

"Yes, Miss Deverill."

The journalist departed, moving past Clara and out of the office, and Irene turned to her sister. "I suppose I have to see him," she said without enthusiasm. "Though I can't imagine why he's back again. Send him in, but for heaven's sake, leave the door open this time."

That last bit of instruction was wholly wasted, for though Clara complied, the duke countermanded the action by shutting the door again after he had entered the room and Clara had departed.

Irene opened her mouth to demand he open it, but then he started toward her, and any thoughts about the door vanished as she remembered Clara's remark from two days ago.

Handsome as sin.

With those words running through her head, Irene couldn't help but notice the athletic grace with which he moved, the perfect way his elegant clothes fit his long legs, lean hips, and the wide shoulders Clara had so admired. As he halted before her desk, she noticed the pale, clear gray of his eyes and the black lashes that surrounded them, lashes far more opulent than any man ought to have. He might very well be, she realized in dismay, the handsomest man she'd ever encountered. How could she not have noticed that fact the day before yesterday? Maybe she'd been working too hard.

He gave a slight cough, reminding Irene that she was staring. Not that all her scrutiny had done her much good, for as he lifted a slim portfolio of black leather and placed it on her desk, she realized she hadn't even noticed until that moment he'd been carrying such an item.

Irene gave herself a little mental shake to bring herself out of this sudden and most aggravating appreciation of the duke's masculine assets. "I prefer the door of my office to remain open."

"And I prefer it closed."

With that, any momentary appreciation of his good looks vanished, and she was reminded that although he might very well be the handsomest man of her acquaintance, that fact hardly mattered, since his good looks took a distant second place to his arrogance.

"I am an unmarried woman," she pointed out. "Isn't a closed door rather improper?"

"Indeed, but since you made it clear in our previous conversation that what other people think is of no consequence to you, why should that matter? And," he added before she could reply, "in addition to your sister, there are presently three other young women seated on the other side of this door, women I have no doubt are gossip columnists."

"Journalists."

He shrugged as if that were a meaningless distinction. "I would prefer not to have them listening in."

"I see. So eavesdropping on other people's conversations is acceptable only when you do it?"

"Rank," he said, smiling a little, "does have its privileges."

"If it's gossip you're worried about, I can assure you

that I have no intention of providing the readers of my paper with the knowledge that you came to see me, much less the details of our conversation."

"Just the same, I would prefer not to risk it."

Irene heaved a sigh and gave up. "Just why have you come to see me?"

"I have a business matter I should like to discuss with you." He gestured to the chair beside him with the other. "Shall we sit down?"

She wanted to refuse, but she couldn't help being a bit curious. "I'd say no," she said as she resumed her seat, "but I doubt it would matter."

"You are beginning to develop an understanding of dukes, Miss Deverill." He pulled out the chair across from her and sat down, then pulled the portfolio from her desk and placed it on the floor beside him.

"Whatever the reason you're here," she said, glancing at the clock on the wall, "it had best not take long, for I have a luncheon appointment at two o'clock. You have twenty-five minutes to come to the point."

"That amount of time will be ample, but first, I wanted to tell you that since my visit to you two days ago, I have had news of my mother, and I thought perhaps you might wish to hear it." He paused, one dark brow lifting in that haughty way of his. "Or perhaps," he said after a moment, "your interest in those who write to you comes to an end once their stories are published?"

"Of course not!" Irene could feel her face and her temper heating up, and she wondered in exasperation how this man was able to flick her on the raw so easily. Whatever the reason, she would prefer not to let him see that he had any effect on her, and Irene strove for equanimity. "You mistake disinterest for knowledge. I own a newspaper, so I probably already know any news you may wish to tell me."

"And yet you could not convey what you knew to me two days ago?" He did not wait for a reply, but went on, "Either way, you must then already be aware that she has not yet taken your advice and married Foscarelli."

"I am, though I confess, I'm a bit surprised. Usually when one elopes, the marriage follows immediately. Is the delay due to your efforts?"

"I'm afraid I can take no credit. Until the day before yesterday, Mr. Foscarelli had been a man without a residence. Now that he has obtained a flat in town, he must wait fifteen days to secure the license."

"I see. Either way, I cannot see that you came here for the purpose of keeping me informed as to your mother's marriage state. Perhaps you could come to the point of your visit?"

"I am happy to do so, but first, I should like to ask you a question, one to which I would appreciate an unequivocal answer."

Irene took a moment to brace herself before she replied. "What do you want to know?"

He reached into the portfolio beside him and pulled out a copy of *Society Snippets*. "I see that in your reply to my mother, you advised her to follow her heart and her passion and not allow superficialities such as position and class to bar the path to true love and happiness."

She grimaced at his dry tone, for he made the words of her column sound like a penny dreadful. "Don't you believe love is important to marriage?"

He didn't reply at once, and the fact that her question

seemed difficult to him when the answer was so obvious to her made Irene almost want to laugh.

"Perhaps it is," he conceded at last. "But there are other things I believe matter more, if one's marriage is to be happy. Things such as compatibility, like minds, similar station—the very things you would no doubt deem the 'superficialities.'"

"You said you had a question to ask me," she reminded. "That did not sound like a question."

He tossed the newspaper onto her desk. "In all this so-called advice you offered my mother, couldn't you have at least suggested she tie up her money?"

Irene stared at him in astonishment. "But I did. I advised her to have her solicitors draw up a marriage settlement."

"That part of your advice did not figure in your column."

"No, because prenuptial agreements are not very romantic, and readers want romance. They want to be swept away by a fantasy. In addition, we have limitations of space. A certain amount of the advice I dispense must invariably be edited out. But in our private correspondence, I was very clear."

"And what of all those who read your column and see a similarity to their own life? What if they act upon what they've read without having had the benefit of a personal correspondence with you?"

"I cannot be held liable for what decisions mature adults make in their private lives as a result of what they read in my newspaper. As for the rest," she went on before he could debate that point, "I advised your mother to give Foscarelli a token sum as a dowry, put him on a quarterly allowance, and keep full control of all her assets in her own hands. I worded my advice in the strongest possible terms."

"And yet, those terms were not strong enough, Miss Deverill, for she has decided to have no marriage settlement at all and to hand over to Foscarelli half her personal capital."

Irene was dismayed, for that was a very unwise proceeding in the circumstances. "Oh, I am sorry to hear it, for tying up the money was one of the points I stressed most strongly in my correspondence with her." She paused, struck by a sudden thought. "But I can't think why you volunteer this information to me, given my occupation. Aren't you afraid it will appear in the pages of my paper?"

He smiled a little, a smile that only increased her uneasiness. "No."

He did not expand on that point, and Irene swallowed, shoving down her apprehensions. "Your mother has the right to make her own decision whom to marry and how much of her own money to bestow upon him."

"No, she does not, not entirely. She is the Duchess of Torquil, and her right to do as she pleases ends when it impinges upon her duty to her family, her good name, and her position. Because of you, she has chosen to cast aside those obligations."

"I fail to see how following her heart prevents her from fulfilling familial obligations."

"Then please allow me to enlighten you," he said smoothly. "As you must already be aware, given your profession, Foscarelli is a lothario who has engaged in countless romantic liaisons, particularly with women of the upper classes. My mother is not his only conquest. He is also seventeen years her junior. He is not, by either birth or deed, a gentleman, and he has no means of his own."

"And yet, your mother is fully aware of all these facts and loves him anyway. In addition, she assured me that there was a great deal more good in his character than anyone knew."

"Yes, yes, I'm sure he's just tortured and misunderstood."

Irene decided to ignore the scathing sarcasm. "Nonetheless, we are not discussing some green girl with no knowledge of the world. Your mother is a mature woman, perfectly capable of deciding Foscarelli's character for herself. He may very well be a rake, but she has every right to wed a rake if she wants to do so."

"You realize that by marrying him, she will be shunned by most of her acquaintances and friends."

"I do. More importantly, so does she, but she seems to feel as I do, that losing such shallow friends as these is no great loss."

"Her daughters, whose entire future rests upon making a good marriage, will share her disgrace by association, and will find their choice of desirable marriage partners much diminished. Their prospects were difficult enough before, given all the American heiresses invading our shores, waving obscene dowries in the faces of the eligible men of our acquaintance—"

"Hardly a testament to the character of those young men, that they would allow themselves to be bought with such ease. But I do see your point. It's not the fact that Foscarelli is a fortune hunter that bothers you. It's the fact that he's a fortune hunter without a title."

Those gray eyes Clara had deemed so beautiful narrowed a fraction. "Do not deliberately misunderstand the cause of my anger, Miss Deverill," he said, his voice low and hard. "Whatever his station, he has chosen not to conduct his courtship in open and honorable fashion. Instead, he has employed concealment and subterfuge, because he knows his intentions are unsavory and the union unsuitable. For that alone, he ought to be tied behind a horse and dragged on his belly to John O'Groats and back."

"A harsh punishment."

"Yes. And one that any man, peer or no, would deserve in such circumstances. God knows, I—"

He broke off, and an expression crossed his hard, handsome countenance, something so stark and bleak that Irene stared in astonishment. This man seemed the last man on earth capable of naked emotion.

It was gone in an instant, however, and Irene could only conclude that what she'd seen was regret and self-recrimination for having not already administered the described punishment to the poor Italian.

"Suffice it to say," he went on, "if Foscarelli were a peer, some restraints of good breeding would be expected of him, one of which would be to cast his eyes upon a woman of an age closer to his own."

"Oh, yes, because peers always do that. The Earl of Plenderith, for example. He is fifty-four, if I recall correctly, and he just married his seventeen-year old ward. He's followed your society's rule splendidly, hasn't he?"

"That is a different situation entirely."

"Why? Because it's the man who is older and not the woman?"

"Yes, as unfair as that might seem. Plenderith is a widower with no heir, and he wouldn't be likely to gain that heir by marrying a woman of his own age. But I suspect you already understand his reasons," he added dryly, "and you are being deliberately disingenuous, though whether it is to tout women's rights, or to justify Foscarelli, or merely to try and prove me wrong, I cannot be sure."

"All three, perhaps? Though I confess, the latter is the most gratifying prospect."

His lips actually twitched at that, but when he spoke, his voice possessed its usual coolness. "Regardless, we have wandered from the point, which is that my mother is about to marry a man with whom she has nothing in common to sustain a happy marriage."

"She has love, a deep and passionate love, it seems."

"Quite," he said, a clipped, polite reply that showed how insignificant he deemed that consideration. "The result of that love shall be a life of disgrace, and—quite likely—romantic disillusionment. My sisters may now never marry at all, for regardless of whatever dowry I might provide, no peer shall want to claim Foscarelli as his stepfather-in-law with so many other eligible young ladies available to wed."

"There are paths in life that a woman might choose that do not involve marriage."

"Not for a peer's daughter. Her destiny is determined by her success in matrimony."

"A point which hardly recommends the institution. Forgive me, but if Foscarelli is so unsuited for your mother, if you are so convinced that their marriage would bring her nothing but disaster, why do you not simply buy the man off? If he's as bad a lot as you believe him to be, that should be an easy thing to do."

His expression became even more bleak, if that was possible. "Give me a little credit, Miss Deverill. I tried that tactic two days ago. My solicitors tell me he has refused the money."

"Good for him."

"You think his refusal admirable?" Torquil gave a humorless laugh. "It isn't, believe me."

Irene knew any discussion of Foscarelli's character was pointless, for it was clear Torquil was determined to think ill of him. "Either way, at this point, the matter has little to do with me."

"No? Your interference shall have been the catalyst, if not the cause, of my family's disgrace. I am here because before that happens, I expect you to rectify the situation."

"Do you, indeed?"

"I do." He reached again into the portfolio beside him, and from its interior, he withdrew a sheaf of papers. "When you sow the wind, Miss Deverill, you should always be prepared to reap the whirlwind."

Irene's amusement faded at once, his ominous words causing a prickle of alarm to dance along her spine. "What . . ." She paused, her voice failing. She swallowed hard, shifting her gaze to the papers in his grasp. "What do you mean?"

He leaned forward and placed the documents on her desk. "That," he said before she could ask, "is a purchase agreement signed by myself and your father."

Her apprehension deepened into dread. "A purchase agreement for what?" she asked, but even as she posed the question, she began to fear she already knew the answer.

"*Society Snippets.*"

If she weren't already sitting down, her knees might have given way. "You are offering to buy my family's newspaper?"

"The offer has already been made, the terms accepted. Once my bank tenders the money, the deed is done."

Irene tried to force down panic and think, but her head was reeling. "I don't believe you," she whispered. "It's not possible."

"It was not only possible, Miss Deverill, it was easy."

"You bastard," she breathed, glaring at him. "Out of a desire for revenge for this perceived slight upon your family, you would take away my family's only source of income?"

"Not at all." He pushed the papers closer to her and leaned back in his chair, looking infuriatingly at ease, while she was sick to her stomach and angry as hell. "The purchase amount is generous, enough to provide a substantial marriage portion for you and for your sister and enable your father to pay off the mortgage held on these premises. In addition, there will still be plenty left to provide him with a respectable income for the remainder of his life."

"So because you are a wealthy duke, you think you can buy whatever you want?"

"Unfortunately, life is never that simple, even for those of us fortunate enough to have wealth. I can't buy my family's reputation back if it is sullied. I can't pay people not to snicker at my mother and call her ridiculous. My money can't spare my sisters the embarrassment and pain they shall suffer as a result of my mother's social downfall. But with my money, I can, if I choose, prevent this newspaper from ruining anyone else's life through its gossip, innuendo, and ill-conceived advice."

"So you intend to purchase it only to shut it down?"

"Just so."

"But you can't! *Society Snippets* is the only remaining trace of my family's newspaper business, a business started by my great-grandfather. The Deverill family has been publishing newspapers for over fifty years."

"Unlike you, your father does not seem dismayed by the prospect of selling the last piece of his family legacy. On the contrary, he jumped at the chance to remove his daughters from a life of drudgery, and he was happy for the opportunity to once again be able to adequately take care of them and provide them with dowries as a responsible father should. He had only one additional request to my proposal."

"Which was?"

"He asked that you and your sister be given some introductions into society. I agreed."

He'd said a moment ago that arranging this had been easy, and she saw now just how easy it must have been.

Everything Papa wanted for his daughters held out to him on a silver platter, and all he'd had to give up in exchange was something that had never been of interest to him in the first place.

"Aren't the daughters of a middle-class newspaper hawker a bit too lowbrow for your class of people?"

"Some might say so, yes," he acknowledged, seeming to miss or choosing to ignore the resentment in her voice. "But the granddaughters of a viscount are not."

She gave a humorless laugh, not surprised that he had learned of her mother's family. "Even if the viscount's daughter married beneath her?"

"Since my own mother may soon do the same, I'm hardly in a position to turn up my nose at what your mother did, am I?"

She frowned. "You seem to know a great deal about my family."

"Private detectives can find out many things."

"Ah, I see. Before a man can exploit another man's vulnerabilities he has to find out what they are."

If her words evoked any feeling in him, he didn't show it. Not a shred of guilt crossed the face Clara had declared so handsome. No apology or regret. He didn't even blink.

"My God," she choked, "does your heart pump blood, or ice water? Or perhaps you don't have a heart at all."

Another flicker of emotion crossed that implacable face, but it was gone in an instant, wiped away by his cold reply. "My heart, Miss Deverill, is not your concern."

"Thank God for that," she muttered, but if her shot hit home she didn't know it, for she looked away, swamped by a feeling of desolation. If this man got his way, everything would be as it had been before her grandfather died, prosperous, comfortable, and mind-numbingly dull. *Society Snippets* was her creation, her vision. She'd poured countless hours into it, working hard to make it solvent. She'd hoped to make it success-ful. She hadn't expected to love it.

And now it would be snuffed out, and she would be relegated back to managing household accounts and doing embroidery for the rest of her days, or—worse—marrying into the sort of world her father wanted for her, the one her mother had lived in and run away from. All she'd accomplished here would be forgotten, thanks to a privileged man who only had to write a bank draft and make a few introductions in order to get what he wanted. She could not let it happen, but how could she stop it?

Irene looked at him again, and as she met those eyes, eyes as cool and unfathomable as the North Sea, she felt so angry and so helpless, she didn't know whether to burst into tears or jump over the desk and go for his throat.

"There might be," he said, watching her, "an alterna-tive."

The very gentleness of his voice sent any impulse to cry straight to the wall. She opened her mouth, but even as the words *go to hell* hovered on her lips, she knew she could not say them.

"I'm listening," she said instead.

He reached out, fingering one corner of the docu-ments he'd placed on her desk. "As I said, I have not yet tendered the money. The contract stipulates that I have fourteen days to do so. If I do not, the agreement is voided, and I would be required to pay your father ten percent of the purchase price for reneging."

"Under what circumstances would you renege?"

"Your advice has wreaked havoc upon my family, and in my view, it is your responsibility to repair the damage done. My mother intends to wed Mr. Foscarelli a fortnight from now, once he has secured the marriage license. That gives you fourteen days."

"To do what?"

"To persuade my mother to change her mind and call off the wedding."

Irene's mind struggled mightily for a way to refuse, but she could see no way that wouldn't lose her all that she had worked for.

"If you succeed," he went on, "I will tear up this document, pay your father the required fee, and all will be forgot. You can continue to advise the lovelorn of London to follow their hearts until the end of your days. But if you fail, if my mother weds that man, you had best give up your journalistic aspirations and your desire to meddle in other people's lives. I will follow through on this purchase of your publication and shut it down, and you will have to begin looking for a suitable spouse to whom to offer your fat new dowry."

"But the paper is my life! I have no desire to be introduced into your set, and certainly not to marry into it!"

"Frankly, Miss Deverill, what you desire is of little consequence to me at this moment."

Frustrated, trapped, Irene tried a different tack. "This is absurd! How can I possibly persuade your mother to go against the very advice I gave her?"

"That, I leave to your ingenuity. My mother has agreed to return home until her wedding, and I have arranged for you and your sister to come to stay with us during that time. With my mother and sister-in-law there, you and your sister will be suitably chaperoned, and I have two unmarried sisters as well, so you will not lack for company and amusements."

"You expect me to stay in your house?" Irene stared at him, appalled by the very idea. "For a fortnight?"

"Yes. That will provide you with many opportunities to use your powers of persuasion on my mother. No one will be told of our little bargain."

"Including my father? If I succeed, his hopes for me and Clara, hopes you put into his head, shall be crushed, for I doubt any reconciliation with my mother's family would continue if I were to remain editor of a scandal sheet."

"You and Viscount Ellesmere shall have to work that out between you. As for your father, he will be adequately compensated. The ten percent fee is already in trust for him should you succeed and keep your paper."

"Compensation or no, you are offering him false hope for a reconciliation with my mother's family. He does not deserve that."

"Does he not?" Torquil leaned forward in his chair, folding his hands over the document on her desk. "Miss Deverill, let us speak plainly. Your father drinks."

Irene's hands curled into fists beneath her desk, her cheeks afire. Not only was this man making her appreciate that she possessed a temper, he was also teaching her just how deeply she could resent another human soul. "My, my," she managed. "Your private detectives have been busy, haven't they?"

"I didn't need detectives to provide that information, merely my own eyes. During the hour I spent discussing this business with him this afternoon, your father consumed an entire bottle of brandy and opened a second one."

Anger and shame roiled inside her in equal measure. "My father's . . . fondness for brandy is hardly the point—"

"It is also public knowledge that your grandfather's newspaper business, once highly successful, was forced into bankruptcy due to your father's mismanagement."

"There are reasons for that—"

"Of course. As I said, he drinks. My point is that he has failed in his primary duty as a man, which is to protect and care for his family. In consequence, I cannot feel much compassion for him, and I shall certainly feel no guilt over crushing his hopes, as you put it."

"You are also deceiving your own relations, including your mother. Have you no guilt there?"

"It is a deceit, I grant you, a deceit of omission."

"A lie of omission is still a lie!"

He moved in his chair and looked away, indicating that perhaps that shot had gone home. But when he looked at her again, any notion that she'd pricked his conscience might just as well have been a figment of her imagination. "It is regrettable, but I do not see any other way. If my mother knew I had tendered an offer to buy your father's newspaper, she would never believe it was simply for investment purposes. She would instantly become suspicious, and any efforts you made to change her mind about Foscarelli would ultimately be futile. I cannot afford the scruple of forthright truth."

"Quite a moral dilemma for you."

If he perceived the sarcasm, he ignored it. "Only you, your father, and I—and your sister, if you choose to make her aware—shall know about this purchase offer. If you tell anyone else what we have discussed, or reveal anything about the situation of my mother and the Italian, I will execute the terms of this agreement at once, and your editorship of this newspaper will end immediately. I hope that is clear?"

"Perfectly." Irene's jaw was clenched so tight, she could barely utter words. "What will you tell your relations?"

He shrugged. "I went to see your father in high dungeon over this Lady Truelove column, and came away appalled by Ellesmere's shameful neglect of his granddaughters and aware of your father's attempts at reconciliation. I was happy to offer my assistance in brokering a peace."

"Out of the goodness of your heart?"

"Your father loathes owning a scandal sheet and would happily shut it down if he knew his daughters would be well-regarded by their relations. Ridding London of a scandal sheet that prints gossip about my family is an endeavor in which I am quite happy to assist, and a circumstance most of my family would not lament."

That was probably the unvarnished truth. She swallowed hard. "It seems you have it all planned out."

"Yes. But the choice of whether or not to carry out this plan rests with you."

That contention provoked her beyond bearing. "Choice?" she echoed, jumping to her feet. "It's a Hobson's choice, which means no choice at all. And how is my newspaper to function for the next two weeks while I am gallivanting around London, being introduced to your acquaintances?"

"That is another thing I shall leave to your ingenuity. If *Society Snippets* ceases to function during your absence, I will not bemoan the fact." He took up that horrid purchase agreement and rose to his feet. "Two weeks is not much time," he added as he replaced the papers in his portfolio. "So I suggest you and your sister come to us as soon as you have made your arrangements here. Around teatime, shall we say?"

"Today?" Irene gave a laugh of disbelief. "You can't possibly expect us to come today?"

"I can, and I do. If you arrive at teatime, you can take refreshment if you choose and still be settled into your rooms before dinner. I do not know if my mother will have returned home by teatime, or what prior engagements the other members of my family have fixed for this afternoon, but I will ensure that my sister-in-law is at home to greet you properly, and I shall also be there to perform the necessary introduction."

"Oh, goody," Irene muttered. "What a treat."

"If you do not arrive," he went on as if she hadn't spoken, "I will present your father with a bank draft tomorrow morning and you shall not be required to come at all. As I said, the choice is yours. My home is located on Park Lane, at 16 Upper Brook Street. Good day, Miss Deverill."

With that, he gave her a bow and turned away, leaving Irene to glare daggers at his back as he departed. Fourteen days under his roof might not seem like much time to him, but to her, it loomed ahead like an eternity of hell.

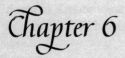

Chapter 6

The duke had barely departed her offices before Irene was also out the door. She strode past Clara's desk, and something in her face must have reflected the emotions roiling inside her, for her sister followed, calling after her as she crossed the foyer.

"Irene, what's wrong? What's happened?"

"Not now, Clara," she called back as she started up the stairs. "Not now, I beg you."

She found her father in the drawing room sipping his brandy and reading a book, his gouty foot propped up on cushions. He looked up as she came in, and the full force of her fury must have been reflected in her expression, because in the face of it, even her father shrank back a little.

"Is it true?" she demanded, halting beside his wheeled chair. "Is it?"

He frowned, but he did not quite meet her gaze.

"Moderate your tone, child, and remember to whom you are speaking."

"Is it true?"

"If you are asking if I've agreed to sell the newspaper to the Duke of Torquil, the answer is yes. He has even agreed to assist in the reconciliation of our family. He knows Ellesmere and has pledged to do what he can to assist. Wasn't that thoughtful of him?"

"Oh, very thoughtful," she shot back. "How could you do this, Papa? How?"

He reached for his glass and downed the contents in one swallow. Only then did he meet her gaze. "Really, Irene, you needn't look as if I've just sold you into servitude, when the reality is the exact opposite. Now, there will be no need for you to labor like a common shop girl."

She ignored his attempt to make his action seem noble. "I enjoy my work. Why can't you understand that?" She watched him shake his head, making it clear he still refused to believe that fact, and she hastened on before the conversation could be diverted from the material point to a debate about women's rights. "I've revived our family business and made it successful again. I created *Society Snippets*, and I've made it a success. And now, after all I've accomplished, you've sold it right out from under me without so much as a by your leave."

"I am your father. I don't require your leave to do anything if I feel it is for your good." Beneath the testiness of his voice, she perceived an underlying guilt, but he gave her no chance to jump on it. "As for the rest, what I have done is what every father has an obligation to do."

"What obligation is that?"

"To secure his children's future, of course. I've secured yours, and Clara's, and I can only hope that makes up for what a dismal mess I've made of things in the past."

Her anger faded with those words, for she knew he believed with all his heart that what he'd done was for her benefit. "Oh, Papa, how many times do we have to discuss this? What you've secured is your vision of my future, but it isn't the sort of future I envision for myself."

"Only because you've never had a taste of it." He nodded, donning a wise and complacent air. "Just you wait. When you are out and about, enjoying the events of the season, dining in a duke's house, going to balls, making friends, you'll be having such an agreeable time, you won't want to come home at all, much less go back to that newspaper of yours. You'll see."

As always when they had this conversation, Irene felt as if she was pounding her head into a brick wall, but she persisted. "I don't want balls and parties. I have no interest in doing the season, and I don't want to go hunting for a husband. I want to publish newspapers."

"And your sister? Is being your secretary and living as a spinster what she wants for her future?"

For the second time today, Irene felt as if she'd been kicked in the stomach. She parted her lips to reply, but no answer came out.

"You enjoy slaving away in that office downstairs, but does she?" he asked. "Is she happy, knowing her life is to be spent taking down correspondence, and typing, and making your appointments?"

He gave her no chance to reply. "She wants to enjoy her life, now, while she's young. She yearns for the amusements of the season as much as any girl."

She shifted her weight, guilt nudging at her. "Clara knows she is free to attend all the parties she wants. Cousin Martha would happily make arrangements among our acquaintances and act as chaperone."

"Clara would have a difficult time in society without you to help her along. We both know how shy and reserved she is. And my cousin, though a worthy woman, would make Clara even more so."

"I'm happy to go with Clara anywhere we are invited," she assured him at once. "But neither of us is in any rush to wed."

"Well, you're not, anyway," her father countered tartly. "Turtles are in more of a rush than you are. And why, pray? Because you prefer running a newspaper to finding a husband."

"Only because society forces me to make that choice."

"Not only society. My dear child, no husband would allow his wife to have a career."

"Either way, we're not talking about me. We're talking about Clara."

"So we are. How is your sister to meet anyone when she spends most of her time working for you? She's twenty-two, Irene, so there's not much time before she's on the shelf. I've arranged things with the duke so that she can have a bit of enjoyment. She can go to balls and the theater, she can dance, and flirt, and enjoy the season as a young woman should, before it's too late."

"Two weeks isn't much of a season."

"But with the duke's help, the viscount might see his way to giving Clara—and you, not that you'd want it—a full season next year. He might forgive, and the breach in our family could be healed."

"And we'll all live happily ever after."

Her father didn't seem to hear that dry rejoinder. "Clara will have the chance to meet worthy young men, and fall in love. She might then be able to marry, and have children and a home of her own. Would you deny her all these opportunities simply because you don't want them yourself? Would you truly sacrifice her youth on the altar of your ambition?"

Irene's eyes stung, and her father's face blurred before her eyes. "That's not fair," she whispered.

"No," he agreed and reached for the decanter from the table beside him. "But then life rarely is, my dear."

She watched him pour the last of the brandy from the decanter into his glass, and she wondered if that was the first one he'd emptied today. Probably not. "You're right, Papa," she said, the words bitter on her tongue. "Life is rarely fair."

IRENE HAD SPOKEN with her father in the hope he could be prevailed upon to cancel the deal he'd made with the duke, but in hindsight, she saw that confronting him in the heat of the moment had perhaps not been the most effective approach for achieving such a goal. And with his talk of her sister's future, he'd taken the last bit of wind out of her sails, for she knew how much Clara longed for society and amusements.

Resigned, she went back downstairs, called Clara into her office, and explained what had occurred. She expected her sister to greet the news that they would be going out into society with a combination of happy anticipation and stark terror, with perhaps some indignation on her behalf at the duke's and their father's high-handed actions. Clara's wail of dismay, however, didn't quite square with any of the responses she'd been expecting.

"Oh, no, no, no." Clara moaned, leaning forward to plunk her elbows on Irene's desk and bury her face in her hands. "I can't believe you agreed to this."

"But I thought you'd like the idea of going into society."

Clara shook her head without looking up, and Irene circled her desk and put a comforting arm around her sister's shoulders. "If it's my feelings you're worried about, there's no need. I have no intention of letting that man buy my newspaper and shut it down, I promise you that."

"That's not it," Clara replied, her voice muffled by the hands covering her face.

"Oh." Feeling a bit deflated by this seeming lack of concern for her beloved newspaper, Irene straightened, studying her sister's bent head as she tried to determine just what Clara found so upsetting. "We'll be all right, you know, however this plays out. Granted, Torquil's the sort of man who thinks he can buy whatever he wants, but even I have to concede that he's willing to pay generously for the privilege. And you'll be taken care of, no matter what—"

She stopped as Clara again shook her head and sat up. "Don't be a goose, Irene. I know you'll take care of us, whatever happens. That is not what distresses me.

And I'm sure you'll find a way out of the mess. You always do."

"But, then, what has you so upset? Is it the idea of meeting new people? I know how daunting that can be for you, dearest, but I'll be right there by your side."

"It's not that either, Irene. We have a much more immediate problem than my stupid shyness. Beginning in only a few hours, we'll be staying in the house of a duke, moving in good society, meeting peers and ladies, and who knows who else."

"Yes, and . . . ?"

"Look at us." The words ended in a wail, as Clara gestured to her brown wool skirt. "There will be social engagements every day, balls and parties every night, and we don't have anything fit to wear for such occasions."

Startled, Irene blinked. "Heavens, I never even thought of that. But it's a problem easily remedied," she added. "The paper is making money these days, so we can afford to spend a bit on ourselves. We'll dash over to Debenham and Freebody this afternoon and buy a few gowns before we go to Grosvenor Square."

"Wear ready-made gowns into a duke's house?" Clara looked at her in horror. "What will they think of us?"

"If they base their opinions of us on our clothes, then their opinions aren't worth having," Irene replied stoutly. "And they can all go hang."

A fine sentiment, in theory, but several hours later, standing in the most richly appointed drawing room she'd ever seen, confronted by the elegant clothes and incredulous gaze of Lady David Cavanaugh, even Irene would have happily traded all her high-minded principles for just one bespoke frock. As the duke's sister-in-law took a glance over the gray-stripe walking suit Irene had purchased at Debenham and Freebody on the way here, she didn't say a word, but she didn't have to. The slight lift of her auburn brows eloquently expressed what was going through her mind. At once, Irene's cheeks began to burn, and she cast a hostile glance at the tall, dark man beside Lady David who had just performed introductions. This was all his doing.

If Torquil perceived her resentment, he didn't show it. "Boothby will have your things taken up to your rooms," he said with a glance at the elderly man who had shown them into the drawing room and announced their arrival.

Boothby, obviously the butler, perceived at once the command that had been given him, and without a word, he bowed and glided from the room.

Irene watched him go with a hint of envy. She'd have gladly carted her own trunk upstairs if it meant she could escape the oh-so-superior scrutiny of Lady David.

"Would you care for tea?"

The other woman's question forced Irene's longing gaze away from the doorway and back to the slim, elegant redhead who was gesturing to the tea tray.

"No, thank you. We have had our tea already."

"I see." There was a pause so awkward that Irene almost winced.

Torquil broke the silence, doing so in a way that—thankfully—didn't make Irene want to go for his throat. "Perhaps you and your sister would prefer to rest before dinner?"

"We would," Irene said without even bothering to

glance at Clara. If she was uncomfortable, she could only imagine how her reserved sister must be feeling. "A rest would be most welcome."

Lady David seemed as relieved as she by this turn of events. "Of course," she said and reached out at once to tug the bell pull on the wall beside her. A footman in livery appeared in the doorway with a speed Irene couldn't help but admire.

"Ah, Edward, there you are," Lady David greeted the footman. "Will you show Miss Deverill and her sister to their rooms, and have their maids sent up to attend them?"

"Oh, we've no maid," Irene interjected with deliberate good cheer. "We'll have to do for ourselves while we're here, I'm afraid."

"You haven't brought a maid?" Lady David's face stilled, her polite smile frozen in place. Guests without maids must be a rare thing in this house.

Irene did not help her, and it was left to Torquil to jump into the breach.

"My mother's maid will be happy to attend you, of course," he said.

This offer, Irene couldn't help but note, did not please Lady David at all, a fact that almost tempted her to accept it. "We would not dream of depriving Her Grace of her own maid."

"It would not be a deprivation, Miss Deverill, I assure you."

"Perhaps not, but we are happy to do for ourselves."

"Yourselves?" Lady David's question betrayed that she was laughing at their lack of sophistication. She must have sensed that she'd shown her amusement too plainly, however, for she went on at once, "No, no. Torquil is right. Of course you must have a maid to attend you. We could never allow our guests to do for themselves."

This gesture, one of accommodation and nothing more, was too much for Irene's pride. "Clara and I are not only sisters, but friends. We do not mind assisting each other. Please, do not distress yourselves about this. If you do, you shall make us feel quite embarrassed."

"Well, we can't have that," Torquil murmured before Lady David could reply, and he closed the topic by offering Irene and her sister a bow. "We shall see you both this evening, then. Dinner is at eight, but the family usually begins to gather about half an hour beforehand in the library." He paused, gesturing to an opened set of doors which led to the room next door. "Please, feel free to join us when you are ready. Edward, see our guests up to their rooms, if you will."

Irene and Clara followed the footman out of the lavish ivory-and-blue drawing room, back to the wide, sweeping staircase, and up to the second floor, where they were shown into adjoining bedrooms.

Irene's room was not as ostentatious as the drawing room. Done up in pale green and white, it was light and airy, and though she loathed giving the duke or his house any credit, she had to admit her room was very pretty indeed. Their trunks had been brought up, and both of hers now reposed on the floor at the foot of her bed, open and clearly awaiting the maid who would never come to unpack them.

The sound of a door opening diverted her observations of her surroundings, and she turned as Clara entered through an adjoining door. "Oh, Irene, isn't it lovely? And we've a bathroom that's just for us. Come and look."

Irene allowed her sister to pull her through the doorway into a bathroom that was substantial enough to possess not only two doors, but also two marble washstands with water taps, a flush lavatory, and an enameled bath with hot water pipes and a mahogany surround.

"My goodness," Irene said, laughing in disbelief. "Are we in a hotel?"

"If we are, it's the Savoy." Clara paused, looking at her. "We didn't have the chance to talk much about it earlier, but I know you aren't happy about this, and I don't blame you. You must be frantic with worry about the paper."

"I'm not ready to wave the white flag on that score just yet. Especially not to that man. You don't mind me fighting to keep it, do you?" she asked. "If I succeed, it'll mean a smaller dowry for you. And Ellesmere might not be prevailed upon to help launch one granddaughter when the other runs a scandal sheet."

"I never expected any sort of dowry, so I'm happy even to receive a small one. And your paper means the world to you, I know. I wouldn't ever want you to lose it."

"You're a darling. But I'm afraid losing it is the most likely outcome at this point, for I don't see how I can change the duchess's mind. And I confess, I'm not happy at the prospect of attempting to do so."

"It was very wrong of the Duke to maneuver you into this, of course, but his actions do seem to stem wholly from his concern for his mother's future happiness.

And even if she does marry the Italian in the end, the Duke surely won't blame you for it."

"Won't he?" Irene made a face. "I'm not as hopeful on that score as you are, I'm afraid."

"He's upset, of course, but once he learns the depth of his mother's feelings for the man, he'll hopefully become more accepting of her marriage, or you'll find a way to persuade her to at least pause and reconsider. Either way, I hope you can find a way to enjoy yourself a little bit, while we are here?"

She thought of the superior Lady David, the dark, arrogant Torquil, and the task that would be required of her, and she doubted there would be much enjoyment to be found. But she looked into her sister's face, and refrained from expressing such a gloomy opinion. "I will try," she said instead. "If only to please you."

Clara smiled, pleased already. "Good," she said and gestured to their surroundings. "Do you mind if I have the first bathe?"

"Not at all. I shall unpack. After all," she added as she turned and started back to her own room, "since we are so déclassé as to possess no maid, we have to undertake that task ourselves. Oh, the horror!"

Leaving Clara laughing, she returned to her room and put the walking suits, tea gowns, ball gowns, and undergarments Clara had insisted she would need in the armoire. The boxes containing her shoes and slippers she placed on the bottom shelf, and the ones containing hats she placed on top. She also made use of the room's chiffonier cupboard for her shirtwaists, skirts, and underthings.

She laid out her new blue silk evening gown on the

bed, then crossed to the bathroom, where her knock went unanswered. Taking a peek inside, she found the room empty, but still steamy, showing that her sister had made good use of the hot water. She decided to do the same, and as Irene sank into the depths of a warm bath a short time later, she was forced to admit that staying in Torquil's house for two weeks did have one favorable aspect.

"Ah," she groaned with pleasure, leaning back and closing her eyes, the tension in her shoulders easing a bit. "Now this I could get used to."

Somehow she drifted off, a fact she realized only when a knock from Clara roused her from her blissful lethargy.

"Irene?"

She jerked upright in the tub, appreciating that the water was now cold and her fingertips wrinkly. How long had she been in here?

"What's happened?" Clara asked, and even through the closed door, Irene could hear her sister laughing. "Did you fall asleep?"

"Of course not," she lied, rising to her feet. "What time is it?"

"Half past six."

Heavens, she'd been in here nearly three quarters of an hour. She dried off, an action that didn't take long, for the towel was composed of the softest, most luxurious cotton she'd ever felt, and it wicked the water from her body easy as winking. When she slipped into her wrapper a few moments later, the muslin didn't even stick to her skin.

She gathered up her discarded clothes and returned

to her room. She donned her underclothes, using the brass knob of her footboard to assist her in lacing her corset tightly enough, then she donned the skirt and bodice of her evening frock, put up her hair, and passed through the bathroom to knock on her sister's door. "Clara, I need buttoning up."

At her sister's urging to come in, she opened the door. "I'm sure you do, too," she went on as she entered the room, but the words were barely out of her mouth before she perceived that her sister wasn't even close to needing her help.

Clara was standing before her dressing mirror in her underclothes, one of her three newly purchased evening gowns clasped in front of her. The other two lay strewn across the bed, along with a variety of petticoats, corsets, and stockings.

"What's all this?"

"Too many choices!" Clara turned, spreading out the skirt of the celadon-green brocade gown she was holding. "What do you think?"

"Very pretty."

"That's the same exact thing you said at Debenham and Freebody this afternoon."

"And it's still true. All the dresses you bought are pretty."

"But which evening dress is the prettiest? On our first night, I want to make the most favorable impression I can."

"The pink, then. Pink always suits you best."

Clara cast aside the green brocade, picked up the bodice and skirt of pink silk, and held them up to the mirror. After a moment, she gave a satisfied nod and began to dress. When she'd finished donning her own gown, Clara did up the hooks down the back of Irene's, then turned so her sister could do the same for her.

"There," Irene said as she fastened the last hook and smoothed the tucks at the back of Clara's dress. "Who needs a maid anyway? Let's go down. We can see just what books are in a duke's library."

Clara turned away, shaking her head. "You go. I still have to dress my hair."

She had no intention of letting her sister go down alone. "I'll wait for you."

"For heaven's sake, Irene," Clara said, sounding exasperated, "I may be a little shy, but I am capable of going down to dinner myself, even in a duke's house. I don't need you hovering at my elbow. I'll join you in the library in a short while."

"All right, if you're sure," she capitulated and started back toward her own room. "Just don't linger up here too long. Heaven only knows what they'll think if you're late to dinner. That would surely be a capital offense."

With that, she returned to her own room, put on her long white evening gloves, and started toward the door into the corridor, but as she passed the cheval glass, she remembered Lady David's incredulous face, and she paused, feeling a sudden, uncharacteristic pang of uncertainty. She took a step back, turned toward the mirror, and immediately wished she hadn't, for the fold lines along her skirt only underscored the reasons for Lady David's incredulous stare.

Still, though the problem could be resolved tomorrow, there was nothing to be done about it now, so Irene gave a philosophical shrug, patted her hair, and left her room. The house was quiet, no servants in sight as she returned to the first floor and started down the corridor she and Clara had traversed earlier in the day.

It was not yet half past seven, and no dressing gong had sounded, so Irene didn't expect that anyone else would be down yet, but as she approached the drawing room and the library beyond, voices told her that some members of the family had arrived before her. The doors to both reception rooms were closed and the voices were low, but given the sultry afternoon, the transoms over the doorways that helped ventilate the house were wide open, and Lady David's voice came to her quite distinctly from the library.

"My dears, you should have seen their clothes! Straight out of a department store, I'm absolutely certain."

Irene stopped outside the door, her hand stilled just above the handle she'd been about to open.

"Not that one ever really expects middle-class girls to dress well," Lady David went on. "But one would expect even the daughters of a newspaper hawker to have their ready-made clothes properly fitted and altered, and to have the creases removed before wearing them out in public."

Irene felt her cheeks growing hot. She lowered her hand to smooth her skirt, but it was a futile attempt, and she saw just how right her sister had been to be so concerned about their clothes. Having come straight here from Debenham and Freebody, they'd had no time to press their new clothes, but that didn't do much to alleviate the discomfort of being ridiculed.

If my mother suffers ridicule and condemnation because of you and your publication, what responsibility do you bear?

Torquil's words from their first meeting came echoing back as if to mock her, and she realized that she hadn't ever allowed herself to consider that question. Nor did she have time to consider it now, for a second female voice entered the conversation taking place on the other side of the door.

"Even if their frocks did come from a department store, why did they not have them altered by their maid when they bought them? A good lady's maid can make even a ready-made dress fit properly. And she can press out the wrinkles, too."

"My dear Sarah, that's just it! They don't have a maid, or if they do, they didn't bring her with them."

"What of it?" an unfamiliar male voice asked. "Many people come to stay without bringing a personal servant along."

"Ladies don't, David," the girl called Sarah replied, "not during the *season.*"

"David may not understand what it means not to have one's maid," his wife went on, "but we do, don't we, sisters? It shall put all of us to great inconvenience, but I doubt these girls have any idea how much trouble their lack of a maid shall cause the rest of us."

Irene failed to see how refusing a maid and dressing herself would be inconvenient to anybody. Unfortunately, that thought only served to send more of the duke's words ricocheting through her mind.

I should like you to consider what impact your decisions may have on the lives of other people.

Really, that man's voice playing inside her head was becoming quite exasperating. She shoved it out again and kept her attention on the conversation at hand.

"I don't mind a little inconvenience," Lady Sarah said, her voice once again intruding on Irene's thoughts. "But I don't see how they can possibly manage. Why, here in town, we change our clothes at least three or four times a day. What young lady would ever attempt to do the season without a proper lady's maid to help her?"

"You've answered your own question, my dear," Lady David replied. "No *young lady* would."

Lady David's acidic comment snuffed out any pangs of Irene's conscience. A little inconvenience, she couldn't help but feel, would do these people a world of good. She wanted to fling open the door and inform that odious woman that, unlike the ladies of the upper crust, women of the middle class didn't change clothes at the ridiculous rate of four times a day, and they certainly had the ability to put them on and take them off without a servant to help. The duchess's maid would not be needed and no inconvenience would be suffered by anyone, thank you very much. But a third woman spoke, and curiosity kept Irene where she was.

"I think you're being terribly unfair. Torquil already explained that they hadn't intended to do the season. It was all a last-minute surprise from their father, and men never understand these things. And anyway, the department stores sell plenty of frocks every day, so how bad could the clothes of the Miss Deverills be?"

"You weren't there, Angela," Lady David replied. "You didn't see them when they arrived. I can really think of no words to describe how they appeared!"

"Then I should advise you not to try," Torquil's voice cut in, and for once, Irene was grateful to hear its cool, incisive cadence. The sound of it acted on her like a splash of water, banishing any embarrassment about her clothes and reinvigorating her fighting spirit. With deliberate care, she opened the door and pushed it wide, her cheeks still flaming, but her chin high.

The duke was seated at a writing desk that faced the doorway, and at the sight of her, he put aside his pen and rose to his feet. He started to bow, but then paused, frowning a little as he looked into her flushed face. He lifted his gaze a fraction, but if the open transom above her head made him realize she'd overheard their conversation, he gave no sign of it, for when he looked at her again, his countenance was as inscrutable as ever. "Miss Deverill," he greeted her and resumed offering a bow. "Join us, please."

Chapter 7

A gentleman, Henry's father had taught him as a boy, never allowed his inner thoughts and feelings to show in his outward expression, and though his mother may have deemed the influence of his father upon his upbringing as too rigid, when Irene Deverill walked into his drawing room, Henry was glad the late duke had been such a strict disciplinarian.

Even if he had not noticed the open transom above her head, the flush of color in her cheeks and the proud lift of her chin made it clear that she'd overheard what had been said, and the sight touched off in him myriad emotions—anger at Carlotta for being such a cat, frustration with himself for not checking her malicious tongue sooner than he had, and—worst of all—embarrassment, a hot, painful sensation Henry seldom had cause to experience.

Displaying any of what he felt, however, was not only

an unthinkable prospect, it would only serve to worsen an already awkward situation, and as he came around his desk, he was grateful for the sangfroid instilled in him during his childhood.

Carlotta gave a shamefaced giggle, and the sound was like paraffin on flames, flaring up his protective instincts and impelling him to move between the spiteful woman on the settee nearby and the proud woman by the door.

"Miss Deverill," he greeted as he halted before her. "It is a pleasure to have you in my home. You are very welcome."

Her brows lifted, her countenance understandably skeptical, but if she was tempted to take issue with his words, Fate deprived her of the opportunity. Her sister appeared in the doorway behind her, and much to Henry's relief, the younger girl's cherubic countenance showed no hint of the bristling resentment displayed by her sibling. She, at least, did not seem to know what had just occurred. "And your sister, too," he went on, offering the girl a bow. "Good evening, Miss Clara."

"Duke," she answered, giving him a quick, nervous bow that caused her sister to move closer to her, and he perceived that he was not the only one with protective instincts. "I hope I am not late?"

"Not at all," he answered her. "It is well before eight. And my mother is not yet down, nor is my brother-in-law. But come," he added, turning to offer the elder Miss Deverill his arm. "Allow me to introduce you to the rest of my family."

As he performed introductions, he began to once again feel in control of the situation, but when they came to Carlotta, he was reminded that any control he thought he had over Miss Deverill was nothing but an illusion.

"I must thank you for your making us feel so welcome upon our arrival this afternoon," she gushed to his sister-in-law. "Why, I don't believe I've ever *heard* so much warmth and consideration expressed for one's guests."

Carlotta's face flushed crimson, and though Henry couldn't help but feel such a set-down no more than his brother's wife deserved, Miss Deverill's impudence also made him appreciate that the next fourteen days were not going to be a stroll in the park, especially since his mother was still in an intractable frame of mind.

He'd taken her aside directly upon her return this afternoon and explained the situation, framing things just as he'd told Miss Deverill he would do, and though Mama had expressed a willingness to introduce the two young ladies into society during the coming two weeks without any indication she'd guessed he had a deeper interest in the Deverill family, Henry felt as transparent as glass. Mama's manner toward him was still cool and a bit wary, and he knew he would be ineffective in any attempts he might make to dissuade her. He could only hope Miss Deverill could do better, though it was perhaps a faint hope. She seemed unable to dissemble, and he knew from personal experience she had no difficulty offering her opinions, most of which flew directly in the face of convention. She was also the most strong-willed and independent woman he'd ever come across, qualities that did not seem conducive to her purpose

here. What would result from all this, he could not begin to imagine, and not for the first time he wondered
why he could never seem to achieve the well-ordered
life he longed for.

He had little time for that sort of wishful thinking,
however, for at that moment, his mother entered the
room on Jamie's arm. She made straight for them, but
though her countenance was restored to the warm and
affectionate one he was used to, Henry feared this display of friendliness was not for his benefit.

"Mama," he greeted her and beckoned to his guests,
who were standing nearby. "Miss Irene Deverill, Miss
Clara Deverill, may I present my mother, the Duchess of Torquil, and my brother-in-law, Lord James St.
Clair."

"Duchess," the Miss Deverills murmured together as
they curtsied. "Lord James."

Jamie bowed, offered to bring sherry for the ladies,
and moved away toward the liquor cabinet as Mama
turned to their guests.

"I am delighted to meet you both," she said, "but
especially you, Miss Deverill. I so enjoy reading your
newspaper."

That, Henry was relieved to note, softened Miss Deverill's defensive stance at once. "Thank you, Duchess.
You are very kind to say so."

"I say it because it's true. I particularly enjoy reading Lady Truelove's column. It is the high point of my
afternoon, much to my eldest son's disapproval. I do
believe he would be more comfortable if the ladies of
his house limited their reading to the *Court Circular*."

Henry stirred. "Really, Mama—"

"Torquil hates being teased, Miss Deverill." She cut him off with an airy wave in his direction. "But I do it anyway, for his own good. Without a bit of teasing now and again to bring him down a peg, he can become somewhat autocratic."

"I quite agree, but—" Miss Deverill broke off to cast a considering glance in his direction. "I fear you have not been teasing him enough, Duchess."

This pert reply earned her a delighted laugh from his mother. "You may be right, my dear, and I suspect you could be of great assistance in that regard, if you chose. Now, Miss Clara," she went on before Henry could remind them that he was actually in the room and there was no need to talk about him as if he weren't, "I do hope you will be comfortable with us during your stay and enjoy yourself. Have you any fixed engagements?"

The girl, who had impressed Henry upon his visits to the newspaper's office as being somewhat tongue-tied, now seemed wholly mute, for though she opened her mouth to reply, no sound came out.

Her elder sister moved as if to come to her aid, but Mama, an excellent hostess, preempted her. "Ah, I see that my son-in-law has been waylaid by Sarah on his way to the sherry. Miss Clara, you and I shall have to remind him of his responsibilities as a gentleman. Come, my dear. Lord James, as you may know, is the second son of the Marquess of Rolleston, whose grandfather . . ."

Her voice faded as she moved out of earshot, Miss Clara in tow, and though Miss Deverill started to follow them, Henry stopped her. "Let them go," he advised. "If your sister is to move in society," he added as she seemed inclined to protest, "you can't be forever dogging her heels, even if it proves to be for only two weeks."

Some of her earlier resentment returned to her countenance. "If I feel impelled to watch over her in this particular company, could you blame me for it, given what I heard a short time ago?"

"No," he admitted. "Your sister did not hear it, too, I trust?"

"Thankfully, no. To her, this visit is the most exciting, glorious, terrifying thing that's happened in years, and if she had heard what I heard, it would have devastated her."

"You need not worry on that score, for once I have spoken with the members of my family on the subject, any talk such as you heard will not occur again in this house, I promise you. Until then," he added as she took another glance past him, "my mother will watch over your sister. You need not worry."

She nodded, seeming satisfied. "The duchess is very kind, but then, I had already guessed that she would be. In appearance, though, she's not at all what I imagined."

"I suppose that's to be expected. When you have a preconceived idea of what someone looks like, the reality rarely matches it. I, for instance, imagined Lady Truelove as stout, red-haired, and swathed in jet beads." He slid his gaze down, a move that reminded him again just how wrong his imagined picture of her had been. The sight of Miss Deverill in an evening frock was a fetching one indeed, and fired his imagination even more strongly than her suffragist shirtwaists and neckties had done. As his gaze slid over the creamy skin of her bosom and caught on the shadowy cleft in the deep V of her neckline, his fancy of her in sheer chiffon flashed across his mind more vividly than ever. His body responded at once, desire flickering up inside him and underscoring the fact that when it came to Irene Deverill, control might be a difficult thing to maintain.

Henry forced his gaze back to her face. "I don't think my imagined picture of you could have been more wrong."

The words were innocuous enough, but he feared his voice may have betrayed a hint of what he was feeling, for her eyes widened a fraction. "But tell me," he hastened on, desperate for a safer topic, "just what did you imagine my mother to look like?"

"Stout, red-haired, and swathed in jet beads."

He smiled at that. "You've taken my mother's words to heart, I see."

That actually earned him a smile. It was a mere curve of the lips, but he'd take what he could get. "As she pointed out, someone has to do it. And if the goal is to bring you down a notch or two, I am happy to make the attempt."

"Of that I have no doubt."

"But to answer your question honestly, I pictured your mother as tall, languorous, and very elegant, not as a petite and lively dynamo. So as you said, one's preconceived ideas about a person can often be wrong. Other than her appearance, however, she is much as I imagined. Of course, we shared a correspondence of letters over a period of several weeks."

"And in these letters—" He broke off, astonished at

himself. "Forgive me. Your correspondence with my mother is no longer my business. It would now be quite uncivil of me to inquire."

"And you are never uncivil," she said, her voice suspiciously bland.

"I try not to be. Although," he added, trying not to smile, for such a response would only serve to encourage her, "sometimes I just can't help myself."

"Rank having its privileges?"

Impertinent minx, to quote his own somewhat arrogant words back at him. "Quite so," he said, refusing to be drawn. "But my rank has tremendous responsibilities as well as privileges, Miss Deverill. My primary one is my family, whom I would give my life to protect. That," he added, watching her closely, "gives me at least one trait you can appreciate, I think?"

She made a rueful face. "Had anyone told me this morning that you and I had a thing in common, I'd have recommended that person for a stay in Bedlam."

"I suspect I would have done the same."

The discovery that they had a shred of common ground was one both of them clearly needed time to digest, for in its wake, neither of them seemed able to think of a thing to say.

It took several seconds before he was able to break the silence. "I hope you find your room comfortable?" he asked, deciding that small talk might be best to preserve what seemed the beginnings of a truce.

"Quite comfortable, thank you. But my bedroom can't hold a candle to that bathroom. I was so impressed by the bathtub, in fact, that I had to have a bathe straightaway."

Henry tensed, those words conjuring more provocative images of her and shredding any notion that there might be safety in small talk. Bathing, he reminded himself, was not a suitable topic to discuss with a young lady. He ought to steer the conversation toward something more appropriate—the weather, perhaps, or someone's health.

"And did you enjoy your bathe?" he asked instead, demonstrating that the erotic pictures of his imagination were impervious to the dictates of good manners.

If she suspected any of this, she gave no sign. "How could I not?" she answered, seeming to take his question at face value. "Soaking in an enormous bathtub, lathering up with French milled soap, drying off with Turkish towels the size of lap blankets—that's heavenly."

She might be thinking about an earthly version of paradise, but Henry's thoughts were much less reverent. The arousal inside him was deepening and spreading, despite his best efforts to check it. "Indoor plumbing," he managed, "is most convenient."

"Oh, indeed."

"In fact, we have"—he paused, taking a deep breath and several blessed moments to count—"four bathrooms in this house. And . . . seven—I think—at our estate in Dorset. One at our hunting lodge in Scotland, and five at our seaside villa at Torquay. I had all of them installed four or five years ago."

"Seventeen bathrooms?" She gave a laugh. "How deliciously decadent of you. It seems, if I may say so, uncharacteristic. I'd have thought you to be a man of much more ascetic tastes."

If she knew what he was feeling just now, she would hardly liken him to a puritan. Still, despite the chaos in his body, Henry couldn't help taking a bit of satisfaction in her reaction. "I seem to have managed to impress you at last, Miss Deverill. My family, unfortunately, did not have the same favorable reaction to the installation of bathrooms that you have displayed. Everyone kicked up the devil of a fuss."

"But why? With our cold and dreary winters, who could object to soaking—"

"We're an old family." Interrupting was rude, but he was desperate. "Old families don't tend to embrace modern ideas. Hot and cold laid on at the turn of a tap is a very modern idea."

Unexpectedly, she gave him a wide smile. "I begin to think I am wrong and you are a hedonist at heart, Duke."

She didn't know the half of it. Her smile—the first full and genuine one he'd seen from her, was a dazzling sight that only made what he felt more difficult to hide. Frantic, Henry glanced around, and when he spied Edward nearby with sherry, he was so relieved that he didn't even excuse himself before turning to snag two glasses off the tray.

"Ah, sherry. Thank you, Edward. Your timing," he added under his breath, "is impeccable."

Ignoring the footman's quizzical glance, he returned his attention to Miss Deverill and held out one of the glasses to her. "Would you care for a sherry?"

"Thank you." She took the glass and lifted it to take a sip, but then she paused, staring at him in astonishment as he swallowed the entire contents of his own glass in a single draught.

Henry was beyond caring about mundane civilities at this point. The wine, however, did the trick, enabling him to banish from his mind erotic pictures of Miss Deverill standing in a bathtub wearing nothing but a filmy layer of soapsuds. He returned the glass to the tray and gave the footman a nod of dismissal, and then, with his body once more under his usual stern regulation, he returned his attention to his guest and decided it was time to broach a delicate topic, one he knew his role as host demanded of him.

"Since we have been talking of family, Miss Deverill, there is something I would like to say about mine before we go in to dinner."

"Yes?"

He paused, choosing his words with care. "I would ask," he said at last, "that you forgive what you overheard just before you came in this evening. My sisters were gossiping about you, that is true, but they did not mean to be unkind."

"No?" She considered for a moment, then she gave a nod. "In regard to your own sisters, I shall take you at your word."

"You are a woman wholly outside their experience, you see, and they don't know quite what to make of you. They are both very young, not yet twenty, and they have led a sheltered life. The latter fact is undoubtedly my fault, and I hope you will forgive them any thoughtlessness in their remarks, for it was borne of naiveté, not unkindness of heart."

"And Lady David?" she asked. "What explanation is there for her behavior?"

"The fact that she is Lady David," he said at once, and at once regretted it.

"I don't understand."

He cursed himself for his impulsive reply and wondered what it was about this woman that spurred him to frank remarks and licentious thoughts. He was usually much more circumspect nowadays. He had no time to ponder his own uncharacteristic behavior, however, for Miss Deverill was watching him, waiting for an explanation. "Carlotta," he said with great reluctance, "married the brother of a duke, when marrying the duke was what she really wanted."

She blinked, staring at him, looking so stunned that if Henry had ever possessed a shred of conceit about himself, it would have disintegrated in that moment. "She wanted to marry you?"

"Hard as that is to imagine, yes."

The dryness of his reply was not lost on her. She bit her lip, looking contrite. "That didn't come out right . . . I wasn't trying to imply anything derogatory about your personal attractions . . . I mean . . . I would hardly criticize your sisters for that sort of thing and then do the same thing to you . . . I didn't intend . . ." She stopped and took a deep breath amid this tangle of disjointed phrases. "Was she very much in love with you?"

"Love?" He gave a laugh, but it wasn't a laugh of amusement. It was a sound so terribly cynical, they both grimaced. "Hardly," he said.

His answer did not, however, deter her. "And you? Were you in love with her?"

"Carlotta?" He gave a shudder at the very idea. "God, no. But I learned long ago—" He broke off and glanced at the door, seeking some sort of diversion. "Where the devil is Boothby? It must surely be past eight o'clock by now."

"What did you learn?" she persisted, demonstrating that she was not one to be easily distracted. Obligated to explain, he went on, "There are many women who would happily marry me, Miss Deverill, but I have always known that ambition, not love, is the usual reason why."

If he hoped she would dispute that view with a tactfully murmured compliment about his personal attractions, she disappointed him, and her silence reminded him that this woman didn't offer banal insincerities for the sake of politeness. That fact alone made her unlike nearly all the other people of his acquaintance.

"A cynical contention," she said. "And yet, one you sound as if you regret."

"I do regret it." He smiled a little. "You seem surprised, Miss Deverill."

"Well, yes. Should I not be?" She laughed a little, clearly confounded. "Given our previous conversations, it has always seemed obvious to me that romantic love doesn't mean anything to you."

It did once, he wanted to say. *That's why I married a poor girl of no significant family and ruined both our lives. It meant everything.*

He felt suddenly, terribly vulnerable, almost as if he'd made his admission aloud, and he hastened into speech. "Do not misunderstand me. While I may regret the fact that most women of my acquaintance would willingly marry me without love, I do not condemn them for it. How can I? Duty requires me to make a suitable marriage, and love cannot be allowed to play any part in my choice of bride. 'A duke,'" he added, quoting his father, 'must marry a woman worthy of his position.'"

"And yet . . ." She paused, tilting her head, her eyes studying him with thoughtful speculation. "And yet, you must sometimes wish it were not so?"

He felt a jolt of alarm. "Not at all," he denied at once. "I accept the fact that for me, love is—must be—a secondary consideration. Wishing it were otherwise would be a waste of time."

"I see."

He very much feared she did see, that those beautiful, discerning hazel eyes had just peeked beneath his smooth, carefully cultivated surface and seen him for what he was: a man who'd once wanted a girl so desperately, desired her so passionately, that he'd thrown away everything else in his world just to possess her, with catastrophic results. He feared he had revealed the essence of himself: a man whose controlled manner, disciplined life, and fastidious rules of conduct were far more than requirements of his position. They were the twines of a lifeline, one he clung to so that he might never again be swept away by his own appetites.

The silence seemed deafening, impelling him to break it. "So there you have it, Miss Deverill," he said, forcing a light note into his voice. "The truth about love and dukes. Terribly unromantic, I grant you, but there it is."

"There's one thing I still don't understand."

"And what is that?"

"You've said that among your kind of people, love is, at best, a secondary consideration to matrimony."

"And?"

She lifted her free hand, a sweeping gesture that encompassed far more than just the room around them. "How could you—or my father, for that matter—possibly think this world, where clothes are more important than kindness, and alliance is valued more highly than love, is a world I would ever want to live in?"

He had no idea how to respond to that question, for women like her, women for whom his world held no appeal, were as rare as hens' teeth. He'd certainly never met one before. Thankfully, however, Boothby's deep voice intervened before he was forced to craft a reply.

"Your Graces, ladies and gentlemen," the butler announced from the doorway with all his customary grandeur, "dinner is served."

Chapter 8

The Duke of Torquil may have surprised Irene with his very modern baths, but she soon discovered that when it came to his dining room, he made no concessions whatsoever to modernity, and the result was beyond surprising. It was stunning.

Old silver gleamed and crystal glittered on a table of pristine white linen, elegant footmen in livery waited to serve, and dozens of candles had been placed in the epergnes on the table and the chandeliers overhead, lighting the room with a soft, ethereal glow.

She'd dined in wealthy surroundings before, of course. When she'd first reached an age to put up her hair and dine with her parents, her grandfather's newspaper empire had enabled them to enjoy a certain number of luxuries, including an excellent chef and a well-set table. And yet, even in her family's most prosperous days, their dining room had never possessed

quite the elegant ambience she felt here. The gleaming
Tass silver and sparkling Irish crystal on the table, the
Reynolds and Gainsborough paintings on the walls, the
thick but faded Axminster carpet beneath her feet—
items every bit as rare and expensive and elegant as
these could have been bought by any new money mil-
lionaire, and yet, somehow, the room would not have
looked like this. The difference was undefinable, yet
unmistakable. Anyone walking into this room knew at
once that these treasures had been handed down for
many generations, not purchased at an auction.

As Irene took her place beside her host at the long
oval dining table, she found in front of her an array
of plates, glasses, and utensils far more elaborate than
anything her family would ever have set out.

She pulled off her gloves and placed them in her lap,
then reached for her napkin, glancing across the table
to see how her sister was faring in the face of this bewildering display of cut glass and cutlery.

Seated between Lord David and the duchess, Clara
had already removed her gloves and was now staring
back at Irene with pleading eyes, clearly looking for
guidance. Remembering the words of her governess
from long ago about starting from the outside in, Irene
tapped her index finger discreetly against the outer-
most utensil to the right of her plate, a tiny, delicate
spoon made of mother-of-pearl, the purpose of which
she could not begin to imagine.

It was, she soon discovered, a caviar spoon. Several
other equally unfamiliar utensils lay beside it; however,
by careful observance of the duke and Lady Angela,
as well as a minimal amount of conversation, Irene

was able to manage not only the caviar spoon, but also the escargot fork and tongs and the pâté knife. Nonetheless, when the hors d'oeuvres had given way to the soup, she couldn't help feeling relieved. Clara, she had no doubt, felt the same.

Once the soup had been served, Irene felt comfortable enough with the accoutrements of her meal that she could devote her attention to the conversation going on around her and be able to converse beyond the monosyllables she'd uttered during the first course.

"What shall we do tomorrow?" Lady Sarah was asking. "We've no fixed engagements, so where shall we take our guests? Shopping?"

"I believe you have several engagements already, Sarah," said the duchess. "Carlotta had your schedule completely full for the entire week, as I recall."

"We cancelled everything this week. We didn't know if—" Lady Sarah broke off, casting an uneasy glance at Lady David. "We thought—that is, we told everyone you were ill. We feared, you see . . ." Her voice trailed off, her floundering explanations fading into an uncomfortable silence.

Torquil broke it at once. "In light of recent events, I believe the young ladies thought it best to remain close to home."

"Oh, my dears," the duchess said, glancing from one of her daughters to the other, then to her daughter-in-law, "there was no need for any of you to cancel your plans."

"Probably not," Torquil said, and though that murmur of agreement was bland, it reclaimed his mother's attention at once. "But I don't think any of us knew quite what to do, Mama. We've all been rather at sixes and sevens this week."

Behind that comment, there was an unmistakable hint of reproof. The duchess glanced away, looking a bit conscience-stricken, and Irene stirred, uncomfortable on her behalf.

"The point is," Lady Angela said, jumping in as another awkward silence threatened, "we've a whole day free, nothing planned, and guests to entertain. So what shall we do?"

"What about an excursion outside the city?" Lord David suggested. "We could take a picnic, make a day of it."

Her hosts, she realized, were unaware of her schedule, and she knew she could not allow them to continue making plans for her in which she could not participate, but Lord James spoke before she had the chance.

"I've an idea. The *Mary Louisa* is docked at Queen's Wharf. If tomorrow is a fine day, we could take her out, sail down to Kew, and have our picnic there."

"But shouldn't we be taking the Miss Deverills about here in town?" Sarah asked. "How can we introduce them to our acquaintances if we are on the yacht all day?"

"You have a yacht?" Diverted, Irene turned to her host, and was at once reminded by his impeccably fitted dinner jacket and perfectly formed white tie that her question was a bit absurd. "What am I saying?" she muttered. "Of course you have a yacht."

"I'm surprised you didn't know that already, Miss Deverill," Carlotta said before her brother-in-law could reply. "After all, *Society Snippets* seems to have found our family and friends quite fascinating during the past year. I'm amazed that tidbit escaped your notice."

Irene was tempted to say that if Lady David continued to be so damnably irritating, the paper just might start to find *her* the most fascinating person in all of society, but for Clara's sake, she refrained, and Torquil spoke before she could think of a more tactful reply.

"I'm sure Miss Deverill is fully aware of what is printed in her own paper, Carlotta," he said, a defense of her so unexpected that Irene couldn't help staring at him in astonishment. "And most of the London papers find us a topic for news. It's part of our life to be talked about. I would think you'd be resigned to that by now."

"Of course," Carlotta murmured, returning her attention to her consommé.

"As for the *Mary Louisa*, Miss Deverill," Torquil went on, turning to Irene, "she's small as yachts go—only 108 feet—but quite well-equipped. She has a full galley and dining room, a parlor, and four bedrooms. She even has"—he paused and took a sip of his wine—"a bath."

"Then you miscounted, Duke," she quipped. "You have eighteen bathrooms."

"Goodness, Torquil," Sarah said, laughing. "What inspired you and Miss Deverill to count up the number of baths we possess?"

"I wanted to know," Irene said before the duke could reply. "And I was so impressed by the number that I deemed him a hedonist."

The absurdity of that description was underscored by a merry round of laughter at the table, and then Angela spoke. "The number's still wrong, though," she pointed out. "It's twenty baths, if you include both yachts."

"You have two?" she echoed, and looked at the duke askance. "Two yachts, and you still say you are not a hedonist?"

He smiled as another round of laughter broke out around the table.

"Each ship has its own purposes," he explained. "The *Mary Louisa* is, as I said, quite small, with a mast short enough to pass under all the London bridges. We use her mostly for sailing the Thames and the canals. The *Endeavour* is a much larger vessel, meant for the sea. And Angela is right about the number of baths, for the *Endeavour* has two."

Irene reached for her wine, beginning to feel staggered by all this opulence. In creating a scandal sheet, she'd known instinctively that this glittering world appealed to a wide swath of people, and the publication's success had proven her right, but she'd never shared the public's fascination for aristocrats and their *ton*. She'd come here certain that nothing about these people, or their wealth, or their style of living could impress her, but in these elegant surroundings, Irene began to fear she wasn't quite so high-minded as she'd thought herself. Two yachts, she had to admit, sounded like smashing good fun. As for the man beside her, she didn't like him, not at all. He hadn't given her much reason to do so. And yet—

She slid her gaze sideways and found to her astonishment that he was watching her, and though his countenance was as impassive as ever, there was something in his steady, unreadable gaze that impelled her to take another gulp of wine, and she decided one of the things about him she found most vexing was his ability to hide what he thought and felt so well. But maybe there was nothing to hide. Maybe he was every bit as cold as she'd first thought him, as emotionless as he always appeared.

Impelled to break the silence, Irene struggled to remember what they'd been talking about. "If you have two yachts, you must love sailing," she said, a comment so inane, she instantly wanted to kick herself.

"We are a sailing family," he agreed, and though his voice was as grave as ever, there was no need to guess that he was teasing her.

Irene made a face at him, but before she could pay him out for it with a suitable retort, another voice intervened.

"There are two kinds of families in society, Miss Deverill," Carlotta said, obviously feeling the need to school her on such matters. "Hunting families and sailing families."

"Well, we are most definitely in the latter category," Angela said, laughing. "So, Torquil, can we take the Miss Deverills out on the *Mary Louisa*?"

"That depends," he answered. "Our guests may not enjoy sailing."

Angela looked from her brother to Irene. "Are you a good sailor, Miss Deverill?"

"I don't know," she answered. "I've never been on a boat, other than a punt on the Serpentine. Does that count?"

"Not if you ask my brother. He thinks if it doesn't have a sail, it's beneath his notice."

"Not true," the duke objected. "I sculled and rowed

at Cambridge, you know. And I've punted you around the Serpentine a time or two, dear sister. But I confess, I do prefer ships with sails. Why do the work yourself when you can let the wind do it for you?"

"As if sailing isn't work!" Angela cried. "If we do go sailing, Miss Deverill, my brother will put us all through our paces. The *Mary Louisa* has been in dry dock all season for repairs, and she was only put on the water a few days ago, which means there's been no time to make her ready. If we take her out tomorrow, we shall all have to help get her underway—except Mama, of course. I doubt being our guest will save you. I expect Torquil will haul the pair of you into service the moment you step on the gangplank. He'll probably thrust a rag and a tin of metal polish into your hand and tell you to get to it."

"I shall do no such thing to guests of ours," he answered. "You may rest easy, Miss Deverill, Miss Clara, for no work on your part shall be required. My saucy sister, however, is a different matter."

"You see?" Angela said, making a face at him past Irene's plate. "What did I tell you?"

"You talk as if there will be so much for you to do," Lord James put in good-naturedly. "Torquil will only make you help until the ship's underway, Angie. After that, he won't demand anything from you or any of the ladies but to sit on the deck chairs, put up your parasols, and sip champagne cups. It's the gentlemen who tack and jibe and take the wheel."

"But what if the ladies want to tack and jibe, too?" Irene couldn't help asking. She looked at Torquil. "What if we want to steer the ship? What then?"

She was challenging him, she knew, but if he intended to take up the gauntlet she'd thrown down, he was given no chance.

"A woman at the helm?" Carlotta said in lively astonishment. "How absurd. Torquil would never allow it."

Irene turned from Torquil to his sister-in-law. "I don't see why not."

"No," the other woman said, the pity in her smile unmistakable. "I should imagine you don't."

"I daresay Irene would like to sail," Clara put in, her voice a bit higher than usual. "So would I. What's it like?" She turned to the man beside her. "Lord David? What is so appealing about the sport that it makes yours a sailing family?"

Irene stared, astonished that her quiet sister had come out with such a lengthy question around people she barely knew, but before she could recover from the shock of that, Torquil was speaking to her.

"I can see, Miss Deverill," he murmured, leaning closer to her, "that Carlotta's tail isn't the only one you intend to twist this evening."

She turned, pasting on an innocent expression. "I don't know what you mean."

"I think you do. As for steering my ship," he added, leaning back and adopting a more conversational tone, "I doubt you'd want to."

"And why is that?"

"It would mean you'd be part of my crew, and if that were the case, you'd be required to obey my orders." He paused, his gaze lowering to her mouth. "Without question."

Her heart gave a sudden, hard thud in her chest. She

felt pinned by that look as if by an arrow, and she was unable to move even after he lifted his gaze again to hers. His words ought to have inspired any suffragist worth her salt with the desire to bash a candlestick over his head, and yet, Irene could not have summoned the proper outrage for such a course. Her lips tingled with heat and her heart raced, not with anger, but with . . . excitement. It was a sensation so unexpected that it took her several moments to recover her wits enough to reply. "A deck chair for me, then," she said at last, "if having you order me about is the alternative."

"Very wise of you, Miss Deverill," Angela told her, laughing. "My brother is a hard taskmaster."

"Very," Torquil agreed, his gaze still fixed on Irene as he spoke, his grave expression and well-bred drawl a sharp contrast to the tumult inside of her. The strangest thing about it all was that she had no idea what had spurred this rush of feeling. She hated being dictated to under any circumstances, and she already knew that from him it was especially aggravating. But just now, aggravation was not at all what she felt. Instead, she felt exhilarated.

After a moment, he diverted his attention, enabling Irene to regain her composure. "And if Angela keeps complaining about what is required of her," he said, leaning around Irene to look at his sister, "she won't be having a deck chair and a champagne cup. Instead, I shall tell Andrew and Fitz and the rest of the crew to take a holiday, and she'll find herself swabbing the decks."

"Oh," Clara breathed on an ecstatic sigh, "it all sounds so lovely. Not the swabbing decks, part," she added at once, making everyone laugh. "But the rest would be heavenly."

"Shall we take up Jamie's plan tomorrow, then?" Angela asked as the footmen began clearing away the soup and serving the fish course.

"We can't," Lady David said. "Even though we cancelled all our social engagements for tomorrow, if we are seen gallivanting out on the water, it would create a most unfavorable impression."

"Oh, but our plans tomorrow were so informal anyway," Angela replied. "Only luncheon at the Savoy with Lady Billingsley and tea with Lady Stokesbury. Those two ladies are like family. Surely they would understand if we—"

"Carlotta is right," Torquil cut in. "These things must be handled in the proper way, regardless of how close the tie. You agree, Mama, I trust?"

"Yes, I'm afraid I do. I wish our social rules were not so punctilious, but Henry and Carlotta have been right to remind us of our duty there. We shall make arrangements to go sailing another day. In the meantime, girls, you must honor your social commitments. I shall write to Lady Billingsley and Lady Stokesbury first thing tomorrow, explain that my illness was merely a headache, and make apologies for our cancelled plans."

She paused as the footman presented her with a tray of sole in sauce. After she had taken a fillet from the tray, the footman moved on and she continued, "I believe I will also happen to mention that Lord Ellesmere's granddaughters are our guests for the next two weeks, and enclose my card to indicate our intent to call on them in the afternoon. We shall then take the

Miss Deverills out for luncheon and some shopping on Bond Street so they might be seen with us in public. Then we shall pay calls on any who might have been inconvenienced by my absence."

Irene knew she had to make her own obligations clear before any further plans were made on her behalf. "It all sounds delightful, Duchess," she said, feeling a hint of regret as she spoke, "but some of these arrangements won't be possible for me, I'm afraid."

Everyone stopped eating, and suddenly, Torquil wasn't the only one subjecting her to full attention.

"I have my duties at the newspaper to attend to," she explained, glancing around with an apologetic smile. "Duties which make me unavailable for any engagements before one o'clock in the afternoon."

There was another silence, this one so lengthy that even Irene began to feel uncomfortable. It was, she was well aware, a most unconventional thing for a woman to have a career, but it couldn't be helped. She did have a career, one that she couldn't simply take up and put down whenever she felt like it.

Carlotta, of course, was the first to speak. "My dear Miss Deverill," she said, setting down her knife and fork with a delicate clink, "you do understand the purpose of the plans the duchess has outlined is to introduce you and your sister into our circle of acquaintance?"

"Of course." Irene smiled, blinking her eyes innocently at the woman across the table, pretending she was unaware of the sudden tension in the room. "But I must also think of my readers. I have a duty to them, and to my newspaper."

"But what will our friends think?" Sarah asked. "They surely would not approve—" She broke off as she looked at her eldest brother, and he must have given her a warning glance, for she bit her lip and returned her attention to her plate.

Carlotta, however, was not so reticent. "Sarah is right. This won't go over well. Heaven knows Ellesmere won't like it."

That was too much for Irene. "Lady David, I have had the same grandfather and the same profession for quite some time now, and I find it odd that despite his disapproval, Lord Ellesmere has never chosen to express to me or my family any concern about how we spend our time. Nor has he shown any concern about how we support ourselves, and he has certainly never offered us a viable alternative to working for our living. So forgive me if I do not deem his opinion of my profession to be of any great importance."

Lady David stared at her, obviously at a loss what to say in the wake of this outburst. "Of course," she murmured after a moment. "Quite."

"Well, I think it very wrong of Ellesmere," Angela said. "Perhaps when Torquil calls upon him, he can impress upon the viscount that he needs do his duty by his granddaughters."

"Of course," the duke said. "That was my intent."

Irene stiffened in her chair, her pride stinging. "We don't need his assistance, nor—" She broke off when Clara's toe nudged hers beneath the table, warning her that she was about to go too far. "That is," she amended, "we don't wish to be any trouble. The duke need not concern himself with our little family squabble."

"It is not a matter of taking trouble, Miss Deverill," Torquil said. "I assured your father that I would attempt to assist him in healing the breach with his father-in-law, and I am glad to do so. But if you think my direct assistance inappropriate, you need only say so."

She might have done exactly that but for Clara, whose big brown eyes were pleading with her across the table. "I appreciate my father's attempt to bring about a truce," she said instead, "for that is probably best for all concerned. But if that truce means the viscount shall expect me to abandon my obligations to the readers and advertisers of my paper, I regret to say that I cannot accommodate him."

"His granddaughter's occupation may be a difficult thing for Ellesmere to accept," the duchess put in, "but he is partly to blame for it. And if Ellesmere wants his granddaughter to give up her journalistic interests, all he has to do is help to bring his granddaughters into society."

Irene wanted to say that she had no intention of giving up her paper, but she did not want to embarrass Clara, so she bit her tongue.

"I'm sure," the duchess went on, "that once Torquil has made the viscount aware of his son-in-law's sincere desire to hold out the olive branch, he'll put things right. In the meantime, he can hardly object if Miss Deverill is unwilling to risk her family's livelihood because his sensibilities are offended."

"But what of society?" Sarah asked. "What will they make of it?"

"They'll be shocked," Carlotta said. "What else could they be?"

"Even if they are," the duchess said, "it is the viscount's intransigence which has forced Miss Deverill out into the world, given that her father is ill and unable to attend to business matters himself. Miss Deverill can hardly be condemned for carrying on in her father's stead. I grow so weary of how unrealistic some in our set can be about the economic realities so many people face." She paused, meeting her son's gaze across the table. "How else but by work or by marriage is a man without inherited wealth to gain an income?"

Irene's gaze slid to the man beside her, but he looked back at his mother impassively and did not answer.

"Oh, lovely," muttered Lord David. "First, professions for women, then another family's private squabbles, and now money. What delightful topics for dinner conversation."

"Well, I don't see why it matters anyway," Angela said. "I think there should be a much wider variety of things for women to do. Well, why not?" she added as all her siblings groaned. "Gentlemen have so many more occupations and distractions available to them than women do."

"Working for a living isn't one of them, though," Lord James replied. "Not in our set, not for either sex."

"No, but, Jamie, surely you would agree that the gentlemen do have more activities available to them than we young ladies do. Paying calls and buying clothes and doing the season is all very well, but it can be so tedious, and sometimes, downright pointless. We can't even vote."

"Ugh," groaned David.

"It would be lovely," she went on, ignoring him, "to have something meaningful to do with one's time."

"Yes," Lady David interjected with a tittering laugh, "because publishing a scandal sheet is so meaningful."

Irene stilled, her hands tightening around her knife and fork, but when she looked at the woman across from her, she made sure there was a bright smile on her face. "Not nearly as meaningful as minute examinations of what people are wearing, though, I daresay."

This time, the silence was not only awkward, but painful, and it seemed to go on forever as glances were exchanged around the table—some embarrassed, and some, like Clara's, understandably bewildered.

As her sister stared at her, looking not only confused but also hurt, Irene's conscience smote her, and any satisfaction she'd felt in standing up to Carlotta's spite vanished.

"Well, of course," Clara said after a moment, breaking the silence. "Fashion is a fascinating topic to all ladies."

"Isn't it, though?" Sarah jumped in at once. "Have you seen the new leg o'mutton sleeves? They're enormous."

With a relief that was palpable, the conversation shifted to a discussion of current fashion, with nearly everyone offering a comment, except Irene, who decided it might be best to pretend vast interest in her fish and say as little as possible.

Torquil seemed to share her disinterest in ladies' sleeves. "Tell me, Miss Deverill," he murmured after a moment, his voice low enough that only she could hear, "do you stir things up everywhere you go or merely within my family?"

"I—" She paused for a swallow of wine. "I don't know what you mean."

"Don't you?" He paused, waiting, and after a moment, she forced herself to look at him.

"I suppose you think I ought to have held my tongue," she said.

"I find it's usually wiser to adopt that course. Carlotta is exasperating, and can often be malicious, but you don't make things easier on yourself by needling her."

"Odd, but I thought she was needling me."

"She was, and as I promised you before dinner, I will put a stop to it the first moment I am able to speak with her alone. My concern at the moment is not her, but you. You shall be moving in high society, Miss Deverill, a place that does not always accept controversial opinions with good grace. That may be a failing of it, I don't know, but for your part, I should advise caution. As for your intention to continue your duties with your newspaper during the coming fortnight, there is no point in discussing it now, but we shall have to come to some understanding about it before the evening is over."

His tone left no doubt what he thought that understanding should be. "I don't see that there is much to discuss."

"In the meantime," he said, refusing to be drawn, "it might be best to have a heed for what you say. A woman born into this world can utter an outrageous opinion on occasion—hence Angela's comment about the vote—

but until Ellesmere comes up to the mark, you are vulnerable to criticism from every quarter. And so is your sister. If you become defensive, people will sense there is something that needs defending. On the other hand, if you do not rise to Carlotta's baiting, she will be the one diminished in the eyes of others, not you."

"The fact that you think the vote for women an outrageous thing does not surprise me, but why should you care how I appear in the eyes of others? It can't possibly matter to you."

"Can it not?"

The question was unexpectedly light, almost careless in its utterance, but his eyes, looking into hers, seemed to darken, turning from the clear, pale gray of a glacier to the murky, turbulent hue of thunderclouds. The transformation was so sudden and so intense that Irene's heart gave another startled thump in her chest.

Everything she'd seen of this man indicated an uncompromising, even ruthless character. He was stiff-necked, old-fashioned, and fastidious beyond bearing. And yet, suddenly, she felt as if she'd just caught a glimpse of something else lurking beneath all that, something completely contrary to everything she knew of him.

He'd swept into her office and into her life two days ago like an arctic storm, seeming the most frigid man she'd ever met, but despite that, strange heat began spreading through her, making her skin prickle and her toes curl in her slippers. He was close enough to her that when she drew in her breath, she could smell the scents of castile soap and bay rum that clung to his skin.

She could almost hear his breathing. Time seemed to hang suspended as he filled her senses with a new and different awareness. The awareness of him as a man.

Irene hadn't much experience with that sort of thing, and it took her wholly by surprise. She'd never been one to be caught up in violent emotions—not until she'd met him, anyway. And in regard to him, those emotions had hardly been pleasant ones, consisting mainly of outrage, frustration, and resentment. She certainly didn't like him, so what was this strange new feeling that froze her in place and burned her like fire?

He spoke before she could get her bearings, his voice possessed of its usual cool, disinterested cadence, making her aggravated all over again. "It matters because you are in my house, and therefore, in my care. It would grieve me to see you or your sister discomfited or embarrassed, Miss Deverill."

With that, he looked away, rejoining the conversation going on around them as if he'd been listening to it all along, when she hadn't heard a single word.

"The boys must come with us, Jamie, or we'll never hear the end of it. They love sailing."

"Which is all very well, except that they've no nanny now. As I recall, a certain person at this table promised to call in at Merrick's Employment Agency and find them a new one, one capable of managing them, yet two days have passed, and we have seen no sign of this august personage."

Torquil made a sound of vexation. "Blast it, I utterly forgot about the nanny. I'll go tomorrow."

"Why don't you go, Jamie?" Sarah said. "They are your boys, after all."

"Yes, but my lack of success with choosing nannies speaks for itself."

"That's only because you always choose the pretty, wholly inefficient ones," Angela said. "Mama and I shall go, for I should dearly love something satisfying to do, and finding Jamie a qualified nanny would satisfy me enormously. My nephews," she added to Irene, "are absolute hellions."

"No, Angela." Torquil overrode her. "I will go, because I promised I would. If you truly yearn for satisfying things to do, however, there are dozens of charities I can recommend that are in dire need of assistance. Would starting your own charity for those less fortunate be satisfying enough for you?"

"It might do," the girl agreed eagerly. "Could I really run my own charity instead of just help Mama with all of hers?"

"Why shouldn't you, if Mama doesn't object?"

The duchess waved a hand airily. "Not at all. I think it a most excellent idea."

"No shirking, though," the duke said, "once you've taken it on. Perhaps," he added, glancing at Irene, "you might ask Miss Clara to assist you?"

Irene looked at her sister, watching Clara's face light up at the prospect.

"Oh, could I?" she asked. "Unless you need me at the paper, Irene?"

"I can manage. I may have to be there nearly every day, but you certainly don't."

"My goodness, Miss Deverill," Lady David said, "you *are* very much the workhorse."

Irene supposed that was an insult to her femininity,

but with a glance at her sister, she remained silent. As Torquil had said, there was little point in talking about it now. "I soldier on, Lady David," she said, pasting on a smile.

"That's very brave of you, Miss Deverill," Sarah put in, her approval perhaps a bit forced. "I couldn't do it."

"Good thing," Torquil muttered.

Sarah did not seem to hear. "It will be exhausting, I warn you, Miss Deverill, to work at your paper and do the season, too. Even though we're coming to the end, there are still many events to attend. I can't imagine how you'll manage."

"I'm sure I shall find adequate time for sleep."

"I doubt it," Carlotta said, overriding her young sister-in-law's attempt to smooth things over. "We are often out past dawn. How shall you participate? Shall you go straight from the ballroom to the newsroom to lunch at Rules?" She gave a laugh and turned to the duke before Irene could reply. "It's absurd. No one could manage such a schedule. You agree with me, Torquil, of course?"

Carlotta was smiling as she looked at her brother-in-law, rather like a cat who'd got into the cream, and who could blame her? Irene braced herself for the duke's inevitable disapproval.

"Whatever Miss Deverill's obligations may be, scheduling them is hardly within my purview," he said, and Irene was so astonished she nearly fell out of her chair. "Either way," he went on, meeting his sister-in-law's gaze across the table with a hard look Irene was coming to know well, "since you spend most of your time prior to luncheon in bed, Carlotta, I cannot see that it is any of your concern."

Those words were like a door slamming shut. Carlotta, suitably chastened, returned her attention to her meal, and Irene, still a bit stunned by this unexpected show of support, leaned closer to her host.

"In cases such as this," she murmured, "I thought it was best to hold one's tongue?"

"There are limits, Miss Deverill," he replied, his voice equally low. "Even for me."

She made a face. "If anyone tests your limits, it's probably me."

"Yes," he acknowledged and looked away, reaching for his wine. "In ways you cannot possibly imagine."

Chapter 9

When dinner was over, the men remained in the dining room for port, the ladies went through to the drawing room for coffee, and the duchess gave Irene her first chance to begin the task that had been forced upon her.

Settling on one of the ivory brocade settees, the duchess smiled at Irene and patted the seat cushion beside her. "My dear Miss Deverill, do bring your coffee and sit down by me."

Irene complied, but as she did, it struck her again just how difficult her undertaking was going to be. Ever since the duke had maneuvered her into this situation, Irene had been racking her brains to determine how best to save her beloved newspaper without compromising her own principles and beliefs, and also without spoiling another woman's happiness.

She had developed a sincere liking for the duchess during their brief correspondence, and now that she had met her, Irene liked her even more. There was a warmth and genuine friendliness in her that one couldn't help responding to. In addition, their meeting had reinforced Irene's opinion of her as a woman of intelligence and sophistication, who was well able to make her own decision about who to wed and how to deal with the aftermath.

So how on earth, Irene wondered, was she supposed to change the other woman's mind? And was it even ethical to attempt it?

The duchess spoke again before Irene could begin to contemplate a course of action. "I am so glad you and your sister have come to us. As I said earlier, your Lady Truelove column is one of the high points of my day."

Beside Irene, Lady Angela wriggled as if uncomfortable with this topic.

Her mother noticed at once. "Angela, my dear, I do believe we need some music. Will you play for us? You play so beautifully."

"Oh, but I—" The girl stopped, seeming to realize that her mother was not really making a request. "Of course, Mama."

She rose and walked to the piano where her sister and sister-in-law were leaning over various sheets of music, leaving Irene and the duchess alone on the settee. The older woman watched her daughter go, smiling a little. "She's a darling girl, Angela."

Irene remembered how she'd overheard the other girl defending her and her sister before dinner, and was happy to agree. "She seems lovely."

"She is. Inside, as well as out. I do hope—" The older woman broke off, her smile vanishing, a thoughtful frown taking its place. "She is worried about her future now, in light of recent events. They all are." The duchess turned to look at Irene, giving her a considering look. "You know, I'm sure, why that is so?"

There was no point in pretending otherwise. "I believe everyone knows your situation, Duchess. I, of course—"

She broke off, feeling as if she was groping in the dark, but after taking a moment to consider, she felt it best to be as frank and aboveboard as possible. "I have a confession to make, Duchess. Lady Truelove has . . . ahem . . . shared your correspondence with me. Lady Truelove shares all her letters with me so that I might best perform my role as editor. In telling you this, I hope you do not feel she has broken your confidence?"

"If I wanted my situation kept a secret, Miss Deverill, I should hardly have written to a newspaper columnist, even one who pledges to keep my confidence."

"Why did you do it? Sorry," she added at once. "I don't mean to pry, but I confess, I am curious. Most of the people who write to Lady Truelove are not likely to be identified by the reading public. Even their nearest and dearest don't usually recognize who they are. You are different. Your name has been connected with Mr. Foscarelli for some time. You must have known that upon reading your letter and the details you provided, many people would know that the 'Lady of Society' is you."

"Just so. But my reason for writing to Lady Truelove was the same as that of most people, I imagine. I was in great distress of mind, and I did not feel there was anyone in whom I could confide, at least not anyone who would listen without judging, and who could offer unbiased advice."

"No close friend, or relation?"

"The life of the aristocracy, Miss Deverill, can often be superficial, and isolating, despite the fact that we are always surrounded by others. My family, understandably, wanted to stick their heads in the sand and pretend their mother did not have a young Italian lover! Discussing it with any of them would have been distressing for them and embarrassing for all of us. As for my friends, I was fully aware of what they would say had I asked their opinion: don't be a fool, Harriet. Have your fling, if you must, but be discreet."

"I see."

"In considering marriage to Antonio, I have been fully aware of what impact it would have on my life and the lives of my children. On the other hand, I have come to realize that to continue with him at all, marriage is the only possible course." She smiled a little. "I have always considered myself a woman of the world, Miss Deverill, but I find that an illicit love affair, however exciting, is not really my cup of tea."

Irene smiled back at her. "My question was not as much why you wrote to Lady Truelove for advice, but why you agreed to have your letter published. Lady Truelove gives all her correspondents the ability to refuse publication. She would have advised you to the best of her ability either way."

"In the beginning, I had thought not to have my letter published, but as Lady Truelove and I exchanged correspondence, I felt more and more strongly that it would be better for all concerned if the news of my marriage came out before the fact, rather than afterward. Otherwise, the members of my family might perhaps feel I had betrayed them and harbor bitterness. By having it come out beforehand, they are able to prepare themselves in advance for what is to come and perhaps forgive more easily. And by the time it happens, society will, I hope, have got over the initial shock, and will regard my marriage as an unfortunate inevitability instead of an appalling scandal."

"Taking the wind out of everyone's sails, so to speak?" When the duchess nodded, she went on, "But you did not wish to tell your family of your decision in person?"

"No. It shall be hard on them, I know, but there are certain points in a woman's life where she must be entitled to consider her own needs, as well as those of her children. They are all very dear to me, but they have no idea how lonely my life has been."

"I understand."

"Given that your mother made a similar decision, I think perhaps you do. Still, if I confessed to such a feeling to my family, they would be deeply distressed and see it as an indictment of their care of me. Torquil, in particular, would take it so."

"He does seem to possess a very strong interest in your personal affairs. Do you not sometimes chafe under such scrutiny?"

She laughed. "I should tell him to mind his own business, you mean?"

"Well, yes, I suppose that is what I do mean."

She shook her head. "It wouldn't matter if I did. Henry takes his role as head of the family very much to heart, and it would grieve him enormously not to have the chance to persuade me against what he sees as a disastrous marriage."

Irene shifted in her chair, hating that she was the means by which he intended to accomplish that task. It was a most uncomfortable position to be in.

"But once the deed is done," the duchess went on serenely, "he will have the comfort of knowing he did all he could to stop me. As will all my children. For I expect every one of them to make various attempts to change my mind during the coming fortnight."

Irene pushed aside for the moment the part she was expected to play in that particular activity. "So the delay in marrying Mr. Foscarelli was deliberate on your part? I was told—that is," she amended at once, "I thought the reason you are not yet married is that Mr. Foscarelli had not yet satisfied the two-week residency a license requires."

"Oh, no. I daresay that's what Torquil thinks, for he has damned Antonio as a worthless scoundrel, whose only intent is to take advantage of me."

"That might be a possible interpretation of events, don't you think?"

The duchess merely seemed amused. "Oh, dear, my poor Antonio has even you viewing him with a jaundiced eye. What does Lady Truelove think of that, I wonder?"

Irene resisted the impulse to squirm again. "Unlike Lady Truelove, I can see . . . ahem . . . at least a little, your son's point of view."

"Torquil's point of view has been shaped by his life and the responsibilities of his position, Miss Deverill, and he has felt it necessary to cultivate a hard, polished veneer. Underneath it, of course, he is a hopeless romantic."

To Irene, there was no "of course" about it. Some of her skepticism must have shown on her face, for the duchess laughed.

"It is hard for someone outside the family to believe, I know, but it's true nonetheless. Still, you mustn't let on that I've given away his secret, for it flies straight in the face of all his efforts to be a hard and world-weary cynic."

"I shan't breathe a word," she promised. *Since it's clear you don't know your son at all.* "But in regard to Mr. Foscarelli," she went on, "do you not ever wonder if Torquil might be right? That the man might be just a fortune-hunter?"

She grimaced, knowing she'd just been unforgivably impertinent, but the duchess laughed again. "Well, of course he's a fortune-hunter, my dear! What else would he be?"

Irene blinked, a bit taken aback. Not that the duchess's words themselves surprised her; on the contrary, they confirmed what she'd suspected all along—that Foscarelli was motivated, at least in part, by monetary concerns. Though she hadn't seen that in itself as a reason to denounce the courtship, it was the reason she'd taken such great pains to underscore the risks and emphasize tying up the money.

"Your silence tells me I've shocked you, Miss Deverill. But I am fully aware that Antonio is a fortune-hunter. Whatever else I may be, I am not a fool."

Irene was dismayed. "Forgive me," she said, mortified that she might have given insult. "I never meant to imply—"

Her apology was cut off by the other woman's pat on her knee. "I know what you meant, and you're a sweet child to be concerned. I love Mr. Foscarelli deeply, as you are already aware from my correspondence with Lady Truelove, but I have no illusions about his situation. If I did not have money, we would not be able to wed. It is as simple as that."

"I am not shocked, Duchess. It is only that most people would not be so frank with a new acquaintance."

"I am not, usually. But when I speak with you, it is almost as if I am speaking with Lady Truelove herself."

Irene felt smothered, embarrassed, and keenly uncomfortable. It was hard to force words out, but she could see only one course open to her, and she willed herself to continue. "I am aware that Lady Truelove was concerned about Mr. Foscarelli's lack of an income."

"She certainly was."

That gave Irene no cues at all. "I take it, then, that you have drafted the—" She stopped, unable to continue, the question caught in her throat, her face growing hot, and she cursed Torquil for putting her in this impossible situation. She had met this woman less than three hours ago. Who was she to ask impertinent questions, and delve into the other woman's motivations and reasons? What right did she have to make trouble between the duchess and the man she loved?

"Forgive me," she said, taking a gulp of coffee. "I don't wish to pry."

The duchess, thankfully, did not seem to perceive her discomfort. "Not at all. You've been a keen observer of

my situation through your columnist. It's understandable you would be curious."

She did not, however, choose to satisfy that curiosity
with any details about the enormous marriage settlement or the lack of a prenuptial agreement, and Irene
could not bring herself to probe any more deeply into
the other woman's privacy. When the duchess changed
the subject, inquiring what social amusements she and
her sister might enjoy, she was relieved, though also
keenly aware of being right back where she'd started.
And when the duchess excused herself from her company a few minutes later and joined her daughters at
the piano, Irene did not follow her. Instead, she stared
moodily down into her coffee cup, considering what
she'd learned.

Nothing earth-shattering—well, except that the
duchess, bless her mother's heart, viewed Torquil as
a romantic, a piece of information so absurd as to be
laughable. As for the rest, she still felt she'd given the
other woman the right advice.

So, what was she supposed to do now?

"Any luck?"

Irene looked up as her sister sat down beside her on
the settee. "I'm afraid not."

"Well, I suppose you can't expect instant success in a
situation like this. Did you—" Clara broke off, glanced
around to be sure none of the other ladies were within
earshot. But they were all across the room, gathered
around the piano, and Angela's playing easily overrode
their murmured conversation. "Did you reiterate that
he might be a fortune-hunter?"

"I did. But she doesn't seem to care. And it's so hard

to speak plainly about these things face-to-face. It was much easier to communicate with her by letter, when I hadn't yet met her. Does that make sense?"

Clara nodded, looking comfortingly sympathetic. "Especially since before you came here, you didn't fully understand the effect her marriage would have upon her family. Whereas now . . ."

"Now, I'm caught between the devil and the deep blue sea. When I first gave the duchess my opinion, I had not thought, it's true, about the impact her decision would have upon her relations," she said slowly. "But, even so, it is still her decision."

"But something troubles you, Irene. I know you too well not to know it."

"She didn't tie up the money as I suggested. I wonder why."

"Perhaps Foscarelli didn't want her to."

Irene pursed her lips, giving her sister a rueful look. "That makes me even more worried. If he was a man of good character, why wouldn't he agree to a prenuptial agreement?"

"Perhaps she didn't ask him. Whatever the reason, she must be very much in love with him."

"I should say so, yes. Definitely." She fell back against the settee with a sigh. "How can I talk his mother out of a course I advised her to take? Such a task forces me to inquire into things that are none of my concern."

"Could you write to her again as Lady Truelove?"

"And say what? That I've revised my opinion and she shouldn't marry the man after all? What excuse could I offer for this change of mind? And she's made up her mind now, so I doubt it would matter. Besides, I still believe she is doing what she thinks is best for her own future happiness." She made a sound of utter exasperation. "This entire situation is impossible. That man," she added, scowling as the door opened and Torquil entered the drawing room with the other gentlemen, "wants the impossible!"

"Goodness, Irene, he does stir you up, doesn't he?"

"To say the least. Oh, dear," she added, straightening in her seat as the object of their conversation started in their direction. "I fear I am about to be called upon for an account of my progress."

She pasted on a smile as Torquil halted in front of them with a bow. "Miss Deverill, have you seen my library?"

"I have not," she said, but she had the feeling she was about to be afforded that opportunity, whether she wanted it or not.

"I have many fine books. Would you permit me to show you?"

"Certainly." Keeping her smile fixed in place, she set aside her cup and saucer and stood up. When he offered his arm, she took it, but neither of them spoke as they strolled side by side past the crowd gathered around the piano and through the wide doorway into the library.

"I am sure you wish for a report on my progress," she said as he led her across the room. "But as yet, there is little to tell."

"I wouldn't expect you to have made any progress in merely one evening," he replied, bringing them both to a halt in a far corner. "I wanted to talk with you about something else, and I think you can guess to what I refer?"

She had a pretty fair idea. Irene slid her hand from the crook of his arm, turning to face him. "If this is about my work, you must see that one cannot simply stop printing a newspaper whenever one chooses?"

"I do. Which means you shall have to determine which member of your staff might best be trusted with your responsibilities until your return."

She almost laughed. "Just when I begin to think you might have some qualities I respect and admire, you display such breathtaking arrogance that I realize I must be wrong. It's amazing."

"You shall be moving in society, Miss Deverill, a place most unforgiving of professions, particularly for women. Carlotta might have been wrong to underscore the fact at the dinner table, but nonetheless, her concern was valid. Ellesmere will not look upon your continuing to work with favor, nor will all the other people who have been subjects of the gossip printed in your paper."

"As you said, your lot should be used to being talked about."

"But they don't like it, especially not in print, and certainly not by someone who is expecting them to welcome her into their circle."

"I don't care if I am ever welcomed into your circle."

"But your sister does, and what you do reflects upon her."

Irene pressed her lips together, refusing to be manipulated by guilt. "I cannot help that. And my sister understands the publishing business well. She understands the demands the newspaper makes upon my time, and that no one can run it for me as well as I can run it myself, particularly now, since we recently lost our most important source of advertising revenue. She also knows that I cannot and will not risk our livelihood for the sake of others' sensibilities, especially when I have received no indication of support from my grandfather. I would be happy to see him do something for Clara—a dowry, perhaps—but either way, if I am successful in what you have demanded of me, both my sister and I will be returning to Belford Row, where I shall continue to run my newspaper to the best of my ability, for I have no intention of depending upon Ellesmere for our support."

"He is your grandfather, and though it might sting to accept help from him, but—"

"Sting? He disowned my mother, disinherited her, refused her a dowry, and never spoke another word to her again for the remainder of her life."

"An action he might have come to deeply regret by now."

"I don't care if he has. Do you think I would ever, *ever*, allow that man to support me or my family?"

"Your pride is considerable, I understand that, and your desire to do right by your loved ones is commendable. I am not asking you to give up your paper, Miss Deverill. If you did, you would have no reason to help me. But I hardly think your paper or your family are put in jeopardy if you hand over its day-to-day operations to someone else for the coming two weeks."

"To what end?"

"I don't know what you mean." But his gaze slid away from hers to pretend a sudden interest in the titles lining the nearest bookshelf, belying his words.

"You know what I mean. It is you, Duke, who has put me in the position of watching my beloved sister stare longingly at the glittering life you dangle in front of her, a life she is unlikely to ever have."

"She could have this sort of life, if she wanted it, with the proper connections and her grandfather's support."

"Oh, could she?" Irene folded her arms. "Even though her sister runs a scandal sheet?"

His lips pressed tight together, confirming that she had a valid point. "Even then, it might be possible, if you were to do as I suggest and be discreet about its ownership."

"So I should hire people to run the paper for me, pocket the profits—discreetly, of course!—and pretend for the world I've nothing to do with it? I should brush my occupation under the rug, relax, and just enjoy the entertainments your connections and those of my grandfather shall provide for me? Is that what you mean?"

He met her gaze again with a level one of his own. "Yes, I suppose that is what I do mean."

She shook her head in refusal before he was even finished speaking. "Never. I created *Society Snippets*. It's my brainchild, my work, my lifeblood. It's as much a part of me as your estates are to you."

"That's a bit of an exaggeration, don't you think?"

With that question, any softening toward him she had felt over dinner crumbled to bits. Her temper—a thing she had never even known she possessed until she'd met this man—began flaring up. "Why?" she demanded hotly. "Because I'm a woman?"

"No—that is, not entirely. The suffragist cause

aside, Miss Deverill, it cannot be disputed that my estates are a far greater responsibility that a sixteen-page newspaper."

"Bigger, perhaps, but not greater. Not more important. I have no doubt," she added before he could reply, "that you will now demonstrate the same disdain for my paper that your sister-in-law displayed at dinner and, like her, deem my creation less than meaningful."

"If I did, could I be blamed for it?" he countered, sudden anger in his voice that matched her own. "Am I not entitled to some degree of disdain for a publication that prints gossip and innuendo about my family and friends and calls it news? Am I unfair for asking that you not flaunt that paper or the fact that you support it with your own labor in my house? Especially at dinner with my family—a family, which you well know is right now being profoundly impacted by what has been written in its pages?"

"I am not flaunting anything," she said fiercely. "Your mother was making plans for my sister and me, making it necessary for me to inform her of which plans for me would not be possible. As for my paper, I refuse to feel either guilt or shame for creating something that saved my family from destitution and provides us with our living. Furthermore," she added before he could get a word in, "I love my work. Nothing in this world gives more pleasure or satisfaction than producing my newspaper and carrying on the publishing business that has been my family's lifeblood for fifty years. I am proud— yes, proud—of what I do and of what I created, and I know my other grandfather, the one who actually cared about me and my welfare, would be proud of me, too.

I will not hide what I do and what I have accomplished as if I am ashamed of it in order to ingratiate myself with a relation who has never displayed the slightest regard for me. I will not even do it to elevate my beloved sister to a higher station in life. And I certainly will not do it because you demand it of me."

She stopped, breathing hard. The soft, lovely notes of a sonata floated through the room as she and Torquil stared at each other, the anger between them rolling like thunder. When the music stopped, neither of them moved or spoke.

"Well done, Angela," Sarah said over the smattering of applause. "Do let me play. I want to do this duet with Torquil. Where is he, anyway? Torquil?"

The duke glanced toward the door and back to her, then he stepped back and gave her a bow, and when he straightened, there was no hint of anger, or anything else, in his face. It was as if she had just seen a slate wiped clean. "Miss Deverill," he said so politely that no one would imagine a single angry word had passed between them. "If you will forgive me?"

He turned and walked away, leaving Irene alone with her anger, which was probably all for the best. If he'd stayed, she might have hurled a book at him.

Chapter 10

As Henry walked away from Irene Deverill and left the library, desire and anger thrumming through his body with equal force, he saw that there was a facet of his own character he'd never acknowledged before. As he strode past the members of his family gathered around the piano and departed the drawing room, oblivious to their voices calling his name, he saw this perverse aspect of his nature with a clarity he'd never before possessed.

He was irresistibly attracted to impossible women.

It was a galling thing to admit. Until now, he'd been able to regard his passion for Elena as a tragic, once-in-a-lifetime incident, a folly borne of lusty youth and romantic ideals that would never be repeated. He thought he had learned his lesson, that he'd become not only an older man, but also a wiser one, and that he was beyond being tempted by women for whom his life held no appeal.

Irene Deverill, however, was forcing him to admit that he'd been lying to himself for an entire decade. For even as she had scorned the civilities and discretions that were a given in society, even as his anger and defenses had arisen in response, so had his desire. To know that he could once again want a woman who had no use for him or the world he inhabited was a shattering, humbling realization.

Henry strode along the corridor, down the stairs, and out of the house, grappling with this truth about himself. What was it, he wondered in exasperation as he stepped out into the fine summer night, that made him yearn for women who were so clearly not for him?

Damn it all, he knew hundreds of suitable girls, girls who would be happy to have him, girls who understood his life and could share it. Why couldn't he lust after one of them? Why this attraction to women so below his station, so outside his circle, so wrong for him?

Perhaps, he thought with a hint of desperation, it was just physical. If so, he ought to acquire a mistress, he supposed. The notion did not appeal. He'd had two since Elena's death, but both had been short-lived, empty affairs, borne of the need for release and nothing more. But even as he hoped that was the case here, he feared it was not. This seemed a deeper yearning, one that lurked in the dark places of his soul. A yearning for something . . . more.

He stopped on the sidewalk, cursing his own greed. Good God, he'd already been blessed with more gifts than most men could dream of. To be unsatisfied showed a callous disregard for the many who were not so fortunate as he. And yet, even as Henry stared into the inky depths of Hyde Park that lay beyond the street lamps and reminded himself to be grateful for all that he had, he felt that same pull within him toward something else, something he wanted and could never have. And he didn't even know quite what it was.

Whatever the reason, Miss Deverill aroused in him passions that he feared could lead both of them down a path he'd walked before, a path that could not bring anything but misery to either party, a path he had no intention of walking ever again.

He rubbed a hand over his face and worked to put things into proper perspective. This situation would only exist for one fortnight. He could withstand even the darkest of desires for two weeks, surely.

With that reminder, Henry resumed walking, his steps carrying him down Park Lane, across Mount Street, up Duke Street, and around Grosvenor Square. He didn't know how long he was away, but by the time he once again emerged onto Upper Brook Street and reentered his own home, the yearning within him was banked beneath his usual surface civility, and he was once again the master of both his body and mind.

Still, he reflected, pausing on the sidewalk to stare up at his well-lit drawing room and one unmistakable, laughing face amidst the others framed in the window, perhaps he ought to avoid being alone with Miss Deverill, if possible. Just to be sure.

THE FOLLOWING MORNING, Irene's day began the same way it always did—with a light tap on her door and the clink of porcelain on a tray. She opened her eyes, but when she did, she found the view a bit disorienting, for the slim girl in cap and apron who bustled in with morning tea was definitely not their rotund parlor maid, Annie, and it took Irene a moment to remember where she was.

In the duke's house. Ugh. She rolled onto her back with a sigh, remembering the events that had brought her here. It might seem like a ghastly dream, but unfortunately, it was all too real.

"Morning tea, miss," the girl said in a soft voice, setting the tray on the table beneath the window and pulling back the curtains just enough to let in a bit more light.

"Good morning," Irene answered, rubbing her eyes with the heels of her hands. She felt terribly groggy, which was understandable, given that it had taken her hours to fall asleep with that man's dismissive opinion of her work ringing in her ears. "What time is it?"

The girl, already by the door, stopped and turned. "Quarter past eight o'clock, miss."

Stunned, Irene shoved back the counterpane and turned, rolling her legs over the side of the bed to stand up. "Heavens," she mumbled, starting toward the chiffonier, "I'm terribly late. I must dress."

"Very good, miss. I'll send Mrs. Norton to you, shall I?"

Irene paused in the act of opening a drawer and straightened, looking over her shoulder at the girl, perplexed. "Mrs. Who?"

"Mrs. Norton, miss. She's lady's maid to the duchess. Her Grace gave instructions that Mrs. Norton was to tend you during your stay since you've not brought your own maid with you."

"No, no, that's all right." She returned her attention

to the contents of the cupboard in front of her. "My thanks to the duchess," she added, pulling out a white shirtwaist and dark blue skirt, "but I wouldn't dream of depriving her of her maid."

This seemed to baffle the poor girl. "You don't want her at all then?"

Honestly, Irene thought in exasperated humor, as she closed one door of the chiffonier and opened another, what did these people find so baffling about dressing oneself? It wasn't that hard. "No," she answered, adding underclothes to the pile in her arms. "Is my sister awake?"

"I don't know, miss. I brought your tea first, of course. When you're ready for breakfast, you'll find it in the morning room. The footmen start bringing it in about half past eight, but you'll find the warming dishes on the sideboard until half past ten."

Irene's stomach rumbled at the mention of breakfast, but she knew she didn't have time for it. "Thank you," she said, setting her clothes on the bed. "You may go."

"Very good, miss."

The maid departed, and Irene went into the bathroom to wash her face, hands, and neck. She then began to dress, glad that for her own daily uniform, she didn't have to corset herself as tightly as she'd had to do for her evening gown last night. Fashionable clothes required such tight lacing, and she wasn't accustomed to that anymore.

After she'd finished dressing, she gulped down her tea, pinned up her hair, and slid a light blue jacket over her shirtwaist. She knotted a tie around her throat, placed a straw boater on her head, and skewered it in place with a hatpin, then crossed back through the bath, intending to say good-bye to Clara. But with her hand raised to tap on the door, Irene changed her mind. Sleeping in was a luxury they hadn't been able to afford for years, and it wasn't as if her sister had to be across town in less than an hour. Why disturb her?

Letting her hand fall, Irene turned away. She left her room, reaching for her handbag and gloves on her way out the door, and strode down the corridor and stairs at a rapid clip. When she reached the ground floor, however, she'd barely taken two steps toward the foyer before the unmistakable scent of bacon wafted to her nose.

Her stomach rumbled again, and she stopped, sorely tempted. What was it the maid had said? Something about warming dishes on the sideboard. Perhaps, if she was the first one down, she could wrap some toast and bacon in a napkin and eat it on the omnibus?

Irene hesitated, but when she saw a footman emerge from behind a nearby baize door carrying a tray laden with warming dishes, she made up her mind and followed him down a short corridor to a room of sunny yellow walls, white plaster work, and dark mahogany.

The footman noticed her behind him, and immediately moved to the side of the doorway to allow her to enter first, but she'd barely taken a step across the threshold before she discovered she was not the first arrival. Torquil was seated at the head of the table, knife and fork in hand, reading the newspaper folded back beside his plate. "Oh," she said and came to a startled stop.

He looked up, and at the sight of her, he was on his

feet at once, setting aside his utensils and napkin to offer her a bow. "Miss Deverill."

After their heated exchange last evening, she had not seen him again, nor had she had any desire to do so. Recollections of his resentment regarding her profession and her own simmering frustration had kept her up half the night. Encountering him now made Irene acutely uncomfortable, and she wished she'd stuck to her original decision to forgo breakfast.

He seemed to be having similar feelings, for he shifted his weight and glanced past her, as if he hoped more people would begin arriving.

"Duke." She bowed, a perfunctory nod of her head and dip of her knees. "I was just coming in search of food."

She grimaced inwardly at her choice of words, appreciating that she'd just described herself as something akin to a scavenging animal, but if Torquil noticed, he gave no sign. Instead, he gestured to the seat to his right. "Will you not sit down?" he asked when she didn't move.

"I . . . no . . . I just . . ." She paused, unable to think of a way to explain her intent had been to take her food with her. Her idea seemed terribly gauche all of a sudden. The clock behind her in the corridor chimed once, and she seized on the sound as the perfect excuse. "Heavens," she said in a strangled voice, "half past eight already? I've no time for breakfast now."

Giving another quick bow, she started to turn away, but his voice stopped her.

"If it is my presence that distresses you, I will leave, of course."

She winced, aware that he sounded almost eager for the prospect, and forced herself to stop and turn around. "No, please, finish your breakfast. I am not distressed. Not exactly. I mean . . ." She stopped again, aware she was stammering, unable to help it, and feeling like a prize idiot in consequence. "It's just that I'm so . . . so late. I am . . . I am always in my office by this time . . . by now. Always," she finished lamely.

A puzzled frown knit his brows. "Does it matter if you are a bit tardy? You do manage the company."

"That's true." She gave a little laugh, one that sounded a bit desperate to her own ears. "But my staff will be arriving at any moment to begin work, and when they do, they will not find me there. They will worry."

"But since you cannot be transported across town by magic carpet, taking an additional half hour to have breakfast will hardly make a difference. I cannot allow a guest of mine to go without breakfast, Miss Deverill," he added before she could reply. "As for your concern that others will wonder where you are and will worry about you, that is a problem easily remedied. Boothby can telephone them."

"You have a telephone?" The moment the question was out of her mouth, she sighed. "Of course you do."

"It's a convenient device."

"Not very convenient. Most other people don't have one."

"Enough do to make it worthwhile. My club, my solicitors, my home in Dorset all have telephones, as do several of our friends, including you. I observed the telephone in your offices when I was there. Please, do sit down."

Deprived of her only excuse, Irene accepted with good grace. "Very well, then. Thank you."

He turned to the footman, who was at the sideboard, arranging warming dishes. "Edward?"

The servant moved to his side at once. "Your Grace?"

"Have Boothby telephone to Miss Deverill's offices and inform them she is delayed, and will be arriving in about an hour. The number to give the exchange is . . . ?"

At his inquiring glance, she turned to the footman beside him. "Holborn 7244."

The servant departed, and Irene accepted the chair Torquil pulled out for her.

"Would you like tea?" he asked, gesturing to the sideboard behind him. "Or coffee?"

"I can wait for my tea," she said as he turned to fetch her a cup, his solicitous manner making her even more discomfited, for it was so clearly for the sake of politeness and nothing more. "Surely the footman will be back in a moment. There's no need to serve me yourself, Duke."

"On the contrary," he said over his shoulder as he poured tea for her from the pot on the sideboard. "The duty to wait upon you falls to me as your host, since no servant is present. And I never ignore my duty. Milk and sugar?"

"A little of each, thank you."

He returned to the table a moment later, setting the teacup and saucer before her. "Would you care for eggs and bacon? Or perhaps you would prefer porridge?"

"Eggs and bacon would be lovely, thank you." Irene

removed her gloves and unfolded her napkin as he filled a plate and brought it to her, and the fact that she was being waited upon by a duke made this entire episode of her life seem even more surreal.

"I'm actually glad of this chance to speak with you," she said as he resumed his own seat. "I have a request to make."

"I will do my best to fulfill it."

"Your mother's maid has somehow become mine, it seems."

He did not seem surprised. "Yes, of course. That is always the case when a guest has not brought his or her own servant. Do you not like her? We can—"

"No, no, it isn't that. I haven't even met her. But we don't need her. We don't need anyone, truly. I meant what I said last night. My sister and I are accustomed to dressing ourselves."

He studied her for a moment, then he said something wholly unexpected. "You're a very proud woman, aren't you?"

Irene's face flooded with color. She could feel it happen, even before he said, "My apologies. I did not mean to embarrass you."

She looked down, pretending keen interest in her bacon. "I have my fair share of pride, I suppose," she admitted after a moment. "I suppose you think that a bad thing?"

"Not at all. I'm very proud myself. I bring it up only because I would like to advise you without hurting your pride, and given what occurred last evening, I am concerned I might inadvertently do so."

She wriggled in her chair, appreciating that after their altercation, he might have a point, and she looked at him again. "Go on, please."

"I suggest you accept my mother's hospitality with good grace. To do otherwise would reflect badly upon her as a hostess, and I'm sure you would not wish to do that."

Irene was confounded. Sometimes, the aristocracy was truly baffling. "I did not understand that it would be discourteous to refuse the use of your mother's maid. I'd have thought the opposite."

"My mother is far too considerate a hostess to see you do without a maid. It would distress her enormously to see two young ladies in the season doing for themselves."

"But what will she do, then?"

"In cases such as this, precedent decides. My mother will take Carlotta's maid. Angela and Sarah, who are unmarried and therefore share a maid, will give their maid to Carlotta, and a housemaid will be brought up to assist them."

Irene groaned. "I now see what Lady David meant about how my sister and I would be causing everyone inconvenience. I thought at the time that she was just being catty."

"You mustn't mind Carlotta, truly. I took her aside last evening, and I don't expect there will be any more trouble from that quarter."

"But it sounds as if she was right. If the staff is short a housemaid, the other servants will have to pitch in to help cover her duties, won't they?" She sighed. "It was a decision of pride," she admitted. "I did not consider the impact my choice might have on other people."

If he discerned that she was acknowledging his words to her from the first time they met, he was too polite to crow about it. "In this case, it's perfectly understandable. Your own household is quite small, I daresay."

"A cook, a housemaid, a housekeeper, and my father's valet comprise the whole lot."

"While we have a staff of over fifty servants, half of whom are here with us in town for the season. You would think in a house like this, a decision so small wouldn't matter, but it's actually the opposite. In a large household, duties demonstrate rank, and rank is every-thing, even below stairs. No servant is happy doing work that might be considered to be beneath him. You would not believe the hard feelings even the smallest decision can generate."

"All the more reason not to deprive your mother of her maid, then, for we are definitely a comedown from a duchess. Can she not be persuaded to take her maid back?"

"I doubt it. And though you don't yet know it, your fortnight in society will be much easier if you have someone to assist you." He paused, then gave a cough. "I should like to make a suggestion, if I may? I am go-ing to Merrick's Employment agency today to engage a nanny for my nephews. I could engage a maid to assist you during your stay. That is, if you're willing to trust such a personal selection to my care."

"Oh, no, please, don't trouble yourself."

"It shall be no trouble, Miss Deverill, for as I said,

I have to be at Merrick's anyway. My nephews simply must have a nanny, for they have been in the care of maids and footmen for several days now. If you want to talk of unhappy servants, let us discuss that! No footman or maid should ever be required to look after my nephews, believe me. They're good boys, but they are a handful. My family has become thoroughly exasperated with them. So has my staff. If I do not find a nanny soon, I expect a mutiny."

"Shouldn't your brother-in-law be the one to find his son's nanny?"

"Yes, but as Angela pointed out last night, Jamie's efforts in that regard have been less than successful. When I offered to assist, he was glad to allow me to do so."

"Do you always feel obligated to solve other people's problems?" she asked, curious.

He shrugged as if that particular obligation was inevitable. "It is often necessary. I am the duke."

"Heavy is the head that wears the crown," she said with mock solemnity. "Or coronet, in this case."

His answering look was wry. "You're misquoting Shakespeare," he told her. "On purpose, I expect."

"Well, yes," she agreed with a grin. "It suits you better that way."

"Because you want to tease me, you mean? That's not very nice, especially since I've just offered to do you a favor."

"Sorry," she said, not the least bit repentant. "But you sounded so preternaturally solemn, I couldn't help teasing you."

"I do take my position seriously, I confess. And solving problems is a great part of what I do. Of all people, you ought to understand that, since solving problems is also what Lady Truelove does, is it not?"

She considered. "Not really. Ultimately, Lady True-love's advice makes little difference. I know you don't see it that way, given the effect your mother's course has had upon your family, but it's true, I promise you. Most people don't write to Lady Truelove because they want advice."

"What do they want, then?"

"Reassurance. By the time they take the step of writing to an advice column, they know—even if they don't realize it themselves—what they are going to do. All they really want is to be told the course they've already chosen is the right one."

He looked as if he might be tempted to debate that point, but before he could do so, a shout was heard, followed by laughter and the sound of running feet along the corridor.

A moment later, two boys of about seven or eight years entered the room. As they came to a skidding halt side by side near Torquil's chair, Irene thought for a moment she was seeing double, so alike were they in their matching dark blue knickers and jackets, with their identical mops of ginger hair and nearly identical smatterings of freckles. Once she blinked, however, Irene was able to discern one distinct difference between them. One of the boys had a covered picnic basket in his hands and the other was clutching the mangled, bright blue remains of what might once have been a kite.

"Uncle Henry, thank goodness you're up," the boy

with the kite said. "We've had a spot of bother and need your help."

"Hmm." Torquil glanced over them. "Yes, so I see. But is your need so urgent that it requires interrupting my breakfast and that of my guests? You don't seem to be bleeding. You don't seem to be ill. And what requires all this running and shouting? Are you being chased by wild dogs, that you behave this way?"

They wriggled. "No, sir," they mumbled together.

More hurried footsteps were heard, and a footman entered. "I am so sorry, Your Grace," he said, panting as he came to a halt behind the boys. "I'll have them out of here. It's just . . . I couldn't quite . . . catch . . ." He paused, obviously trying to regain his breath.

"It's all right, Samuel. I'm sure you've had a difficult time with them, for they seem determined to break rules today, behaving like heathens instead of gentlemen and with no consideration of the others who live here."

This withering speech caused both boys to hang their heads, and Irene quite felt sorry for them.

"I am sorry they disturbed your breakfast, Your Grace," Samuel apologized again, still breathing hard. "Sorry, Miss Deverill. They wanted to fly kites, so I packed up a breakfast for them and we went across to the park. Owen's kite crashed into a tree and got broken, and while I was trying to mend it, Colin's kite got . . . ahem . . . lost . . ." He paused again, looking pained. "So we came back, but before I could catch my breath, they decided they needed to see you, and came racing up here before I could catch them. Again, I am so sorry they disturbed you."

"Please, do not distress yourself, Samuel," Torquil said. "This is not your fault in any way. It is mine. By tomorrow, they will have a new nanny, and you will no longer be required to go chasing them hither and yon, I promise you. You may go."

The footman straightened with a nod, but instead of departing, he hesitated, opening his mouth as if he wanted to say more. He glanced at the boys, however, and seemed to change his mind, for he closed his mouth again, gave another nod, and departed.

"Miss Deverill," Torquil said, gesturing to the boys standing on the other side of the table from her, "may I introduce my nephews, two of the finest scapegraces in London? Colin, Owen, this is Miss Deverill."

"How do you do?" they mumbled, not looking at her, clearly knowing they were in trouble.

"It is a pleasure to meet you," she answered, trying not to smile.

"Well, gentlemen," Torquil said, tossing down his napkin, "you've had a very exciting morning." He rose and moved to stand before the two apprehensive boys, hands on his hips. "You've lost a kite, broken another, run Samuel ragged, shouted and run through the house, and disturbed Miss Deverill's breakfast and mine. What have you to say for yourselves?"

They hung their heads, silent and chastened. Irene, who knew very well what it was like to be caught in his sights, looked at the twins with sympathy.

He turned to the boy holding the basket. "Colin, what happened to your kite?"

"It got caught in a tree. I went up and tried to get it—"

The boy stopped abruptly and bit his lip, his blue

eyes widening with the unmistakable realization that he'd just said something unwise.

"You climbed a tree?" Even in profile, Torquil's disapproving face seemed rather daunting, but then, a slight curve tipped the corner of his mouth upward, making Irene aware that he wasn't quite as disapproving as he wished to appear. "Did we not make a rule about this last summer when Owen broke his arm? No climbing trees until you're how old?"

"Twelve," Colin said.

"Just so, and have you turned twelve since that rule was made?"

"No, sir." Colin looked up, his face brightening as if he'd been struck by a sudden idea. "But I had a good reason for climbing the tree, Uncle Henry. It wasn't just to get the kite."

Torquil's mouth twitched unmistakably. "Indeed? And what reason could possibly justify breaking the rule about tree climbing?"

Colin set down the basket and bent over it, disappearing from Irene's line of vision. When he straightened, he had in his hands a small bundle of gray-and-white fur which he held up for his uncle's inspection. "I had to get this."

Irene stifled a laugh with her napkin, and Torquil pressed his lips tight together, clearly trying not to do the same. It took a moment for him to speak. "You rescued a kitten from the tree?"

Colin nodded. "It was stuck, and crying, so I had to rescue it. I couldn't just leave it up there, scared and all alone, Uncle Henry, could I?"

The kitten blinked up at Torquil and gave a soft mewl.

He made a choked sound. Pressing a fist to his mouth, he turned away from the boy and the animal, and only Irene caught his expression.

He was laughing. She stared, amazed, for she'd never seen him laugh before. He wasn't looking at her, but down at his plate. He made no sound, but his fist was pressed against a wide smile, and his shoulders worked with silent but unmistakable laughter that he was trying desperately to hold back. The sight had the strangest effect on her; her amazement ebbed away and another sensation took its place, one both sweet and painful that pinched her chest and made it hard to breathe.

After a moment, he lifted his head, gave a cough, and lowered his hand. "Rescuing an animal is a commendable thing," he said gravely, returning his attention to his nephew, no trace of laughter in his face now. "But should such a circumstance occur in future, you will fetch an adult to assist you in your rescue attempts. The rule about tree-climbing remains in effect. Is that clear?"

"Yes, sir." Colin lowered the animal, hugging it to his chest. "Can we keep it?"

Torquil frowned, but though Irene knew firsthand how intimidating his frown could be, it didn't seem that way to her at all after what she'd just witnessed. "With all the rules you've broken today, I see no reason to think you can be trusted with the welfare of an animal."

They wilted, poor boys, and Irene had to press her hand to her mouth to prevent a sound of commiseration from escaping her lips.

"On the other hand," he went on, "you did save the

animal's life, which means you are now responsible for its future well-being. So, if your father does not object, and if you promise most sincerely to take proper care of it—see that it is fed and groomed and if you handle it gently and with respect when you play with it, you may keep it."

With a shout of happy celebration that was quickly smothered, a chorus of promises to always care for it and never break any rules ever again, the two boys departed for the kitchens with their new friend to obtain for it some milk and gruel.

The moment they were safely gone, all the humor Torquil had been holding back was unable to remain suppressed. He fell into his chair with a full-bodied, merry laugh.

Irene laughed with him, but after a moment, her laughter faded. His did, too, as he turned his head to look at her, and Irene's heart seemed to stop beating in her chest. Time seemed to halt as well, and the silence, as it had last night, seemed to fill the room, every bit as charged as before, but in a very different way.

His face bore its usual impassivity, and she had no idea what he was thinking, but just now, that didn't seem to matter. She'd seen him laugh. Her heartbeat resumed, quickening until it was a hard, panicked thrum in her chest, so loud to her own ears that she feared he might be able to hear it.

"So," he said, breaking the agonizing silence and giving a cough, "you've now met my infamous nephews, Miss Deverill."

After what had just happened, the use of her surname seemed strangely impersonal, almost disappointing, which was absurd. He could refer to her no other way, for it wasn't proper for a man to address a woman he barely knew by her Christian name, and Torquil was all that was proper.

Irene dismissed this nonsensical feeling of disappointment from her mind and forced herself to pick up the thread of the conversation. "You do realize Colin climbed the tree to get the kite, then saw the kitten, and used the animal as his excuse for breaking the rule about tree-climbing so he wouldn't get into trouble?"

"Of course, but if one intends to issue a reprimand, one has to sound at least somewhat severe." Torquil laughed again, shaking back his hair as he leaned back with his tea, and Irene felt again that strange, piercing sensation in her chest. "Assuming such a stance at that moment was, I confess, beyond my ability."

"What was all the shouting?" asked a voice from the doorway, and they both looked up as Angela came in. "The boys, I suppose? I could hear them all the way upstairs. What are we to do with them?"

"Don't worry, Angie," Torquil replied. "I am hiring a nanny today, as I promised." He shot Irene a questioning glance, and when she nodded, there was no need for her to guess what he might be thinking. He smiled, and that strange pang once again twisted in Irene's chest.

Suddenly, it seemed impossible to sit here. "I should go," she said, grabbing her handbag from the floor beside her and rising to her feet. "I'm so late already."

He rose at once. "Of course. Shall I have one of the footmen hail a taxi for you?"

"I can easily do that. We're on Park Lane, after all, taxis everywhere. Besides, you shall have need of all the footmen, I fear, to keep an eye on those boys. Good morning."

She bolted, not realizing until she was out of the house that she'd left her gloves behind. She didn't go back for them. Being in his sights was hard enough when he was being impossible. When he was being nice, it was devastating.

Chapter 11

The day before press time, there was always a great deal to do, but when Irene reached her offices and began work, she found it impossible to concentrate on any task for more than a few minutes at a time. At every turn, her mind insisted on going back to Torquil and what she'd witnessed at breakfast.

She'd already noted how good-looking he was, but that hadn't served to elevate him much in her opinion, for she'd still found him hopelessly rigid, snobbish, and dictatorial, even ruthless. And yet . . .

Irene stared down at the pages in front of her, their typewritten lines fading, superseded by his face, lit by suppressed laughter. In that moment, his mask of stone-faced civility had slipped, showing the man underneath, and suddenly, he had become far more than the arrogant, good-looking duke. He had become human.

Even now, the image of him in her mind was enough

to turn her topsy-turvy, and if anyone asked her opinion of his character at this moment, she wouldn't know what to say.

He could be so infuriating, so damnably rigid. And yet, she could not deny his love for his family. It was, she now knew, absolute and all-encompassing—the center of his world. Until now, she hadn't really appreciated how deeply ingrained in him that quality was, or how attractive it could be. In truth, she hadn't known such men as that existed at all.

She loved her father, and her brother, too, but neither of them could be described as protective in any way. Jonathan, five years younger than she, was on the other side of the world, and who could blame him? He'd tried to warn their father that the business was headed for queer-street, but Papa had refused to listen and refused to change course, and after many lurid quarrels on the topic, Papa had tossed Jonathan out of the house. Her brother had gone off to make his way in the world as best he could, and though he inquired after them in his letters to her and Clara, neither she nor her sister had ever told him how dire things were. He could have done little about it but come home, which would only have made their father even more irritable and even less inclined to see reason.

As for her father, he was fixed on one idea for his daughters' future, and no other. He was convinced—probably rightly—that elevating them into society was the only way he could help them. His wits addled by drink and pain, he had no other solutions to offer, no other abilities to draw upon, no other vision for their lives. And Irene had long ago resigned herself to the fact that, given her father's love of brandy, she would have to be the one to protect him, not the other way around.

Torquil was an entirely different sort of man, a man with whom she felt wholly out of her depth. She was used to being the one holding everyone together. It was, as he had pointed out, a trait they shared. To not be the one in charge was a frustrating thing for her. She wasn't used to it, she didn't like it, and she resented like hell that Torquil had been able to maneuver her into a situation where she didn't have it. And yet, now—

Her door opened, and Josie stuck her dark head into Irene's office. "Can we run with it?"

"What?" Irene blinked, roused out of her reverie slowly, like coming out of a dream.

"My column. Can we run with it?"

"Oh, right." Irene straightened in her chair, rustling the pages in front of her with a brisk air. "About that—"

She broke off, vexed with herself because she couldn't even remember if she'd read Josie's latest Delilah Dawlish column, and a glance at the first page told her that even if she had done so, she hadn't bothered to do any editing. "Give me a few minutes more, Josie," she mumbled, rubbing four fingers over her forehead. "I haven't got to your piece yet."

The other woman seemed to sense something amiss, and that, of course, sparked her excellent investigative instincts. "You've been in a fog all day. What's wrong?" She gave Irene a knowing look over the gold-rimmed spectacles perched on her nose. "Headache from too much champagne? Too much high living and too many late nights without enough sleep?"

Irene gave her a look of reproof. "It's only been one night," she reminded. "And if I find that my stay in the duke's house has been mentioned in your column, I shall edit it out and give you the sack."

"No worries there. We're all keeping mum, since you've ordered us to, though we can't think why."

"I like our paper to talk about other people. Not about me."

"Well, it'll be in all the other society papers by the end of the week. *Society Snippets* will be the only one not talking about it."

That was a nauseating fact she preferred not to dwell on. "In this case, I am happy to have it so."

"Very well, but I hope you come back from this so-journ with some juicy tidbits to share with our readers."

Am I not entitled to some degree of disdain for a publication that prints gossip and innuendo about my family and friends and calls it news?

Irene tossed down her pencil in exasperation, and the unexpected gesture caused the other woman to raise an eyebrow.

"Sorry, sorry," Josie said. "No need to be so touchy."

"It's not you," she said, pushing Torquil's words from the night before out of her mind. "But let's get this clear. I'm not spying on these people. That's not why I'm there."

"I know it's for Clara's sake and family unity, and all that. Though how your father managed to gain any favor from the duke after our Lady Truelove column, I can't imagine."

Irene did not enlighten her.

"But still," Josie went on when she didn't speak, "this stay in the duke's house would be a perfect opportunity, Irene. Very Robert Burns." She nodded with a worldly-wise air. "'A chield's amang you takin' notes.'"

"That will be enough, Josie. I shan't be 'takin' notes,' as you put it, so stop quoting Robert Burns and do me a favor. Read over Elsa and Hazel's stories and ensure they are ready for tomorrow. I've been dithering so much today, I fear I won't have time, since I have to be back at Upper Brook Street in time to change for dinner, and it's nearly five o'clock."

"Wait." Josie's dark eyes widened in shock. "You want me to edit Elsa and Hazel's stories for you?"

"Yes, if you think you can do a proper job of it."

"You just watch me! Heavens," she added, still looking amazed, "you are allowing me to edit. Who'd ever have predicted that? I think the planets have stopped moving in their orbits."

"Yes," Irene agreed with a sigh as an image of Torquil's devastating smile flashed across her mind again, evoking all the same heart-stopping emotions as before. "I rather think they have."

IT WAS A quarter to six by the time Irene reached Upper Brook Street. She went straight up to her room, hoping to have time for a long soak in that glorious tub before dinner, but as soon as she entered her room, her plan went straight out the window.

The doors through to Clara's room were open, and she'd scarcely tossed her handbag onto a chair and removed her hat before her sister came through from her own room, already changed for dinner in green brocade. "Thank goodness you're back. I thought you'd have returned long before now."

"Everything took forever today. I couldn't . . . umm . . . I couldn't concentrate. And then, traffic was beastly. It took me ages to find a taxi, and when I did, it crawled around Trafalgar, absolutely crawled—"

"Never mind that now," Clara cut into these explanations. "You've got to change straightaway, for the duke's carriage will be coming around from the mews in less than half an hour to fetch us. We're going out." She waved a hand toward the bed. "I've had your gown pressed and everything laid out in the hope you'd be home in time to come with us."

Irene glanced over her shoulder to find her midnight-blue silk gown spread out on the bed with various undergarments beside it. "In time for what?" she asked, slipping out of her jacket. "Where are we going?"

"Dinner at the Criterion first, then the theater, then supper at the Savoy. Isn't that wonderful?"

Irene thought of the Duke, and she wasn't sure if wonderful was the right word. "Is everyone going?"

Clara shook her head. "Just the ladies."

Irene's breath escaped in a rush of relief. After last night and this morning, she felt at sixes and sevens, and she welcomed the chance to get her bearings without him around to muddle her thinking. "What play are we seeing?"

"Oscar Wilde. *A Woman of No Importance.* Do stop talking, Irene, and hurry up."

The next twenty minutes were a mad dash as, with Clara's assistance, she changed into evening clothes.

Silk shawls in hand, they raced down the corridor, encountering Angela and Sarah, who were also late, along the way. All four arrived in the foyer together, out of breath and laughing, just as Boothby announced the arrival of the carriage from the mews.

The frantic rush that began their evening continued for the next seven hours. The glittering, noisy Criterion, the wicked wit of Oscar Wilde, the excitement of sitting in the duke's box, and the elegant private dining room at the Savoy—all went by in a dazzling whirl, leaving Irene exhausted, exhilarated, and a bit dazed by the time they returned to Upper Brook Street just before half past one.

"Oh, my word." Irene fell back onto her bed with a sigh, as Clara followed her into her room and closed the door. "Was this a preview of things to come?"

"I think so," Clara answered, moving to sit on the edge of the bed beside her. "Did you enjoy it?"

"I did, I must confess. Especially the Criterion. Such lovely, lovely food. And the Savoy, too." She groaned, pressing a hand to her stomach. "I fear I shan't eat again for days."

She turned her head to look at her sister. "You seemed to enjoy yourself. I saw you and Lady Angela with your heads together several times."

"We were discussing the charity she wants to start, though we weren't able to talk very much—the Criterion's so noisy, and no one wants to talk during a play."

Irene groaned again. "Right now, I feel as if I can't talk at all. I can't even breathe." She rolled, working to stand up as Clara moved aside. "You must help me out of this corset before I burst. By the way," she added, turning around so her sister could undo the buttons at the back of her gown, "I forgot to tell you earlier— we're to have a maid while we're here."

"Yes, the duchess's maid. She assisted me to dress three times today. It was most helpful."

"I'm sure. That's why we'll be engaging a maid of our own, through an agency."

"We will? You hired someone? What a splendid idea."

"I can't take the credit, I'm sorry to say. It was the duke's suggestion." She paused to pull off her gloves, toss aside her bodice, and step out of her skirt. "I tried to give the duchess's maid back at breakfast, and he recommended this course instead, so as not to offend her—at least, I think that was the reason." She frowned, then gave a shrug. "I really don't understand the aristocracy and what offends them, honestly. Ah," she added on a sigh of relief as her stays loosened. "That's better. How do women lace like this every day?"

Clara laughed, giving her a hug, propping her chin on Irene's shoulder. "They eat less creamed lobster at dinner."

"Did I eat too much? I probably shocked all the ladies at the table." She sighed and turned around as her sister's arms fell away. "You're fortunate to be such a quiet, self-contained person. Even if you tried, I doubt you could offend anyone. Whereas I, alas, seem to give offense at every turn."

"I doubt that."

"Still, the sooner I accomplish my task and return to our old life, the more comfortable I shall feel."

"Well, you spent a great deal of time talking with the

duchess," Clara pointed out as Irene unhooked own her corset busk and tossed the offending garment onto the bed. "Are you making any progress?"

"Unfortunately not. Turn around and I'll undo you. We couldn't talk openly about Foscarelli, of course," she went on as her sister complied, "since we were surrounded by her family."

"I suppose he is a bit like the elephant in the drawing room," Clara said.

"Yes, exactly." Irene laughed. "Everyone knowing he's there, but no one wanting to admit it. Whenever I did have the chance to slip in a word or two of concern about him, all she did was tell me how marvelous he is, or how lovely the house is that she's bought for them, or how exciting it is to be wanting to marry instead of dreading it. Her first husband, I gather, was not an easy man." She paused, her hands stilled on her sister's corset laces. "I'm not sure I can dissuade her. I'm not sure I even want to try. She seems so happy. Oh, Clara what am I to do?"

Her sister considered for a moment, then said in a small voice, "Must you do . . . anything?"

"Of course I must. You know what's at stake for me."

"If you don't succeed," Clara said, turning around to put a hand on her arm, "would that be so terrible?"

"Yes! I could lose the paper altogether."

"True, but . . ." Clara's arm slid away and she gestured to their surroundings. "Would a life such as this truly be such a bad alternative?"

"It wouldn't be like this, not for us, whatever happens. We won't be eating at the Criterion and going to the theater all the time. Ellesmere isn't nearly so rich as the duke. Unless you are clever enough to snag an enormously wealthy peer, we shall never have a life like this."

"You know what I mean."

"I do. But . . ." She paused, trying to find a way to explain her point of view. "A life of engagements and amusements, doing the season and raising funds for charity and giving house parties—it's a busy life, certainly, but it's not . . . substantial enough to satisfy me. A year or two ago, it might have been, but now? No. I love what I do." She tilted her head, studying her sister's face. "It's different for you, I know. You dream of a life like this."

Clara bit her lip, telling Irene the truth even before she lied. "I shall be content to return to our life as it has always been."

"But not as content as you'd be if you had a place in society."

"I'm not sure. I doubt I'd have the nerve for it without you close at hand." Clara looked pained. "Is it selfish of me to want it for both of us, knowing you don't want it at all?"

"Of course not. But I can't bear the idea that my life would be one of observing rules that seem so trivial, or even downright silly, and obsessing about what dress to wear at this hour and to this ball, and who sits by whom, and watching as conversations come to a stop the moment someone—probably me—says anything controversial. Everything controlled for me, nothing controlled by me. Do you see at all what I mean?"

"I suppose I do."

"Still," she added at once, "I will do what I can to see

that you do not suffer for my choices. Ellesmere may not like having his eldest granddaughter publishing a newspaper, but if he can be made to overcome that scruple enough to grant you society, I will be delighted. You, dear sister, deserve all the balls and plays and dinners at the Criterion you can stand."

Clara laughed. "And water parties, too, I hope? Did the duchess tell you about that?"

"She mentioned it was being arranged, but that was all."

"Torquil is arranging it for five days hence. If it's a fine day, we shall set sail from Queen's Wharf at ten o'clock, journey down to Kew Gardens and have a picnic luncheon, then sail back. Do say you'll take the day and come with us. It'll be lovely."

"Only if we don't become seasick." She grinned. "That would put a damper on the party."

"The duchess did warn me that could happen, but she also said it's unlikely on the river. Sailing on the ocean is the real worry. But just in case, she said I should eat several soda crackers the moment we come on board. And she assured me that if I were to become ill, the ship would dock immediately. You will come, won't you?"

"The important question is: Do you need me to come?"

"It isn't that. There shan't be any other guests, I'm told. Just us and the family, and I shall do well enough in their company, now that I've come to know them a little. Lady Angela and Lady Sarah are ever so nice. But you ought to come, too."

Irene was tempted. Sailing on a yacht, with a nice deck chair and a champagne cup and the river rolling by, sounded just as delightful now as it had yesterday. And how often would she have the chance for such an excursion? Before she could decide, however, Clara spoke again.

"There is another thing you should know. Torquil has called on Ellesmere, and the viscount has agreed to be at Kew for luncheon at the same time as we. His home, I'm told, is very near there, at Brentford, so Kew shall be an easy distance for him. He has promised to bow when he sees us, making the acknowledgement."

Irene snorted. "How good of him. I know, I know," she added as Clara started to speak. "I understand how these things are done. First the bow, then the introduction, then the calls, then the invitations . . . I comprehend it all. It's just . . ." Her voice trailed off and she sighed, remembering Torquil's words from breakfast. "Oh, Clara, I'm just so devilishly proud. I hate that a man who never took any notice of us is now inclined to do so because a peer of higher rank has asked him to."

"I know. But if our grandfather bows to us, will it be so very hard for you to return it?"

"Oh, terribly," she said with cheer. "I shall do it, of course, for your sake."

Her sister smiled, making the sacrifice to her pride a small one. "Then it's settled, and you will come sailing with us?"

"I suppose I have to, now. Josie can handle things for one day."

"Couldn't you take more time than that? Say . . . two weeks?"

Torquil's words from the night before rang through her mind again. "Do I . . ." She paused and swallowed, finding it hard to ask the question she wanted to ask, afraid to hear the answer. "Does it embarrass you that I intend to keep on with the paper while we are here?"

"Embarrass me? Oh, no."

"But what about afterward? If things go well, you are hoping I won't continue it, aren't you? You'd be happy to see me give it up altogether."

"I have not thought that far ahead. I am just enjoying myself. And the only thing I know is that I would prefer it if you took some time to enjoy yourself while you have the chance. Lady David is right, you know. To have a foot in both worlds, even for two weeks, will be exhausting."

Irene made a face. "Lady David is all the more incentive for me to find a way to change his mother's mind so I can be gone from here. But either way, you needn't worry about your future. If I fail, Ellesmere will have accepted us. If I succeed, Torquil still has to pay Papa a portion of money, all of which will go to provide a dowry for you. Don't argue," she added as her sister started to protest, "for my mind is made up."

"But it sounds as if the duchess's mind is made up, too, Irene. I don't see how you'll ever persuade her."

Suddenly, an idea flashed through Irene's mind like a bolt of lightning, a solution so profoundly simple, she was stunned she hadn't thought of it straightaway.

"That's just it," she said with a jolt of excitement. "I've been looking at this situation the wrong way around. The *duchess* doesn't need to be persuaded of anything."

Clara stared at her, looking understandably bewildered. "I don't under—"

"It won't be an easy thing to manage," she murmured, her thoughts racing as her idea took shape. "But it'll be much easier on my conscience. It'll take time, though." She paused, musing. "How am I to find that?"

"As I've just been trying to tell you, you could take the time. A two-week holiday—"

"A holiday? By heaven, you are absolutely right. A holiday is just what I need." Irene chuckled at her sister's obvious bafflement. "You will be delighted to know that I've changed my mind. I won't be working as much as I had intended. I'll have to return home for an hour or so each day, of course, just to be sure things are running smoothly and Papa hasn't converted the newspaper office back into a library during our absence, but other than that, I will hand things over to Josie for the next two weeks, and spend the remainder of my time moving in society with you."

"You will?"

"Yes. And I shall also be making my best effort to be nicer to the duke." She couldn't help laughing at her sister's stupefied expression. "I must. It's the only thing to do, don't you see?"

It was plain that Clara didn't. She was looking utterly fogged.

Irene laughed again and gave her sister a smacking kiss on each cheek. "And you are the one who has made me realize it. Oh, Clara, you're brilliant!"

"I have no idea what you're talking about, but . . ." Clara paused, yawning. "But I fear you'll have to explain it all in the morning, for I am going to bed. And after working all day, you should go to bed, too," she added as she gathered up her discarded clothes and started toward her own room.

"I will, I will," Irene agreed, but her mind was still racing even after she had slipped on a nightgown and slid between the sheets of her bed. The clock ticked seconds and minutes as she stared up at the ceiling, trying to determine her best approach.

It was going to be every bit as difficult as the course Torquil had intended her to take, perhaps even more so. But, in following it, her conscience would be clear, for she wouldn't be interfering with another woman's happiness, and she wouldn't be going against what she still felt had been correct advice.

But how to manage it? Irene turned on her side, considering. It would be like scaling a Nordic glacier. Not impossible, perhaps, but by no means easy.

That was the challenge of it, but though Irene was seldom intimidated by anything, even she had to admit she found this particular challenge a bit daunting. In fact, the more she thought about it, the more daunting it became, making her even less inclined for sleep.

Finally, Irene gave up. Whether it was the idea racing through her mind, or the rich food she'd consumed, or the excitement of the evening, she was just not sleepy. Flinging back the covers, she got out of bed. Perhaps a book would help, she thought as she lit a lamp. Something deadly dull. *Fordyce's Sermons*, perhaps, or an unedited version of Chaucer's *Canterbury Tales*. Those would put anybody to sleep.

She replaced her nightdress with a tea gown, just in case the hall boy wasn't asleep at his post, then she picked up the lamp, and left her room, padding down the corridor in bare feet.

She needn't have worried about the hall boy, for he was bent sideways in his chair by the stairs, eyes closed and mouth open, snoring quietly. She tiptoed past him and down to the floor below, but as she turned into the corridor where the library was located, the faint light pouring through the doorway of that room told her she was not the only person in the house who was still awake.

Irene stopped, hesitant. It wasn't, she knew, quite the thing to be wandering about at this hour. Oh the other hand, she was already here, and she did not want to go back up and stare at the ceiling for the rest of the night.

Irene resumed walking, but when she reached the library, she was forced to halt again when she found that the very glacier she intended to climb in the morning was squarely in front of her right now.

Torquil was facing the doorway, seated at his writing desk and composing a letter, just as he had been the evening before, though less formally attired in a smoking jacket and shirt instead of dinner suit and white tie. Preoccupied with his task, he had not yet noticed her standing there, and she knew she ought to turn around before he did. It was the middle of the night. She was supposed to be in bed. This wasn't proper.

She moved to turn away, but the very movement caught his attention and he looked up.

He went utterly still, and something very much like dismay came into his face. That, she feared, did not bode well. She ought to go, but his gaze seemed to pin her in place.

"I couldn't sleep," she blurted out. "I came down for a book."

He stood up, and if he felt any dismay at the sight of her, it vanished at once, replaced by polite disinterest. "Miss Deverill," he said and bowed.

She cleared her throat. "I hope I'm not disturbing you?"

"Not at all," he said, and stretched out his arm toward the bookshelves lining the walls behind him, inviting her to help herself to any book she might wish.

She hesitated, knowing she had two choices. She could mumble some terribly lame excuse and duck out like a frightened rabbit, or she could begin climbing that glacier. Irene lifted her chin, took a deep breath, and started forward.

Chapter 12

$\mathcal{H}$enry had never been the sort to believe in fate. Destiny, he'd always felt, was in one's own hands, by choice of will, with perhaps a bit of divine assistance from time to time. Tonight, however, with Irene Deverill standing before him in her loose-fitting gown, her gold hair falling around her shoulders, he began to fear that will was useless and the divine had a damnable sense of what was helpful.

After his walk last evening, he'd slept a good night and woken this morning sure he was back on solid footing. Even at breakfast with her, he'd been well enough, and throughout the morning, he'd been able to keep the image of her stunning face, lit with laughter, out of his mind for almost the entire day. But then, he'd arranged the water party and wondered if she would like sailing. He'd called on Ellesmere, a feat which had forced him to talk about her. Worse, he'd then gone to Merrick's and chosen her a maid, an act which had led his imagination to images of her dressing and undressing, very shaky ground indeed, and he'd decided it would be best if he did not attend the theater with them this evening. Given his desire for her, steering clear was his only honorable course.

Denied that just now, he forced his face into the polite, disinterested expression required of a civilized gentleman and stood up. "Miss Deverill," he said and bowed, but as he did, he caught sight of her bare toes peeking out beneath cerise pink silk, and his body at once began a rebellion against civility. He jerked upright.

She gave a slight cough. "I hope I'm not disturbing you."

Disturbed, he supposed, was one way of describing how he felt. "Not at all," he lied and forced himself to remember what she'd come for. He turned slightly, again inviting her to peruse the bookshelves.

She walked past him, and as he turned, he prepared to excuse himself and escape before his much-too-vivid imagination led him to more agony, or worse, to actions he would regret.

"I'm glad to have run across you, actually," she said. "This might be an excellent moment for us to talk."

"Talk?" That impossible notion spurred him to action. He dredged up his honor, and prepared an excuse—the lateness of the hour and how tired he was. But when he turned around, excuses to leave went straight out of his head.

She was bending down, perusing the lowest shelves, the lamp on the floor nearby. He froze, staring at the unmistakable outline of her hips and buttocks, plainly visible through the thin layer of pink silk, making him fully aware that she had nothing on underneath. No petticoats, no drawers, no . . .

Oh, God, have mercy.

Riveted, he stared, arousal rising and fortitude cracking. "It sounds as if you have something important you wish to discuss."

"It can wait, if you prefer. It's just that . . ." She bent down a little farther, stretching to reach a book, and he knew he wasn't going anywhere. "This meeting is rather fortuitous."

"Fated, you might say," he said as he crossed the room toward her, his gaze on her hips, his thoughts in the gutter.

"Exactly." She straightened and turned toward him as he paused beside her. "Everyone else is in bed, so we won't be overheard."

The baser side of Henry's nature was already well aware of that point. "And what you want to discuss is a forbidden subject?"

For some reason, that made her laugh. "Forbidden? Oh, no. It's just that it's easier to discuss your mother with you if there's no chance she can overhear."

"My mother?" He felt as if he'd just been doused with ice water. "You want to talk about my mother?"

Talking, particularly about his mother, seemed ludicrous just now, but it was a much safer topic than the one he'd been contemplating. Not knowing whether to be relieved or disappointed by that fact, Henry tamped down lust and resigned himself to conversation. "What about her?"

"It's really Foscarelli I want to know more about. You've met him, I trust?"

Startled, he blinked. "What on earth gave you that idea?"

"Well . . . I assumed it. You did tell me you tried to buy him off."

"So I did. Through my solicitors."

"Solicitors?" She stared at him, shaking her head and giving a laugh as if she couldn't believe what she was hearing.

"That amuses you, Miss Deverill?"

"Your assessment of this man's character and suitability are based on what you have heard, not what you have concluded from your own knowledge and experience. You condemn my poor paper for engaging in gossip when it's about your family, yet, you seem able to embrace gossip wholeheartedly when it's about someone you don't wish to like. A bit hypocritical, don't you think?"

"That is ridiculous."

"Is it? You profess to despise rumor and innuendo, and yet those criteria seem to form the entire basis of your opinion of the man."

"And?"

"Don't you think you should meet him for yourself before you judge his character?"

"I cannot do that." The very idea appalled him. "It isn't possible."

She laughed again, lifting her hands in a gesture of bafflement. "Why not?"

"We have never been introduced. No introduction has been offered to me on his behalf, and if it were, I should refuse it. Even my mother would not suggest it."

She made a sound of impatience and turned her attention back to the bookshelves. "You aristocrats and your rules," she muttered as she pulled a volume halfway out and glanced at the title. "So damnably silly."

"Perhaps they seem so to you, but they exist nonetheless, and I must follow them, for unlike you, I am unwilling to suffer the consequences of not doing so."

She shoved the book back into place and turned to him again. "How did your mother meet him, then, if these rules are so important?"

"She wanted her portrait painted. She commissioned him. Then she decided to have him teach her to paint in oils. One thing led to another, and here we are."

"She was attracted to him and she wanted a fling, you mean." She laughed. "How delightfully naughty of her. Oh, Duke, I do like your mother!"

"I'm gratified to hear it, but I don't see what is delightful about having a fling."

Even as he said it, he knew how idiotic that comment was. So did she.

"Don't you?" Her hazel eyes sparkled with mischief. "Don't you, really?"

He stiffened, sensing danger to his newly acquired equanimity, and he feared he was every bit the hypocrite she'd accused him of being as desire for her flickered to life again. "I would prefer not to discuss the circumstances of my mother's fling, if you don't mind. She is, after all, my mother."

"It's terribly romantic, isn't it?" Miss Deverill went on, oblivious to his request for a change of subject. "Having a fling, and then falling in love."

"I don't see how," he mumbled, shifting his weight,

keenly uncomfortable with this topic. "Since one can hardly call it love."

She sighed. "I fail to see how your mother could ever think you a hopeless romantic."

Henry couldn't see it either, for his thoughts about the woman in front of him were anything but. His gaze slid down, his body began to burn. "The material point," he said, jerking his gaze back up to her face, "is that no conversation between Foscarelli and myself can take place. Propriety forbids it." As he spoke, he was well aware of how haughty he sounded, but it seemed his only refuge at the moment. "I suppose you think me overly fastidious."

She pulled out another book, opened it, and began to scan the pages. "That's one way of putting it."

That dry rejoinder, a reminder of his so-called hypocrisy, raised his defenses at once. "Foscarelli is a rake of the first water, with many feminine conquests. He is also, to put it crudely, on the make. If I allow myself to be introduced to him, I send a message to the world that I approve of such behavior. I cannot do that. And even if I did meet him," he went on as she opened her mouth to argue, "it would hardly change my opinion. If a man has behaved like a wolf, if he has preyed like a wolf, and feasted like a wolf, does it matter if he baas and bleats to me as if he were a sheep?"

"Oh, for heaven's sake," she said in exasperation and snapped the book closed, "this man may soon be a member of your family."

"I would prefer not to be reminded of that possibility, a possibility, I might add, that you are supposed to be helping me prevent from becoming reality."

She made a face and put the book away. "That's proving somewhat difficult, as you might imagine. You are her son. If your efforts to persuade her against this course have failed, I'm not sure what you expect me to do."

"Point out his flaws, stress his reputation. Urge caution. You are Lady Truelove's editor. One might infer you are also her confidante. Stress your friendship with your columnist and her trust in you. That might persuade Mama to listen."

Miss Deverill shook her head. "It's clear to me—it has been all along—that advising your mother not to marry him is a waste of time."

"Because people don't want advice," he said, remembering her words at breakfast, words even now he did not want to accept. "They want reassurance of what they've already decided."

"Just so. Which is why I strongly advised her to tie up her money. The fact that she didn't follow that advice, withhold a dowry, and restrict him to an allowance surprises me, I confess. Your mother seems a keenly intelligent woman. I don't understand why she agreed to give him so much money as a marriage portion."

"I do." He sighed. "She did it to spike my guns."

"What do you mean?"

"She knew I would try to buy the man off, and she circumvented my ability to do so."

"I don't understand. You're rich as Croesus, aren't you? Surely you're richer than your mother. If Foscarelli is truly the blackguard you think he is, why don't you just keep raising the amount of your offer until you reach a figure he finds acceptable?"

"It's not that simple. Most of my mother's wealth—

which is considerable, by the way—is in funds and shares which can be easily converted to cash."

"Surely you have funds and cash, too?"

"Yes, but most of mine is tied to the estates and the title in some way, either through the lands themselves, most of which are entailed, or in funds and shares that support the estates with their earnings."

"And converting those funds to cash would be a problem for you?"

"Not for myself. One man can live very well on a very small income. But if I liquidate assets, many others would suffer. There are hundreds of people who depend upon me and the income generated by my estates. I won't hollow out the title and risk the livelihoods of all those who depend upon me in order to buy off a fortune-hunter, not even for Mama, and she knows it. She knows her offer is a better one than I can ever make him. She is buying him, and as a result, she will be chained for life to a man wholly unworthy of her."

"A conclusion you cannot possibly make until you have met him. For myself, I refuse to believe things are as black as you paint them. It's clear that she loves him."

"But love is not always tied to happiness. He is a fortune-hunter. Do you really think my mother could be happy with such a man?"

"Maybe." She gave a shrug. "My mother was."

"Your father was a fortune-hunter?" He stared at her, astonished. "But your family had money when your father was young, didn't they?"

"Did your private detectives tell you that?"

He saw no point in prevaricating. "They did, yes. My

understanding is that Deverill Publishing was once a thriving, prosperous concern. Your father surely had no need to marry for material considerations."

"Oh, but he did. You see, as a young man, my father was a wastrel—wild and irresponsible. He was also terrible with money—still is, I'm afraid. He had the unfortunate habit of spending every penny of the very generous salary my grandfather paid him in the company. He had no interest in the newspaper business, and no desire to arrive for work every morning on schedule after drinking himself under the table the night before. My grandfather—who was quite a tartar, by the way— became thoroughly exasperated with him. He gave my father the sack, disinherited him, and tossed him out of the house. He told Papa not to come back until he had accomplished something in the world besides gambling, drinking, and chasing women."

"So your father went to find an heiress, and the result was that he married Ellesmere's daughter? But it didn't work," he pointed out when she nodded. "After your parents eloped, the viscount disinherited his daughter and refused to provide a dowry."

"True, but that wasn't the point. Grandfather was proud that we had a real lady in the family, a viscount's daughter, and that installed my father back in his father's good graces. And he actually managed to stay there. My mother, you see, was able to do the one thing my grandfather never could: keep my father up to the mark. He gave up drink and worked hard to live up to what she expected of him."

A man who consumed enough brandy to remain

drunk every waking moment could hardly be described as up to the mark, but he did not point that out.

"It was only after my mother died," she said as if reading his thoughts, "that Papa took to drink again. For the fifteen years they were married, he didn't touch a drop of liquor or sit at a single gaming table. But when she died—"

Miss Deverill paused, a hint of pain crossing her face, and she looked away.

"Go on," he said. "When she died . . ."

"You've undoubtedly seen the result for yourself." She faced him again, shrugging as if it didn't matter, but he knew it did. "Papa fell completely apart. Grandfather tried to help him—he didn't want to see his son backslide, I'm sure. But then Grandfather died, too, and my father had no one who could help him after that. My brother tried, but after a series of violent quarrels, my father disowned him, and he went to America."

"And your brother left you here on your own?"

"Papa wasn't so bad then as he is now. And since Papa tossed him out, what else could he do but go off to make his own way? I tried to help my father as well, but that was no good either. I think Papa just didn't see the point of being responsible anymore, not without my mother." Irene looked at Henry again, and there was unmistakable affection in her face that he felt her father did not deserve. "He loved her, you see. He may have been fortune-hunting when he met her, but he also fell in love with her. And she loved him."

"But after your mother's death, things went downhill, I take it?"

"Yes." She gave a laugh, forced and devoid of humor. "Despite all my grandfather's efforts to teach him, my father never could develop a head for business, poor lamb. He began drinking again, and making reckless, unwise investments. The more he lost, the more he drank, and the more reckless he became."

"Yes, chasing losses is very common for men who are fond of gambling, I'm afraid. And drinking heavily impairs the judgment. Hard on you and your sister, though."

"That doesn't matter. I can take care of myself and my sister. But don't you see why I'm telling you all this? While my father may have been a fortune-hunter and a rake, he nonetheless made my mother happy."

"Against tremendous odds."

"Perhaps, but that's not the point. My father is weak, no doubt about that. And some women would not be happy with a man like that, or a man like Antonio Foscarelli, for that matter. But not every woman is the same."

He rubbed a hand over his forehead, striving to decide what to say. He recalled his own less-than-favorable impression of Irene's father, and he felt it was open to question just how happy with the fellow her mother could have been. To him, the picture she had just painted of her family was a sentimental one that ignored the hard reality: a rake could not ever really reform. He might have the intention to do so, he might even hold his life together for a time for love's sake, but he was first and last and always, a rake. Pointing that out would have bolstered his argument against his mother's marriage, but when he looked into Irene's face, soft with compassion for her parent, he couldn't do it. "I begin to understand," he said instead, "why you felt comfortable giving my mother the advice you did. You thought she was like your mother."

"Not precisely. What I thought was that your mother, like mine, ought to be given credit for knowing her own heart and mind, and for being the only one who could or should decide where her true happiness lies."

"With that man."

"He might genuinely love her, you know."

Henry couldn't help a laugh. "You believe that?"

"It's possible. As I said, my father fell in love with my mother. It was after he began courting her, but nonetheless, he did fall in love with her. As to Foscarelli, I can't say what he might feel, for unlike you, I believe one should actually meet someone before passing judgment on their character, and I have not met the man. I'd like to, for I am curious about him, I admit."

Henry could not believe what he was hearing. "You can't meet him."

"Why not?"

The idea of Miss Deverill, who was not only an unmarried woman, but also a stunningly beautiful one, in the sights of that blackguard was enough to make Henry feel absolutely savage. "No," he said, shaking his head. "He is just as unthinkable an acquaintance for you as he would be for me. More so, in fact, for you are a young lady."

She laughed, making short shrift of the rules that governed his world. "A fact which makes me want to meet him all the more. He's said to be a fascinating man."

"Cobras are fascinating, too, but they are still poisonous. Meeting him would put your reputation in serious jeopardy. He's a libertine, a sybarite, utterly immoral."

"Hmm . . ." Her lips tipped in a sideways little smile that told Henry he was making no impression whatsoever. "With every word, you give me a greater understanding of the man's appeal."

"Do be serious," he admonished. "You publish a scandal sheet, so you surely know Antonio Foscarelli is a notorious man, though whether that reputation is due in greater part to his affairs with women or to his nude portraits of them, I cannot say."

"Affairs? Nude portraits?" She lifted her hands, fanning herself in a pretense of being thoroughly shocked. "Oh, my heavenly days."

He watched her, unamused. "You have taken my mother's words about teasing me to heart, I see."

Her hands stilled, resting against her bosom, drawing his gaze at once to the creamy white skin beneath her fingertips. All the arousal he'd been fighting since she walked in the door flared up again, hotter than ever, and it occurred to him that no woman he'd ever known had the singular talent of provoking both his desire and his temper simultaneously. "Miss Deverill," he began.

"Any artist of good character is celibate, of course," she went on with deep solemnity. "And paints breathtaking, brilliant bowls of fruit."

His aggravation faded into bemused chagrin, and as he slid his gaze up from her collarbone, along her delicate throat, over her stunning face, and into her eyes, his body didn't care a jot that all her merriment was at his expense.

His head, however, worked to remind them both of what was important. "Your idea isn't worth discussing, since what we are attempting to do is prevent her from marrying him at all."

"Which, as I am trying to tell you, isn't going to work. I could list his flaws to her from now until the end of time, and so could you, and everyone else in your family, and I doubt it would impair her feelings for the man in the slightest degree."

"Then you had best come up with another way to change her mind."

"Or you could just resign yourself to her decision, attempt to persuade him to sign a settlement, and make the best of things."

He didn't credit that suggestion with a reply, but his expression must have conveyed his opinion clearly enough. "Really, Torquil," she cried, "you are the most impossible man. You can't control everything and everyone, you know."

"Apparently not," he muttered, glaring at the woman who seemed able to rob him of all his control in the wink of an eye. "And yet, I am undeterred."

"If your mother wants to marry him, who are you to say she can't? If she's in love with him, who are you to judge her for it?"

"Love?" He made a sound of disdain, shaking his head violently. "It's not love."

"Of course it is. She's about to sacrifice everything, risk everything, to be with this man. What else could it be but love?"

He made a sound of impatience. "It's passion. Raw, unbridled passion."

"Passion. Love." She shrugged, laughing as she looked up at him, shaking back the loose gold waves of her hair, harkening to the darkest lusts inside him. "Is there really so much difference?"

"All the difference in the world. One is stable, lasting, sane. The other is wild, ungovernable, mad—"

He stopped, struck by the innocence that shone in her laughing, upturned face. She did not know what he was talking about. He wanted her with a fierceness that took his breath away, a woman he'd known five days. Hell, he'd wanted her when he'd known her five seconds. But she knew nothing of that sort of feeling. The hunger, the desperation, the aching need—these were sensations she had not yet experienced.

"You want to know the difference between passion and love?" He wrapped an arm around her waist, pulled her hard against him, and bent his head. "This is passion," he said, and kissed her.

Chapter 13

Having been kissed once, at the tender age of thirteen, Irene would have thought she'd be somewhat prepared for her second such experience. That tentative press of lips with the boy next door, interrupted almost at once by the approaching footsteps of her governess, had been tender, sweet, and, truth be told, vaguely disappointing.

Torquil's kiss was nothing like that.

It was neither sweet nor tender. Instead, it was hard and hot, not tentative at all, and it brought a thrill she'd never felt in her life before.

She closed her eyes, and the moment she did, he overwhelmed her senses. There was nothing else in the world but him. His scent—castile soap, bay rum, and something deeper. His taste—port and fruit. His arm like a steel band around her waist. His clothes, soft velvet and crisp linen against her palm, and beneath them, his heart, thudding hard in his chest.

His lips parted, urging hers to part as well, but when she complied, his tongue entered her mouth, and she jerked in shock, breaking the kiss. At once, he went still, his mouth a fraction from hers, his quick breaths mingling with hers. He was waiting, she realized. Waiting for what?

She didn't know, but she did know she didn't want this to stop, so she slid her arm up around his neck, and rose on her toes to touch her lips to his.

He groaned against her mouth, and as if that was what he'd been waiting for, his arm tightened around her waist again, and he pushed her backward, following her into the corner of the room.

Her shoulders hit the shelves behind her, and books toppled out of the bookcase as his other arm came around her back to hold her tight. He deepened the kiss again, his hand tangling in her hair and his tongue in her mouth.

Pleasure began spreading throughout Irene's body as he tasted deeply of her, a dark, heavy wave of it. She wrapped her other arm around his neck, wanting him closer. She stirred, pressing against him, relishing the feel of his hard, masculine form. The feelings within her grew hotter, stronger, and yet, she still yearned for more. She wrapped her leg around his, wanting him even closer, and as she rubbed her foot along the back of his calf, the feel of his trousers against her bare skin somehow heightened her pleasure and made it even more acute. She moaned against his mouth, wanting this to go on forever.

Without warning, he tore his lips from hers, an abrupt, almost violent withdrawal that forced her to open her eyes.

"Good God," he rasped, his breathing harsh and quick. "This needs to stop."

He grasped her arms, pulling them down from around his neck, but despite his words, he did not let her go. "For both our sakes, this needs to stop. Surely, Miss Deverill, you think so, too."

Irene couldn't think at all. Her head was reeling, her heart was pounding, and her body was on fire, and yet, despite all that, she felt absolutely glorious. The last thing on her mind was calling a halt to this wondrous experience and returning to sanity, so she shook her head, closed the scrap of distance he had put between them, and slid her arms back up around his neck again.

"Given what just happened," she said, breathless and laughing, "I think you should probably call me Irene."

A shadow crossed his face—guilt, perhaps, or regret—and Irene's blissful euphoria began to evaporate. He stepped back, out of her embrace, shaking his head. "I cannot do that," he said. "It would be . . ."

His voice trailed into silence, and he came to a stop several feet away. He rubbed his hands over his face as if trying to think. "It would be an unpardonable liberty. And far too intimate."

His sense of right and wrong and what was proper was something Irene had never found more baffling than she did at this moment. "Too intimate?" she echoed, not quite believing she'd heard him right. "You were kissing me, Henry."

He grimaced, clasping his hands behind his back, tilting his head to look at the ceiling. "Yes."

"You were holding me in your arms," she went on, blushing as she said it, her words fanning the erotic flame he'd started. "Your tongue was in my—"

"Yes," he cut her off, and though he seemed to lose his fascination with the ceiling, when he tilted his chin down, he did not quite look at her. His face, usually so implacable, was twisted a bit, as if he was in pain. "I must beg you to forgive me, for I have subjected you to masculine attentions which any young lady would find unwelcome."

Her blush deepened and spread as she recalled those thrilling masculine attentions, and her opinion was re-inforced that the life of a young lady must be terribly dull. "I wouldn't necessarily say that—"

"By doing so," he went on as if she hadn't spoken, "I have also exposed to you an unsavory facet of my character, one I would have preferred to keep hidden." Taking a deep breath, he raked his hands through his hair and met her bewildered gaze head-on. His light eyes seemed to darken, becoming a deeper, more tur-bulent gray. "The truth, Miss Deverill, is that, though I am a gentleman, I am also a man possessed of deep carnal appetites."

Irene's toes curled into the carpet beneath her feet. "Yes," she said faintly. "So it would seem."

"I have had, from the moment we met, an ardent de-sire for you, one which I am finding nearly impossible to contain."

She stared, beginning to feel as if she was in some

strange and crazy dream. He was the last man she'd ever have expected to possess carnal appetites, though with his kiss still burning her lips, she could hardly deny it. He spoke of passion, and after what he had just done, she knew he must feel it, yet he looked as if he welcomed that feeling as much as he might welcome tooth drawing. And she was the object of all this? She still couldn't seem to take it in.

But in this series of shocking happenings this evening, the notion that he had felt these things for her from that first moment in her office was perhaps the most astonishing of all. "Wait," she pleaded, desperate for a moment to think. "You have felt this way about me from the beginning?"

His lashes lowered, then lifted. "Yes."

She looked into his eyes, so cool, so remote, and yet, they flared the spark in her that his kiss had ignited, and her body responded at once with a strong, answering thrill. She took a step toward him. "But—"

She stopped as he took another step back.

"No doubt, this feeling I have is temporary," he said. "It will pass, but until it does, I fear you may be vulnerable to further attentions of this sort from me, for as I said, I am finding them difficult to master. In light of that, I suggest that for the remaining time you are here, we should maintain as much distance as politeness and civility will allow."

That was rather less thrilling, particularly since he spoke of his lack of control as if it were a compulsion to eat sour persimmons. "I see."

"I will do all that I can, Miss Deverill, to ensure that

tonight's events are not repeated. Of course you cannot be expected to forget my conduct, but I hope you can forgive it. Good night."

He offered her a stiff bow and turned away. Irene, stunned, bemused, and still unmistakably aroused, could only watch him as he walked toward the door, his most unaccountable admission still ringing in her ears.

I have had, from the moment we met, an ardent desire for you.

She'd only imagined such words in dark, half-formed thoughts in the privacy of her own room, and she certainly never would have thought they could come out of this man's mouth.

He vanished out the door, and Irene stared at the empty doorway. She blinked, she shook her head, she laughed in disbelief, and only now was she able to articulate precisely why she found this entire situation so absurd.

"But we don't even like each other."

Even as she said it, she was acutely aware of the feelings he had brought about within her, feelings which she had never experienced before, nor had even known existed. Passion, it seemed, did not require liking.

She pressed her fingers to her lips, wincing, for they felt puffy and tender to the touch. Her plan, she noted, had gone quite awry. She'd gotten the crazy idea that it might be easier—or at least, less impossible—to reason Torquil into accepting the marriage than it would be to dissuade his mother from entering it, and encountering him here had seemed a perfect opportunity to begin implementing that strategy. She had certainly not been attempting to attract him; she'd never even thought of such a harebrained idea. Torquil attracted to her would have been a ludicrous notion ten minutes ago. And though she'd begun to discern that he had certain appealing qualities, she'd never have imagined in her wildest flights of fancy that such scorching heat existed beneath his icy surface.

I am a man possessed of deep carnal appetites.

So much for scaling the glacier, she thought wryly. Tonight, she might very well have melted it instead, something she'd never dreamt was even possible.

Life, she appreciated, was sometimes utterly unpredictable.

For Henry, the next five days were agony. Whenever he saw her, he was the perfect gentleman. His conversations with her were superficial and amiable. His manner was impeccable, his attitude toward her so scrupulously polite that no one could have faulted it.

But in his heart, he lusted.

Alone in his rooms, he closed his eyes and imagined her with him—what her magnificent body would look like if she were naked before him, her gold hair tumbled down around her shoulders. He imagined the texture of her bare skin and the sounds she might make, and the feel of her body moving beneath him—and above him, and in front of him. His imagination, the tool of his lust, seemed to know no bounds.

In front of others, he was careful. He was discreet. He never looked at her for more than a few seconds, and when he did glance her way, he made sure that his expression revealed nothing, ensuring that no one, not even those nearest and dearest to him, could guess what had occurred between him and Irene Deverill in a darkened corner of the library.

But in his mind and body, he knew.

He knew every detail because he relived it, over and over. The scent of her hair and the taste of her mouth and the tease of her foot riding up the back of his leg. Instead of the exquisite pain of his own withdrawal, he fashioned different, much more satisfying endings.

None of this, of course, made his pretense of polite disinterest toward her any easier. But he could not stop the willful licentiousness of his thoughts. He didn't even want to.

This situation could not continue for long, he knew that. If it did, he'd go mad. But his only other option was to send Miss Deverill home, and he had no intention of doing that.

He was not ready to give up on the only means he had of separating his mother from her Italian. If anything, the incident with Miss Deverill made him more convinced than ever that his mother was making a mistake. Lust was no basis for a lifetime commitment.

Nor was he sure sending Miss Deverill away would make a particle of difference. He feared the distance from Upper Brook Street to Belford Row wasn't nearly enough to suppress his appetite.

No, he was caught, like a fly in treacle. But he had to admit it was a damned sweet way to drown.

By the morning of the water party, however, Henry had managed to achieve a stable, if agonizing, equilibrium, and he felt that he just might be able to withstand the next eight days without ravishing Miss Deverill in a corridor or hurling himself off a cliff.

The morning was clear and warm, promising the sort of fine summer day so rare in England and so splendid when it occurred. The wind, too, seemed amenable to a day on the water, brisk enough to carry them to Kew and back with a minimum of effort, but warm enough to make the journey pleasant.

Still, the *Mary Louisa* was just out of dry dock after extensive repairs, and to make sure she was fully ready for the day, he arrived at Queen's Wharf several hours ahead of the rest of the party.

It wasn't as if he'd been sleeping much anyway, and he hadn't been sailing since early spring, so readying the ship was a welcome distraction. He supervised Andrew and Fitz and the other members of the crew, and did his own share of work as well, for despite several days of preparation, the ship wasn't as up to par as he'd like. When ten o'clock came and everyone else arrived at Queen's Wharf, there was still enough to do that it was easy for Henry to stay well away from Miss Deverill, and he left it to his siblings to give her a tour of the ship, finding excuses to be busy elsewhere every time conversation with her became a possibility. If this trend could be made to continue, he might be able to get through the entire day without imagining Miss Deverill naked, and all would be smooth sailing.

They'd barely passed Battersea Park and cleared the Albert Bridge, however, before he made the mistake of taking the helm from Andrew, and his first mate had barely departed to the galley for a cup of tea before he saw the object of all his thoughts coming along the starboard deck straight toward him, no one with her and a determined look on her face. Henry glanced around, but no member of his crew was close enough that he could hand over the helm, and he knew all his efforts to avoid her had been an exercise in futility.

So much, he thought, for smooth sailing.

IN THE NORMAL course of events, Irene would never dream of forcing her company on anyone who didn't want it, and as she walked along the deck toward him, it was obvious that Torquil would prefer to be anywhere but in her vicinity. He'd been making that fact plain for five days now. Given his confession that night in the library, she couldn't blame him, and if this had been any other man, she would never dream of inflicting further embarrassment upon him by her presence, but in this case, she had no choice.

Time was going by, and she was no closer to a happy exit from this situation than she'd been when she'd arrived. Half her allotted time to find a way out of this mess was gone, and after five days of being avoided, she was determined to force her company upon him, whether it pained him or not, so that she could make him see sense.

He might have taken some comfort in the knowledge that he was not the only one who would have preferred no reminders of that night. He might have derived some satisfaction from knowing that ever since that extraordinary kiss, her nights had been restless ones. He might even have relished the fact that his voice, thick and dark, had insisted upon coming to her again and again in dreams, arousing in her all the dizzying feelings he had evoked with his kiss and his erotic confession.

I am a man possessed of deep carnal appetites.

He might have savored the knowledge of her sleepless nights, of how his lush kiss and passionate words had called to something carnal inside of her, too. But he was never going to know any of that because she'd have died rather than tell him.

As it was, by the time she reached where he stood at the helm, he was wearing his usual countenance of cool disinterest. But it didn't matter, for now she knew what lurked beneath.

Her face was growing hot before she'd even reached him, but she could not avoid this. Plucking up her courage, she said in as normal a voice as she could muster, "I am glad to find you alone. I need to speak with you."

"Unless the ship is on fire," he said, "I would prefer you didn't."

Her face was what was on fire, but she persevered. "I have no doubt of that, and I'm sorry for it, but it cannot be helped. At some point, Duke, we must have a conversation."

He wanted to refuse, that was clear. But in the end, perhaps due to a lifetime of civility, restraint, and politeness, he did not.

"Very well," he said and stepped to one side. "Would you care to take the wheel?"

"I beg your pardon?" She looked at the helm, then back at him, her frustration with him momentarily forgotten in her surprise. "You'd let me do that?"

"I would."

She frowned, suddenly a bit suspicious. "Why? Because the moment I put my hands on the wheel, you'll dash off and leave me stuck?"

That actually made him laugh, and the sight and

sound of it made her laugh, too, easing the tension between them even as the sight of his smile and the sound of his laugh made her tummy give a nervous dip. He was handsome enough when he bore his usual expression of cool indifference, but when he laughed, when the edges of his eyes creased a little and his eyes glinted brilliant gray, and his mouth curved in that heart-stopping smile . . . goodness, he was a treat to look at.

"I wouldn't dash off and leave you, Miss Deverill," he said.

Given that he'd been doing just that for five days, she couldn't help raising a skeptical eyebrow.

"My ship," he explained, still smiling a little, "is at stake."

"It might be anyway, if you let me steer. What if I wreck it?"

"You won't," he promised. "I'll help you."

He was, at least, talking to her about something besides the weather. "All right. What do I do?"

"Stand here." He moved aside, gesturing for her to take his place before the large wheel of smooth, polished oak. "Now, pretend you're first mate."

"First mate?" she cried with mock indignation. "Why not captain?"

He frowned, looking stern. "Don't push your luck."

"Oh, very well. I had so hoped for the chance to order you about, but I suppose it's not meant to be." She faced the helm. "What do I do?"

"First, determine your direction." He put his hands on her shoulders and turned her toward a round oak stand behind and to her right, on top of which reposed a large brass device with a dial she recognized even before he added, "The compass says you're heading southwest. But look what's ahead of you."

He turned her to face the bow again, then let go of her shoulders and moved to stand slightly behind her. His arm stretched out above her right shoulder grazing the side of her neck as he pointed to the shoreline, which was directly in front of them, though still some distance away. "You stay on this heading, and you'll run aground."

"So I have to turn the wheel to the right?"

"To starboard, yes. Chiswick is to the right of us, just there." He pointed to the northern bank. "The river takes a turn to the northwest here, so you'll need to alter your course ninety degrees, changing direction until the compass points northwest. Do you understand?"

She nodded, glancing ahead, then back toward the compass, then ahead again. "Yes, I think so."

"Good. Now, take the wheel by the handles and turn it slowly starboard. As you do, you'll feel the ship start to turn."

She felt more than a little nervous, but she did as he instructed.

"Be patient," he cautioned, stretching out his arm again and leaning in. His body brushed hers as he put his own hand on the wheel, and suddenly every nerve ending in her body was tingling with awareness. "We're not in the Henley Regatta, not today anyway, so there's no need to rush it."

He helped correct her course a little, then eased back. "Good," he said, his arm sliding away from above her shoulder as she let out her breath in a slow sigh of relief. "Keep turning, and keep an eye on your compass.

Once you see that you're pointing northwest, straighten out, and you'll be fine for a bit."

She navigated the turn as he directed, her gaze travelling back and forth between the compass and river ahead, until the ship was on a northwest course and sailing parallel to both banks. "I did it." She grinned, glancing again at the compass, just to be doubly sure. "I did it."

"So you did. And splendidly, too. You might be in the Henley yet."

She laughed, exhilarated, and turned her head to look at him. He was watching her, his eyes darkening to a smoky gray, and when he spoke, his voice had a hint of dark confession in it.

"You were wrong, by the way."

Her throat went dry. "About what?" she whispered.

"That you wouldn't ever be able to give me orders. I can think of a few I'd comply with if they came from you. You have more power than I care to contemplate, Miss Deverill."

Irene's heart gave a jolt of panic. "Do I?" she said, laughing to hide her sudden nervousness. "I don't suppose if I ordered you to just accept your mother's marriage and give me back my newspaper, you'd do it?"

Suddenly, his countenance was the cool, remote one she'd seen in her office that very first day. "Is that why you came back here?" he asked, his voice deadly quiet. "After the admission I made the other night, you thought I might perhaps be vulnerable to a bit of persuasion on that score?"

That sent Irene's already teetering emotions straight over the edge. "You are the most impossible man!" she cried, aggravated not only by that accusation, but also by the fact that whenever she started liking him, he managed to say something that made her feel as if tea dregs had just been thrown in her face.

"Unlike you," she said, "I have already faced the fact that your mother will not be moved to change her mind, no matter what I say. I admit that I came back here hoping I might have a reasoned word with you on that score—though how I ever thought I could possibly reason with a man as hardheaded and arrogant as you, I can't think!"

She paused to glance over the bow, then returned her attention to him and went on before he could get a word in, "I did not seek you out for the motive you cite. No, I came back here because the only way I can discuss this topic with you at all is if I can catch you alone, something that for the past few days has proven a difficult task. So when I saw the chance to speak with you with some degree of privacy, I took it. But it was not in any way because of the other night, and I certainly gave no thought whatsoever to . . . to . . . employ feminine wiles on you."

She paused, sucking in a deep breath before she started off again. "For one thing, I wouldn't know how. I've no experience with that sort of thing, no gift for flirtation, and certainly no desire to wield this power you have laid at my door. And I should not dream of taking advantage of anyone in such a condition of vulnerability as you described. It would be cruel. Besides, if we are talking about being vulnerable, you are not—"

. . . the only one who feels that way.

She stopped, her unsaid words hanging in the air, bit

back by a sudden acute need for self-preservation. She could not, she simply could not, confess to him that she was equally vulnerable to him. That his kiss had been the most exciting, extraordinary experience of her life. It would be too humiliating to admit she found this man so damnably attractive, when she was also well aware of his low opinion of her, her work, her beliefs, and her life. She hated even admitting to herself the aggravating fact of his attraction.

"You are not so vulnerable as you think," she said instead, glaring at him as she shored up her pride. "You have your powerful position in this world and your rank, where I have neither. Although, while we are on that subject, let me say that as much as you think your position entitles you to dominate everything and everyone, it doesn't, and you can't. Even your mighty ducal authority doesn't extend that far. Perhaps you ought to start accepting that fact with better grace. About your mother, and about me."

She stopped, breathing hard, and she waited, not sure if she ought to stalk off now, while she had the last word, or wait for him to say something else equally insufferable so she could light into him again. When he did speak, it was not at all what she would have expected.

"You're quite right."

She blinked. Her anger faltered a bit at this unexpected admission. "I am?"

"Yes, and it seems I must again ask your forgiveness, Miss Deverill. What I said was unpardonable and arrogant, and you are perfectly within your rights to dress me down. In my defense, I can only reiterate that where you are concerned, as we both now know, I am . . ." He paused, swallowing hard as if he found it difficult to continue. "I am painfully aware of my susceptibility where you are concerned. I find myself doing all manner of things I would not usually do because I am feeling things that I don't usually allow myself to feel."

"Yes, well," she muttered, a bit mollified, but still prickly and terribly self-conscious, "that makes two of us."

"Yes." His face gave nothing away, but his gaze lowered to her lips. "I rather thought that might be the case."

She wanted to ask what made him think so. How had she given herself away? But then, she remembered how she'd twined her arms around his neck and rubbed her foot along his leg, and she saw how stupid that question would have been. How could he not have known what that kiss had made her feel?

Heat flooded her face, but she could not move. Panic made her heart race, but she could not run. He was thinking about that kiss, perhaps about doing it again, and she could not help thinking about how it would feel if he did.

Her lips began to tingle and her heart hammered like a mad thing, but then he returned his attention to the bow, and she felt a stab of disappointment.

"You're drifting."

"Hmm?" Irene frowned at his profile, trying to regain her scattered wits. "What?"

"You're drifting." His arm stretched out over her shoulder again to realign the ship to a course parallel to shore, then slid away again at once. "Best watch where you're going."

At once, she returned her attention to steering the ship, realizing much to her mortification that if he had kissed her right then and there, she would have let him, even though practically everyone on the ship could see them if they'd chanced to turn around and look to the stern of the boat, and she discovered a new appreciation for his suggestion that they maintain a discreet distance.

"This is a tricky part of the river," he said, interrupting her thoughts. "I should take over."

Irene was happy to let him. She excused herself and rejoined the others, accepting a champagne cup from the footman along the way, in the hope of steadying her frayed nerves and highly strung emotions.

She sank into her deck chair, where the talk of the others flowed around her, but though the other ladies tried to bring her into their conversation, Irene remained preoccupied, appreciating that she had a serious problem on her hands.

Her plan to persuade Henry to change his mind instead of having his mother change hers wasn't going to work. For one thing, it was exactly what he would be expecting her to do. And besides, it wasn't playing the game fair, given his *ardent passion* for her, as he put it. Just the memory of those words was enough to rekindle the feeling, and Irene hastily got to her feet and walked to the rail before the other ladies could see her blushing. This situation could not continue. But what, she wondered as she stared moodily out at the water and sipped her champagne cup, could she do about it?

Her first line of attack—Henry's plan—had been doomed to fail from the start. Her second plan was also out the window. She had no third. And despite the unexpected events of a few days ago, if the duchess married her Italian, Irene had no illusions where Torquil was concerned. He might have a passion for her, but it would not stop him from putting an end to Lady Truelove and *Society Snippets*. For those, she well knew, he had nothing but disdain. And worst of all, every time she looked at him, she found herself longing for him to kiss her again.

Irene leaned her elbows on the rail with a sigh. How on earth was she to get out of this mess?

Chapter 14

As a boy at Eton, Henry had first learned that many Catholic priests of the Middle Ages made a daily ritual of flogging themselves. He'd found that a baffling fact, not only as a staunch Anglican, but also as someone who'd always possessed a great deal of common sense.

Now, however, with the fragrance of Irene's skin and the warmth of her body so vivid in his memory, Henry began to understand the compulsion of self-torture. And he'd certainly been living like a priest for far too long.

No wonder he'd asked her to take the wheel. He'd known it would give him the perfect excuse to stand behind her, inhale the scent of her, touch her, however fleetingly. And he'd been awash in lust as a result.

As if that wasn't bad enough, he'd taken out his self-inflicted frustration on her with his boorish accusation, providing her with all the more reason to resent him, and providing himself with all the more cause for self-condemnation.

Yes, he was a glutton for punishment.

A cough brought him out of this reverie, and he glanced up to find his mother a few feet away, an expression on her face that all sons of loving mothers know. He tensed, but when he spoke, he worked to make his voice light, hoping to keep his secret well-hidden. "Mama, what are you doing back here? Want to be like Miss Deverill, do you, and have a go at steering the ship?"

"Would you allow it?" she asked.

For some reason, he was a bit nettled by that question. "Why wouldn't I? Why does everyone think I'm such a tyrant?"

That made her laugh. "Not a tyrant," she said, moving to stand beside him. "Just a man who is the admiral of his fleet, and who believes it is his sworn duty to ensure that all his ships sail in what he feels is the proper direction."

His defenses faltered. "Yes, well, if that's what I believe, I fear I'm doomed to disappointment," he muttered. "The women in my life, alas, don't seem willing to be as predictable as my yachts."

"No," she agreed and paused beside him. "Miss Deverill in particular," she said after a moment, "is a woman who charts her own course. And does it rather well, too."

Even the mention of her name was enough to threaten his tenuous hold on self-possession. He kept his attention fixed on the helm. "Stop matchmaking, Mama," he said, hoping he sounded as indifferent as he wished he could feel. "Miss Deverill is not, by any stretch of the imagination, in my life. Nor would she ever wish to be. She has no use for our sort. She's made that clear enough."

"You may be right."

She didn't broach the topic he'd attempted to lead her toward, so he turned his head and met her gaze, tackling it for her. "In mentioning the women in my life, I was referring to you."

She turned away, running her gloved hand over the brass surface of the compass behind them and rubbing her fingertips together as if the instrument had dust. "Oh?"

"Don't be coy, Mama. Not with me."

"Very well." She turned back around and looked at him again. "I suppose I couldn't avoid this moment for two entire weeks. Just don't let it become a row, dear. We have guests."

"Do you love him?"

"Yes."

He nodded. He'd expected no other answer. "Even though he wants your money?"

"It's not a matter of want. He has no means or income of his own, and he has relations to take care of. He can't afford to marry a woman who doesn't have money. Fortunately for both of us, I have plenty to support us, for otherwise I fear we should have had to part. A peer isn't the only sort of man who has duties and responsibilities to the members of his family, you know."

"And despite the mercenary aspect of his courtship, you trust him with your future?"

"Yes. You see, he loves me, too, Henry."

Her voice was steady, her gaze unwavering. He found that incomprehensible, given the man's reputation with women. "How can you know it's love? How can you be so sure?"

"I am as sure as one human being can ever be about another."

"Given human nature, that's not so very sure. Even if it is love, how do you know it will make you happy?"

"I don't. Nothing in life is absolutely sure. Sometimes, I think you find that a difficult thing to accept, Henry."

He swallowed hard, afraid she was right about that. But he liked predictability, damn it. "And your daughters? We have already discussed how their future will be affected. What of that?"

"There will be scandal, but we shall do what we can to mitigate the damage. And if the result is that Angela and Sarah find men who care for them enough to marry them in spite of their mother's choice, then my marriage will have been a good thing for their future, not a bad thing. Position and suitability are not everything when it comes to matrimony. In spite of your own unfortunate experience with marrying for love, you do see that, Henry, surely?"

"Position and suitability are not the only considerations, no," he allowed with a sigh, "but I doubt Angela and Sarah will see it that way."

"I can make them understand that, if you help me."

"I'm not sure I should," he grumbled. "Or one of them might take it into her head to run off with the chauffeur, and then where shall we be?"

She laughed. "Oh, my dear. I shall have to caution

them against that, for I fear a chauffeur in the family would be too much for your nerves."

He sighed, studying her face. "I'm not going to win this fight, am I?"

Her laughter faded, but her smile lingered, a faint, knowing curve. "Which fight are we talking about? The one you are having with me?" She turned her head to glance at the ladies gathered near the front of the boat, and at one in particular who stood a little apart, staring out over the starboard rail. "Or," she went on, looking at him again, "the one you're having with yourself?"

He stiffened, appalled that he might be more transparent than he'd thought, at least to his mother's keen observation, and it was his turn to look away. But he could still feel her gaze on him and sense the understanding in her smile, and it made him hotly uncomfortable to think she might know the true cause of his torment. "God, Mama," he managed, "I hope you're not intending to be indelicate."

"I could, I suppose. But I won't."

He thanked God for that small favor.

"But," she went on, "I am worried, I confess."

Of course she was. "I know what worries you."

"Do you, indeed?"

He squared his shoulders and looked at her, facing the fear rattling around in his own mind even as he gave his mother the credit of it. "You fear I shall make the same mistake twice. Lose my head."

"I'm not afraid about you losing your head, Henry. I'm afraid of what might happen if you lose your heart."

He wasn't surprised that she would attempt to put

romantic connotations to what he felt about Miss Deverill when there was nothing romantic about it, but he could hardly articulate what he actually was feeling to his own mother in order to argue the point. "If it were about my heart," he said instead, "why should that worry you? In our last conversation on this topic, you seemed to feel I should make better use of that particular muscle than I have been."

"So I do. But I fear you persist in viewing the loss of one's heart as a mistake, and for you, a mistake is something to be avoided at all cost. I wish I could make you see how wrong that is." She turned away before he could argue. "Losing one's heart is never a mistake, Henry," she said over her shoulder. "No matter what may come afterward."

A convenient philosophy, he supposed as he returned his attention to the river, and no less than he would expect, given her current situation. Mama was in a romantic—and to his mind, unrealistic—haze. He knew how that felt. All was bliss, and everything in the garden lovely, and following one's heart seemed as inevitable as breathing. There was nowhere to go from that height of dizzying, unreal happiness but back down to earth, where one usually landed on the bedrock of reality with a bone-shattering crash.

"My heart, Mama," he said at last, "is in no danger of being lost."

She didn't answer, and when he turned his head, he found that she was walking away, already too far away to hear.

"Miss Deverill's virtue," he muttered with a sigh, "might be a different matter entirely."

IRENE DECIDED IT was probably best if she avoided Henry for the remainder of the day. When they docked at the yachting station at Kew, and journeyed to the pavilion, she walked with Clara, behind him and his mother. The more formal rules of seating that applied at dinner were not followed for a picnic luncheon, and she was glad of it, for that meant she did not have to sit at the duke's right hand, and she chose the very opposite end of the table. No doubt, he was as relieved as she.

When they took a stroll through the famous gardens after their meal, they had only been walking for a few minutes when the duchess moved to fall in step beside her. "Now, Miss Deverill," she said, taking Irene's arm, "we are approaching the Italian knot garden, and that is where Torquil arranged for Ellesmere to be after luncheon so that we shall run across him. The viscount is amenable to the introduction, Torquil has assured me, so when the moment comes, I shall introduce him to you and your sister. He may only bow, accept the introduction, and go on, or he may wish to converse for a bit. He was of two minds on that when Torquil met with him."

"If he does wish to converse with me, I shall have to let him," Irene said, making a face. "And for Clara's sake, I shall be all that is polite. But I hope you do not expect me to like him."

The duchess laughed and patted her arm. "Of course not, my dear. I have many relations I don't like. Ah, there he is."

The man coming toward them along the path was old, and though Irene had expected his appearance to reflect that, she hadn't expected him to be so thin and frail. He moved slowly, making good use of a cane, and leaning on the arm of a man perhaps two decades younger. His son George, Irene supposed, Mama's brother.

The approach was leisurely, but when they were abreast, the duchess took a step forward. "Ellesmere, how delightful to see you," she said. "And your son, too. How lovely."

She turned, drawing Irene and her sister forward. "Viscount Ellesmere, Lord Chalmers, please allow me to introduce you to my friends, Miss Irene Deverill, and Miss Clara Deverill. Ladies, Lord Ellesmere, and his son, Lord Chalmers."

The viscount sniffed, looking them over as they bowed. "I shan't bow to you," he said as they straightened, and Irene glanced over her shoulder at Torquil, still several yards behind them, wondering if all his good work had been for naught. If the man wouldn't even bow—

"Getting too old for that sort of thing," he went on gruffly, regaining her attention. "Hurts my back. Bad enough I'm walking around on this hard ground."

He turned to the duchess. "I've never met your friends, Duchess," he said gruffly, "but the Miss Deverills and I are actually related."

"Indeed?" She made a show of surprise, then one of enlightenment. "Oh, good heavens," she added with a little laugh, "I do believe you are. I'd forgotten."

Irene watched this little exchange with mixed feelings. They all knew the facts, the whole meeting had been prearranged, and yet, they all had to pretend it was a happy coincidence. A week ago, she'd have condemned such a charade as hypocritical, even downright silly, and yet now, as she was taking part in it, she had to admit that such pretenses probably made things easier on everyone. Perhaps some of these social rules weren't as useless as she'd thought. Sometimes, she thought, sliding a glance at her shy sister, they might even be useful.

The old man gave a cough, bringing her attention back to him. He was peering at her sister, and Irene tensed as he gave a harrumph. "You look like your mother, girl, you do, indeed."

Fully aware the viscount might think that fact something for which to denigrate his younger granddaughter, Irene moved to jump in, but to her astonishment, she saw his face and stopped. His pale blue eyes were watery, but not, she realized, because of his advanced age. Astonished, she stared as he blinked several times, then looked away, out over the gardens.

But if she thought that sign of tender sentiment would extend to her, she was mistaken. When his gaze swerved to her, he gave another sniff, one she suspected was less favorable. "You, young woman, look far more like your father. He was a handsome fellow."

As was her custom, Irene took refuge in a pert reply. "Was that a compliment, Grandfather?" she asked, pasting on a smile. "I shall take it as one, for no girl can have too many compliments."

"You've a saucy tongue in your head, girl," he said, but somehow, she fancied that he didn't seem to mind. For Clara's sake, she was glad. Nonetheless, when he returned his attention to the duchess, Irene couldn't help being relieved.

"Your friends seem a genteel pair of girls," he said grudgingly.

Irene resisted the impulse to express the hope he'd recover from the shock.

"Duchess," Lord Chalmers said, entering the conversation, "my father doesn't entertain much anymore, and prefers to remain at his house in Brentford, but I am thinking to give a house party once the Twelfth sends us all to our estates. Mine, as you may know, is in Surrey. If you would honor me, I shall send your family an invitation."

Upon the duchess receiving that idea with favor, the viscount glanced over Irene and Clara, and gave his son a nudge with his elbow. "Invite her friends, George," he added. "Girls need society. It's good for them. Now, if you will forgive us, Duchess, we must return to our guests."

He turned, and leaning heavily on his son's arm, he walked away. Her party did the same, turning in the opposite direction.

As they walked back to the pavilion, the duchess once again fell in step beside her. "That went well, don't you think?"

"Yes." Irene turned her head, looking back over her shoulder at the frail old man who had disinherited his daughter for running off with a man whose family printed newspapers, and she couldn't help wondering how long Ellesmere's good opinion would last if she managed to keep her paper and continue publishing it. "It went well for now."

WORD OF ELLESMERE's acknowledgement spread, and over the next two days, as Irene and Clara were taken to the theater and the opera and to various other engagements, they were introduced to more people than either of them could possibly remember. Their days were long, and full of activities, and amid that social whirl, even Irene was grateful for the help and valuable advice of her new lady's maid, Mrs. Holt.

She continued to supervise the paper, making liberal use of telephones and messengers. She missed her work, but it was nice, she had to admit, to have a holiday. She did not refer to her profession while in company, and thankfully, no one asked her about it. As Henry had said, even if one had to have an occupation, one could be discreet about it. Irene managed to be discreet.

Henry avoided her as much as possible, which was the proper thing to do under the circumstances. He seldom accompanied them as they mingled with his acquaintances in society. What he did with his time, to the best she could determine, was go to his club, conduct business of one sort or another, and stay away from the house in Upper Brook Street for as many hours a day as possible. He was, no doubt, happy to steer clear of her, but for her part, Irene was frustrated. His avoidance of her made things less awkward, certainly, but despite his efforts to absent himself from her company, his erotic confession still haunted her, and his kiss tormented her.

As the days went by, however, she became obsessed by a different, much more serious problem.

She was running out of time.

When subjected to Irene's delicate inquiries on the

subject, the duchess showed no signs of diminishing affection for her Italian or any inclination of changing her mind, and Henry gave her no indication he was coming to accept that fact.

She racked her brains for a solution. She talked it all over with Clara numerous times. To no avail.

She began to feel quite desperate. With only a handful of days left before her deadline was up, Irene lay in bed, wide awake, and not because of any delicious memories of kissing the Duke of Torquil. But even after going over the whole business again and again, she had no solution. If only she could seek out someone's advice.

Advice. Was that a possibility?

Irene shoved back the counterpane, got out of bed, and lit a lamp. Padding over to the writing desk beneath her window, she sat down, pulled out notepaper, and took a moment to compose her thoughts. Satisfied, she inked her pen and began to write.

Dear Lady Truelove . . .

She began at the beginning, putting the whole business down in a letter to her famous literary creation. As she wrote, she couldn't help feeling this was a pointless exercise, but she continued on. Her brain began to chide her that it was silly to think that writing herself a letter was going to resolve anything, yet she continued.

"You see, Lady Truelove," she murmured out loud as she wrote, "Torquil is convinced that Foscarelli is out only for the money, but I am not. The duchess's judgment is sound, I am sure, but what if she and I are both wrong and Torquil is right? And even if he is the one who is wrong, what would convince him that money is not this man's only motive? I had advised no dowry, only an allowance, but—"

She stopped talking and her pen stilled, and suddenly in her mind, her next move lay before her, bright and shining like a new penny. "Foscarelli has to agree to forgo the dowry," she murmured. "It's the only way Henry will let me off the hook."

Relieved that at last she had a plan, Irene put her pen down, blew out the lamp, and returned to bed. She didn't know if she would succeed, but her worry had vanished, for when her head hit the pillow, she fell instantly asleep.

The following day, she put her plan into action. Josie obtained Foscarelli's address for her, and though her face was alight with curiosity, she asked no questions. That evening, when everyone else went out to a concert and supper, she pleaded a headache, dressed herself all in black, and took a taxi up to Camden Town.

Antonio Foscarelli lived in a modest, but respectable service flat. As the taxi pulled up in front and came to a halt, Irene pulled the black veil attached to her hat down over her face. With her identity disguised from any journalists who might be watching Foscarelli's residence for signs of the duchess, or any other female who might call upon the artist, Irene stepped down from the vehicle. She paid the driver, then handed him an additional shilling. "Wait here. I will return in half an hour."

The driver tipped his cap in agreement, and she entered the building. She took the stairs to the second floor and paused in front of No. 2, the suite of rooms to the right of the staircase. Upon her knock, the door was opened by a well-dressed, very superior-looking man-servant, who took in the appearance of a veiled woman in dark clothes on his master's doorstep with perfect equanimity. She hoped that was due to his excellence as a servant and not as a testament to his master's character.

"May I help you, madam?"

Safe from prying eyes now, Irene pulled back her veil. "I wish to see Mr. Foscarelli, please."

"Whom shall I say is calling?"

"I am a friend of the duchess."

The manservant gave a slight bow and opened the door at once. "This way," he said, leading her into a parlor that, to Irene's middle-class eyes, seemed daringly bohemian. The walls were painted a vivid emerald-green and hung with gilt mirrors, evoking the mood of a Parisian salon. Tall peacock feathers stood in a vase, there were stacks of books and distinct traces of cigarette smoke, and a painting of a partially clad woman hung on the wall above the fireplace.

Irene smiled a little at the sight of it, recalling Henry's words about the artist. His intent had been to lower her opinion of Foscarelli, of course, but if this was an example of the man's work, she could see why women liked to be painted by him, for the image was excellently rendered and not at all salacious. It was, in fact, a tasteful rendering, and the subject, though beautiful, was not one of those pubescent girls that artists seem so fond of depicting in the nude. She was, perhaps, about Irene's own age, or a bit older.

"My late wife."

She turned at the sound of a man's voice, and found herself face-to-face with the man considered to be one of London's most notorious bachelors. With the fair coloring and pale skin of northern Italy, he was good-looking, but not extraordinarily so, and he was shorter than she might have expected. "A most excellent work," she answered.

"Thank you." He gestured to a settee of dark blue velvet, and Irene sat down, settling her dark skirts around her. He took the chair opposite. "My valet tells me you are a friend of the *duchessa*?"

She smiled a little. "And perhaps a friend of yours, as well."

That, understandably, surprised him. He tilted his head, studying her with a puzzled frown. "Do I know you, Signora?"

"Yes, you do, in a way. I am Lady Truelove."

Chapter 15

$\mathcal{H}$enry stared out the window as the taxi in which he was riding pulled into Thornhill Square in Camden Town. He hadn't planned to come here, and even now, after nearly forty minutes in the taxi, he wasn't the least bit sure he was doing the right thing.

He was ignoring the rules of his upbringing, the good manners and restraint of a lifetime, and his own common sense. Self-doubt wasn't an emotion he often allowed himself, but given that his whole world was a bit topsy-turvy at present, he supposed he was entitled to a little self-doubt.

Irene, of course, was the cause of much of that.

Don't you think you should meet him for yourself before you judge his character?

A question he really hadn't wanted to explore, and given all the other things that had happened that night in the library, it had been an easy one to ignore. The sailing trip, however, had forced him to accept that his mother was not going to be swayed from her course, and his only choice now was to attempt to mitigate the damage. To that end, meeting Foscarelli was no longer a choice. It had become a necessity.

The taxi stopped in front of his destination, and Henry reminded himself that even if Foscarelli turned out to be every bit the scoundrel he expected, he could not, under any circumstances, put his fist through the other man's face.

The driver opened the door. Henry drew a deep breath, put ducal pride in his pocket, and stepped out of the vehicle. Paying the fare, he instructed the driver to wait, then he entered the building and crossed the foyer to the stairs. But before he could ascend, he heard footsteps above him, and when he looked up, he saw a woman in black coming down. She turned on the landing, facing him, and he froze. So did she, hand on the balustrade, one booted foot suspended over the step in front of her.

"Henry?" she gasped, staring at him.

Appalled, he stared back at her. "Miss Deverill? What in blazes are you doing here?"

She lifted her chin, giving him a look he was coming to know well as she came down the rest of the stairs. "I might ask you the same question."

It was a question he was in no frame of mind to answer. He strode forward. "Come with me," he said, then took her arm and began pulling her—none too gently—toward the door, his only thought to get her out of here. "A woman, alone, in Camden Town, after dark," he muttered as he opened the door. "Good God, are you mad?"

"Wait," she ordered in a sibilant whisper and yanked a veil down over her face just before he propelled her out the door and down the steps.

"Do you know the risks you've taken?" he said as they crossed the sidewalk to his waiting taxi.

Her taxi was also waiting at the curb, and he waved to its driver. "Walk on," he ordered, and the man on the box gave a shrug, snapped the reins, and started his vehicle down the street.

His own driver had already climbed down and opened the door. "Sixteen Upper Brook Street," he said tersely, removed his top hat, and shoved Irene into the carriage. He followed, tossing his hat into a corner and taking the seat opposite her as the driver closed the door behind them.

"Good grief, Henry," she grumbled as he jerked the curtains closed. "There's no need to manhandle me."

"I thought I was very clear when I said you could not meet Mr. Foscarelli. It's obvious you had no compunction whatsoever about disobeying that instruction, so I have no reason to believe you would willingly obey one to accompany me into a taxi."

"I am happy to accompany you for my business here is finished." She pulled back her veil and settled her black crepe skirts around her. "I certainly never dreamt I'd encounter you here, though. I thought you couldn't meet Foscarelli without an introduction."

"I suppose that in spite of my very specific instructions, you chose to pay a call on Mr. Foscarelli out of curiosity, with no regard for your reputation or any consideration for the people who are currently introducing you into society. There were two young men lounging in doorways across the street, and I would wager my last quid that they are employed by your competition. Or do you think your fellow scandal sheets will refrain from writing about you because of some notion of professional courtesy?"

"Oh, stop exaggerating. It's dark out. I came in a taxi." She reached up, yanked out her hatpin, and removed her hat, waving the mass of black straw and chiffon at him. "I wore a veil, for heaven's sake! Really, Henry, you might give me a little credit," she added, sticking the pin through the crown and tossing the whole ghastly contraption to a corner of the carriage, where it landed on top of his own hat. "I know how to take precautions to protect myself from gossip. No one will ever know it was me."

"I'm not so sure about that. You're staying in my house, and I'm sure they saw me."

"Well, the fact that you can't be discreet isn't my fault! Besides, if anything, they'll think I'm your mother."

"Odd, but I don't find that possibility particularly comforting. And," he added, his ire rising higher, "discretion isn't even the most important consideration. What about your safety? You would put that at risk just to satisfy your curiosity?"

"I didn't go to see Foscarelli out of curiosity."

"Why, then?"

"I'll tell you my reason if you tell me yours. Are you here to try again to buy him off? Because you won't have any success."

"I know that. As I told you, Mama spiked my guns on that score. I was hoping, however, that he might be persuaded to accept a smaller dowry than the one he'd finagled out of Mama."

She blinked, startled. "So you've accepted their marriage as inevitable?"

"I'm not waving the white flag just yet, trust me," he muttered. "But there's no harm in preparing for the worst. And now that I've explained my reason for being here, I'd like to hear yours. What reason could you possibly have for jeopardizing your safety in this way?"

She sighed, looking away. "Thornhill Square is a perfectly respectable neighborhood," she said, but the diffidence in her voice told him she knew he was right about the risks involved. "It's safe enough."

"Safe enough?" He studied her lovely profile, reminded of what consequences might have resulted from her decision to go gadding about northeast London alone at night. He leaned forward and grabbed her arms, forcing her to look at him. "Thornhill Square might be safe, I suppose, but the neighborhoods you traversed to get here are most definitely not. What if the cab had broken a wheel, or one of the taxi's horses had gone lame? God—" He broke off, for contemplating what might have happened to her was more than he could bear, and he gave her a little shake. "Where are your wits, Irene?"

She smiled at him, and Henry sucked in his breath. Even in the dim light, her smile disarmed him, and his anger faded into bewilderment. "Why in heaven's name are you smiling like that when I'm chiding you up hill and down dale?" he demanded.

"You called me Irene."

"Sorry," he apologized at once, and let her go, feeling as if he were coming utterly undone. "I know you gave me leave, but nonetheless, I should not have done it. Put it down to frayed nerves. This week's events have worn them to a nub."

"You're concerned about me." The notion seemed to please her. Her smile widened, and he felt the warmth of it seeping into him, settling into his very bones and bringing a pleasure borne not only of desire, but of something deeper and more profound that he wasn't sure he wanted to explore.

He looked away, embarrassed. "Of course I am. Any gentleman would be."

"You say that with such conviction," she murmured, "and yet, there are many gentlemen who wouldn't care two straws."

That was truer than he liked to think.

"I'm not used to that," she said musingly.

He looked at her, curious, and found her smile had faded to a serious expression. "Not used to what?"

"Having someone be concerned about my well-being. It's . . ." She paused. "It's nice," she whispered, sounding surprised.

"Yes, well . . ." He took a moment, working to regain his equilibrium. "I hope, now that your curiosity has been satisfied about the man who aspires to become my stepfather, you won't be making any more jaunts to Camden Town after dark?"

"I already told you, it wasn't curiosity that brought me here. I came for much the same reason you did. I was hoping to persuade him to accept an allowance in lieu of a dowry."

"I see. And did you have any success?"

"No, because he needs a substantial capital sum. It's not for himself—"

Henry interrupted with an unamused laugh. "Of course not."

She ignored the sarcasm. "Did you know he has land in Italy? And twelve brothers and sisters? They have an olive farm near the Amalfi coast that his grandfather let go to rack and ruin. His father's dead, and since he's the eldest, it's up to him to support them all. That's why he needs a dowry."

"And I daresay he tells this heartbreaking story to anyone who will listen. Something, no doubt, about his poor but lovely mama, widowed so tragically, and of his dear, dear siblings—perhaps one a young sister with consumption? He may have mentioned royal blood, too—his family's long-lost—and wholly fabricated—connection to the duchy of Milan, perhaps?"

She made a face. "No royalty, no consumption. Just six hundred acres of olive groves and grape vines. They are neglected and overgrown, but could be made profitable, if only—"

"If only he had money. Without that . . ." He paused for an exaggerated sigh. "I fear doom is upon his entire family."

She frowned. "Really, Henry, I'm trying to explain his circumstances."

"About which I assume I am supposed to care?"

"Well, you should," she flared, positively scowling

now, "since he is likely to become a member of your family in a few days, a possibility you have acknowledged yourself. The point is that he has land. Surely that raises him a notch or two in your aristocratic circle?"

"Land doesn't make a man a gentleman."

"So what does? A title? A proper place in the stud books? God, Henry," she added before he could answer, "you are the stuffiest, stubbornest, most aggravating man I have ever met." She fell to her knees, grasping the facings of his evening jacket in her fists, crushing the flower in his buttonhole and filling the carriage with the heavy scent of carnation.

"And do you want to know the most aggravating thing about you?" she demanded, punctuating each word with another tug on his lapels. "It's that every time I start to think what an amazingly attractive man you are, you open your mouth and *ruin* it!"

Henry blinked, startled, certain he hadn't heard correctly. "You think I'm attract—"

"Henry?" She eased between his legs before he could think to stop her, and pulled him closer. "Just shut up," she said and kissed him.

Her lips were every bit as soft as before, but even hotter, even sweeter, and the pleasure of it was so acute, it was like pain. Desire began coursing through his body at once, hammering through his brain, pulsing through his blood.

He grabbed her arms while he still could, and pulled back. "Irene, for God's sake."

She followed his retreat, and cut off any more words with another kiss, a quick one to his mouth, but whatever he'd intended to say went straight out of his head as she trailed soft kisses along his cheek, to his ear and back again.

He could not find the will to shove her away again. He could not move at all.

She tilted her head and left another trail of kisses along his opposite cheek, then she pressed another to his lips. At last, she drew back. Her lips a few inches from his, she waited, and he knew if he was going to call a halt to her sweet seduction, now was the moment.

Inside, he began to shake.

She was so close to him that her breathing mingled with his. Along with the scent of his boutonniere, he could smell the fragrance of her skin, her hair. Desire was clawing at him now, blurring with his reason, blotting out his good sense.

At last, she moved to withdraw, but it brought no relief. An agonized sound tore from his lips, his hands gripped her arms, and he shoved her back onto her own seat, but instead of letting her go, he followed her, falling to his knees as he maneuvered her body onto the seat of the growler.

He captured her mouth with his. Her lips parted, and at once the kiss was deep, open, and lush, unleashing all the lust he'd been battling since they met. The need for her that raged through his body right now shocked even him, and he couldn't imagine what she felt. When she made a wordless sound against his mouth, he forced himself to slow down.

He cupped her face in his hands and gentled the kiss, tasting her in soft nibbles, suckling her lower lip. He pressed kisses to her chin, then her neck, but though he'd thought to work his way down, her high collar prevented him from that exploration. If he was going to inflame her as he was inflamed, he had to start lower and work his way up.

He slid his hand down from her cheek, over the full curve of her breast, cursing whoever had invented the corset, and moved farther down, over her thigh and down to her knee. Grasping folds of black crepe and linen in his fist, he slid her skirts up and slipped his hand beneath.

He cupped his hand around her calf and glided upward along the side of her leg to the top of her stocking, where his fingertips worked beneath her garter and stocking hem. When he touched bare skin, it was like hot silk.

Still kissing her, he grazed the back of her knee with his fingertips, and she moaned against his mouth. Her hands raked through his hair. She cupped his head, pulling him closer, wanting more.

He gave it, moving his hand higher, gliding his palm over her hip, and then moved to ease between her thighs.

She jerked in shock and broke the kiss, crying out. Her hands came down, flattening against his chest.

He went still, knowing that if maidenly panic impelled her to call a halt now, he'd have to let her go, and if that happened, he'd have to climb out of the cab and hurl himself into the path of oncoming traffic.

Given the confined space and her many layers of clothing, his options for arousing her were limited. He decided words were his best bet.

"Irene, I want to touch you," he said, his hand working between her closed thighs in infinitesimal increments. "Just let me touch you. It's all I've thought about."

She relaxed a little, and then a little more, and he was able to push his fingers inside the slit of her drawers.

She was hot, slick, fully aroused, inflaming his senses. She moaned as he began to caress her, slowly at first, and then faster.

"Oh!" she groaned, her arms tightening, her hot face buried against his neck. "Oh, oh."

She moved on the seat, her hip brushing against his groin, and a shudder of pure pleasure rocked his body, forcing him to stop. "Christ," he muttered, and straightened on his knees, striving to hold back.

After a moment, he leaned down, pressing kisses to her face as he began to caress her again.

"Irene," he murmured, saying her name as he'd been saying it to himself for a week of tortured nights, while the tip of his finger slid back and forth between the secret folds of her, spreading her moisture, until her body was moving in desperate jerks and her every breath was a pant.

She was close to orgasm, he knew, and he pulled back so that he could look into her face. Her eyes were closed, her lips parted, a fine bead of sweat on her brow as she strove toward climax.

"That's it, Irene," he murmured, coaxing her, wanting more than anything to see her come. "That's it. You're almost there."

He didn't know if she knew what he meant, if she had ever pleasured herself, but when she cried out, her hips arching into his hand, he knew her face was the most beautiful thing he'd ever seen, and the soft cries of her pleasure were the sweetest thing he'd ever heard.

He worked to give her every bit of sensation her body could derive, and when at last she sagged back against the seat with a sated sigh, he kissed her mouth again and pulled his hand from beneath her skirt.

He'd have liked to think he could have resisted taking her virginity in a carriage, but as many times as he'd reflect on this moment later, he'd never be absolutely sure he could be that heroic. Either way, Fate never gave him the chance to decide.

The carriage jerked to a halt.

Quick as lightning, he yanked her skirts down. He flung himself back, away from her, and it felt as if he were tearing himself in two. "Go in the servant's entrance," he told her as she sat up and he reached for her hat. "And up to your room as fast as you can. If anyone sees you and asks where you've been," he added as he plunked the black monstrosity down on top of her head and tugged the veil into place, "you were working, and visiting with your father. Since you're wearing mourning, you'll have to make up a dead relative and wear black for a month, so let's hope no one sees you. No matter what, you did not go to Camden Town."

The carriage door opened, but she didn't move to get out. Instead, she stared at him, wide-eyed and flushed, looking deliciously tousled and completely overwhelmed.

"Yes, I know," he said, and leaned forward, grasping her arms and pulling her toward him. "It's rather shattering, isn't it?" He kissed her, hard, before she could answer and released her. "Go."

This time she obeyed, clamoring out of the growler,

crossing the sidewalk, and descending the steps to the servant's entrance. He waited until she was inside and the door had closed behind her, then he looked at the driver waiting by the taxi door. "White's," he said. He needed a drink.

Chapter 16

*T*he family was out, and the servants were having their evening meal when Irene entered the house, and she was able to traverse the downstairs corridor, pass the servants' dining room, and race up the backstairs to her bedroom without encountering anyone.

In leaving the house to meet with Foscarelli, she hadn't given much thought to what the servants would think of her going out or coming in at night. They were already aware of her occupation in the City, and though they surely disapproved of it and of her just as much as anyone upstairs might do, Irene had never been all that concerned about having anyone's approval, above stairs or below. In this particular circumstance, however, she was heartily grateful to get into her room sight unseen.

She shut her door behind her with a shuddering gasp of relief, and leaned back against it, a move that tilted her enormous hat up behind her head.

She ripped it off and tossed it aside, then once again fell back against the door, panting not only from her race to her room, but from everything that had gone before.

What Henry had done to her—oh, God, what had he done? His kiss, his hands, wringing sensations from her she'd never felt in her life, sensations she'd never have dreamt were possible. Such wicked, delicious excitement, catching her in a swirling vortex of pleasure that had carried her higher and higher, until . . . she couldn't think how to describe it. There were no words for what Henry had done to her.

It's rather shattering, isn't it?

"To say the least," she whispered, pressing a hand to her chest and taking in deep breaths of air, trying to curb the chaos inside her. But it was no good. Her heart was racing, her body was tingling, her skin was flushed with heat. Every cell of her seemed lit from the inside with a blissful euphoria. She laughed and fell back against the door. She felt absolutely glorious.

HENRY FELT LIKE hell. He had his drink—in fact, he had three, but even three whiskies proved a wholly inadequate remedy for what ailed him. He ordered a room prepared and sent one of White's footmen for his valet and a change of clothes, for he knew there was no way he could go home in this condition. He could not bear the thought of sitting across from Irene at the breakfast table tomorrow, drinking tea and eating toast and making conversation with her and her sister and his siblings as if it were just an ordinary morning. He'd been doing that for nearly a fortnight. He couldn't endure doing it again.

He took his bath cold, which helped a bit, and he spent the night at his club, though sleeping had little to do with it, for the image of her face and the echoes of her passion haunted him all night. But he finally drifted off about dawn, and by midmorning, after a hot breakfast and a shave, he felt ready to do what he knew needed to be done. It was vital that he talk with her, and for that, he needed all the resolve he could muster. Otherwise, he might very well pin her to the nearest wall and ravish her on the spot.

In the early afternoon, he went home, where his mother immediately pulled him aside for a brief conversation, and what she told him underscored the fact that he needed a private word with Irene as soon as possible. Unfortunately, she was not in the house. She had gone, her sister informed him, to work at the paper.

He had his carriage brought around, and twenty minutes later, he was standing on the sidewalk in front of the plate glass door that led into the offices of *Society Snippets*.

How strange life was, how unexpected. Two weeks ago, he'd thought he was the master of his world and what happened in it. And then Irene Deverill had come along, obliterating that illusion. In many ways, he was an utter mess as a result, but when he thought of her as she'd been last night, he wouldn't change a thing. The problem was, chaos, unsated desire, and torture, however sweet, could not be borne indefinitely. He had to get clear. If he did not, his annihilation or her ruin would be the result.

He opened the door. The bell jangled as he went inside, a faint sound barely audible above the din of the printing press that was thundering away at one end of the room, but the dark-haired young woman operating it heard the bell just the same. She glanced over her shoulder, and he recognized her as one of the journalists he'd seen on his second visit here. She stopped the press at once and came bustling over to him, and above the gold-rimmed spectacles perched on the tip of her nose, her dark eyes studied him with all the avid interest of her profession.

"Miss Deverill?" he inquired, handing over his card.

She took it, but didn't read it. "Of course, Your Grace," she said, making it clear she was already well aware of who he was. She shoved up her spectacles and pasted on an expression of brisk efficiency. "If you will follow me?"

She led him to the closed door of Irene's office, gave it a sharp knock, then opened it. "His Grace, the Duke of Torquil," she announced, then stepped aside to let him pass through.

Irene stood up as he came in, and as the door closed behind him, her radiant smile hit him with all the impact of a kick in the stomach. "Henry."

He set his jaw and removed his hat. "Miss Deverill," he said and bowed.

When he straightened, her smile was gone. Her chin went up a notch, reminding him of her pride, and it hurt him to know he was wounding that pride. After last night, she had reason to expect more of him than ducal formality, but though he felt like a cad, he could not allow, he did not dare allow, any intimacy between them now. He wasn't strong enough to stand it.

"I hope you are well," he said, taking refuge in polite civilities.

"I am. And you?"

"Perfectly sound," he lied. He gave a cough and paused, looking down at his hat, working to come up with another polite inquiry so that he might ease his way into his reason for coming. "Quite busy. We are preparing to leave London for Ravenwood."

"Your estate in Hampshire?"

"Yes. We go on Friday. That's the Twelfth, you know."

"Ah, yes," she said, a strangled sound that told him small talk was proving as difficult for her as for him. "The Glorious Twelfth. Will . . . will your family be hunting the grouse, or sailing the Solent?"

"Oh, sailing, of course." He smiled a little, remembering her first evening in his home. "We are a sailing family, after all."

"Yes." She shifted her weight and glanced around, reminding him this aftermath must be as embarrassing for her as it was agonizing for him.

He forced himself to come to the point. "Mama is to marry Foscarelli. She—" He broke off, for he still found his mother's marriage a difficult thing to accept, but after a moment, he forced himself to go on. "She wanted to marry him on Tuesday, but I have persuaded her to wait one more week. Since we are decamping for the country, there is a great deal to do, both here and at Ravenwood, and it would be a great burden on Carlotta to supervise the entire settling-in. I cannot be of help, for I have far too much to do with the estate to assist with the household."

"So . . ." She paused, seeming puzzled. "Are you requiring me to go with you, then? Do you think another week will enable us to change your mother's mind?"

"No, I fear we are past that point. She is determined, and I doubt any persuasion will avail. Mama will journey down to Hampshire with us on Friday to help at Ravenwood, then return on Monday and marry Foscarelli on Tuesday at the Registry Office. They will, she has told me, stay at their new home in Chiswick for a week or two, then they plan to take a honeymoon to Italy, meet his family, that sort of thing."

His words were stilted, awkward, and something of what he felt must have communicated itself to her, for she said, "I know it is a serious concern and disappointment to you, and I'm sorry for that."

"You mustn't think I blame you in any way."

"That's a change from twelve days ago."

"Yes."

"I've failed in the task you set me on." She looked down at her desk, making a show of straightening her blotter, then looked up, squaring her shoulders. "Are you going to take my paper?"

The question shocked him, though he knew it should not have done. He'd set these stakes, and he certainly hadn't given her any reason to believe him too much of a gentleman to follow through. He could never take from her something she loved. "I never would have taken it, Irene," he said. "I know you probably don't believe that, but I was angry, and desperate, and—I am not ashamed to admit it—afraid for my mother's future. In hindsight, I see that my expectation that you might be able to persuade her against her course was unrealistic, not to mention unreasonable. And I am sorry for it."

"You were only trying to protect her. I see that now."

"Yes, but one can't protect everyone all the time. Not

even me." He managed a laugh. "Especially not me. Which brings me to what I really came here to say."

She frowned, looking understandably bewildered.

He crossed the room, moving to stand before her, glad there was the barrier of a desk between them. "As I said, we go on Friday. Angela wondered if your sister might come, too, if that would be acceptable? I do not think," he added before she could answer, "it would be appropriate for you to accompany her."

The hurt that shimmered across her face hurt him, too, like a knife in his chest. "Right," she mumbled and looked away. "Of course not."

"Irene, you mustn't misunderstand—"

"I couldn't anyway," she said, her voice overly bright. "I've been away from the paper far too much as it is. And there's my father to consider. He's not well, as you know, and . . ."

Her voice trailed off, and for the life of him, he could not mask what he felt. "I can't have you there, Irene," he said, throwing his own pride to the winds, his voice a harsh and desperate rasp. "I can't. Not under these circumstances. My past conduct makes it clear I cannot be trusted in your company."

She ducked her chin. "Because of last night," she whispered, pink tinting her cheeks.

"Yes. And because of that night in the library, and the images of you with me that plague my imagination, images you would find even more shocking than my deeds thus far have been."

"Oh." The sound was faint, hushed, and it was a long moment before she spoke again. "And yet," she whispered, looking up, "all I can think about right now is throwing my pride out the window, coming around this desk, and flinging myself at you in the most immodest way."

Henry froze, riveted, staring at her. The floor felt if it was slipping out from beneath him, along with all his honorable resolutions. "Irene, you have no idea what you're saying. My . . . desire for you remains unabated."

The blush in her cheeks deepened. "Yes. I . . . after last night, that fact is rather self-evident."

"When you are near, I forget that I am a gentleman, and if distance is not put between us, I fear that I will continue to impose my attentions upon you. What do you think will happen to you if that continues?"

"I . . ." She paused, licking her lips as if they were dry, a gesture that drew him like a moth to flame. "I'm not exactly sure."

"Forgive me, then, for I must be blunt. You are a virgin. You've never lain with a man. I'm right in assuming that, aren't I?"

Her cheeks were scarlet now. "Of course I haven't! Heavens, do you think I could ever let any other man touch me the way you—"

"Just so," he cut in. "I must get clear of you, for if I do not, I will continue to seduce you. It is a galling thing for me to admit," he rushed on before she could reply, "but I doubt I would be able to stop myself, and I fear I will bring all the advantages of my superior experience to bear. If you do not succumb, I will continue to be in torment, and if you do, the consequences for you—for both of us—would be dire."

"Sometimes, I think you think too much about consequences, Henry."

"Yes, well, I have good reason to do so, given my past."

"What do you mean?"

He looked down at his hat, crushing the brim in his fists. He did not want to tell her, but he knew he had to. He had to make her understand what, precisely, he was capable of. He looked up and met her gaze. "I was married once."

"What?" Her pretty hazel eyes went wide. "But—"

"No one knows. Well, Mama knows, but no one else. Not even my brother and sisters. It was a long time ago. I was at university. I was only nineteen, she was seventeen. She wasn't my sort. I persuaded her to elope, and we kept the marriage dark. It was not—" He paused, drawing a deep breath. "It was not a happy union. We separated completely within a year, and we did not see each other again after that. She died the following year. Cholera."

"I see." She bit her lip. "I'm so sorry."

He shook his head, waving aside sympathy. "It was a long time ago. It doesn't matter now."

She frowned, puzzled. "If it doesn't matter, then why tell me? What does it have to do with us . . . with our situation?"

That, of course, was the tricky part, the sordid part. He did not attempt to coat it with sugar. "She was the daughter of a shopkeeper at Cambridge, a tobacconist. I fell for her, utterly and completely, the first time I ever saw her over a counter, before I even knew her name. I do not pretend that my intentions were honorable; indeed, they were not. I was the son of a duke, we were not suited at all, and I knew it, but I was determined to have her. The problem for me was that she was a virtuous, innocent girl, and I was wild with passion, oblivious to reason—Irene, why the devil are you smiling?"

"Because I'm so very glad you are telling me this."

"Glad? Good God, why?"

"Well, to be honest, Henry, you play your cards far too close to your chest for my liking."

Since he felt as if he must be emanating lust twenty-four hours a day for all the world to see, the knowledge that he wasn't was rather a relief. "I am not the most open of men, I grant you."

"That's putting it mildly. Most of the time, I've no idea at all what you're thinking or feeling."

"Given the things I'm thinking about you," he muttered, his gaze sliding away, "that is probably a good thing."

"No, it isn't. And that's why I'm glad. The idea that you would trust me with such personal information, particularly in light of my profession . . . it is . . . quite astonishing." She paused, laughing a little. "Extraordinary, really. I'm honored that you trust me to that extent, and I promise you, I shan't tell anyone."

"Of course you won't. I mean, I know that." He shifted his weight, keenly uncomfortable, and looked at her again. "But given the situation, and what is between us, it's necessary for you to know my history."

"Why? Because you think that history is repeating—" She broke off, her eyes going wide again. "Good Lord, Henry, you're not thinking of marrying me, are you? You're not . . . are you falling in love with me?"

"It isn't love, Irene. At least, not the sort that would make for companionable marriage. That's what I'm trying—badly, I admit—to explain. You are only the second woman I have ever met for whom my feelings have been too strong to be denied." He gave a humorless laugh. "I have a penchant, it seems, for women who are not suited to my life, and it is a life I cannot change. I want you, yes. I want to kiss you, lay my hands on you as I did last night, ravish you, and bed you, and—forgive me if I presume too much—if I am near you for much longer, that might happen. If it does, I will have ruined you, just as I—" He stopped, for even now, over a decade later, it hurt to say it. "As I ruined her. We would then have to marry."

"I don't see why—"

"And yet," he interrupted, feeling like the lowest cad a man could be, "I would do it. At this moment, I am so vulnerable where you are concerned, so weak, that if you agreed to do it, I would marry you, just so that I could have you. Yes, I would make that exact mistake all over again."

"I see," she said, her voice cool, hot gold sparks in her eyes. "So marriage to me would be a *mistake*?"

He did not want to argue. Normally, he did not shy from battle with her, but today, he had no stomach for it. "I know that I always manage to say the wrong thing with you, and I don't know precisely why that is, but either way, do you not also think it would be a mistake for us to marry? Putting it another way, would you want to marry me? Join your life forever with mine? Be my duchess?"

The appalled look on her face told him with brutal clarity the answer he already knew. "God, no."

Despite the fact that he had expected no other answer, he was a bit nettled by such an emphatically negative reaction to a position that thousands of other women would jump through fire to attain.

"I'm not a tobacconist's daughter, granted," she went on, "but I'm not society, and I've no desire to be."

"Just so," he said, still nettled.

"I'd no longer be able to demonstrate for women's rights."

"My duchess could certainly not march in the streets, if that is what you mean. And our family is political. We have always supported the Tories, but none of the parties advocate suffrage—"

"Well, there you are! I won't give up fighting for the vote, Henry. Never. And I'd have to give up *Society Snippets*, something I cannot ever imagine doing. I love my work, far more than I could ever enjoy being a duchess. Not that I really know what duchesses do, exactly, other than go to Ascot and hold dinner parties, and I only know that because we report on those sorts of doings all the time. But I know enough to know I should hate being a duchess, and I should make an utter mess of it and be bored silly, and—"

"We seem to be in agreement, then," he said, mustering his dignity in the face of this withering assessment of what being his duchess would be like. He also attempted to accept with grace the humbling fact that she'd prefer to run a scandal sheet rag than be his wife. But then, he'd known that all along. From the beginning, that particular fact was one of the things he found so damnably attractive about her. "And that leaves us nowhere, as I've been trying to explain."

"There is another choice, one it's clear you haven't thought of. We could have an affair."

It was his turn to be appalled. "We can't do that."

Much to his consternation, she gave a laugh. "Why not? It isn't a sin, what we feel."

"Isn't it? Find a vicar who agrees with you, and I'll concede the point."

"What I mean is that I don't regard it as a sin, regardless of doctrine. Do you?"

"I don't know." He tried to consider the question rationally, but he knew his ability to be rational could not be trusted, not when it came to her. "I was raised to believe it a sin, as I'm sure you were. More importantly, most other people think it is—and that goes straight to the heart of it. We are both unmarried. In everyone else's eyes—if not our own—an affair between us is fornication, and unspeakably immoral."

"When you touched me, Henry, I did not feel immoral." She looked at him, her face softened and lovely, calling to the devil inside him.

He persisted, as much to remind himself as to explain to her. "The consequences would be dire, especially for you. You've been accepted into society through your grandfather, and if anyone found out we were intimate, you would instantly become soiled goods. You would come to bitterly regret it, and I would hate that—"

"I would not," she interrupted. "I can't imagine any circumstance in which I could ever regret a love affair with you, Henry."

The tenderness in her voice was almost his undoing, and he worked to push her further away before he gave in to this unspeakable idea. "Such lofty sentiments are easy to say, but what of your family? What happens when the world finds out, you are disgraced, and your family is disgraced along with you? What happens when your competitors splash your ruined name across their papers and discuss our sordid affair with relish? Do you think they wouldn't?"

"Well, of course we'd have to be extremely careful! I shouldn't like anyone to find out, for Clara's sake. And for yours."

"But not for your own?"

She smiled, as if her own ruin was a trivial concern. "Society isn't going to accept me either way, Henry. These two weeks have been more enjoyable than I had ever thought they would be, granted, but this sort of thing can't last, not for me. I run a scandal sheet newspaper. I have a career. I am a suffragist. How long do you think it will be before Ellesmere finds out I have no intention of giving up these things or my radical views? Clara will be all right. He's taken a shine to her, and she can still benefit from his good will and that of your family, regardless of the outrageous things I do."

"I'm not sure how much use my family will be in regard to protecting your sister once Mama marries her Italian. But of course, we would do what we could for both of you."

"As I said, it's wasted on me. Society, I fear, will never accept me, regardless of whether anything happens between us or not."

"That doesn't have to be the case. As we discussed before, you'd have to avoid flaunting your profession, and you'd have to soften your views, but—"

"Soften them how? By not doing work I love? By abandoning a cause I believe in? I won't, not for you, not for my father, not even for Clara. I am working to form a union with other women to petition for the vote, and when that happens, my competitors, I have no doubt, will take great delight in writing accounts of my un-womanly doings in their papers, especially when I've been arrested and the police have dragged me to jail."

"Oh, God," he groaned, terribly afraid that prediction might one day come true.

"So you see? I fear condemnation and ruin are inevitable for me, one way or another, and I do not want to miss this chance with you in order to avoid what is inevitable. Such an association between us is also a risk for you, however, so if you . . ." She paused, looking suddenly uncertain. "If you don't want me under those conditions, I would understand."

Not want her? God, that she could think such a thing, even for a moment. Didn't she know by now he'd crawl to the devil on his belly in order to have his way with her? But it wasn't only about him and what he wanted. He knew that well enough. He forced himself to remain on honorable ground.

"There are different kinds of ruin, Irene." He paused, considering how best to say it, but there was no delicate way to conduct an indelicate conversation. "Even if we are discreet, even if can conceal our affair from all prying eyes—which is difficult enough—there is always the possibility of a baby to consider. At that point, discretion goes to the wall."

She blushed again, and he hoped perhaps he was finally making her see sense, but her next words told him otherwise. "Yes, well . . . ahem . . . I've already thought of that."

He was never, he decided, going to understand this

woman. That fact, alas, did not dim his desire for her in the slightest degree. "You have?"

She gave him a look of reproach. "Well, really, Henry, I may advocate following one's passions, but I'm not an idiot."

"Of course," he agreed at once, not knowing what else to say. "But you are an advocate of free love, apparently. What of the love children that accompany it?"

"Well, as we've been discussing, I do think people ought to be free to love whom they choose, as long as it truly is a choice by both parties and neither are already married to someone else."

Despite the damnable circumstances, he couldn't help a laugh. "You realize your view on this is completely opposite that of society? Among my set it's perfectly all right for married people to have affairs, just not the unmarried people."

"All the more reason your set has its priorities completely backwards. But as to children, no, given society's strictures, bringing children into such a situation would be cruel. For they would be illegitimate and condemned for what is not their fault."

"And, therefore . . . ?"

"I seem to recall at the last suffragist meeting I attended, there was mention of . . . of . . ." She stopped, her gaze veering away as she touched a hand self-consciously to the back of her neck. "Ways to . . . umm . . . prevent that . . . ahem . . . particular eventuality."

Two weeks ago, Henry would have been shocked all out of countenance that a young lady would know about such things, that anyone would tell her about them or that she would be talking about them, especially to him. He'd have been appalled to learn he'd be discussing openly such topics as illegitimate children and free love, or that he would be considering the possibility, even theoretically, of deflowering a woman to whom he was not married. Even with Elena, he'd at least waited until after the wedding to claim that honor. Having an illicit affair with a heretofore innocent, unmarried woman was so far beyond the pale, it was unconscionable. But his conscience, he knew, was weak as water where this particular woman was concerned. As for her, he was coming to accept that Irene was a law unto herself. She had a way of blowing all his notions of proper behavior to bits. Rather like dynamite.

Perhaps he was suffering from some form of shell-shock as a result, because his brain was not willing him to slam down this topic and make his body walk out the door. And since he was well past the point of refusing to discuss it altogether, there was no point in dancing around what she meant with the use of silly euphemisms. In for a penny, in for a pound. "You are talking of prophylactics," he said bluntly. "Granted, they prevent pregnancy as well as disease, but they are also illegal. You know that, surely?"

"Well, yes. Which is why you'd have to be the one to procure them. You're a duke. The police would never arrest you."

That, he was forced to admit, was true. "You seem to have given this a great deal of thought," he said slowly.

"Yes," she said. "I have. Oh, Henry, you said yourself it's proving impossible for you to stay away from me, and you must know that I am finding it every bit as hard to stay away from you."

He started to speak, but she leaned over the desk, putting her fingers to his mouth to stop him. "If that kiss in the library didn't make it plain enough, surely that carriage ride did."

At any other time, he might have found it very gratifying indeed to hear her make such an admission aloud, and the touch of her fingers was sending dangerous impulses through him, but at this moment, his conscience could not be allowed to savor either of those. He grasped her wrist, pulled her hand down, and let her go. "And after last night, you feel overwhelmed. I understand that, and it is completely my fault—"

She laughed, much to his consternation. "Why? You are wholly to blame because in the face of your attentions, I'm helpless to resist you? I shall have to purchase some sol volatile, I can see, or I shall faint dead away the next time you kiss me."

"Please, Irene, do not tease me, I beg you. Not now."

She sobered at once. "I'm not overwhelmed, Henry. I know just what I'm proposing, and I'm making that proposition freely, that I promise you."

He turned away, walking to the tiny window of her office and staring out at the brick wall of the solidly middle class house next door, appreciating all the ramifications as he knew she could not. "But what I'm trying to explain to you is that it is not an informed choice. Not for you. It can't be."

He forced himself to turn and meet her eyes, to face in her gaze the same yearning he felt inside himself and turn it down. "You can't even begin to know what losing your innocence feels like, Irene. No one can, until it happens. And once it's done, there's no going back, regardless of the consequences. You have no idea what giving up your innocence to a man really means."

"That's true, Henry. But," she added softly, "you are the only man I have ever met that I have imagined losing my innocence to. If it isn't you, I doubt it would ever be anyone. I don't want that."

With those words, so simple and so sweet, he'd lost, and he knew it. From the very beginning, even before that kiss in the library and that hot, sweet carriage ride, even when all this had been nothing but his own erotic imaginings, he'd wanted this very thing from her, and despite the fact that it went against everything he'd been raised to believe about right and wrong, he knew his answer was inevitable. Perhaps he'd always known that.

"Very well," he said. "I will make the arrangements."

He turned abruptly away before either of them could change their minds, but he did pause at the door for one more thing. "You'll need that god-awful hat," he said without looking at her, then he opened the door and walked out.

Chapter 17

$\mathcal{A}$s Irene watched the door swing shut behind Henry, she felt so dizzy, she had to sit down. Suggesting an illicit affair, after all, wasn't the sort of thing a girl did every day.

Still, her bold suggestion wasn't the only thing that was making her wobbly at the knees. The knowledge that he had wanted a girl with such passion that he had defied all the dictates of society in order to have her was every bit as stunning. Irene thought of that day two weeks ago when he'd come storming in here, when she'd thought him so cold, and she wanted to laugh at the idea. Henry, she was now discovering, was as cold as wildfire. Who'd ever have thought it?

She knew the course they were about to embark upon was a reckless one, mad, foolhardy, even. And yet, she did not care. She was so exhilarated by the thought of it that she could barely breathe. She was willing to take any risk, pay any price. For to not be with him seemed unthinkable now.

By the end of the day, she had moved back into the house in Belford Row, after assuring Clara that of course she must go to Hampshire on Friday with the duke's family, and happily refusing all the entreaties from her sister to journey down with them to Ravenwood.

She also ignored her father's disappointment and disapproval at her decision to return home. Papa, as fond as she was of him, had long ago ceased to be someone whose approval she required. In the past, that fact had always made her feel both sad and a bit guilty, but now, in light of the course she was about to embark upon, she was glad of the emotional distance that had long existed between them, for it made what she intended to do infinitely easier.

The wait was the hardest part. All day Sunday, she could think of nothing but Henry and what it would be like to have his hands on her. Even during church services, God help her, she had thought only of him.

On Monday, she received a letter from him with instructions, and that evening, she packed a small valise and informed her father that she missed Clara so much she was going back to spend the remaining nights before the other girl's departure at Upper Brook Street. She then slipped a long, dark cloak over her clothes, donned what Henry had called her "god-awful hat" with its concealing veil, and took a taxi to a small hotel in an obscure street of St. John's Wood. There, she presented herself at the front desk as Mrs. Jones. Mr.

Jones, the expressionless concierge informed her, had already arrived and was in his own rooms—rooms that adjoined her own. He hoped Mrs. Jones found that an acceptable arrangement?

"Of course," she said, trying to sound wholly natural when she felt as if hundreds of butterflies were fluttering around in her stomach.

Her case was taken by the bellman, who led her up to the second floor, and down a short, dimly lit corridor to a pair of doors at the end. He unlocked the door to the right, opened it, and stepped aside for her to enter. When she did, he followed her, setting her suitcase beside a closed door that she could only conclude led to the room next door.

"Shall you be needing a maid, madam? If so, I can have one sent up."

She tore her gaze from the closed door. "No, I shan't require a maid, thank you," she said, looking around as he began to draw the curtains closed. It wasn't a large room, but it was unexpectedly pretty, with walls of robin's egg blue and darker blue draperies. There were gilded wall sconces, walnut furnishings, and a sizable brass bed.

Irene's heart thumped hard in her chest.

Behind her, the bellman gave a delicate cough. "Will there be anything else, madam?"

She turned, realizing he had moved toward the door and was waiting, his white-gloved hand poised by his side in a discreet fashion. At once, she opened her handbag. "No, thank you," she answered, pulling a shilling from her coin purse and placing it in his palm. "You may go."

"Very good, madam. If you require anything, the bell pull is beside the bed."

He departed, closing the door behind him. Irene removed her cloak and hat, but she'd barely tossed them onto a chair before a knock sounded from the adjoining room. She crossed over to the door, and with a deep, steadying breath, she opened it to find Henry on the other side, and the sight of him in his shirtsleeves gave her a jolt of such surprise, she laughed.

His mouth curved up a bit. "Nervous?"

"Terribly, but—" She paused, studying him for a moment. "I just realized," she said, still smiling a little, "that this is the first time I've ever seen you without a jacket."

That particular fact seemed to underscore the intimacy of their situation and reminded her of the ramifications of what they were about to do. But he spoke again, giving Irene no time to think about how nervous she was. "I hope the bathtub meets with your approval?"

"The what?" She watched him nod to something behind her, and she turned to find that her room possessed an adjoining bath. Through its open doorway, she could see copper pipes and a white, enameled tub. "Heavens, when I came in, I didn't even notice it."

"You wound me, Irene. It took me all afternoon to find an appropriately discreet hotel that possessed a private bath."

Laughing, she turned and looked at him again. "Thank you. That was a very chivalrous thing to do."

He didn't laugh with her. "Not so chivalrous," he said, looking into her eyes, and her laughter faded at the intensity she saw in his. "I'm hoping you'll share it."

At those words, Irene's heart slammed hard against her ribs, and the butterflies in her stomach transformed into a flock of panicked birds. He seemed to sense it, for he reached through the doorway and cupped her face, his palm warm against her cheek. "Are you absolutely sure you want to do this?"

"Yes." She nodded, confirming it to herself as well as to him. "I don't think I've ever been more sure of anything in my life, Henry. So . . ." She paused a moment. "What happens now?"

"There are several ways we can proceed. If you're hungry, I can order dinner, and we can dine first." His hand slid to her neck, his fingertips lightly caressing her nape. "Or you can put that tub to good use, have a bathe, and then change into more comfortable attire. I'd suggest a loose-fitting gown that doesn't require a corset. Or . . ." He paused, and his fingers stilled. The intensity of his gaze deepened, darkening his eyes to smoke. "Or you can allow me to undress you."

Irene didn't need any time to decide which course she preferred, and as his hand slid away, she caught it in both of hers, then lifted it to the top button of her walking suit. "I think," she said, "I prefer the third option—"

His mouth was on hers before she could even finish, his hand pulling out of her grip, his hands caressing her face as he kissed her. The kiss was both tender and hot, and her lips parted at once, opening to him and to whatever experience he was giving her tonight.

Henry tasted her mouth in soft, lush kisses as he began maneuvering her backward into her room, and he tried not to think about the fact that he was pushing her across the Rubicon. Once they were both inside her room, he kicked her door shut behind them, and deepened the kiss even more, inflaming his own lust to blot out his conscience, his past, and any inconvenient contemplations of right and wrong.

But this strategy for dealing with his conscience had its own drawbacks, for within seconds, he was fully aroused, and if he kept up this pace, tonight would not be the extraordinary experience he wanted for her. He had to slow down.

He broke the kiss, working to balance between the two opposing forces within him as he began to unbutton her jacket. It was slow going, for his hands were shaking with the effort to contain his moves. Of course, she noticed.

"You're not nervous, too, are you?" she whispered, sounding surprised.

"Are you joking? Of course I am," he muttered, sliding her jacket down her shoulders and tossing it aside. Then he looked at her again, raking his hands through his hair and drawing a profound, shaky breath. "I'm nervous as hell."

For some reason, that made her laugh.

"Go on, then," he said as he started on the buttons of her shirtwaist. "Laugh at my expense. You do seem to enjoy that particular sport."

"Well, yes," she admitted. "I am fond of teasing you, it's true. But I do like that you're nervous."

"Why, in heaven's name?"

"Because it proves you're not always as in control as you pretend."

He suspected she wouldn't say that if he lost his control as completely as he wanted to and let what was raging in him have free rein, and he was glad she'd chosen to let him undress her. Had she slipped into a loose-fitting garment with nothing underneath, he feared it would have been his undoing, and her deflowering a short, very unromantic experience. As it was, the act of unfastening buttons and untying ribbons enabled him to curb, bit by bit, his own urges, and by the time she was down to chemise and drawers, he was prepared to concentrate fully on what was most important: arousing and pleasuring her.

For the first time since he began to undress her, he looked into her face. She was flushed, her breathing quick—a good sign she was already partway there, but it wasn't enough. Not nearly enough. He cupped her chin, and kissed her, then drew back again. "It's all right if you tease me and laugh," he told her as he reached behind her head and began pulling the pins out of her hair. "For before the night is out, Irene, I will have my revenge."

"Heavens," she murmured, her lashes lowering. "It seems I shall need that sol volatile after all."

Despite her light words, he felt the tremors running through her, though whether it was due to apprehension or anticipation, he couldn't be sure. Probably both.

He turned to toss the pins onto the dressing table beside him as his other hand raked through her hair, bringing it tumbling down around her shoulders, just as it had been that night in the library, just as it had been in all his dreams of her since then.

He grasped a handful of gold silk in his fist and pulled her head back. He kissed her, his free hand undoing the buttons at the neck of her chemise. He wanted to touch her breasts, cup and suckle them, but the modest neckline of her garment prevented it. He trailed kisses along her throat and over her collarbone as he moved both hands to her waist. He grasped the hem of her chemise, then moved to draw it upward, but suddenly, she grasped his wrists to stop him. He tilted his head, pressing a kiss to her ear. "It's all right. Don't be afraid."

"I'm not afraid. It's just that . . ." She paused, then gave a little laugh. "We both know I'm not experienced in these matters, but surely I'm not the only one whose clothes come off?"

"No. But it's probably best if I stay dressed as long as possible."

Being Irene, she couldn't just accept this explanation. "I don't think that very fair."

It wasn't fair, no, but it was far easier for him to hang onto restraint if he kept his clothes on. He wanted all of this, every second of it, to be something she would treasure, without regret, and putting her hands on his body, he supposed, was part of that for her. He'd have to bear the tension. "Very well," he said and spread his arms. "If you wish to undress me, I won't object."

She lifted her hands to the top button of his waistcoat. "I don't know anything about men's clothes," she said. "I fear I shall prove much less skilled at this than your valet."

"You'll do fine. Our clothes are like everything else about us." He smiled at her questioning look. "Straightforward. Uncomplicated."

She made a skeptical sound as she slid his waistcoat off, but she didn't stop to debate the point.

He had already removed his necktie, collar, and studs, so she only had to remove his cuff links, slip down his braces, and undo the buttons of his shirt. She did not, however, notice the front tab button that hooked his shirt to his drawers, and he couldn't help laughing at her consternation when his shirttails failed to come out of his waistband.

"Let me do it," he said and finished for her, doffing both his shirt and undershirt in the space of a few seconds. He tossed both aside, but when he looked at her again, her face made him go utterly still.

Her lips were parted, her gaze unwavering as she studied his naked chest, seeming fascinated. She flattened her palms against his pectorals and ran her hands over his shoulders, and down his arms. The slow, warm caress felt so good that Henry groaned, tilting his head back, letting her explore him and satisfy her curiosity even as he struggled to keep his arousal in check. She ran her hands over the muscles of his chest, shoulders, arms, and abdomen. But when she reached the waistband of his trousers, he knew that was as much as he could bear.

"That's far enough," he said, and ignoring her protest, he grasped her wrists and pushed her exploring hands firmly away. "You'll be able to have more explorations later. It's my turn."

He glanced down, noting the full shape of her breasts and the jutting outline of her nipples beneath the thin lawn of her chemise, a sight that deepened his arousal, and he knew he could not wait any longer to see what until now he'd only been able to imagine.

"Raise your arms," he told her as he grasped handfuls

of delicate lawn fabric in his fists, and when she complied, he pulled the garment over her head and tossed it onto the growing pile of garments near their feet.

But when he looked at her again, the sight of her was so lovely, so breathtakingly lovely, that haste went out the window, and he had to stop and just look at her. Her skin was pale as cream, with a delicate flush of pink. Her breasts were full and round, the nipples hard and aroused, with velvety pink areoles.

His throat went dry.

He sank to his knees in front of her and cupped her breasts in his hands. She inhaled sharply, tilting her head back, arching into his touch. Her skin was like warm silk, and he toyed with her, brushing his thumbs back and forth across her nipples, rolling them between his fingers. She began to moan, soft and low, cradling his head, her fingers working in his hair, but it wasn't enough. He wanted her so hot, so aroused, that when the moment came to take her fully, she would be as ready for it as he was.

He leaned closer, shaping one breast in his palm as he opened his mouth over the other. She cried out, her body jerking in response. He suckled her, gently, then not so gently, scoring her nipple with his teeth.

"Henry," she cried softly, stirring, agitated. "Oh, God, Henry."

He toyed with her a moment longer, then he eased back, but he had no intention of relenting, for he wanted her even hotter. He reached for the button that held up her drawers and freed it, then he jerked the garment down her legs. Wrapping his arm tight around her hips, his forearm beneath her bum, he began pressing kisses to the bare, silken skin of her stomach. She stirred, agitated, but he held her fast, knowing it would fan the flames within her to tormenting heights if she could not move. He kissed her stomach and tongued her navel and slid his hand between her thighs.

He pressed his thumb up into the crease of her sex, and she moaned, her knees caving, but he held her upright, his arms a tight band around her hips, and moved his thumb along the crease of her sex.

Her hands raked through his hair. Her hips jerked against his imprisoning arm as she instinctively strove for climax, but he kept firm hold of her, preventing her from gaining her peak. She moaned in protest, the agitation in her growing stronger as he caressed her with his thumb.

He lifted his head to look at her. He couldn't see her face, for her head was flung back, but that was all right with him, because what he could see—her flushed skin, her long, slender throat, her full, jutting breasts—was splendid enough.

She was slick, and hot, and he pushed his thumb into her just a little, then out again, spreading her moisture to enhance her pleasure. She moaned again, her body shuddering. "Henry," she wailed. "Oh, God. Oh, God."

"Now who's being teased, hmm?" He kissed her stomach as he caressed her clitoris. "I warned you," he went on.

She was panting, desperate. "Please," she moaned. "Oh, please."

"Please, what?" He circled her clitoris with the pad of his thumb. "Do you want me to stop?"

She shook her head violently. "No, no, don't stop. Oh,

God, please don't stop. I just want . . . want"—her hips writhed helplessly—"more. Please, Henry."

"Not yet. Wait." He kissed her stomach and stroked the crease of her sex without letting her move, fanning the flames of her desire, and his own, as her sweet, sweet pleas for more drove him to the brink. Only when he knew she was on the verge of being unable to bear it, did he relent, easing his hold. At once, her hips rocked hard against him, her thighs squeezed tight around his hand, and with a low keening wail and a shuddering gasp, she came in a rush, her knees collapsing beneath her.

He rose, pulling his hand from between her legs and catching her in his arms. He kissed her, then lifting her in his arms, he laid her on the bed.

Irene could only stare at him, dazed and wordless as he moved to lie beside her. After what she'd just experienced, she couldn't imagine what strange and beautiful sensations could possibly come next.

She'd known her knowledge of physical relations between men and women was incomplete, gleaned as it was from one painfully embarrassing conversation with her mother when she was fifteen, a few whispered consultations over the years with some of the married ladies at suffragist meetings, and snatched peeks at forbidden books when she could lay hands on them. But combined with the wild, wonderful carriage ride with Henry the other night, she'd come here tonight thinking she had a pretty good idea of what to expect. But now, shamelessly nude before him, all her senses in a dazed, euphoric tumult, she appreciated that she knew nothing about this at all.

But there was more to come, she knew that, for Henry was watching her, his glittering gray eyes pinning her to the mattress as he began to unbutton his trousers, and when he pulled them down, Irene could only stare at his groin, stupefied as, at last, she began to see what all the whispered, embarrassed conversations had really been meant to explain. For the first time, she felt a hint of panic. Her gaze flew back up to his face. "Henry?"

He shoved his trousers and linen all the way down to his ankles, then stepped out of them, and when he straightened, she saw that in his hand was a small, red envelope. She swallowed hard, trying to shove down this sudden bout of panic.

He must have seen what she felt in her face, for he leaned down and kissed her mouth. "It'll be all right," he said.

He stretched out beside her on the bed, slipping the red envelope beneath his pillow, and when he turned toward her, she felt the hard erect part of his body pushing against her thigh. "Henry?" she said again, feeling a sudden frantic need for reassurance.

He lifted up to rest his weight on one arm and look into her eyes as he reached out and caressed her face. "God, you're lovely," he said, his hand sliding down, his gaze following as his palm glided over her breast, along her ribs, over her stomach, and down her thigh. "In fact," he said, laughing a little, "I think you are, truly, the most beautiful woman I have ever seen."

Suddenly, his hand stilled at her hip, and a shadow seemed to cross his face. "If you want to call a halt," he said, his voice a harsh whisper as he looked into her eyes, "you can, Irene. It would be . . . easier for me if you did it now, rather than later."

She turned her head and kissed his palm. "I don't want to call a halt."

"You might," he said. "Before the end."

"Why would I?"

Instead of answering, he slid his hand beneath the pillow. He retrieved the red envelope, opened it, and removed what was inside.

"Is that . . ." She paused, lifting her head to have a better look, but he had already tucked it into his palm.

"Yes," he said and began easing his body on top of hers, moving slowly as if to give her plenty of time to change her mind, until he was fully settled between her legs, and she felt him, hard and erect, against the place he'd kissed so intimately moments ago. His hand slid between them, and after a moment, he touched her where he had before, caressing the folds of her most private place with his fingertips, stirring those amazing feelings again. She lay back, closing her eyes, but his voice prevented her from sinking into the passion his caress always seemed to evoke. "Irene, listen to me. Look at me."

She obeyed, opening her eyes.

"There will be pain for you," he said. "There's no way around that. But if, at any point, you want me to stop, say so, and—" He paused and kissed her, hard. "And I'll stop. I promise. All right?"

His voice sounded strange, strangled and harsh, and his breathing had quickened, but she was not afraid. "I don't want you to stop," she whispered, and as she spoke, any vestige of panic faded away. For she wanted this. More now than ever.

He moved, and she could feel the hard part of him rubbing against her. The place between her thighs seemed keenly sensitive to sensation now, and the hardness of him felt scorching hot against her, and deliciously sensual. She moaned, her hips pressing up against him.

"Irene?" His voice was urgent now as lifted himself above her, resting his weight on his forearms. "I can't hold back any longer. I'm coming inside you."

Inside? Her eyes flew open to the vision of his face, taut and unreadable above her, but before she could utter the question on her lips, she felt him pushing against her. Into her.

She sucked in a startled gasp as her body stretched to accommodate this large, uncomfortable invasion. He went still, hovering above her, waiting. She knew what he waited for, and she nodded, urging him on, her hips lifting.

That seemed all he needed. Suddenly, with a rough sound, he gave a powerful thrust of his hips against hers that brought the hard, erect part of him into her fully, and though he'd warned her, she couldn't help crying out at this sudden assault. He caught the sound of her pain, capturing it in his own mouth with a kiss, as her arms tightened around him. He stilled again, kissing her, deep, slow kisses as he brushed his palm against her hair. Then he pulled back, and began kissing her everywhere he could reach—her throat, her cheeks, her mouth, even the tip of her nose.

"It'll be all right, Irene. I promise it will."

But even as he soothed her, the pain was receding. "I'm all right, Henry," she whispered, and tentatively, she moved beneath him, trying to accustom herself to him coupled with her in this way.

He buried his face against her neck and began to move within her, quickening his pace, and as he did, his thrusts against her grew stronger and deeper, and she knew he was feeling the same sort of pleasure he'd given her. She pushed upward, tightening and flexing her hips, and when he groaned in response, she smiled, beginning to like this part. The pain had eased to a mild soreness deep inside, nothing intolerable, and she worked to move with him, trying to match the rhythm of his thrusts.

His breathing was ragged, and his hips were pushing hers hard into the mattress with quick, urgent thrusts. Irene began to feel again that wondrous pleasure that he'd given her before, but even hotter and deeper.

But then, suddenly, shudders rocked him. He let out a hoarse cry, thrust against her one last time and went still, his body covering hers, breathing hard against her neck.

She caressed him, liking the feel of the hard, smooth muscles of his back, and when he lifted up and looked into her face, she found herself seized with an overpowering tenderness that was like nothing she'd ever felt in her life before. It squeezed her heart and made her want to laugh and cry. It seemed to fill her very soul.

So this was what it was to be a ruined woman. She felt no regret and no shame. She just felt an overwhelming happiness that bubbled up within her until she couldn't contain it, and she laughed out loud. Being ruined felt ripping wonderful.

Chapter 18

"Irene?" Henry lifted himself above her, looking dubious. "You're laughing?"

"Well . . . yes." She'd confounded him, she could tell. "I'm sorry, if that's a rude thing to do at a moment like this. It's just . . . I don't know what all the repression and censure is about, honestly." She paused, laughing again. "This is glorious. Why don't people do this all the time?"

That made him laugh, too, a deep, hearty laugh, and he liked the sound of it. "Many people do," he said, cupping her face with his palms. "Believe me, there are people meeting in hotel rooms and bedrooms all over London as we lie here talking about it."

Her laughter faded as she studied his face. "What about you? Have you been with many women? Besides your wife, I mean."

"No, not many. I mean, enough to know what I'm doing. But not enough to be cynical about it, thank God."

"And some people are cynical?"

"Far too many, I'm afraid." He studied her, and his smile faded to a thoughtful expression. "You're a very unusual woman, do you know that?"

"Why? Because after knowing you less than two weeks, I've taken you as my lover?"

She tried to sound nonchalant, but she feared the breathlessness of her voice spoiled the effect.

"In a way, yes. You are very unexpected, Irene. I never can seem to predict what you'll think or feel about anything. Or what you'll take it into your head to do."

"That's part of my charm."

She was being facetious, but he did not laugh. "Indeed, it is. I think I'm coming to like it, actually." He kissed her, then lifted himself away from her, and she let out a startled breath as his body slipped free of hers.

His hand reached between them, stirring between her thighs, but it wasn't a caress, and she knew he was retrieving what had been in the red packet. Strangely, knowing that made her feel shy all of a sudden. "What happens now?" she whispered.

"That depends on where everyone thinks you are."

"If you mean Clara, she thinks I'm at Belford Row. If you mean Papa, he thinks I'm spending the night at Upper Brook Street."

A frown knit his brows. Abruptly, he rolled away, and she felt a strange shiver of apprehension as he sat up, his back to her, the contents of the red envelope in his closed fist.

"What's wrong?" she asked.

"Nothing. It's just a bit awkward." He gave a short

laugh. "Talking about your father at this particular moment."

"If you think I regret what happened, Henry, I don't."

"I'm glad." He turned his head, smiling a little, and with his free hand, he reached for one of hers. He kissed it, then let her go and rose from the bed. Irene sat up, allowing herself a good, long look as he walked to his own room. His body was really quite splendid, she thought, craning her neck. His wide shoulders, his muscled back, his bum. He vanished through the door, and she gave an aggrieved sigh before falling back against the mattress.

When he returned, he was clad in a long, dark red dressing gown, much to her aggravation. He resumed his seat on the edge of the bed. "If you don't need to be back home straightaway, shall we have dinner up here?"

"Oh, can we? What a lovely idea. I'm famished."

That made him laugh, and she smiled at the sound. "As much as I like to make you laugh," she said as she sat up, "why was that amusing?"

"Because I know the reason you're hungry." Smiling back, he kissed her, and then he looked down, and his hand cupped her breast.

Her body responded to his touch at once, arching into his hand, but her delicious anticipation was quashed before she had the chance to savor it.

"You'll have to give me a bit of time to recover, darling," he said. "Men need that."

"Oh." She blushed, realizing there was a great deal about men she did not know. Then she frowned, tapping his wrist. "If that's so, then why are you teasing me this way?"

His eyes widened, and for a moment, he looked as innocently disingenuous as one of his naughty nephews. "Is that what I'm doing?" he murmured, his fingertips brushing over her nipple, stirring heat inside her.

"Yes," she said firmly and pushed his hand away. "Besides, you promised me food."

"So, dinner for two, then? Do you trust me to order for you?"

"Certainly. Being a duke, you're sure to know what food goes with what wine, and all that, so order whatever you think best. But no dessert," she added as he started to rise.

He sank back down, giving her a puzzled little frown, the one between his brows that told her she'd confounded him yet again. "Why not dessert?"

"I don't need any." She smiled, wrapped her arms around his neck and kissed him. "You're my dessert."

AND SO IT began, the life of Mr. and Mrs. Jones. Henry would telephone from his club which hotel they would be staying in, a different hotel every night. He arranged for the transportation of her suitcase and the laundering of her discarded clothes, so that no matter where they spent the night, she always had fresh garments without anyone in her household or his being given cause for suspicion while doing the laundry. And he assured her that he never came in his own carriage and that he always took a circuitous route to their destination. They met after dark and parted before dawn.

These illicit arrangements were a facet of life she already knew something about, for the bread and butter of gossip columns involved the love affairs of vari-

ous members of the aristocracy. And that knowledge
served her well in guarding against any gossip being
directed at her and Henry. She was always sure to leave
him shrouded in her dark cloak and veil. Train stations
served as desirable places to slip out of her distinctive
veiled garments and into her usual shirtwaist and skirt,
a uniform indistinguishable from the shop girls, telephone operators and typists who scuttled about London
late at night and early in the morning. Even her hair
color was easily hidden beneath a plain straw bonnet.
Despite these precautions, one of Irene's competitors
did make mention in its Wednesday edition of the Duke
of Torquil's sudden interest in a mysterious veiled lady,
forcing Irene to make sure that Josie's next Delilah
Dawlish column did the same, for a failure to mention
it would be noticed by her competitors. She even began to fabricate an identity for Torquil's mistress. His
family, of course, asked him no questions about this
woman, for as he assured her, among his sort of people,
a man's mistress was never discussed.

Her father, who didn't read any of the gossip rags and
had long been accustomed to Irene coming and going
at odd hours, was given no cause for suspicion, and as
long as Clara didn't visit Belford Row, the secret of
Irene's sleeping arrangements would be able to remain
intact.

For Irene, their nights together were wondrous, not
only because of the sweet bliss she felt in Henry's
arms, but also for their conversations, for she had never
in her life had the chance for open, honest debate with a
man. She'd had a suitor or two, respectable young men
introduced through her cousins or because they lived

in the neighborhood and she'd known them all her life. They had all been polite, earnest, and dull. Any feminine dissent on her part to their opinions and advice had made them uncomfortable and inclined to change the subject. Never had she had any interaction with a man who could meet her on her own ground as Henry did. He did not find her feminine brain at all intimidating, nor inferior to his own masculine one. Nor was he wont to patronize or humor her to avoid discussion, and their conversations were often as heated as their lovemaking. As he had from the moment they'd met, he was able to provoke her, and infuriate her, and make her think.

"But why should women have the vote?"

Irene set down her knife and fork, happy to take him on over the breakfast trays spread out between them on the bed of their third hotel room in a week. "Why shouldn't they have the vote? Answer me that."

"That's not an argument." He leaned back against the brass headboard with his tea, preparing to get comfortable. "Make your case."

"Why should I have to? Did men ever have to? Or did they just decide—we're bigger, we're stronger, we win?"

"Well, yes, that's probably exactly how it happened, but again, that's not an argument. If you want the vote, you'll have to do more than march and protest and declare some sort of moral high ground, you know. You'll have to convince men in power to cede power to you, and to accomplish that, you've got to do better in forming your argument. It'll get you nowhere to complain about how unfair things are and how men have had it all their own way for too long. If you ever get the ear of an MP and you say rot like that, he'll laugh in your face and tell you that what you need is to be married with a brood of children so you'll remember your place."

She grimaced. "That's more true than I like to think."

"So, answer my question. Why should women have the vote?"

Breakfast forgotten, she set down her utensils and shoved aside her tray. "I believe if women had the vote, it would be a better world."

"That's sentiment, and I don't care what you believe. Remember," he added at her sound of outrage, "I'm your opponent. I'm the MP you've got to convince. Try again."

"I will try, Henry, but in all seriousness, don't you think women having the vote could bring about changes that are good? Forget the notion of making argument, just tell me what you think, you personally."

"Honestly? I don't know." He ignored her sound of exasperation and considered for a moment. "If it happened," he said slowly, "the change would be enormous, chaotic even. Would they be good changes? How can I answer that? All my life, I have been raised by a certain code. I am the duke, it is my responsibility to keep my world stable, to take care of all those who exist within my sphere. The tenants of my farms, the servants in my employ, the tradesmen in my village— all these people depend upon me to keep their world as reliable as possible. That is a fact of my existence. I am keenly aware that the economic condition of all these people, particularly the women and children, is to a great extent dependent upon decisions I make."

"But put your title aside. What of yourself?"

"Speaking as a man, I have always believed it is my

duty, my responsibility, and my honor to take care of the women in my life, and the children. If I do not have that, if I am not allowed that, then—as a man—what am I? What is my purpose in this world, if it is not to protect and care for those I love and hold most dear?"

Watching him as he spoke, Irene felt a powerful ache in her chest. She could not reply, for she was overcome by myriad emotions. Bafflement, for he truly did not see that he was so much more than the caretaker of others. Confusion, for she'd never known any man for whom caring for others meant so much. And, yes, she felt a hint of envy, too, envy of those who were fortunate enough to have him as their champion.

She couldn't think of how to say all that, and as she watched, that puzzled little frown etched between his brows. "Why are you looking at me that way?" he asked.

"Because, Henry," she said softly, "you are not like any other man I have ever known."

That embarrassed him, she could tell, for he looked away with a cough. "Yes, well, I don't think I'm so rare a chap."

"But you are. And because not all men are like you, where does that leave the women who are not fortunate enough to be within the realm of your responsibility?"

He raked a hand through his hair and gave a laugh. "God, Irene, I don't know. You confound me at every turn, you truly do. Why is it that with you, I am always questioning what I think, what I believe, what's right and wrong? Until I met you, I was absolutely sure I knew all these things."

"And now?"

"Now, I'm not sure of anything, to be honest. You provoke me and madden me and arouse me and impel me to question everything I know and believe. I find myself engaged in debates on issues I never considered before, and you shred ideas about my life I have always taken as truth."

"You do the same to me. But that's a . . . a good thing." As she said it, she felt a sudden prickling along the back of her neck, as if an ill wind were brushing through the room. "Isn't it?" she whispered.

"Is it?" He frowned, glancing around the hotel room, and as she followed his gaze, she noted the evidence of their frantic rush to lovemaking a short time ago—the scattered clothing, the red envelope. "I am enmeshed in situations that I never would have dreamed of only a few weeks ago," he went on, musingly. "You delve, Irene, into the very bedrock of my existence."

She forced herself to look at him again. "You said you wouldn't regret this," she whispered. "What we have."

"I don't." He set down his tea and leaned forward, cupping her cheek. "Not at all, not for a moment. But knowing you is a bit chaotic to my sensibilities. You want to change the world, darling," he added, smiling so tenderly that her moment of apprehension floated away and disappeared. "And I'm far more accustomed to being content with the world as it is. And on that note," he added, leaning back, his hand falling away, "you still haven't convinced me of why women should be granted the vote. So carry on."

She thought for a moment, trying to form her argument as he expected her to do. "Because what is decided by men on our behalf takes no account at all of what we want, of what we know is best for us."

"But as a man, I know what you really want and what's best for you."

"Really, Henry," she choked, any notion of reasoned debate going straight out the window. "You don't really believe that, do you?"

"Of course I do," he said, his expression impassive, and yet, she knew without appreciating just how, that he was provoking her on purpose. It was working, too, for she was now furious and spluttering, and completely inarticulate.

She scowled, frustrated by the skill with which he was able to turn the discussion in his favor simply by using her own emotions against her. "This isn't fair. You men go to university, spend four years learning and practicing how to debate—"

"I didn't." He grinned. "I had nine years, not four. Before Cambridge, there was Harrow. And before that, my tutors. And yes, at Cambridge, I was a master of oratory debate. Champion class four years running. So, you're right—you are completely outmatched and outgunned. Which is a given anyway," he added, grinning, "since I'm a man and you're a woman. You haven't a prayer."

"Stuff," she said, fully aware now that he was toying with her. "Give me over nine years of hard training at debate and oratory, and see how you fare then."

"I'm not sure that matters. Irene, I am surrounded by women, and I can assure you, every member of your sex is well able to create an argument at the drop of a hat. It may not be a logical one—"

She remonstrated by giving him a nudge with her foot. "You know what I mean. Your sex is taught debate and oratory at university. We women are denied that opportunity."

"Not denied it. Not always, anyway."

"Mostly, though. It's only allowed us if the men in our lives—who nearly always have charge of our money—will consent to pay the fees. So again, it's our men—husbands, brothers, fathers—who decide for us how much education we receive. Most of us are allowed little more than the elementary aspects."

He smiled. "You sound like my sister. She wanted to go to university."

"Angela?" Irene froze, dismayed. "Henry, you didn't refuse your sister a university education, did you? Please, tell me you did not do that."

"No, no, not Angela. Patricia. She was mad, absolutely mad, on chemistry. She wanted to go to Girton and become a doctor. But my father—he was alive, then—would not hear of it. Bad enough if a man in our family had wanted to be a doctor, but a woman? God, no. It was a crushing disappointment for her. It broke her heart."

Irene's point had just been made, but she didn't care about that just now, for she was looking into his face, and any academic debate on women's rights and education was pushed aside. "Patricia? She died, didn't she?"

"Two years ago, yes. She died in childbirth. Eclampsia. The baby, too." He stirred, then gave a cough. "If you wish for women's rights, I can assure you I would happily advocate giving women better access to university education, especially if it meant more female doctors and better medical care for your sex."

He was clearly attempting to return the conversation to politics because it was safer for him than talking of personal loss and private pain, but Irene would not let him make that diversion. "What was she like?"

"Patricia?" He smiled, but in it there was unmistakable sadness, and she wondered how she could ever have thought this man icy or unfeeling. "I think you might be able to guess what she was like." His smile turned wry. "You've met my nephews."

Irene laughed. "Oh, dear."

"Exactly. Pat was the most adventurous member of our family. She was always wanting to know the why and the how of everything. And she had a first-class brain. She's a woman who would have made the world a better place, to use your argument. Well," he amended, "except that she did almost blow up the summerhouse once."

"Heavens. Like mother, like sons."

"Yes. A chemistry experiment gone wrong. But despite the summerhouse incident, she was brilliant. Had she gone to Girton, she'd have loved every minute of it. Still, she loved Jamie madly and adored her boys, and she—I won't say she got over not going to university, for one doesn't simply get over the crushing of a lifelong dream, but she was able to be happy in spite of that loss."

Irene nodded. "Yes. One has to go on, doesn't one? I mean, what else is there? Other than to be like my father. He'll"—she broke off and looked down at the breakfast plates—"he'll kill himself with drink," she whispered. "I know it."

Henry grasped her chin, lifted her face. "If he does,

as you are well aware, there is little you can do to stop him."

"Yes, I know. I've done all I can. I used to go through his rooms every day, toss out his bottles. I'd order the servants to keep liquor from him, told the tradesmen never to bring liquor into our house, for I wouldn't pay the bill if they did, but . . ." She shook her head. "None of it did a bit of good. Papa always managed to get drink from somewhere, and eventually, I just gave up. I accepted the fact that if a person is determined to go down a certain road, no one else can really prevent them from it."

"I think," he said with a sigh, "that we have both come to accept that fact about people."

"You're thinking of your mother, I know." She pushed trays out of the way and rose onto her knees, moving forward to wrap her arms around his neck. "But you mustn't worry, Henry. Her course may be perfectly right, for her and all of you. Only time will tell."

"I can only hope you are right, for I have been forced to concede that her marriage is not my decision to make."

"So I can win arguments with you." She grinned. "How gratifying to know."

"You haven't won the one we've embarked upon," he reminded her. "You still haven't made a case for women having the vote."

She sighed. "The problem is that any time a woman makes such a case, or even attempts to debate any issue in a public forum, we're told that's not womanly, dear, and to stop being so resentful and angry."

He tilted his head, studying her. "Irene, you could

stand on the street in your shirtwaist and necktie, and even—God forbid—a pair of trousers, holding a placard over your head that demands all men's heads on platters as a policeman drags you off, and I could never think of you as unwomanly. And right now," he added, glancing down, "when you're not wearing much of anything, I really can't think at all."

At once, all her womanly instincts stirred up, but then she perceived what he was doing, and she frowned. "You are trying to distract me again."

"Well . . ." He paused, his fingers pulling apart the edges of her dressing gown to take a peek down her bosom, "diversion is a fundamental tactic of debate."

She slapped his hand and sat back. "It won't work, Henry. I'm on to you now."

"Oh, very well. Distracting both of us would have been deuced good fun. On the other hand, you are in desperate need of training in debate. Where were we?"

"You were making the preposterous argument that you are somehow entitled, by the mere fact that you are a man, to make my decisions for me."

"So you feel that I should cede you power and give you the vote because you don't believe I have your best interests at heart?"

"No! That's not it at all. Oh, I wish I could make you understand. The power over my best interests isn't yours to cede or keep, to take or give. You don't have the right to decide what I want or what's best for me. Only I have that right."

"But legally, men do have that right, when it comes to the women in their care."

"And the law is wrong. Wrong the same way slavery

is wrong, and indentured servitude is wrong. I am a human being, with my own soul, my own thoughts, my own opinions, and my own will. Those things do not belong to you, or to my father, or to my brother, or to anyone else, man or woman, and whether you agree with me or not, Henry, my destiny is mine, and the choices that determine that destiny are also mine. They are mine alone."

He smiled. "Now that, my darling," he said softly, "is the basis of a sound argument."

THOUGH HER PAPER might speculate on the naughty doings of others, Irene had never been involved in anything naughty herself, nor had she dreamt she ever would be, but her secret assignations with Henry were so deliciously naughty that they filled her with anticipation when she wasn't with him, and delight when she was. Perhaps it was a flaw in her character, but she found the whole thing terribly exciting. Henry did not share her view.

He regarded the secrecy of their liaison as a necessary evil. As fond as he was of discretion, he did not like secrecy. Sneaking around and midnight adventures made him very uncomfortable, and the whole prospect of being caught worried him for her sake. She also suspected he harbored some sense of guilt. He must have done, for he was so upright and moral. And yet, in their secret nights together, Irene also began to discover a great deal about the other side of his nature, the dark, sensual one he'd warned her of that night in the library.

From him, she learned that there were an amazing variety of positions in which two people could make

love, and that his favorite was to have her on top so that
he could see her face and stroke her breasts as she cli-
maxed. She learned how to hold his erect penis in her
hand, and how to stroke him until it drove him to the
brink. She learned that lying beside him with her head
resting on his bare chest was the best thing about the
blissful aftermath because she loved the sound of his
heartbeat. And she learned that he always reserved a
room with a bathtub because he loved to help her bathe,
lathering soap over her skin and caressing her, and she
learned he'd been imagining that particular activity
since the first night in his home when they'd talked
about bathrooms.

And best of all, she learned that she could set aside
any missish behavior with him, that she could take the
lead any time she wanted to. It was humbling and amazing when she learned that his most fervent wish in all
of this was to please her, but to her delight, she learned
that it aroused and pleasured him if she told him what
aroused and pleasured her. He loved hearing that.

"What about this?" he asked, his fingertips caressing
the back of her bent knee.

"Hmm . . ." she murmured on a sigh, settling more
deeply into the mattress beneath her, pretending indifference. "That's nice."

"Nice? Nice?" He kissed her shoulder. "No man can
take such lukewarm commentary lying down."

She giggled. "Henry, you *are* lying down."

"Nonetheless, I take issue." He rose, naked, and
moved to the foot of the bed. "I must insist upon a full
exploration of this topic."

She lifted her head. "Exploration?"

"Oh, yes." He smiled, his gaze locked with hers, and he grasped her ankles. Slowly, he began pulling her legs apart.

"Henry?" She felt a little thrill—anticipation mixed with a hint of alarm for she was completely naked at the moment. "What are you doing?"

"What about this?" he asked, his fingertips gliding up and down the inside of her calves and over her shins. "Do you like this?"

When she didn't answer, he bent down, pushing her knees a bit farther apart and easing his body between them. "Or this?" He pressed a kiss to the inside of one knee, then the other, then he lifted his head. Looking into her eyes, definite purpose in his expression, he moved his body another notch higher between her thighs and slid his arms beneath her legs.

"Henry?" Her throat went dry. Her tension increased.

"What," he asked and bent his head, "about this?"

He pressed his lips tenderly to her most intimate place, and the sensation was so piercingly sweet that she cried out. Instinctively, she squeezed her thighs. "No, no," she wailed softly, shocked and embarrassed and aroused all at once.

He stopped and lifted his head, but she couldn't look at him. She could only squeeze her eyes shut.

"You don't like it?" He leaned down again, nuzzling her.

"I don't . . . I don't know. I'm sure it can't be . . . oh, God, Henry, no. That's wicked."

She was blushing all over, she must be, for her embarrassment was so acute, she could hardly bear it. This was beyond anything they had done, beyond any sensation he'd given her yet.

"Irene," he said, his breath warm against her dampness. "I want to do this. I want to kiss you here. I want to taste you. Let me."

And then he did, and she gasped, a deep, shuddering gasp that jerked her hips against his mouth. "Oh, oh."

He lifted his head again. "Should I continue?" he asked tenderly, nuzzling her, teasing her. "Do you like it? Not sure?" he added when she didn't answer.

"Not sure," she managed, her insides like molten jelly. "More."

He laughed softly. "More it is."

Her hands clenched the counterpane as he kissed her with his lips and caressed her with his tongue, tasting deeply of her, while she could only lie there, awash in sensations so exquisite she couldn't form words to tell him so. "Oh, oh, oh," was all she could manage, as the sweet sensations rose, peaked, and broke over her—not a new sensation, no, but more powerful, more intense, more shattering than ever before. And then it came again, and yet again, and all she could do was sob in helpless ecstasy as his shameless carnal kisses wrung every bit of pleasure from her body.

At last, he lifted his head. "I want to be inside you," he said.

"Yes," she panted, opening to him at once, spreading her legs wide as he moved his body on top of hers. He paused only long enough to find the red envelope, retrieve the condom—the shield that preserved her pretense of virtue. He slipped it on, and he took her, a hard, full thrust that drove the air from her lungs and made him groan.

"I can't hold back," he muttered against her throat as

his hips rocked against hers again. "Sorry, Irene. Just can't."

Two more thrusts, and then, his arms were wrapping tight around her, and he came, his body shuddering with the force of his orgasm, then he collapsed, panting, on top of her.

She lay there, running her fingers through his hair, still stunned by what he'd just done. She thought of all the times this week she'd sat in her office, staring out her little window to the brick wall next door, dreaming of their next rendezvous, but no daydream she'd had, no matter how erotic, had come close to this.

I am a man possessed of deep carnal appetites.

Yes, she thought, smiling. He certainly was.

Chapter 19

Henry stirred, pressing a kiss to her hair as his hand slid between them to retrieve the condom. Hiding it in his fist, he got out of bed. Naked, he walked to the window, and while she admired the view she had, he took a look between the drawn curtains. "It'll be daylight soon," he said, letting the curtain fall and starting toward his own room. "We'd better dress."

He vanished into the adjoining room as Irene got out of bed. She moved slowly, her mind drifting back again and again to what had just happened and all the other sensual experiences he'd given her during the past four nights. He really was such an unexpected man. The things he knew, especially about women. From being married, perhaps, or the others he'd been with.

Not many. *Enough to know what I'm doing. Not enough to be cynical about it.*

She liked that about him. Some men, particularly

of the aristocracy, were notorious philanderers. He wasn't. In fact, she thought as she reached for her corset and began to put it on, he was not one to be in the pages of her paper much at all, and when he was, the gossip about him was of the tamest variety, the occasional speculation about which young lady he'd danced with at a ball, and could she be the one he might marry, that sort of thing.

He would marry, of course. Eventually, he'd have to, wouldn't he?

A duke must marry a woman worthy of his position.

His words the first night she'd been in his home came back to her, and Irene's hands stilled on the clasps of her corset busk. She was definitely not that woman.

She didn't mind that, she told herself at once. Why, she'd scoffed at the notion of marrying him just a few days ago. They weren't suited in any way. She knew it, and so did he.

I have a penchant, it seems, for women who are not suited to my life, and it is a life I cannot change.

Irene stared down at the floor, looking into the future, and it was a bleak point of view. She didn't know how long this affair would last, but it would end. And then what would happen? She hadn't allowed herself to think about that. During the past few days, she hadn't thought about anything beyond the night ahead, and now she knew why she hadn't indulged in that sort of speculation.

What would happen was inevitable. He would find someone suitable, and she would go back to the life she'd had before she'd met him, a life with work she loved in a world she understood. A life without him.

Irene felt suddenly dismal.

"Lord, Irene," Henry said, his voice breaking into her thoughts as he reentered her room and scooped up his studs from her dressing table, "is that as far as you've got? We really must hurry. It'll be light soon. And I've got to have at least a bit of sleep, for I've heaps of things to do before I leave for the country."

He was leaving today for Hampshire. Another thing she hadn't allowed herself to think about. Her corset fastened, she stopped dressing and turned, following him as far as the door as he returned to his own room. "What time is your train?"

"Two o'clock, out of Victoria." He dropped his studs onto his dressing table, then reached for his collar.

Watching him, the realization of impending separation fully hit her, deepening her already dismal feelings. "Until this moment," she said slowly, watching his back as he fastened his collar, "I didn't think about the fact that I wouldn't be seeing you tonight."

"Neither did I," he confessed. "It's been a wild week, rather."

"Perhaps I could come down with you and your family. I know you hadn't wanted me to do that," she added, hoping like hell she sounded indifferent enough for pride's sake, "but that was before we . . ." She paused as she watched him go still, but she forced herself to finish. "But that was before. Now, it's different, surely?"

"Is it?" He turned, and Irene wished suddenly that she had not become more skilled at reading his expressions, for she knew before he spoke what he was going to say. "You can't come to Hampshire, Irene," he said gently. "It won't do."

She looked down, her heart stinging at the rebuff. "I understand," she mumbled, though she really didn't.

In an instant, he was in front of her, putting his hands on her arms. "Look at me."

Pride forced her to look up even though her eyes, damn it, were stinging.

"It is far, far more difficult to be discreet in the country, particularly in a part of the country where everyone knows me. In London, there are hotels, taxis, and some degree of privacy and anonymity. In my village, there would be none of that. We might be able to sneak off for a bit of time together, but the chances are high that we would be seen. And even if we do not make any attempt to be alone together, I fear—"

He broke off and drew a breath. "I am, as you know, a man who does not show his feelings openly, and I have always found that to be useful talent, but since I met you, Irene, that sort of sangfroid has become harder and harder to maintain. It wears on me. My desire for you has not abated these four days. It has only grown stronger, and I fear that I will not always be on my guard to conceal it. I live every moment with this fear—that someone will look into my face, and see what I feel. That I will one day forget discretion, forget caution, and people will know the true nature of what is between us. Can you say, honestly, that you would always be able to hide the desire you feel for me?"

"No." It was a difficult thing to admit. "I don't think I could, not every moment."

He kissed her, then his hands slid away from her shoulders and he turned away. "In light of that," he said as he returned to his dressing table and reached for one of his shirt studs, "I suppose it is a good thing that I shall be in the country for the autumn. It will give us both time to get our bearings."

Irene stared at him in dismay. "The entire autumn?"

His hands stilled. "We'll have to see," he said after a moment and resumed fastening shirt studs in place. "I have a great deal to do at Ravenwood, and the other estates as well. I'll be able to come to town occasionally, but not too often, or it will cause gossip and speculation. I have no reason to be here at this time of year, you see."

"So where does that leave us?" Even as she asked the question, she knew the answer, and her dismay deepened. "I won't see much of you at all, will I?"

He picked up his tie and looped it around his neck before he answered. "I'm afraid not," he said at last. "Not until spring. And even then, we shall have to continue to be as discreet as possible."

"Of course, but . . ." She paused, the ramifications of the situation truly sinking in for the first time, cutting through the blissful haze that had surrounded her these past four days. "Oh, God, we can't ever really be seen together in public again, can we?"

He paused, his hands still at his collar. "Do you think we can?" he countered as he finished knotting his tie. "You know, better than anyone," he said as he reached for his waistcoat and put it on, "how gossip starts, how fast it spreads. You are an unmarried woman, and I an unmarried man. Given how we feel, do you think we can risk ever being seen together, even chaperoned, without causing gossip? People will begin speculating about us. Your competitors may catch the scent of a story and start following you, and we'd be in the devil of a mess."

She would never, she realized, be able to see his home. She would never be able to sail with him or sit at dinner with him again. She looked over her shoulder at her hotel room and the scattered clothes, remembering the aftermath of their first night together, and she knew, suddenly, what he'd known all along.

"So, this is all we have," she said, returning her attention to him. "Sneaking in and out of hotel rooms in the season, and perhaps a few times the rest of the year."

He turned from the mirror and came to stand in front of her again. His hand cupped her face, but she did not look at him. Instead, she stared at his shirt front and the elegant silver stud with the ducal coronet. "Do you remember, Irene," he murmured, his fingertips caressing her cheek, "what I told you when you first proposed this arrangement?"

"One can't go back," she whispered. The moment she said it, everything in her rebelled, anger and frustration flaring up. "God, is there no place for us, other than this?"

"There is. You could marry me."

Irene stiffened. "We've talked about this already."

"Perhaps we should talk about it again. I know you do not want to give up your work, but as we've discussed, you could continue it to some extent, if you were discreet. And though I know you do not want to be a duchess, I'm not sure you've considered the job in a very objective light."

She moved uneasily, not sure she wanted to rehash this topic. "I am not convinced I want to live in your world, Henry. I confess, I'm not all that taken with it."

"Shall I move into your world instead? A world of scandal sheets and occupations for women and suffragists and middle class terrace houses? Where in that world would I fit? I am a duke, not a clerk at Lloyds. I cannot set aside my position. There is no means of doing so. And even if I could do it, I would not, for there are far more people than the two of us that must be considered. Those people depend upon me, Irene, to be just what I am and who I am and where I am. I cannot leave my world."

"I know that. I wouldn't ask it of you."

"So your question is answered, then. We are now in a place between our worlds, a place of nighttime assignations, of hotel rooms and risk and secrecy, and unless you change your mind and marry me, this is all we have."

"And that," she whispered, forcing words out, "is not enough for you, is it?"

"For now, perhaps it is enough. But it cannot last, Irene."

She looked up, startled, but before she could reply, he went on, "As much as I want you, I do not know how long I can exist here. The strain of it wears on me, even after less than a week, for I feel history repeating itself. I am treating you just as I treated my wife—hiding you away, keeping you as a secret pleasure and an object of shame. It is harder than even I expected, and with every moment that goes by, the guilt of what I am doing weighs on me more heavily."

Irene stared at him, shocked and dismayed. "All this time," she murmured, "through these nights we have been together, I have been so happy. But you . . ." She stopped, finding it hard to say the words out loud. "But you have not."

"I have." His voice was fierce, harsh. His gray eyes were dark and turbulent, but in his face, there was pain, pain that hurt her, too, that made her feel as if her heart was being ripped out of her very chest. "Here in this room, when it is just us and there is nothing else, this time has been the happiest of my life, Irene. But life cannot just be this room. And out there, I am in agony."

With that confession, her heart seemed to part from her completely, tearing out of her breast and tumbling straight into his hands. In that moment, she fell in love with him.

The sensation was overwhelming, and it took her a moment before she could think of anything to say in reply. "And here I thought I was learning to discern your feelings. I had no idea of this. Why did you not tell me?"

"Tell you what? I tried to explain beforehand how this would be, but I knew you did not understand. I should have walked away, but I agreed to this arrangement because, God help me, I wanted you so much, I could not stand not having you. I still feel that way, as selfish and dishonorable as it is."

"We chose this together. You must not berate yourself and feel guilty for what is between us."

"Must I not? Even though I wholly deserve my own recriminations? I am torn, not only by my desire for you, but also by suspense and fear on your behalf and the dictates of my conscience, as well I should be. If we are discovered, then you would be proclaimed a strumpet, and I would deserve all the blame for having made you so."

"That hasn't happened, Henry," she reminded. "We cannot torment ourselves with worry over things that have not happened."

He looked as if he wanted to say more on the subject, but he nodded instead. "Very well," he murmured and turned away, returning to the dressing table.

"At least our first separation won't be too long," she said, trying to put the best face on things as he buttoned his waistcoat. "I'll see you when you come back on Monday with your mother and my sister."

He didn't reply. Instead, he reached for his pocket watch, but then he paused, and though his head was bent and she couldn't see his face in the mirror, she felt a little shiver of apprehension again along the back of her neck. "I don't think," he said after a moment, "that I will be coming to town as soon as that."

Irene was astonished. "But what about your mother's wedding?"

"I won't be at the wedding." He tucked his watch into his waistcoat pocket and fastened the fob. "No one in the family is going."

She could not believe what she was hearing. "But you said you've accepted her decision to marry him."

"So I have. But attending would imply to society that I approve." He lifted his head and met her gaze in the mirror. "I don't."

"Oh, Henry, really!" she cried, aggravated beyond bearing. "I cannot believe you can still be as fastidious as this."

"You abhor playing the hypocrite, yet you think I should do so?"

"I suppose I thought you'd be more charitable," she shot back, stung. "More forgiving."

"It's not a matter of charity or forgiveness, Irene. Such condescension on my part would further tarnish the family in society's eyes."

"Oh, hang your image and your precious society! This is your mother we are talking about."

He ignored her scowl and her aggravated words as he picked up his cuff links and began to put them on. "My attendance would further damage Angela and Sarah's chances. It would mean even fewer invitations arriving for them, and therefore, even less chance of them being considered for suitable matrimony."

"Marriage isn't everything," she cried. "Suitability isn't everything."

"My sisters would not agree with you there, Irene."

"What about you?"

He went still for a moment, then he tugged his cuffs into place and turned around. "I don't agree with you either."

Those words felt like a knife going into her chest, and he seemed to sense their impact, for he sighed. "Surely you could not expect me to offer any other answer?"

"I don't know what answer I expected," she countered, stunned, her chest aching. "Perhaps one that wasn't so damned disappointing."

"I'm sorry to have disappointed you," he said, and with that cool reply, all the bliss of the past few days began to crumble.

What had she been thinking to expect him to be anything but the man that he was? Had she really thought a couple of weeks in her company and a few nights in her bed could overcome the strictures of a lifetime? Had she really dared to hope that a few spirited discussions could imbibe him with some of her working-class views and modern values? Had she ever believed that she possessed sufficient influence to make him see beyond rules and traditions and what others might think? If that was what she'd been thinking, she'd clearly been lost in a fantasy. The place in her chest where her heart had been now felt like a gaping, empty hole.

If this was what it felt like to be in love, she thought, then she wanted no part of it. A sound very much like a sob escaped her.

In an instant, he was in front of her again, his hands on her arms. "Irene—"

"And you wonder why I refuse to consider marrying you?" she choked.

His head turned a fraction, almost as if she had slapped him, and it was a long moment before he spoke. "If we continue as we are, the time will come when you will not have a choice. When we are caught, your name will be dragged through the mud. Your competitors will reveal all the lurid details of our affair to everyone in my world and yours. What then, Irene?"

"That hasn't happened!"

"But it will. It is, I fear, inevitable. That is what I am trying to make you see. At that point, circumstances will force your hand. You can refuse me, live in shame, and leave me to endure all my life the knowledge that I have dishonored you and sent you down the road to ruin. Or you could then marry me, and both of us would have to live with the fact that you were forced to do so by circumstances. You would resent it, that resentment would grow, and whatever you feel for me would eventually turn to ashes."

"You are talking of your late wife now, not of me."

"I am talking about the inevitable course of a love affair that is not conducted in honorable fashion!" He gripped her arms when she tried to turn away. "Listen to me, Irene. If you chose to marry me now, freely, of your own will and consent, without waiting for circumstances to force you, then it would be different."

"Would it?" she cut in. "You talk of my free choice, yet you work to influence me with the dictates of your conscience. I know you think I ought to feel the same shame that you do, but though it is perhaps a flaw in my character, Henry, I do not feel shame. You talk of my consent, yet you do not ask me what I want. You talk of honor and duty, and obligation, because those are important to you, but you never ask what is important to me."

He took a deep breath and let it out. "I don't ask because . . ." He paused, his hands sliding away from her shoulders. "I fear the answer would break my heart."

"Do you have a heart?" she cried. "Forgive me for being skeptical, but I have never seen much evidence of it. And that is the crux of the problem. I want to love you, Henry. And you make it impossible."

Her voice broke, and to her mortification, she began to cry. He moved to touch her, but she took a step back and his hands fell to his sides.

"I want to love you, and I don't just mean here in this room. I want to love you because I am in love with you."

Even as she said it, the pain in her chest shimmered

through her entire body, for she knew love did neither of them any good. "And don't tell me," she went on fiercely before he could reply, "that what I feel is merely passion, or that I am overwhelmed, or swept away, for what I feel is none of those things. I love you. I know it as surely as I know my name, and yet I can see by your face that you do not believe me."

"How can I?" he muttered, rubbing his hands over his face as if trying to think. "You say you love me, but you will not marry me and share my life?"

"No, Henry, I won't. It isn't because of my work," she added at once, "for as much as I love what I do, I would give it up if I had to, in order to follow my heart. And it isn't because I'd be a duchess, for though I don't relish the prospect, I daresay I could manage the role if it came to it. No, I will not marry you because you cannot bring yourself to attend your own mother's wedding."

He stared at her, looking utterly baffled. "What on earth does Mama's wedding have to do with us?"

"She is your mother, Henry. She needs you, she needs your support, but you withhold it, and for what? You say you do it for other members of the family, but have you asked them if they want to attend?"

"No, because I know what their answer would be."

"And perhaps your conclusion would be proved correct, but my point is that you have not asked them. In fact, I doubt you even considered their right to be consulted on the subject. And even if you are right in this particular case about what they would decide, did it ever occur to you that as head of the family, your own best action might be to support your mother and attempt to persuade the other members of your family to do the same? Of all the duties you may hold, surely the greatest one must be to show others, by example, what is right. And in this case, that means standing by your mother when she needs you, not turning away from her."

"Irene," he began.

"Do you see now why I refuse you? If I married you, what would become of me?" She pressed a hand to her chest. "Me, Irene? What would become of what I think is right? Of what I aspire to and dream of and believe in? Would you ask me what I want, would you consult with me and gain my opinion, or would you simply decide what was best for me?"

She didn't wait for him to answer. "And what of children? If I marry you, and we have a daughter, what will she be in your world? What of her hopes and dreams? What if she comes to you one day and she says, 'Papa, I don't want to do the season and find a husband; I want to go to university and become a doctor and make the world a better place'? What will you tell her?"

"I—" He broke off and swallowed hard. "My position would obligate me to discourage any daughter of mine from such a course."

"Oh, God, Henry!" Even though she was not surprised by his answer, it infuriated her and deepened her resolve. "With every further thing you say, you cement my conviction that I am right in refusing you. For though I love you, you break my heart with your rigid and uncompromising view of the world. As for what I want, I would happily live in sin as a strumpet and a man's guilty pleasure, if my only other choice was to be his obligation and his duty. And if all that is not enough reason to refuse you," she added, choking back tears, "I could never marry a man who desires me but cannot bring himself to love me—a man, in fact, who does not even seem to know what love is!"

With that, Irene stepped back and shut the door in his face, perfectly certain she'd done the right thing, even as she burst into tears and her heart shattered into a thousand pieces.

Chapter 20

*T*he gallery at Ravenwood was a long, wide corridor. One side, lined by a balustrade of intricately carved oak, overlooked the main entrance hall, which was the original castle keep. Along the opposite side, hundreds of images lined the wall, portraits painted in oils and framed in gilt-covered wood. Henry walked along the gallery, passing the faces of the previous Dukes of Torquil, along with their wives and children, and though he glanced at them as he passed, he did not stop until he came to one image in particular.

The face that stared back at him looked like his own—the same black hair, the same gray eyes, the same square jaw. He began to fear that the similarities did not end with looks.

You break my heart with your rigid and uncompromising view of the world.

He thought of his boyhood, and the terror that would

strike his heart any time he did something against the rules and had to face his father.

The rules. It always came back to that. His whole life was lived by rules and codes of conduct. Of honor. And duty.

Of all the duties you may hold, surely the greatest one is—must be—to show others, by example, what is right.

But how did he know what was right? Ever since Irene's stinging set-down, he had been pondering that question. On the train journey to Hampshire and during the three days since, he had thought of little else. Haunted by self-doubt, he'd wandered the woods of his ancestral home, toured the farms and the cottages, walked the house and the gardens, trying to regain amid these touchstones his sense of right and wrong, a renewing of his purpose, and the meaning of his place in the world. He'd never had cause to doubt or even consider these things until a fiery beauty with radical views had come along, questioning everything he thought he knew, and pressing him for answers that could not be found anywhere in his previous experience. Irene shook the very foundations of his existence.

Now, he was standing in front of the previous duke, hoping that in his father's face, he would find answers, but instead, he felt more than ever before the burdens of his position.

Mama was to marry Foscarelli tomorrow, and when she did, the lives of all the family would be forever changed. He could not prevent that. The only thing he could do now was set the best course for the future of his family. But what was that course? Only a few days ago, it had seemed self-evident, but now it was lost in a sea of conflicting interests.

Did it ever occur to you that as head of the family, your own best action might be to support your mother and attempt to persuade the other members of your family to do the same? She is your mother, Henry. She needs you, she needs your support, but you withhold it, and for what?

For rules, of course. To preserve the way things ought to be. For tradition and duty. But not, in this case, for what was right. Irene's words had stung like a whip, but he'd wholeheartedly deserved the lashing. For now, looking into his father's implacable face, he knew his decision had been his father's, not his own, and it had been the wrong one. He was not his father, and he did not want to be.

He looked at the portrait beside his father's, and the sight of Mama's beloved face gave him all the more reason to berate himself. His mother had not loved his father. She had tried, but Papa, as everyone in their family was well aware, had been a difficult man to love. Henry had always known his parents had married for suitability and duty, but he had never dwelled on it, for in his world, love was a secondary consideration in marriage, and if it happened, it was a happy accident. Mama had done her duty; she had married the suitable man, provided him with the required heir and four other children besides, but she had never been allowed to love him.

Now, she had her first and perhaps only chance to marry for love, and his way of dealing with that fact had been his father's way—to block her at every turn.

He looked again at the stern-faced image beside his mother's, and he feared he was more like the man before him than he'd ever wanted to believe. *I want to love you, Henry. And you make it impossible.*

Irene's words echoing through his mind forced him to think of Elena, for a decade ago, his wife could have said those very same words to him. As a youth of nineteen, he'd been inflamed by passion for a sweet and innocent girl. He had married her, he had bedded her, but he had never given her his heart. Instead, he had hidden her away, a shameful secret to be kept from the world, and passion had not transmuted into love; instead, it had crumbled into dust. He had always blamed the failure of his marriage on the fact that he had married out of his class, but now he knew that was not his true sin at all.

Do you have a heart? Forgive me for being skeptical, but I have seen little evidence of that particular organ.

Henry lowered his head into his hand. He had a heart. He knew that because right now it ached in his chest like an open wound. But of course Irene had never seen it. How could she, when he took such pains to keep it hidden, to keep it in his own hands and under his own control?

He loved Irene. He had been in love with her almost from the very beginning—falling, he suspected, just about the moment she'd called him a lily of the field and denounced him and everything he stood for. And ever since, he'd been doing all he could to bring her closer, maneuvering her into his world and even into his very house just to be near her, but he hadn't deemed what he felt to be love. No, in his own mind, he'd called it lust, and by doing that, he'd been able to convince himself that giving his heart would not be required.

Footsteps sounded at the end of the gallery, and he lifted his head, turning as Angela came down the stairs. She caught sight of him and paused on the landing, frowning. "Henry? What are you doing over there?"

"Thinking about my life, my duty, and what it all means."

She frowned, understandably puzzled by such an enigmatic answer, and started down the gallery toward him. "What's brought this about?" she asked as she halted beside him. "Some ducal crisis?"

"You could say that."

She turned toward the painting all the wall. "And you're looking to Papa's portrait for guidance?"

"In a way, though not perhaps in the way he might have hoped. I am thinking of the man that I am, and what of me I will be passing on to the next generation."

She gasped, turning to look at him, her gray eyes filled with delight. "Henry! Who is she?"

"Women," he groaned. "You jump from an innocuous statement to a foregone conclusion in the space of a heartbeat."

"It's Miss Deverill, isn't it? Oh, I hope so, for I do like her."

"You do?"

"Yes. Sarah does, too. Carlotta doesn't," she added, laughing. "A fact which makes me like her ever more. And if you love her, then, well, of course, I shall adore her."

She gave him an inquiring glance, but he refused to rise to the bait. "All my life," he muttered, "I've prided myself on my circumspection and discretion. I am humbled at every turn these days, it seems."

"Well, you've hardly made a secret of your interest."

Fear clutched at him. "What do you mean?"

"You let her steer the ship, Henry! Good God, I saw that, and I about fell over the side, I was so shocked. When's the wedding?"

"You go too fast, Angie. There is no wedding."

"Oh." For a moment, she looked thoroughly let down, then she brightened. "You're right. I go too fast. You have only known her a few weeks. But she is from a respectable family, on her mother's side anyway, though she is a bit more . . . independent than our lot's used to."

"That's one way of putting it, yes," he said with a sigh.

"But she's such fun. She makes the talk at dinner much more interesting. Well, she does," she added, laughing as he laughed. "It's usually so boring—talk of the season and the latest dresses, and such, while she talks about jobs and what it's like to work—things that matter. It's fascinating."

"Is it? Angie," he added before she could respond, "what do you want for your life?"

"What?" Her voice held lively astonishment. "What do you mean?"

"For your life. What do you want?" He waved a hand to their surroundings. "Do you want all this? To be married and have a husband from the right sort of family and your portrait on the gallery wall?"

She frowned, looking bewildered. "I suppose. I mean, what else is there?"

"I don't know. But it's a question, I think, that you

should ask yourself, from time to time, and consider seriously. Promise me you'll do that."

She still looked puzzled, but she nodded. "All right."

"Don't just choose your course because it's the easy one, or the obvious one. Don't . . ." His voice broke, and he swallowed hard, appreciating that loosening the reins of his control over those so dear to him was a damned difficult thing to do. "Don't just choose what I would want for you, or what our friends might think is right. And whatever you choose, you may be sure I'm behind you, and I support you. I will always support you."

"Thank you, but . . ." She paused, giving him a doubtful look. "Are you . . . are you afraid I'm falling in love with an unsuitable man, or something?"

"No," he said with a laugh, and then a thought struck him, his laughter faded, and he frowned at her. "You're not, are you?"

"No, although if I were, I should hardly tell you. You'd hit the ceiling."

"No, I wouldn't. All right, maybe I would," he amended as she gave him a skeptical look. "But I would always want you to be happy. You and your sister, and every other member of our family." He paused, then added, "Including Mama."

Angela sighed and jerked her chin, looking away. "She seems to care very deeply for that man, although I don't know why she has to marry him." She paused, then burst out, "It's a hard thing to swallow!"

"I know. But it is her decision, and we'll not sway her from it. All we can do now is accept it." He paused, considering the ramifications of what he was about to do, then he took a deep breath and reached for his sister's hand. "That's why," he said, "I'm going back to London. I'll take the evening train."

"London?"

"Yes. I'm going to the wedding tomorrow."

"But why?" she cried, pulling her hand from his. "You can't possibly approve!"

"No, but it doesn't matter if I approve."

"By going, you indicate that you do. That is what everyone will think."

"I realize that." He glanced at his father's portrait, Irene's words in his ears. "But I don't ever want to become so wedded to what people think that I fail to do what is right."

"That won't happen, Henry," she said. "You always do what's right."

"Do I?" He thought of Elena, and of Irene, and of his heart, and he grimaced. "Not always."

"Yes, you do," she insisted. "Although, that's sometimes only after you've tried everything else."

He smiled a little. "Yes," he agreed. "Perhaps that's true."

He sobered. "And in this case, I feel that the right thing for me to do is to stand by Mama."

"But only a few weeks ago, you were adamantly opposed to the marriage."

"I am still not convinced it is the right thing, but that does not matter, for it is not my decision to make. I am going to the wedding not because I approve, but because I must stand by Mama, as I would stand by any member of our family who needs my support."

"Don't Sarah and I need your support, too?"

"Yes, and afterward, I will do all I can to mitigate any damage Mama's wedding or my attendance there may cause you and your sister."

"But you won't stay away?" Her face crumpled when he shook his head, tearing at his heart. "You know my ability to find a husband shall now be utterly out the window?"

"It's not quite as dire as that," he said gently. "You're a beautiful girl from an influential family, and as I said, I'll do what I can for you."

"The only thing you can really do is raise the dowry."

"Which I will not do," he said. "That would only attract fortune-hunters."

She tossed her head. "A fact that hardly matters, since our own Mama is marrying one. An act that I cannot help but feel is very selfish of her."

"Perhaps . . ." He paused, looking at the portrait of his mother's face, forcing himself to consider as objectively as he could what marriage to his father had been like for her. "Perhaps after twenty years in a loveless marriage," he said gently, "Mama has earned the right to be selfish, at least about whom to marry. She loves Foscarelli, and love is important, though our sort always try to pretend it isn't."

"Mama says that, too. She says with her marriage, I will be free to find a man who truly loves me for myself and not for my position. Do you think that's true?"

"Yes, I do. Though I suspect that's not much comfort to you just now. I'm sorry."

"People will ridicule us, laugh at us."

"Yes. But we have each other, and we shall have to brave that storm together. As head of the family, it is my job to guide the ship through that storm, but it would mean a great deal to me if I knew I could count on my crew."

She grimaced. "By that, I suppose you mean you want all of us to go to the wedding together as a show of solidarity."

"You must do as your conscience dictates, Angie. I shan't tell you what to do."

"Heavens," she murmured, making a face. "There's a first time for everything."

He smiled at that, but he didn't reply. He simply waited, watching her, and after a moment, she capitulated.

"Oh, I suppose you're right to advise that we stand as a family. Especially since we'll be persona non grata anyway. I'll go down to London with you, and I'll try to persuade Sarah to come as well. You'll have to work on David and Jamie, if you want them to come. As for Carlotta, I'll talk to her, too, thought I don't know how much good it will do."

"You're a brick, Angie."

"And since we shall be in London, anyway . . ." She paused and gave him a sidelong glance. "Perhaps you should call on Miss Deverill? But," she added as he sighed, "whatever you do, you mustn't rush things. I know that's hard for you, for you are a bit impatient sometimes. But you barely know her. Best to wait a bit, until you're sure, before you go proposing, or anything like that."

"I'm afraid it's a bit too late for that advice. The deed is done." He grimaced, turning away before she could see his pain in his face. "She refused me, Angie."

"What? No!"

He couldn't help laughing a little. "Your surprise is gratifying, dear sister."

"Well, who wouldn't be surprised? You're the greatest catch in England!"

"Am I?" His amusement faded, and he stared at the wall of dukes and duchesses before them. "I don't feel like such a prize."

"Oh, my dear." Angela wrapped an arm around his shoulders in a comforting hug. "Did she say why she refused you? Does she not love you? Is that it?"

"It's not that simple, I'm afraid."

"Well, you are asking her to take on an enormous job, and she may not feel she's up to it. Or that she's ready. Wait a bit, and then try your suit again. You're not giving up after one refusal, surely?"

Instead of answering, he gestured to the face before them on the wall. "Do you remember Papa?"

"Of course."

"Do you think . . . am I like him?"

"You look like him. So do I, for that matter."

"But in character, am I like him?"

If he'd hoped for an immediate and decisive negation of that possibility, he was disappointed. Instead, his sister turned toward him and studied him, pondering the question for a long moment before she answered.

"A little, I suppose. You are very strict, and you can be very severe, sometimes. So was he. But . . ." She paused to consider further, then she said slowly, "But you're different from Papa, and that's because I know, I have known throughout every moment of my life, that you love me. Knowing that makes all the difference."

"Does it?" He stared at her, and suddenly, he knew just what he had to do, and what he had so dismally failed to do. "Angie, you're a darling," he cried and grabbed her arms. Laughing at her astonishment in the wake of this fervent declaration, he gave her an appreciative kiss on the forehead. "And I hope like hell you're right."

Chapter 21

Irene was doodling flowers and hearts and little stick men on the sheet of notepaper in front of her. The stack of work to her right hand remained untouched. Her face, she hoped, was no longer puffy with tears after her crying jag this morning. On the other hand, since it was the latest in a week-long stretch of crying jags, it hardly mattered. And given the pain in her heart, she hardly cared what her face looked like anyway.

She ought to be glad—glad, damn it—that he'd come back to town for his mother's wedding. At least some of the things she'd said had gotten through his thick skull. And the breach in his family was apparently healed. How could she not be glad?

The fact that three entire days had passed since then and he had not come to call on her was not at all surprising. His sisters had come twice to see Clara, but he had not come with them. Still, what else could she expect? He had offered her honorable marriage; she had refused him, giving him a blistering tongue-lashing in the process. From his point of view, what more was there to say?

She doubted she would ever see him again. Even if he might, perhaps, want to see her, there was probably some stupid rule against it in the ducal book of ethics.

Her throat closed up, and a tear plopped on her sheet of paper, blurring the lines of her stick man.

It wasn't as if she regretted her decision, or the things she'd said. It wasn't as if she wanted to be a duchess. She didn't. The problem was that she'd fallen in love with a duke. One couldn't, it was evident, have one without the other.

And the duke, worse luck, did not seem to be falling in love with her. He probably still wanted to bed her. He might still be prepared to marry her so that agreeable situation could continue. What girl wouldn't swoon at such an offer?

Just thinking about it made her angry all over again. And more convinced than ever that she'd done the right thing. Refusing him, in fact, had been the only thing in this crazy three weeks she was absolutely sure of.

She nodded, decisively, and felt no better. Instead, she felt even more dissatisfied, not only with him, but also with the world and everything in it, including her own life. She'd been perfectly content with her life just as it was, happy even. Until Henry had come along.

As a result, she'd lost her virginity and gotten her heart broken. Just as catastrophic, she'd lost all interest in her work. Now, it seemed pointless and trivial. Why should anyone care how many silly ghosts were supposedly floating around Berry Pomeroy Castle? Did it matter if Lord Bransford was attending Sir John Falk's house party? Lady Mary Bartholomew's engagement had been called off? No matter. Irene scowled. There was a duke, eligible, wealthy, and impossible, who was available at present. Perhaps Lady Mary could throw in her lot with him. Lady Mary was the daughter of a marquess, after all. A perfect duchess in the making.

Irene paused in her doodling and wondered if maybe she ought to take a real holiday. Give up the paper altogether. Go to America and see Jonathan, or defy Papa's wrath and bring Jonathan here. He could run the paper, and she could go off to Paris and regain her zest for life. She could sketch, or something.

Irene looked at her stick men and flowers with doubt. No, she supposed, a life of sketching wasn't the best idea. And if Jonathan entered their house, Papa would probably call the police. Besides, she doubted going off anywhere in a fit of heartbreak would solve anything. She wanted to go back to being the person she had been before, someone who'd been happy and fulfilled and perfectly content here, in her own sphere. But one could not go back.

She squeezed her eyes shut, but the moment she did, she had to open them again, for thinking of secret nights in hotel rooms with Henry was not going to make her feel better. He was ashamed of those nights, torn by self-recrimination and guilt, and she'd had only the vaguest idea of it. How could she marry a man when most of the time she had no idea what he really thought and felt?

Why, she wondered for perhaps the hundredth time

in the past week, couldn't she have fallen in love with someone comfortable? Someone easy and amiable. Someone who loved her? Henry was impossibly stuffy and arrogant as the devil, and in his entire marriage proposal, there had not been even the barest mention of love. The closest he'd come had been one short reference to his heart. And any man who could not even see his way to allowing a daughter of his to go to university, even if it was the dream of her life, didn't have a heart.

Another tear plopped onto the page, turning her painstaking sketch of a daisy into a gray cloud, bringing a pair of gray eyes to mind. With an abrupt move, she shoved her pencil behind her ear and put the sheet of doodling aside.

This had to stop. For heaven's sake, she had work to do. She had to stop being this unholy mess of a girl. She had a life to live, and it did not, it could not, include him. His life did not include her. It was as simple and awful as that.

She reached for the list of companies that had advertising contracts up for renewal, but before she could peruse it, there was a knock on her open door, and she looked up to find Josie in the doorway.

"You wanted to see me?"

Irene straightened in her chair. "Yes, Josie. Come in, and close the door behind you."

The gossip columnist's dark brows lifted in surprise at her request about the door, but she complied, shutting it and coming to sit on the other side of the desk. "What's all this?" she asked, peering at Irene over the rims of her spectacles, no doubt noting her puffy face and despondent air. "Missing high society, are we? Or perhaps," she added, her shrewd gaze meeting Irene's, "just one particular member of it?"

"Not at all," she lied, working to put Henry out of her mind and don the brisk demeanor a newspaper publisher ought to have. "I wanted to see you because I'm going to be making a change to the content of the paper. A change that will profoundly affect you."

"That sounds ominous." Josie took a deep breath. "Just tell me straight out . . . am I getting the sack?"

"No, no," she hastened to say. "Although after this conversation, it would be perfectly understandable if you wanted to leave, and if that's the case, rest assured you'll receive the most gushing, praiseworthy letter of character you can imagine."

"Thanks, but now you're really alarming me. What's in the wind?"

"I'm changing the editorial content a bit." She took a deep breath, bracing herself for what she knew she had to do. "I'm getting rid of all the gossip. No more Delilah Dawlish, I'm afraid."

"My column?" Josie stared at her, understandably stunned. "But outside of Lady Truelove, it's the most popular column you've got. Everyone loves it."

"I know."

"And the gossip is all true. Irene, I never bring you anything that isn't absolutely on the up-and-up."

"I know that, too. This decision has nothing to do with you or the quality of your work. I just . . ." She paused, working to find a way to explain that wouldn't give her away. "I just don't want the paper to gossip about the *ton* anymore."

"The *ton*, my foot." Josie wagged a finger at her.

"What you really mean is that you don't want to print any gossip about the Duke of Torquil and his family."

So much for not giving herself away. "It's isn't just Torquil's family I'm thinking of."

"Tell it to the marines! You've been mooning over that man ever since you moved back from the West End."

"I have not been mooning over him," she denied, but that was such a blatant lie, she gave up and veered away from the topic of Henry. "This isn't just because of Torquil, Josie," she said instead, trying to sound as indifferent as possible. "I have to think of Clara. Ellesmere's come up to snuff, I'm happy to say. He seems willing to pay a bit of attention to her, bring her out, that sort of thing, so she'll only continue working for me until I can hire a new secretary, then she'll become quite the social butterfly."

"What about you?"

"Me?" She shook her head with a laugh. "Ellesmere won't be launching me into society, not when he learns I won't give up the paper. But it's different for Clara. He'll be able to do great things for her, and the duke's family is willing to help. I can't jeopardize her chances by printing gossip about Ellesmere, and Torquil, and their set. I can't. Delilah has to go."

"I see." Josie chewed on her lower lip, considering for a moment before she spoke again. "So where does that leave me?"

"We'll be keeping everything else pretty much the same, so you can write the same sorts of stories Elsa and Hazel do."

Josie took a deep breath and met her gaze steadily.

"Or I could take Delilah to a competitor. The *Social Gazette* or *Talk of the Town* would love to have her."

"I'm sure they would. And if that's your choice, then I would completely understand. And as I said, I would give you an excellent letter of character. Not," she added with a smile, "that the notorious Delilah Dawlish needs a good character to find work."

Josie smiled back at her. "No, it's probably better if she has a bad character, in fact. But . . ." She paused, her grin fading. "But I believe I shall want the letter just the same."

"So you intend to go?"

"I have to, Irene. I can't let Delilah go. She's my creation, my invention. She's something of me—oh, how can I explain?"

"You don't have to explain. I understand just what you mean, Josie. I truly do."

The other woman nodded. "Delilah's latest thrilling installment of life among the nobs is sitting on Clara's desk awaiting your edits. Are you going to print it tomorrow, or can I take it with me?"

"I won't be printing it, and you're free to take it with you. But you don't have to leave straightaway, Josie. You're welcome to stay on the customary fortnight, with wages, of course."

"Thanks, but I don't like long good-byes. And with that dramatic line," she added, rising to her feet, "I make my exit. Send the letter to my flat, will you?"

"Of course." Irene stood up and held out her hand. "Good-bye, Josie. I wish you nothing but good luck and literary success. Just try not to write anything catty about Clara."

"I won't." She grinned. "I'm never catty about people I like."

With that, Josie gave her an impudent salute and departed, closing the door behind her, but Irene had barely resumed her seat before another knock sounded on her door and Clara came in.

"Here's everyone's work this week, all typed and ready to edit," Clara said, dropping sheaf after sheaf of clipped pages in front of her. "Elsa's column, *Doings in Devon*, and her piece, *England's Most Haunted Places*. Fran's *News from the North*, and her article on a day in the life of a lady's maid. Which was a brilliant idea, Irene, I must say."

Any other time, Irene might have been gratified to hear it. "Thanks," she mumbled, trying not to sigh.

"And here's Josie's *News of St. James Square*," Clara went on, dropping another sheaf of papers on Irene's desk. "And her Delilah Dawlish column—"

"We won't be needing that," Irene cut in. "Josie's leaving, so you can give it back to her on your way out."

"Leaving?" Clara paused, but only for a moment. "Never mind. You'll have to tell me about that later. I'm too busy to stop and hear about it now." Retaining Josie's infamous column in one hand as she dropped the last remaining article on Irene's desk. "And lastly, that's Hazel's interview with Lord Pomeroy about the workings of Parliament. She asked him if they'll be taking up the issue of women's suffrage in the next session, but the old curmudgeon told her they weren't inclined to it at this time. Sorry, Irene."

"No surprise there," she mumbled, gathering all the articles Clara had just dropped on her desk, unable to summon a speck of interest in any of them, and she wondered how long her life was going to seem dry as dust and dull as paint. And how long her heart was going to feel as if it was rattling around inside her in razor-sharp pieces.

"That's the lot," Clara said with a sigh of relief. "I know we're terribly busy today, but would you mind if I take a few minutes and have tea with Papa?"

"Of course not." She waved a hand toward the door. "He'll be delighted."

Clara turned away, but paused by the door. "Oh, one other thing."

Irene looked up. "Yes?"

"I forgot to mention your Lady Truelove column. It's in there, too. I typed it up this morning."

Just the mention of Lady Truelove was enough to make Irene's chest feel as if it had just been sliced open, but she tried not to show it. "Thank you, Clara. Go have your tea."

"You might want to look it over first thing. I'm not sure about it at all."

Irene frowned. "You didn't like the letter from 'A Knight in Knightsbridge'?"

"I'm concerned about it, I'll say that much. And I think upon reflection, you might want to reconsider using it at all."

Irene was astonished enough to be pulled a bit out of her lethargy. Clara seldom criticized, but when she did, her instincts were always sound. "But I can't change it now," she said, dismayed, flipping through pages in search of the relevant ones. "We go to press tomorrow."

"Which is why you should edit it straightaway. I'll

return in a short while, and you can tell me what you want to do?"

Irene waved an absentminded hand toward the door as she pulled her pencil from behind her ear and continued to flip through sheaves of pages, scanning the top of each one for the famous salutation that always opened her advice column.

But when she found what she was looking for, it was not what she expected. Clara had said she'd typed it, but the words, 'Dear Lady Truelove' at the top of the page and all the words below them were handwritten, and it wasn't her own handwriting.

Baffled, she pulled the letter out of the stack and began to read it, but she had only got to the third line of perfect copperplate script before shock hit her like electricity and her pencil dropped from her fingers.

The pencil hit the desk, rolled off the edge, and bounced across the floor, but Irene scarcely noticed, for she was staring at the page in her hand, transfixed. Her heart must have put itself back together, because it began to pound in her chest like the piston of a steam engine. A roar was in her ears, and she couldn't seem to quite take in what she was reading. She felt dizzy—from a lack of oxygen, probably, because on top of everything else, she couldn't seem to breathe.

At the end of the first paragraph, she had to stop long enough for a deep gasp of air, but she could not resume her task. As she stared down at the page, the beautifully curving letters seemed to blur before her eyes, and she blinked several times, trying to clear her vision, but she had no chance to continue reading this astonishing epistle.

"'Dear Lady Truelove,'" an unmistakable male voice said, and she looked up to find Henry standing in the doorway, hat in his hand, his face so gravely handsome that her poor heart nearly broke all over again. And when he spoke, the pleasure and pain of his voice and his words were so acute, she feared it would stop beating altogether.

"'I have fallen in love,'" he continued to quote from the letter before her, watching her, "'truly and completely in love, for the very first time.'"

At this narration of what she'd just read, Irene gave a shuddering sob.

He didn't seem to notice. "'The woman whom I hold in such passionate regard, however,'" he continued as he entered her office and began walking toward her, "'is not of my station. She is a publisher, a brilliant businesswoman, and a staunch suffragist. Needless to say, society would not approve.'"

He stopped in front of her desk. "'But my passion will not be suppressed. With each passing day, the deeper it becomes. I have offered her honorable marriage, but she has refused me.'" He paused, swallowing hard, and looked down at his hat. "'She does not wish to be my wife or the mother of my children.'"

Irene opened her mouth, but she could make no words came out. She was mute, and before she could master the emotions overwhelming her, he resumed his narrative.

"'Nor can I blame her, for I have been improper in my courtship, arrogant in my manner, and oblivious to her concerns about what a marriage to me might mean for her future and that of any children which might bless our union,'" he went on, still staring down at his hat. "'I fear she thinks I would be a tyrannical husband and an even more tyrannical father, and when confronted with these understandable concerns, I failed to adequately address them. Given her refusal, the proper course would be that I withdraw completely from her life, and no longer impose my attentions upon her. But that I cannot do.'"

He looked up. "'For I love her. And it is a love unlike anything I have ever felt. It is deeper than any mere physical passion. It is stronger than my pride, and deeper than a lifetime of convictions, and wider than the world in which I live. It is soul-deep and life-long, and I have come to understand that all the other aspects of my life—my wealth, my position, what others think of me, and even my duty to my title and my estates—mean nothing without her by my side. I shall do what duties of my position I can fulfill, but if I cannot, by some miracle, convince her to change her mind, marriage shall not be one of them, and I shall go on alone all my remaining days.'"

Irene gave another sob. "Henry—"

He leaned across the desk, and cupped her face, caressing her mouth with his thumb. "'I have never been one to give my heart, nor even to acknowledge the existence of it, and I fear that as a result, the woman I love is wholly unaware of my true feelings for her, for I have not been eloquent in expressing them.'"

His hand slid away, and she bit her lip as he went on, "'You see, I am sometimes inclined—so I have been told—to speak when I should not, and in my speech to be quite aggravating, and in consequence, I have been known to spoil a romantic moment with my oratory. As a result, I fear I may say the wrong thing yet again and further harden her resolve against me. I am writing this letter, Lady Truelove, in the hope that you will print it, for I do not know any other way but this to make her aware of what I feel. If she sees this letter, she may soften enough to allow me time to court her properly, and therefore, enable me to convince her of the depth of my affections and the sincerity of my suit. To that end, I would be most grateful for any insight or advice you can offer me. Signed, A Duke in Distress.'"

"Henry, I swear," she cried as she began circling her desk, trying to wipe away the tears on her cheeks only to have fresh ones take their place, "if you don't shut up and let me get a word in, I shall fall into a weeping, muddled mess right here on the floor!"

He complied, saying nothing more as he turned to face her, and Irene's heart ached with such powerful longing that she couldn't think of what to say to him in reply. After such a speech, what could any girl say? But as beautiful as it was, it was still just words.

"You broke my heart, Henry." Her voice cracked on the admission, all the pain of that moment flooding back. She clenched her hands into fists and struck them against his chest. "You broke my heart, damn you, just at the moment I realized it was in your hands."

"I know." He caught her wrists. "And I'm sorry. I'm so very sorry. In my defense, all I can say is that from the moment our affair began, protecting you became my primary responsibility, and the more it went on, the more unbearable it became to have you as a shameful secret."

"But you didn't say a word, not one word, about loving me at all, Henry. I was so angry, and so hurt." She wrenched free. "I still am."

"And you were right to turn me down, Irene, because when I proposed, even I didn't understand my own feelings for you. Only after you refused me, and I knew I'd never be able to have you in my life, did I begin to understand the true depth of my love for you. It's not just physical desire or infatuation, but I wasn't prepared to acknowledge that until you refused me. And I didn't know after what happened between us how I could make you believe me. All I could think at the time I proposed was that I wanted to make you openly mine, and I wanted to be openly yours. I am not the sort of man for an affair. It's marriage or nothing with me. I'm old-fashioned like that." He paused, and slowly, he reached for her hands and took them in his. "So, will you, Irene? Give me the chance to court you properly and honorably, and prove to you that I would be a better husband than I have heretofore demonstrated?"

She looked up at him, into his brilliant gray eyes, and she was still baffled as to how she could ever have thought him cold. "As long as you understand that our daughters will have a university education if they want it," she burst out, "and I don't give a damn if you like it or not."

His face twisted, went awry, and only then did she realize he'd been dead scared she'd refuse him again. He let go of her hands, cupped her face, and kissed her mouth. "They'll have it," he promised and began pressing kisses to the tears on her cheeks. "If they want it. They shall be the ones to decide the issue, not us, for they will be possessed of their own thoughts, their own opinions, and—given their mother—their own will."

She nodded, laughing. "I agree. They shall choose."

"One thing, though. I have no intention of risking that any of our children are created on the wrong side of the blanket. So until the wedding, we will be properly chaperoned, and your reputation protected. Carlotta shall be chaperone."

"Carlotta?" Irene was appalled.

"Well, it can't be Mama. She'll be in Italy. By the way, you know she married Foscarelli, of course?"

"Yes, I know. And," she couldn't help adding, "I also know that you and all your family went to the wedding."

"We did. You may be glad to learn that afterward, I requested that Mama introduce me to her husband."

"Goodness," she murmured, smiling as she pressed a kiss to his mouth. "I'm surprised the earth didn't stop revolving. And now that you've met him, have you softened your opinion of him?"

"No," he said promptly. "He's a bounder, Irene, and he makes my boot fairly itch to kick him."

"You didn't kick him, though." She eyed him with doubt. "Did you?"

"No. I shook his hand in the proper manner, welcomed him to the family, and assured him that he'll be under my protection—and my eye—from now on."

"Oh, dear." She laughed. "That probably made the poor man quake in his boots."

"He did go a bit pale, now that I think on it. I just hope I impressed him enough with the threat of my wrath that he behaves himself."

"I'm sure he will. Speaking of wrath . . ." She paused

and grasped the facings of his gray morning coat in her fists. "I believe you still deserve some of mine. The wedding was Tuesday, and it is now Friday. Friday, Henry," she repeated for emphasis, tugging on his lapels. "Which means three full days before you came to see me, and I've been in utter misery the entire time."

"Have you?" He looked far too pleased by that news. "That's unfortunate."

She scowled. "Damn it, Henry, what took you so long?"

"I needed the time. Not only to write my letter, but also to commit it to memory."

She laughed, picturing him pacing back and forth at Upper Brook Street, saying the words he'd recited over and over. "But how did you slip it in here?"

"Your sister. We arranged to substitute my letter for the column you'd written, and timed it properly so that I was in the outer office when she brought you the stories for editing. My sisters acted as intermediaries."

"It was"—she stopped, her throat clogging up—"a beautiful letter."

"Yes, well . . ." He shifted a bit, embarrassed. "Thank you. Romantic speeches are not really my gift. You may never hear another one."

She smiled. "What changed your mind about your mother's wedding?"

"You, of course. You think I was eloquent in my letter to you? Your words to me a week ago were scathingly eloquent, and they have haunted me ever since you said them. I deserved every condemnation you hurled at my head. I was wrong in my decision not to attend her wedding, for it is impossible for me to serve the interests of the family while simultaneously turning away from any member of it. I realized you were quite right, that my first duty was to stand behind Mama in her decision. And when it was put to the family, they all agreed with me. Even Carlotta, although I suspect that was only because David threatened to petition for legal separation if she did not. I've never seen anything shut Carlotta up so quick."

"Good for David. That's what she needs, for him to stand up to her. But does she really have to be our chaperone?"

"Well, as I said, Mama can't do it. Nor can your grandmother, Viscountess Ellesmere. She is going blind, and she's deaf as a post, and not the least bit reliable as a chaperone. And I need someone who will keep me sternly away from you and make me behave myself. It's Carlotta or no one, I'm afraid."

"I prefer no one. We've done all right so far."

"No, Irene, your reputation hangs in the balance, and my nerves won't stand the suspense."

"Very well," she capitulated with a sigh, "but you shall make it clear to her that she's to turn a blind eye if I pull you shamelessly behind a hedge for some passionate kissing."

He groaned. "Not only my nerves shall be tested, I see, but also my masculine fortitude. Very well. I will endure what I must. And during our engagement, the whole family will help you learn everything you need to know about what duchesses do, so you'll know just what you're in for. Mama, too, when she returns from her honeymoon, will help you prepare a bit before the wedding. That is, if the rest of us haven't scared you off by then."

"You won't," she promised. "I'm not easily frightened."

"Thank God, because if you don't marry me six months from now, I fear I shall have to jump off a cliff."

"There'll be no cliff, Henry, I promise you. If you can promise me one thing."

He nodded as if he knew what she meant. "Keep the paper. I shan't care."

"Even about the gossip?"

He grimaced. "I shan't like it, I confess, and it will be rough on the family, but—"

"Don't worry, Henry," she said, laughing, taking mercy on him. "Before you even walked through that door today, I had already decided to eliminate gossip from the paper's content."

"You did?" He looked so relieved that she laughed again. "What prompted that decision?" he asked.

She sobered. "Believe it or not, I don't like gossip. Other people do, of course, which is why I chose to include it, for when I started the paper, I desperately needed it to be a success. But now that the paper is doing so well, I can afford to eliminate it. We'll still have fashion news, what the ladies are wearing at Cowes Week, who's going to which house party, that sort of thing. We might even add interviews with members of the aristocracy—a day in the life of a duchess, for example. But no more gossip."

"This wouldn't—" He broke off and tenderly kissed

the tip of her nose. "This wouldn't be out of consideration for my family, would it?"

"You know it is," she whispered. "I couldn't bear to see anything scandalous about your family in my paper."

"Thank you, darling." He kissed her, a long, deep kiss this time.

"But," she added, when she was allowed to breathe again, "since I shall soon be a duchess, I'll have to bring in a partner to run the paper for me."

"Hang discretion. If what I said to you that night in the library is the only reason you're bringing in a partner, don't. Run it yourself if you want. I don't ever want you to feel as if you have to play the hypocrite."

"It isn't that. I shall be very busy, I expect, being a duchess. Which brings me to my request." She took a deep breath. "I hope you are not expecting me to give up working for the vote, Henry? Because I won't," she said before he could answer her. "I can't do that, not even for you. So if I am arrested for protesting and marching in the street, I'm afraid you shall have to get your wife out of jail."

"Don't be absurd, darling. Duchesses are like dukes. Our sort don't get arrested. It's not done. But," he added, sliding his arms around her waist, "I'm not sure marching will be necessary. As a duchess, you will have far more effective ways to change the world at your disposal. Gaining the ear of the Prime Minister over dinner, for example. Or endorsing candidates for the Commons who share your views."

Such exciting possibilities made her catch her breath,

but she knew it wasn't only her influence that would be needed. "That will only make a difference if you're with me, and if you will support me. Will you?"

"Always," he said quietly. "I will always be there to help and support you. Even about the vote, though I've no idea what it will be like to live in a world where women vote. It'll change everything, I expect. As for your paper, I can't help being curious. Who are you thinking to make your partner? Clara?"

"She wouldn't want it. No, I think I shall write to Jonathan, and see if he might like to come home and run things. He'll be keen, I suspect. We might even start another paper or two, or a dozen. Revive the family business on a grand scale. If the estate would back these ventures long enough for us to make a profit? I won't ask it, if—"

"Of course we shall back you." He kissed her. "I believe in family and family loyalty very strongly, you know."

"I should like to keep Lady Truelove, too."

"I think you must. Especially since you have to print my letter."

"I'm not going to print it, Henry. It is for my eyes, and mine alone. But I will keep it until its paper is yellow and crumbling and the ink is faded. I will keep it," she added tenderly, "until the day I die. And I will read it every single day."

"And any time I start to become autocratic and tyrannical, you can pull it out, read my own words back to me, and put me in my place."

She smiled, lifting her hand to curl a lock of his hair in her fingers. "Well, yes, that, too."

"As to printing it, nor not, that's your decision, darling. As long as you know I'm sincere, that's all that counts. And I agree that you must keep Lady Truelove alive. She's what brought us together. We can't let her go now. Speaking of which . . ." He paused, his arms tightening around her. "She never did give me the benefit of her advice."

"As if you need it! You've done pretty well on your own, I think. All Lady Truelove would tell you, anyway, is to follow your heart, and love me. Love me, Henry, and marry me, and teach me how to be the best duchess I can so that together we can take care of both our families and make the world a better place."

"Now that," he murmured, bending his head to kiss her mouth, "is the best advice I've ever heard."

Next month, don't miss these exciting new love stories only from Avon Books

Blame It on the Duke by Lenora Bell

Nicolas, Lord Hatherly, never intended to marry, but now he must honor his father's debt to a social-climbing merchant or lose the family estate. Alice Tombs has spent the past three seasons repelling suitors like the wild marquess so she could explore the world. Until Nick proposes a tempting arrangement: just one summer together. It'll be easy to walk away after a few months of make-believe—won't it?

Ride Rough by Laura Kaye

Maverick Rylan won't apologize for who he is—the Raven Riders Motorcycle Club Vice-President, a sought-after custom bike builder, and a man dedicated to protecting those he loves. So when he learns that the only woman who has ever held his heart is in trouble, he'll move heaven and earth to save her.

The Enforcer by HelenKay Dimon

Security expert Matthias Clarke's latest prey is the sole survivor of the massacre that killed his brother. Kayla Roy claimed she was a victim, but then she disappeared. Matthias thinks Kayla may be the killer—and he wants justice. Kayla never lets a man get close, but keeping Matthias away might be impossible, as their mutual attraction feels overpowering—and very dangerous.

Discover great authors, exclusive offers, and more at hc.com.

REL 0417

At Avon Books, we know your passion for romance—once you finish one of our novels, you find yourself wanting more.

May we tempt you with . . .

- **Excerpts** from our upcoming releases.

- Entertaining **extras**, including authors' personal photo albums and book lists.

- Behind-the-scenes **scoop** on your favorite characters and series.

- **Sweepstakes** for the chance to win free books, romantic getaways, and other fun prizes.

- Writing **tips** from our authors and editors.

- **Blog** with our authors and find out why they love to write romance.

- **Exclusive content** that's not contained within the pages of our novels.

Join us at
www.avonbooks.com

AVON

An Imprint of HarperCollins*Publishers*
www.avonromance.com

Available wherever books are sold or please call 1-800-331-3761 to order.

FTH 1013

*G*ive in to your Impulses!

**These unforgettable stories only take a second
to buy and give you hours of reading pleasure!**

Go to *www.AvonImpulse.com* and see what we
have to offer.

Available wherever e-books are sold.

AVONIMPULSE

IMP 0811